hb

Beautiful Lady

Beautiful Lady

Patrick Read

Kingsfield

First published in 2002 by Kingsfield Publications
1 Kingsfield Close, Bradford on Avon
Wiltshire, BA15 1AW

British Library Cataloguing in Publication Data
A catalogue record for this book is available from the British Library

ISBN 1 903988 01 2

Printed and bound by Antony Rowe Ltd, Eastbourne

Introduction

by George Digby
Librarian, The University of Wessex, England

Violent death is commonplace – so much so that nowadays we are hardened to it. We have only to switch on the television news and we see can the bloodstained bodies. We see them through the eye of the camera, of course, and hence at one remove; perhaps mercifully so.

Since violent death is so familiar to us, it is surprising that we can still be affected by it – that we can still feel any concern about whether particular individuals live or die. And yet we do feel such concern. Which is why I have devoted time and energy to arranging the publication of the book that you are about to read.

It all began with an e-mail. (Because we librarians are right at the cutting-edge of information technology, you know.)

Who was the beautiful lady? it said. And that was all. But it was, of course, possible for me to see that the message had been sent by a.dorner@uncoll.cam.ac.uk, i.e. it had come from my old friend Anthony Dorner at University College, Cambridge.

Old friend is right, I thought to myself. I hadn't seen Anthony for years. I'd sent him the usual Christmas cards, of course, with duplicated news of my family and a personal note at the bottom, but never got anything back. He might have been dead for all I knew, so it was nice to hear from him.

As for the message – who was the beautiful lady – well, at first I didn't respond. It didn't mean anything to me, so I just sat and looked at it for a while. And then I got called away, distracted by my duties. I forgot about it.

The next day, when I opened up my e-mail again, there was another message from Anthony. This time it was accompanied by personal abuse, so it was quite obvious that it came from my old friend. *Joe loves Wallis, true*, the screen told me. *Wake up you stupid bastard and get in touch.*

Well, nothing for it of course but to lift the telephone and speak to the old boy.

Anthony seemed in good form on the phone. He was a bit mysterious, wouldn't say anything about Joe and Wallis, whoever they were, but he did say that he had something urgent he wanted to speak to me about, and he invited me to visit him 'soonest'. Naturally I agreed immediately. I didn't need much encouragement, because I hadn't been back to Cambridge for some time.

Anthony suggested that I should stay overnight, and I assumed at first that he would be able to book me a guest room in the Master's Lodge. But no. He positively hooted with laughter when I suggested it.

'Good grief, George,' he said, 'you are out of touch. All guest rooms were seized by the state years ago. Nowadays every broom cupboard is occupied by a Peruvian economist and an East German specialist in early Welsh poetry. Go to a hotel, dear chap, like everyone else.'

So I did.

The following Monday I travelled to Cambridge by train. This is not a journey I would recommend. Even with a first-class ticket the phrase 'cattle truck' keeps entering the mind. However, I buoyed my spirits up with the thought that Cambridge in the autumn would be beautiful – and it was.

Especially beautiful was the sight of my alma mater – University College – five hundred years old, but still a wonderfully inspiring sight, despite the worst that our useless politicians can throw at it by way of financial cuts.

I made a mistake at first. When I had last visited the College, Anthony's rooms had been on G staircase, in the Elizabethan court. But I discovered that he had moved; his former rooms were now occupied, it appeared, by a Peruvian economist. I made enquiries of a passing Porter, and was directed round the corner, through an arch, and across the frontage of a hideous 1950s block to the Founder's Quad.

It was the first time I had been in this Quad for perhaps

twenty years, and I could quite believe that the Founder had once lived there. It proved to be one of the darker and gloomier corners of the College, and rather spoilt the good impression conveyed by the main entrance.

I made my way up a dingy wooden staircase, the walls lined with electrical wiring which seemed to have been installed in the nineteenth century. This staircase constituted the sole entry and exit point for a few rooms which would have been instantly condemned by the New York fire authorities.

Eventually I found Anthony's name painted on an old oak door set in a low stone entranceway. I knocked and he let me in.

After the usual greetings we relaxed over a glass of sherry.

By way of breaking the ice I asked him why he had moved from his old rooms – which had always seemed very comfortable to me – into quarters which were so obviously inferior.

Anthony seemed a little disconcerted by the question. 'Oh,' he said with a wave of the hand, 'you know how it is. I haven't been to a College Council in fifteen years, or read the agenda for ten. And if you don't keep up with the paperwork you suddenly find there's been a "reorganisation" – which is to say a coup – and suddenly you're moved out of your nice comfortable quarters and exiled to Siberia. It's the College's way of trying to tell me something.... Actually it's not too bad. I've got the study here, a bedroom next door, and the loo and so forth across the landing. Quite adequate for an old bachelor.'

It was obvious to me, despite Anthony's protestations, that the question of where he was housed in the College was a touchy subject, and I was sorry I'd raised it. Even I could see, reading between the lines, that his career had not prospered of late. Or even of early. The room looked sparse, bare and cold. There wasn't a picture anywhere, not even an illustration cut out of a magazine. There was no television, no radio, no record-player – and not even many books. There was, however, a computer, so at least he was moving with the times after a fashion.

I had to remind myself that once upon a time Anthony Dorner had been a coming man. He was a scholar at Winchester; winner of a major scholarship in History at University College in 1957;

and got a most distinguished First. For a while he had seemed destined for greatness, but somewhere along the line things had gone wrong. His charming wife left him quite quickly for a whiz-kid businessman. And the books, the fruition of all his promise, somehow did not appear. And then there were the stories of the heavy drinking, and the unfortunate extempore speech at the Founder's Dinner one year. And various other incidents, which I had heard about third-hand, and which were not likely to endear Anthony Dorner to the more sober Fellows of the College. He who might once have hoped to be a Regius or Chichele Professor had ended by not being offered a chair at all. Not even, as he once put it, at an inferior university like Wessex. Which was a joke, of course, but one made with a good deal of bitterness underlying it.

So, there the two of us were. Anthony Dorner, a man with so much hope behind him who had got nowhere very far. And I, the dull plodder, who had ended up in quite a senior – well, actually *the* most senior post – in the Library of what is, when all is said and done, quite a respectable university even if it is a former polytechnic.

And to cap it all, when I came to examine him closely in the fading afternoon light, I realised that my old friend looked quite ill. He always was a bit on the tall and thin side, but now he looked pale and haggard. His hair was greying all over, though he hadn't lost it like me. He was still reasonably well dressed (sports jacket and cavalry twills from one of the better Cambridge tailors), but the golden young man had departed.

Despite the circumstances, Anthony put a brave face on it all, and after a bit of chit-chat I asked him to explain his mysterious e-mail: *Joe loves Wallis, true.*

'Oh that,' he said casually. 'That was just to get you interested, George. But it's true, I think. Or it was. He did love her, after a fashion. Admired her, anyway.'

'Who admired whom?' I asked patiently. And Anthony began to explain.

'I've written a book, George.'

At last, I thought.

'It's a study of political thought in the nineteen-thirties. Complicated era. There were lots of well-meaning chaps who remembered the slaughter in the first world war, didn't want a re-run, and made asses of themselves by supporting appeasement. In particular, I've been concentrating on some very odd events in December nineteen-forty. It's taken me about fifteen years to research it all, but now I've written it up, and I want you to get it published for me.'

'Well, that shouldn't be too difficult,' I said confidently. 'What about the Press?' I meant the Cambridge University Press of course – a most distinguished firm.

'Er, no,' said Anthony. 'No, I fell out with them some time ago. And in any case they wouldn't be interested. You see, I've written it up in the form of a novel.'

Oh, had he. My heart fell. A novel, indeed.

Anthony did not appear to notice my reaction. 'It seems to me,' he continued cheerfully, 'that you're just the man to place it for me. Act as my agent so to speak. You're quite a well-known novelist yourself – I'm sure you've got lots of contacts.'

This was flattery of the crudest kind, and I told him so. 'My two novels,' I reminded him firmly, 'were detective stories, published nearly twenty years ago, and not very well received then. The firm that published them went bust two years later.'

Anthony dismissed these objections. 'No, I'm sure you're just the chap. Experienced librarian, ear to the ground, all that sort of thing. Besides, the villain of the piece lived out your way.'

'Villain?'

'Westrow, Earl of.'

'Never heard of him. Didn't know there was one.'

'Well, there isn't now,' Anthony admitted. 'The line died out in nineteen-forty, to tell you the truth.'

'Was his name Joe?' I asked.

'Oh, read the book, George,' said Anthony. 'Read the book.'
Reluctantly, I agreed to. But first we went down to dinner.

It was many years since I had dined in the College Hall, and I was pleased to see that most of the old traditions were still observed. The Fellows still wore gowns for dinner, grace was still recited in Latin, and at the end of the meal the students still climbed over the long refectory tables, muddy Doc Martens boots and all. If there's one thing I do like it's tradition.

Unfortunately I noticed that the other Fellows studiously ignored poor Anthony. I don't consider myself particularly sensitive to nuance, but even I could see that most people simply pretended he wasn't there.

During dinner, Anthony pointed out the Bursar to me. He was a short, slim little chap, with a rather fancy waistcoat under his gown. Watching him, I wouldn't have been at all surprised to be told that the man was gay. Oh, I know what you're thinking – impossible in a decent College. But some very odd people have been offered Fellowships in the last few years, I can tell you.

'The Bursar is keeper of the archives,' Anthony told me. 'He's the one who's got all my research papers tucked away safely, if I should fall under a bus.'

Afterwards, Anthony succeeded in nobbling the Bursar to introduce me, though the weaselly little chap very nearly escaped.

'University of Wessex?' said the Bursar after we had – very perfunctorily – shaken hands. He wrinkled his nose as if he could smell something nasty. 'Yes, I seem to have heard of Wessex.'

I didn't bother trying to explain that some of the newer universities have many virtues: such as devoting time and attention to teaching the students instead of publishing papers on the frequency of commas in Wordsworth. With some people such explanations are a waste of time. Anyway, the Bursar soon made an excuse and left.

I had noticed during dinner that Anthony wasn't eating very much, and I now realised that he was looking distinctly unwell. He had turned a very strange colour, so I suggested we should return to his room.

He seemed relieved. 'Yes,' he said. 'Good idea.'

Back in his quarters Anthony went into his bedroom and emerged shortly with an A4-sized box in his hand. 'This is the manuscript,' he said. 'Text of my novel. I do have another copy, but take good care of it. Be a good chap, read it as soon as you can and let me know what you think. Having worked on it so long I'd like to make some progress fairly quickly.'

I could sense that he was anxious to be rid of me so that he could retire to his bed, so I made my departure at once.

'I think I ought to be off pretty early in the morning,' I told him.

'Oh, that's all right. I've got to go to Addenbrooke's myself anyway. Booked in for some tests.'

'Oh,' I said, a little taken aback. 'Well... I'll be in touch then.' And we left it at that.

The following morning I set off for home. As soon as the train left Cambridge I began to read the manuscript. Or typescript to be exact.

It was a very tidily presented piece of work, but I hadn't been reading long before I found myself muttering a bit, and at one point I must have groaned aloud. 'Oh dear oh dear,' I think I said. 'Oh dear oh dear oh dear.'

My sole companion in the first-class compartment looked across at me. I think he was a Prof. 'As bad as that, is it?' he asked sympathetically.

'Well yes,' I said. 'I'm afraid it is.'

Back at the University of Wessex Library I cancelled a few appointments and concentrated on Anthony's book. Then, when I'd finished it, I went out into the stacks and checked a few facts here and there.

His manuscript wasn't *bad* exactly, despite my groaning. In fact it was quite good. But it seemed to contain a curious mixture of verifiable fact, wild speculation, and sheer invention. It was a disturbing work to come from the hand of a professional historian, and I simply didn't know what to make of it.

That evening I telephoned Anthony to give him my initial reactions, but I couldn't get a reply. The following morning I tried again, also without success. Finally, after making myself thoroughly unpleasant, I bullied the Head Porter into making some enquiries, and he rang me back to say that Dorner (not even *Mr* Dorner) had been detained in hospital for further tests.

This was definitely not good news, and I cancelled some more appointments, booked myself back into the same hotel in Cambridge, and began that dreadful train journey once again.

The weather had changed for the worse. The wind was now from the east, sweeping across the Northern European plain, with nothing to stop it between the Urals and Cambridge; the air was bitterly cold.

The trek through the corridors of Addenbrooke's hospital was exhausting in itself, but eventually I found Anthony's ward. The Sister in charge, a pleasant and friendly woman, assured me that he was well enough to talk, but asked me not to tire him.

The ward was a small one, with just three other occupants, all of them elderly men. Two were apparently comatose, and the third had a nasty cough. I sat down beside Anthony's bed.

My old friend looked even thinner than he had two days earlier, and paler too. I asked him how he was and he told me in a rather weak voice that he had seen better days. I asked him if he was well enough to discuss the book, and he said he thought he'd better, while he had the chance. At the time I thought he was joking, and smiled. He always was a joker.

'Well,' I said, getting down to business, 'I've read the book twice now, and I've got lots of notes scribbled in the margins, so I'd like to clear up a few points I'm doubtful about.... I think it's rather a good novel, on the whole, but there are one or two things that worry me. This use of historical personages for instance. Joe Kennedy, Wallis Simpson, the Duke of Windsor and so on.'

Anthony looked up at me sharply. 'What's wrong with that?'

'Well,' I said, as tactfully as possible, 'it seems a bit unnecessary, that's all. Why don't you call the American Ambassador by a fictional name?'

Anthony began to get agitated. He pulled himself up in the bed and started to berate me. 'Look, you stupid bastard, that's the whole fucking point. I've written the book in the form of a novel so that the ordinary man in the street can read it without sweating. But it's not fiction, it's true! That's the whole bloody point! It's all based on documentary evidence. In particular it's based on Jane Padget's report for the King.'

I glanced around rather nervously, but no one in the ward seemed to have noticed Anthony's raised voice. The comatose chaps were still comatose, and the cougher appeared to be stone deaf.

'I see,' I said slowly. 'But you're awfully rude about some of these people – Joseph Kennedy and Wallis Simpson in particular.'

'That's because they were shits,' said Anthony forcefully. 'Four-star, high-grade shits. Joe Kennedy was as crooked as they come. He was a Fascist, a liar, and a hypocrite. Wallis of course was a whore. And a German spy.'

'I see,' I said cautiously, not sure how to respond to this outburst. 'And, er – you're sure you can prove what you say about them?'

Anthony turned his eyes sideways to look at me, and I was shocked to see how bloodshot they were. 'The dead cannot sue,' he reminded me.

'Well yes, I know that. But isn't it a bit, well, unethical to malign those who aren't here to defend themselves?'

Anthony's lip curled alarmingly. 'Malign?' he snarled. 'You think *I* malign *them*? Jesus Christ, George, you seem to have lost whatever marbles you ever had.'

He sank back under the sheets, as if exhausted by our brief exchange.

I tried to appear more reasonable. 'Well,' I said, 'I will admit that some of our boyhood heroes turned out to have feet of clay. Lloyd George, Malcolm Muggeridge, General Montgomery. People like that – they all turned out to have, well, shortcomings.'

'Shortcomings?' echoed Anthony. 'Feet of clay? George, they were solid bloody ceramic, all the way up to their shoulder-blades.'

I moved on. 'I myself,' I said, 'have had a look for some supporting evidence for some of your claims, and what really worries me is that I can't seem to find anything about the central event in your book – all this business involving the kidnap of Princess Elizabeth.'

A great sense of weariness passed over Anthony's face, and I became quite worried about him. Perhaps I was pressing him too hard.

'George,' he said, as if addressing a very small child, 'that is the whole point. The incident involving Princess Elizabeth was hushed up. Kept secret. You understand? D-noticed out of history. I myself am the sole discoverer of the truth, nearly sixty years after the event. And it's taken me over a decade to unravel it all, moving inch by inch.'

'And you have the evidence?' I asked cautiously.

'I have the evidence. It's all on my computer, or in the archives. The chief source, of course, is Jane Padget's report for the King. Only one copy of that exists, but I've read it.'

'Jolly good,' I said, as encouragingly as I could. 'I only ask these things because I'm sure a publisher will want to know, that's all. I tell you what, though....'

'Yes?'

'I think what your novel really needs, especially in view of what you've just told me, is an introduction at the beginning. I think the reader needs to be told point blank, right at the beginning, that all this really happened, and that you've only written it as a novel to give it a sense of immediacy, as it were.'

Anthony made no objection, so I continued.

'And then at the end,' I said, 'I think it needs a sort of epilogue, to round it all off. People like to know what happens to the characters at the end of a book.'

Anthony sighed deeply. 'I haven't the strength,' he said. 'I can't do any more.'

'Oh no, no, no,' I said hastily. 'I wasn't suggesting that you should do it, Anthony. I thought it was something that I could do for you.'

Anthony opened one eye, very slowly, and turned its baleful glare upon me. 'George,' he said. 'If you write an introduction and an epilogue to my novel, all you will do is prove to the world that you really are the pompous ass that we all thought you were when we were undergraduates.'

And it was then that I knew he was seriously ill, because he didn't smile at the end of his joke, as he always did when he was well. And I don't mind telling you that this realisation shook me.

'Well, Anthony,' I said, trying not to show how shocked I felt, 'I make you a solemn promise, here and now. Whatever else happens, I will get your book published. One way or another.'

He closed both his eyes and sank even lower in the bed. 'I'd be very grateful,' he said. 'I really would.'

'Would you mind if I went and had a look at some of your working papers – notes and things, on the computer and so forth?'

He seemed to be falling asleep. 'Help yourself, George. Be my guest. But get the damn thing published.'

I thought about patting him on the shoulder as I left, but I didn't. Englishmen of our generation are not terribly comfortable with physical expressions of affection.

I went straight back to the College, made my way to the Founder's Quad, and went up the staircase to Anthony's room.

It occurred to me as I got there that the room would almost certainly be locked in Anthony's absence; I ought to have called at the Porters' Lodge first, to get them to lend me a key. But as it turned out that wasn't necessary – the door of the room was open.

I went in and found a student busy emptying Anthony's possessions into boxes. I could hardly believe my eyes.

I could tell he was a student, and probably a postgrad., because of the long, dirty hair, the grubby T-shirt, the faded jeans, heavy boots, acne, nasty unwashed smell and generally surly expression. A typical specimen of the genus *studentum pauperum*. I didn't like him.

'And what,' I demanded, 'do you think you're doing?'

'None of your fucking business,' said the student, without even pausing in his work.

'It most certainly is my business. Mr Dorner is a close friend of mine, and you have no right to be handling his belongings.'

'Bursar's orders,' said the young man abruptly.

Oh, I thought. So the Bursar was responsible. He of the fancy waistcoat. I might have guessed.

I decided to ignore the removal man. I had to admit to myself that it was possible – just – that the Bursar had been told that Anthony would be in hospital for some time, and that this student had been deputed to ensure that Anthony's possessions remained in safekeeping while he was away. That was what I hoped at the time, anyway. But I was reminded once again, now that the room was almost stripped, that Anthony had precious few belongings to be stored, and that upset me.

I turned my attention to the computer, which was still where it had been on my previous visit.

'I need to examine Mr Dorner's computer files,' I said. 'I suppose there's no objection to my having a look?'

The student shrugged. 'Please yourself. It's a dead parrot anyway.'

'I beg your pardon?'

'There's nothing on it. Hard disc's wiped. I've had a look at it myself, ten minutes ago. Bloody thing's obsolete anyway. It's only a 386.'

I was astonished, yet again, by the young man's arrogance and general rudeness, but I ploughed on regardless. I booted the computer, waited for it to warm up, and was distressed to find that the wretched youth was absolutely right. The hard disc *was* empty. I couldn't find anything on it.

I turned away, deeply disturbed.

'Finished, mate?' asked the spotty one.

'Yes, thank you,' I said.

Mate, he called me. And I mean really, this used to be quite a good College.

Later that day I tried to see the Bursar myself, but he was apparently in London, or so his secretary alleged. I stayed in Cambridge overnight, and I could have tried to see the Bursar again the following morning, but I'm afraid I simply went home. I did, after all, have other things to do.

Professional and personal matters occupied me for a couple of days, but over the weekend I rang Addenbrooke's to see how Anthony was. The admissions people couldn't seem to trace him on their records, which I took to mean that he had been discharged, and it wasn't until a further two days had elapsed that I rang the College and tried to get in touch with him.

The Porter who answered the phone told me that Anthony had died, the day after I had last seen him.

I'm afraid I was too shocked to say anything. I just put the phone down.

When I had recovered a bit, I looked up the College membership in the Commonwealth Universities Yearbook, found the name of the Chaplain, and gave him a ring.

The Chaplain (a Reverend Walshbee) told me that Anthony had left his body to medical science, so there would be no funeral. But, under the College Statutes, there was a requirement that there should be a memorial service in the chapel, and it would be held on the following Friday at 2.30 p.m.

Well, of course I attended. It was my third trip to Cambridge in two weeks, but the circumstances were exceptional after all.

Not many other people bothered to attend, I'm afraid. There were four elderly gentlemen, whom I took to be senior Fellows, and one lady, probably the wife of one of them. No sign of the Master of the College, Sir Arnold Webbster FRS, or indeed anyone else of note.

As I went into the chapel I heard a man who later turned out to be the choirmaster say to one of the choristers, 'Just treat it as a practice,' and that, I'm afraid, is more or less what they did. It was a truly tragic occasion.

Thirty minutes. That's all it took. Thirty minutes for a handful of friends and colleagues to say goodbye to a man whose career had once seemed to offer so much.

At the end I sat quite still for a few moments, savouring the beauty of the chapel and letting the last of the music echo in my ears. But this pause proved to be a mistake, because by the time I got to my feet and went outside, everyone else had gone.

Well, I was damned if I was going to put up with this

nonsense. I knew perfectly well where the senior common room was, and I went there and walked straight in, bold as brass.

The Chaplain was the only other person there, pouring himself a cup of tea. He was about twenty-eight, I would guess, but losing his hair already. 'Ah, Mr Digby,' he said, 'I hoped you'd find your way here.' He was quite obviously a shameless liar, and yet supposedly a Christian, too. 'You were an old friend of Anthony's, I believe.'

'And his literary executor,' I said, because by that time I had been told so by a solicitor.

'Well.... Jolly pleased you could make it.'

We chatted for a few minutes, rather awkwardly, and then the chap decided he must go. 'Oh,' he said, with a rather embarrassed look. 'There's something I was told to tell you, if I saw you. By the Bursar.' Not *asked* to tell me, you notice – *told.*

'Oh yes?' I said, rather coldly.

'Yes. The Bursar said to tell you, quite definitely, that there are no papers of Mr Dorner's in the College archives. He said you'd be sure to ask, and that I must make quite sure to tell you. Whatever Mr Dorner may have said – and I'm afraid he wasn't a terribly reliable sort of person – the College has no papers of his. None at all.'

'Well thank you,' I said. 'I'm so pleased to know how things stand.'

By now you will have gathered that I am the kind of chap who does not give up easily. If I make up my mind to do a thing, I jolly well stick at it until it's done. And it wasn't an easy task getting Anthony's novel into print, that I can tell you.

I don't think I can remember quite how many publishers I approached, but eventually I found a young fellow who seemed quite keen on it. So the book is in print at last, and – as I promised Anthony – I've written an introduction and an epilogue, just to put the thing in context.

I was a bit worried, you see. Anthony had insisted to me that every word of his book was true, and that he had the evidence to support it, based on some fifteen years' research. And I have no reason to doubt his word. But unfortunately, I couldn't find the actual evidence that he had assembled; and if I were paranoid about it I might put that down to some sort of conspiracy to suppress the truth. However, I have found quite a lot of support for Anthony's story, derived from general history books. And I have also done a little bit of research of my own, which is referred to in the epilogue.

One thing you might like to know about now is the reaction of the authorities whenever I tried to establish the most basic fact of all – whether or not Princess Elizabeth actually was kidnapped in December 1940.

No comment was largely the order of the day. A suspiciously tight-lipped 'no comment', at that. So, right at the very end of my labours, after I'd done all the proof-reading, I did take my courage in both hands: I wrote to Her Majesty the Queen herself.

I didn't really expect to get a reply, but curiously enough I did receive one. I had a letter from a chap called Reginald St John Francombe, who is apparently Comptroller of the Queen's Correspondence. He wrote to me as follows:

> Dear Mr Digby,
>
> Her Majesty has asked me to thank you for your recent letter, enquiring whether she could confirm your friend's account of certain events which may have occurred in December 1940. Her Majesty has commanded me to say that her own memories of that year are now rather faint. However, she awaits publication of your friend's book with considerable interest.

I suppose it was as much as I could hope for.

And so now, Dear Reader, I will detain you no longer. Here it is: *Beautiful Lady* – a novel by my dear friend, Anthony Dorner, sometime Fellow of University College, Cambridge, an historian, scholar, and gentleman. I miss him enormously.

Part One

23 December 1940

Chapter 1

Internal Memorandum **BUCKINGHAM PALACE**

To: His Majesty the King
From: Miss Jane Padget
Date: 3 January 1941

TOP SECRET
For the King's eyes only

May it please Your Majesty -

You have commanded me to set down in writing, while the memories are still fresh in my mind, an account of the kidnapping of Her Royal Highness the Princess Elizabeth.

My report is set out below. If you require any further information, please let me know.

This report has been drawn up not only from my own recollection but also with the aid of material supplied by MI5. Where appropriate, the MI5 reports have been supplemented with information from U.S. Military Intelligence and the Federal Bureau of Investigation. I am grateful to the Officers of all these bodies for allowing me access to some of their files.

Your Majesty - you encouraged me to tell the story in my own words, and that I have done. But you will know that an American citizen, Mr Seymour Jensen, was with me throughout almost all the events described. I therefore took the liberty of allowing him to read a draft of the report. Mr Jensen has corrected me, or augmented my comments, on a few points of detail.

I would like to take this opportunity of recording my view that we all owe Mr Jensen a profound debt of gratitude, myself perhaps most of all. I am anxious that you should be left in no doubt about his contribution to our nation's welfare.

I will begin my report by giving an account of

```
what happened on Monday 23 December, 1940. A
number of events occurred in the afternoon of
that day.  At the time, many of them did not
appear to be important. But, with the benefit of
hindsight, they obviously were....
```

'Seymour! Seymour! I'm over here!'

Jane Padget was standing outside the Hans Crescent entrance of Harrods as she waved frantically to attract Seymour Jensen's attention. He was just across the road, looking towards Sloane Street, which was the direction she would have been coming from if she hadn't arrived before the arranged time.

'Seymour!' Honestly, the man *was* a bit slow sometimes even if he was very sweet. He had obviously heard her shouting this time, but he was still obstinately looking in the wrong direction – he was looking up at the windows of the houses nearby, if you please. As if she were likely to be there!

'SEY-MOUR!' she shrieked, and at last he turned round. He smiled with relief, looked the wrong way to check the traffic, *of course*, because he was still a dim-witted colonial who hadn't realised that cars came at you on the left-hand side of the road – and then, having risked life and limb unwittingly, he trotted across the road to greet her.

As she saw him run, Jane gave a little intake of breath. He was absolutely *gorgeous*, there was no doubt about that. A tall, fair-haired, blue-eyed, Swedish-origined American, and a Harvard man too. Well, just. At the end of his first term actually, whereas she of course was in her second year at Oxford, and was therefore, by definition, infinitely more sophisticated than a Harvard freshman. But, nevertheless, he was terribly sweet and *very* good-looking.

Seymour trotted up and gave Jane a dazzling smile. She hoped for a moment that he might kiss her. Nothing elaborate, just a dab on the cheek would do, and she half-turned to give him an opportunity. But no. Mr Beautiful Dimwit passed on that. He was obviously worried about frightening the horses. He just said, 'Hi,' and smiled again, and she forgave him instantly.

'Well,' she said after a moment. 'Shall we go shopping?'

There wasn't a lot to buy, if truth be told. England in December 1940 was fifteen months into the war, and rationing was well established. The German U-boats were very successful at sinking the ships bringing food from abroad, and even in Harrods there was little to be had.

Jane took Seymour towards the meat counter, and found a lengthy queue waiting patiently. The lady in front of them turned round. 'The young man in charge thinks a lorry has just brought in some chops,' she said confidentially.

This was good news, and they decided to wait. Jane noticed that the lady who had spoken to them was immaculately dressed. Two years earlier, her maid and butler would have done all the shopping. Now, the butler was probably in the army and the maid was a Land Girl – and the lady of the house was talking to strangers in the street, something she would never have dreamed of doing before.

For ten minutes Jane and Seymour chatted about the film they had seen the previous evening, and then their patience was rewarded. They were able to buy three pork chops, which Jane would cook for dinner – one for herself, one for Seymour, and one for her father, Alastair Padget.

They left Harrods and began to walk towards Jane's home, which was in Eaton Square.

'I wish you'd let me bring you meat from the Embassy,' said Seymour. Frederick Jensen, Seymour's father, was Defense Attaché at the American Embassy in Grosvenor Square, and therefore had almost unlimited access to steaks, ice-cream and other luxuries unheard of in wartime Britain. But Jane would have none of it.

'Seymour, darling,' she said, 'I've explained to you before, and as a Harvard man you really ought to be able to remember. I do not approve of the black market. Neither do I approve of people with connections in your Embassy making improper use of those connections to stuff themselves silly. As it is we've got three perfectly good chops, plus some very nice vegetables, and we didn't even have to queue for very long. So stop moaning.'

Seymour, she noticed, was about to complain that he hadn't

been moaning at all, but then he changed his mind, in case he offended her. Jane had her work cut out not to giggle. Poor Seymour, he just hadn't got the hang of English girls – not yet.

It was about half-past four on a cold, gloomy, December afternoon. The light was fading, and most pedestrians who did not have to be out and about had already arrived home. In pre-war days, the last few days before Christmas would have seen the streets packed with shoppers, but now there were few people about. The traffic was also light, with only an occasional taxi passing by. Petrol rationing meant that people did not use their cars unless they absolutely had to, and the black-out regulations made driving after dark hazardous.

Seymour and Jane walked briskly to keep warm.

As they turned into Pont Street, the air-raid sirens began to wail. One siren, close at hand, was very loud, and rather frightening; others, further away, could also be heard, rising and falling with their warning of an imminent bombing raid.

Seymour seized Jane's arm and began to look around for the nearest air-raid shelter: they were usually sign-posted. 'Quick,' he said, 'we must run and take cover.'

'Why?' said Jane calmly. She resisted the pressure on her arm as Seymour tried to get her to break into a trot.

'Why?' Seymour repeated. His eyes bulged in astonishment. 'Well, because the bombs are going to fall any minute. I've only been in England two weeks, but I've already been caught in several raids, and they're not a lot of fun.'

'Yes, I know that, darling,' said Jane patiently. 'But why run? If a bomb's going to hit us it's going to hit us, whether we're in a shelter or anywhere else.... You only die once, Seymour, and if I'm going to die today I'll die with dignity if you don't mind. We won't *run* anywhere.'

Seymour knew when he was defeated. 'Oh, very well,' he groaned. But they were passed by several other pedestrians who took quite a different view and were moving at unaccustomed speed.

'Where shall we go then?' Seymour asked. 'Shall we just wander along, hand in hand, giving Mr Hitler a clear target?'

'Yes,' said Jane. 'Why not?' But actually she was looking for somewhere quiet. Somewhere warm. Somewhere private.

Shortly she spotted a small hotel on the other side of the road. She was about to lead Seymour over to it when there was a sudden squeal of tyres. A black car, driven extremely fast, rounded the corner of Sloane Street and began to advance upon them, accelerating rapidly until it was doing about sixty.

This display of high-speed driving was most unusual in any circumstances, and Jane could only think that the air-raid siren had put somebody into the most frightful panic. She held Seymour's arm, restraining him in case he might once again have forgotten about which side of the road to look at first, and she stared at the windscreen of the fast-moving car as it roared past them and flashed straight through the red traffic-lights at the junction fifty yards ahead. Then the car roared on up Beauchamp Place, eventually disappearing as it turned left.

Jane was quite taken aback. 'Well!' she said. 'What do you think of that?'

'Very odd,' said Seymour, frowning. 'Do English people often drive so fast?'

'The driver looked awfully familiar,' said Jane. 'I'm sure I've met him at a function of some sort. All red face and pomposity. And he was certainly in a great hurry.'

'Yes,' said Seymour slowly. 'And what about those two women fighting in the back seat?'

'What about the what?'

'The two women,' Seymour repeated. 'Struggling in the back seat.'

'Nonsense.'

'There were!' Seymour insisted. 'I saw them. You were looking at the man, evidently – ' He gave her a hard look, as if to say *You would always look at the man.* Then he continued: ' – and I was looking at the women. Two of them, in the back seat. One of them blonde, the other dark.'

'Nonsense.' Jane took Seymour by the arm and led him across the road towards the hotel which she had spotted a few moments earlier. 'I cannot vouch for what happens in Cambridge,

Massachusetts, or for that matter in Cambridge, England, but in London ladies do not fight in the back seat of cars. Especially when the car in question is a Bentley driven by a peer of the realm.'

'Oh, so you do know the driver?' said Seymour.

'Sort of. I remember his face. He had House of Lords written all over him.'

'Oh, well, that would explain it then.'

'Explain what?'

Seymour Jensen paused on the pavement outside the hotel. 'Well – ' He hesitated.

'Spit it out, Seymour darling, you'll feel *so* much better afterwards.'

'Well – it's just that I thought the darker woman in the back seat was more of a girl, really. And she reminded me very much of Princess Elizabeth. And before you say anything,' he added hurriedly, 'let me say that I have seen the Princess – she was at a reception at the Embassy only two nights ago. And I was very nearly introduced to her.'

'Hmmph,' said Jane, which meant that she didn't believe a word of it.

Jane took Seymour by the hand and led him into the hotel.

'What are we going in here for?' squeaked Seymour.

'We are going in here,' said Jane, 'to shelter from the bombs, to get out of the cold, and to have a madly passionate snogging session all on our own.'

She glanced at Seymour and saw that he had gone quite pale, which caused her to burst out laughing.

Still holding him by the hand, she stood in the deserted hotel lobby and looked around.

'Where is everybody?' asked Seymour, voicing her own thoughts.

'Sheltering in the basement probably. Not a place I would care to be myself. It takes too long to dig you out if there's a direct hit.' Then Jane found what she was looking for and pulled Seymour along behind her.

‘Come with me,’ she said. ‘We’ll go in here.’

Seymour proved unco-operative. ‘But... but... ’ he stammered. ‘This is the ladies toilet!’

Jane looked at the sign on the door, as if seeing it for the first time. ‘So it is,’ she said, and pulled him in after her.

To her delight, Seymour was clearly far more frightened of being found in a ladies toilet than he was of being killed by German bombs. ‘We can’t go in here!' he hissed.

‘Of course we can,’ said Jane. ‘There’s a war on. Things are different in wartime. And why are you whispering?’

‘Because I don’t want anyone to hear us.’

‘But nobody can hear us, Seymour, we’re alone. Look, there’re only three stalls and they’re all empty.’

‘But what if someone finds us?’

‘They won’t,’ said Jane. ‘I’ll put the light out.’ And she reached over and clicked off the switch.

Seymour groaned and Jane chuckled. As usual, she was persuading him to perform acts which were in total conflict with the way he had been brought up, and few things amused her more. She took a firm grip of Seymour’s hand and pulled him into one of the stalls. She locked the door, sat him down on the seat of the toilet, and then perched on his knee.

‘There,’ she said, nibbling his ear. ‘Isn’t this cosy?’

‘Oh God,’ groaned Seymour. ‘*Cops nab Yank perv in dames’ can*. I can see the headline now.’

‘Shut up,’ said Jane. ‘And kiss me.’

It took a minute or two, but eventually Jane got Seymour going. The warm contact of her own flesh against his proved to be a more powerful stimulus than his nineteen-year-old self-control could deal with – which was exactly what Jane had anticipated. Soon she could feel a pleasingly firm erection pressing hard against her thigh.

‘Stand up,’ she said.

‘What?’

‘Stand up, Seymour. Don’t argue. And don’t say *What*. It’s vulgar.’

‘Why do I have to stand up? Are we going?’

'No,' said Jane. 'We're going to come.'

'Oh God,' breathed Seymour.

'Sshh, my darling,' said Jane softly. 'Sshh. Sshh. Sshh.'

Seymour stood up. Jane unbuckled his belt, reached in through the fly of his trousers, and drew out his erect penis. She squeezed it and Seymour gave an involuntary sob.

'Oh I know, darling,' said Jane sympathetically. 'I know.'

Now that Seymour was ready, Jane unzipped her own skirt and stepped neatly out of it. She pushed down her silk knickers (Fortnum and Mason), and deposited them on top of her skirt on the seat of the toilet.

The darkness hummed around them. Outside there were four successive crunches as bombs fell some streets away. Seymour flinched instinctively.

Jane reached up and pulled Seymour's head down. She kissed him passionately, pushing her tongue into his mouth. She desperately wanted him to do the same to her, but he didn't seem to understand that. Well, never mind, she would teach him some other time.

Then while gently squeezing and stroking his cock, she took his hand and drew it down between her legs. She felt the tension in his arm, a tension which reflected the conflict between Seymour's desire and dismay. Half of him wanted – *oh* how he wanted – to feel her and grope her and play with her. But the other half of him clearly couldn't cope.

Jane had only known Seymour about two weeks, but already she knew him well enough to be aware that he had been brought up to believe that you just didn't *do* these things. You just didn't suck girls' nipples while you were pinching them hard between the legs. Especially not when they were nice, well-bred English girls, who were supposed to be terribly shy and retiring and introvert. But Seymour was learning, slowly. This time, when she placed his hand where she wanted it, he didn't move it away.

'There,' said Jane with a sigh. 'Now you play with me nicely, Seymour. Just the way I taught you. And if you're very very good I might even play with you.'

Which, of course, she did immediately. She began to stroke his cock, rhythmically, firmly, and steadily, but controlling him all the time. Not letting him get too far gone until she was good and ready.

Eventually – Jane had no idea how long it took – she opened her legs just a little bit wider, and then she closed them tight, gripping Seymour's fingers in her groin. And she sighed with pleasure as her brain fizzed and her pulse pounded.

Then, with a quiet laugh, she began to quicken the movement of her own hand.

Seymour squirmed, and she sensed that he was still sufficiently under control to be concerned about where his ejaculation would go. 'Just let it come,' she said fiercely. 'Just let it squirt wherever it wants.'

And then, with a practised movement, she went on flicking and fondling his cock until she felt a powerful throbbing in her fingers and he almost fell against her.

Chapter 2

The bombs seemed to have stopped falling, so Jane and Seymour left the hotel. No one saw the two of them depart, and the streets remained almost deserted.

They walked in silence for a while, Seymour in particular moving like a zombie.

Then Jane glanced at her watch.

'It's nearly five already,' she said, 'so let's go round by the Palace and pick up my father. It's a bit out of our way but you'll enjoy having a look round inside.'

'The inside of Buckingham Palace?' squawked Seymour. 'They'll never let me past the door.'

'Oh yes,' said Jane confidently. 'If I vouch for you.'

As they approached the Palace, the nearby air-raid sirens gave out a high, steady-pitched note. This was the so-called 'all-clear' signal, indicating that the danger of an enemy attack from the air had passed, for the time being at any rate.

Seymour had said nothing while they walked through the enclosing darkness, and as they neared the Palace gates Jane asked him what he was thinking.

'Do you want the truth?'

'Of course.'

'Well – to be honest – I was thinking that you're kind of weird.'

Jane laughed. 'No, darling. I'm not weird. I'm just English.'

Jane led the way round the front of the Palace to the private entrance in the south wing. In the black-out it was hard to see where they were going, but with the aid of a small torch, which she had carried in her handbag ever since the beginning of the war, she found the door without difficulty.

Once inside, Jane introduced Seymour to Mr Redpath, a grey-haired security guard who was an old friend of hers.

'You remember Mr Jensen from the American Embassy?' she

said. 'This is his son, Seymour.'

'Well, how do you do, sir,' said Redpath. 'A pleasure to meet you.... I expect you'll be going up to see your father, Miss?'

'That's right.'

'Just sign in, if you will.'

Jane and Seymour signed the proffered visitors book, and then she led the way into the main building. Seymour was most impressed, she could tell.

'Gee,' he said. 'I've been inside the White House, but I never expected to come in here.'

They climbed a flight of stairs, and as they were walking down one of the long corridors leading to the King's business offices, a woman with an agitated air rushed out of an adjoining corridor and almost bumped into them.

'Oh!' she said. 'Oh, I'm so sorry.' And then: 'Oh, it's you, Jane.' And she went on hastily, without any preliminaries, 'Tell me, you haven't seen Lillibet have you?'

'No, Crawfie, I'm afraid not,' said Jane.

'Oh. Oh dear,' said Crawfie. 'She should have been back ages ago.' And she dashed off immediately, her unbuttoned cardigan flapping in the breeze she created.

'Who was that?' asked Seymour, as they continued their trek down the corridor.

'That was Crawfie. Miss Crawford to you. She acts as governess to the two Princesses. A real mother hen.'

'Ah. And who is Lillibet?'

'Short for Elizabeth.'

'*Princess* Elizabeth?' Seymour paused and gazed back the way they had come, but Crawfie had long since disappeared.

'God, Seymour, your powers of deduction are amazing.'

'But if she's looking for, er, the Princess Elizabeth, shouldn't we tell her that we saw her in the back of a car?'

'No, Seymour, we should not, because *we* did not see her. You simply imagined that you had.'

In December 1940, Jane's father, Alastair Padget, was Legal Secretary to the King. He had served three Kings in this capacity:

George V, from 1933 to 1936; Edward VIII, during his reign of a few months in 1936; and now the 'new King', George VI.

When Jane and Seymour arrived at Alastair's office he was just pulling on his overcoat, and so almost immediately they all three retraced their steps to the south entrance.

As they approached Mr Redpath, in order to sign out, the door swung open and in came the formidably tall and well-built figure of Commander David Mantle, the uniformed officer from Scotland Yard who was responsible for the security of the royal family.

'Evening, Alastair,' boomed the Commander, as he scribbled his name in Redpath's book.

'Hello, David,' said Alastair. 'What brings you here?'

Commander Mantle lowered his voice. 'Oh, some sort of panic about Lillibet,' he said, as if he wasn't taking it very seriously. 'She went out for a dancing lesson earlier on, and now Crawfie is frantic because she's late getting back. I don't suppose you've seen the Princess have you?'

'No,' said Alastair. 'I haven't seen her all day.'

Jane realised at once that if Commander Mantle had been sent for, there was genuine concern about Princess Elizabeth at a high level, so she decided to put aside her own private doubts about what Seymour had seen. She put a hand on the police-officer's arm as he made to move by.

'Er, Commander,' she said, 'if you've really been sent for to look for the Princess, I have to say that Mr Jensen here thought he caught a glimpse of her in the back seat of a Bentley, at about half-past four.'

'Oh? Where was this?'

'In Pont Street,' said Jane. 'We were just about to cross the road, and the Bentley came by very fast.'

'Heading which way?'

'West.'

'Oh....' The Commander looked doubtful. 'Wrong way entirely, really. The dancing class was in Belgrave Square. And she went in a Rolls. You say this young gentleman saw her – so you didn't see the Princess yourself, Jane?'

'No. I was looking at the driver, because he was driving so recklessly and I thought he was a menace to society. But it was just after the siren went, so I suppose he must have been in a bit of a panic.'

The Commander turned to Seymour. 'And you, young man. Are you sure of the identification?'

Seymour turned slightly pale. 'Heavens, no, Sir. Not really sure. I've only seen the Princess once, at a reception at the American Embassy. And I only got a glimpse of the two women in the back of the car. But one of them sure looked like the Princess to me.'

'Well, thank you for your help,' said the Commander. 'I may come back to you. But I'll go upstairs and see what the King has to say. I expect it's just the raid that's caused the problem.'

Jane, Alastair and Seymour made their way on foot to the Padgets' flat, which was in a house in Eaton Square. It wasn't far, about half a mile, and Jane and her father knew the route intimately. This was just as well, because in the black-out a stranger would soon have got lost.

Once home, Jane set about cooking dinner, while Seymour and her father sat talking over sherry.

Jane wondered if Seymour realised what was going on during this preprandial chat. Probably not. But she knew perfectly well what her father was up to. In suggesting that they should all three have dinner together, Alastair Padget was achieving a number of ends at once.

First, he was making his daughter happy, because he knew that she was fond of Seymour, although she hadn't known him very long. Second, he was flattering a young man, making him feel important by discussing the progress of the war with him on confidential terms, just as if he were a man of the world much older than his actual years. This was a good way to make a friend, possibly an influential friend, for the future. And third, Alastair was finding out, very tactfully, what Jensen Senior at the US Embassy had been telling his son about the political situation in Europe.

In December 1940 the United States of America had not yet entered the war, and was, strictly speaking, a neutral party; hence it was useful for the British to know what Washington was *really* thinking and intending to do. And in return Alastair Padget was subtly feeding into Seymour's memory a few bits of information which he wanted passed on – passed on indirectly and discreetly of course – to the US government. Alastair had no doubt that, later on in the evening, Frederick Jensen would ask his freshman son what had been talked about over dinner.

Jane smiled as she cooked. He was a devious so-and-so, her father. But then he had once worked for MI5, and still maintained close links with that organisation.

'Chops!' exclaimed Alastair with delight when his meal was served. 'Haven't seen a chop for a fortnight. What did you have to do to get these?'

'Had to promise the butcher the use of my body three times a week,' said Jane, and was gratified when poor Seymour nearly choked on his wine.

Her father sighed. 'Jane,' he said, 'I do wish you would remember that you are not among your left-wing Oxford friends now, but in the presence of a guest.'

'Yes, Daddy,' said Jane dutifully.

Discussion turned to the former King, Edward VIII. Since his abdication in December 1936, he had been known as the Duke of Windsor, and Seymour was astonished to hear that the Duke and his then mistress, Mrs Wallis Simpson, had on several occasions been entertained to dinner in this very room.

'In fact,' said Alastair, 'he sat in the same chair as yourself.'

'And Wallis Simpson sat in mine,' said Jane. 'The seat is still warm.'

'Gee whiz!' said Seymour. 'Just wait till I tell Pa!'

Alastair laughed. 'You'll find he knows already. He and your mother have been here on several occasions.'

Seymour became thoughtful. 'There's been an awful lot about the Duke in the American press, you know. He's been giving interviews and making statements that even I thought were a bit...'

'A bit what?' asked Jane.

'Well...' Seymour paused. 'Disloyal? Out of line?'

'The Duke makes no secret of the fact that he wants this war to end,' said Alastair. 'We haven't been in any doubt about that for some time, and he will tell anyone prepared to listen that he wants a negotiated peace between Great Britain and Germany.'

Seymour hesitated again, as if worried about offending his hosts. 'And isn't there... some sort of idea about him becoming King again? Or not so much King perhaps, but a President of England?'

'Well,' said Alastair carefully, 'it isn't very widely known, but the Duke of Windsor would apparently be willing, as part of a peace treaty, to see his brother King George packed off to Canada or Australia – with the royal family given safe passage as well, of course. And it appears that, in those circumstances, the Duke would be prepared to return to England as some sort of head of state. Whether as King, or President, or whatever, would remain to be seen.'

The phone rang, and Jane left her chair to answer it.

'Are you two planning to go out tonight?' Alastair asked, after Jane had disappeared into the hall.

'Er, yes, I think so,' said Seymour. 'Jane has promised to take me to the theatre. I gather it's quite a cultural evening. At the Windmill, I believe it's called.'

What response Alastair Padget might have made to his daughter's suggestion for the entertainment of Seymour Jensen that evening will never be known, because Jane called him to take the telephone.

When Alastair returned a few moments later his expression was grave. 'I'm afraid I've got to go back to the Palace,' he said. 'There's some sort of crisis blown up.'

'Oh dear,' said Jane. 'And you haven't had your pudding yet, either. Never mind, Seymour and I will share it between us.'

'No you won't,' said Alastair. 'Seymour must eat on his own. Because you, Jane, have got to come too.'

Chapter 3

The black-out meant that there were few taxis to be had after dark, so Alastair and Jane walked to the Palace. Alastair set a brisk pace, and they soon became warm despite a touch of frost in the air.

Just after they set off, Alastair said: 'Are you serious about that young man?'

Jane didn't answer directly. 'Why do you ask?'

'Well, because if you are, you're awfully hard on him. If there's anything to him he won't hang around to be treated badly.'

Jane took the view that she'd always been rather nice to Seymour. Perhaps teased him a little, but that was all. However, she made no reply.

For the next ten minutes Jane and her father walked in silence, each wondering about the particular nature of the crisis which had led to their being summoned back to the Palace.

When they arrived they were asked to go immediately to the King's study.

The King looked up as Alastair knocked and entered first. 'Ah, Alastair,' he said. 'Thank you for coming. And you too, Jane.'

Jane noticed at once that the room was thick with tobacco smoke. As usual, the King was smoking full-strength Capstan – an open packet lay on his desk – and Commander Mantle was joining in. By the look of them both, they'd been chain-smoking for hours.

Also on the King's desk was a large whisky and soda, apparently untouched. The drink looked flat, as if the King had poured it much earlier, and had then decided that he needed a clear head more than he needed a drink.

Alastair and Jane were asked to sit down, and were put at their ease. Then Commander Mantle began to speak.

'Now, Jane,' he said, 'you and I bumped into each other briefly, just as I arrived, and you made a few comments that I want to go over with you again.'

During the next few minutes, the Commander carefully drew from Jane a repeat of the story about the Bentley hurtling past herself and Seymour in Pont Street. He questioned her about Seymour's possible sighting of Princess Elizabeth, and about her own view of the driver.

Eventually the Commander paused, and there was silence for a few moments. The blue-uniformed man more than filled his chair, but there was no fat on him. Jane recalled the story that, years earlier, when he was a beat constable in the East End, he had chased and caught two thieves. Grabbing one, he had tucked him under his arm and then sprinted on to capture the other.

The King spoke, addressing himself to Alastair and Jane. 'I think you both ought to know,' he said slowly, 'that this afternoon Princess Elizabeth went out for a dancing lesson at an academy in Belgrave Square. She's been going there for some months, every Monday, regular as clockwork. Perhaps too regular. Anyway, she was accompanied as usual by Sergeant Wilson, the detective responsible for her safety. He drove the car, which was a Rolls.... Well, to cut the story short, Lillibet and the Sergeant didn't arrive back at the Palace at the expected time. No one worried at first – there was an air-raid on, they could have decided to take shelter, that sort of thing. Crawfie panicked, of course – was convinced her beloved Lillibet had been hit by a bomb – but then Crawfie's always panicking.... Time passed, until it was obvious that something was wrong. I sent for Commander Mantle, and a search was started. Very discreetly.'

The King hesitated, and struggled to control his emotions. This was a man, Jane recalled, who had never expected to be King, but on Edward VIII's abdication he had been obliged to take the throne, largely against his wishes. He had always found it difficult to carry the burdens of office, and tonight he looked more care-worn and worried than usual. He dragged on his cigarette.

Commander Mantle took up the story. 'We've found Sergeant Wilson. Found him in an alleyway round the back of a shop, quite near the dancing academy. It's where the car would have been parked. He'd been shot in the back of the head. Dead, of course.

Very professional job, and quite ruthless. But we haven't yet found the Princess.'

'And you've had no communication about her?' asked Alastair.

'Oh yes,' said the King. 'We've had a comm... a comm... a communication.' The King's agitation was making his stammer worse than usual. 'A phone call, to be precise. Very brief, and much too quick to be traced. Came through on my direct line, missing the switchboard, so someone's jolly well informed. Not many people have that number. Anyway, the blighter had the insufferable imp... imp... impudence to tell me – '

For a moment the King was unable to continue, and Jane noticed that a nerve in his cheek was twitching.

'The message was,' said the Commander, 'that the Princess was safe. She was being held by the speaker – who was a man, by the way. And that – quote – a letter is in the post.'

'A letter is in the post?' echoed Alastair incredulously.

'That's right. If it weren't for the death of Sergeant Wilson I'd be inclined to think we were dealing with a crank, or a lunatic. But all the signs are – despite the eccentric approach – that these people know exactly what they're doing.'

'You say these people,' said Jane. 'There's more than one person involved?'

'I would guess so,' said the Commander. 'It's almost certainly a man who did the shooting, probably the same man who phoned His Majesty, and your friend Seymour saw a woman struggling with the Princess.'

'Oh,' said Jane in a small voice. She was a little taken aback to discover that the Commander seemed to accept Seymour's evidence at face value, whereas she herself had poured scorn on it. But of course the circumstances were a little different now.

'I don't suppose,' said the Commander to Jane, 'that you remember any of the registration number of the car you saw?'

'No,' said Jane. 'But it was a black Bentley, four and a quarter litre engine, with a Park Ward body. They don't make a thousand of those every week.'

'How come you know so much about Bentleys?' asked the Commander.

'Both my uncles have got them.'

'Well done, Jane!' said the King. 'You see, Commander, I told you she had to come!'

'And I think,' said Jane, 'that if you can show me some photographs, I might be able to identify the driver.'

'Photographs?' said the Commander. 'You mean the rogues' gallery?'

'No, no, he's not a convicted criminal. Not yet. But I have a strong feeling that I've seen him before. In fact, my impression is that he's a member of the House of Lords.'

'Well there's some pretty criminal chaps in there,' grunted the King.

Alastair addressed the King. 'I wonder if you could bring me up to date on the action taken so far, Sir?'

The King waved at the Commander, authorising him to speak.

'Very well,' said Mantle. 'One, a cover story has been put out, within the royal household, to the effect that the Princess has been taken ill with suspected appendicitis. We've put a D-notice on it, in case it leaks, so the newspapers won't print a word. Within the Palace, only the King and the Queen know the truth. Two, on the assumption that this crazy story about a letter in the post is true, we've got the Post Office doing a double-quick delivery of the Palace's mail. Normally it would be brought in about four o'clock tomorrow morning, but we're expecting the first sackful any time now. Of course there are also quite a lot of letters handed in at the Palace gate by members of the public – messages of goodwill and so forth. Christmas cards at this time of year. We're having them brought up also. The fact that the Post Office is clogged with Christmas mail doesn't help – but they're doing their best.'

The King rose to his feet. 'Alastair,' he said, 'pretty soon the Commander will have to go back to Scotland Yard to co-ordinate the operation there. What I want you to do is to be in charge of things here.'

'Gladly,' said Alastair.

'And what I'd like you to do, Jane,' the King continued, 'is come with me.'

Jane glanced at her father, who nodded, and she rose to her feet. She followed the King into an adjoining sitting-room, where he crossed to a bookcase.

'House of Lords, you say?'

'Well, possibly,' said Jane faintly. She was beginning to wish that she'd never mentioned the possibility of identifying the driver, because the King appeared to be building up his hopes.

The King pulled open a drawer in the lower part of the bookcase. Then he stood up, clutching a photograph album. 'Yes, this is it. We had most of the House of Lords here for one of last summer's garden parties. It was a relatively small affair – there is a war on, after all – but Lillibet was trying out her new camera. One of these Leica things. German, naturally, but don't tell anyone, and she was so proud of the results that we had them put in an album....' He placed the book on a table. 'Now, let's see. You sit down here, Jane, and make your way through it.'

'Yes, Sir,' said Jane.

Her heart was beating so loudly in her ears that she could hardly hear any normal sounds at all. And the chop which she had eaten with such enthusiasm only about an hour ago was beginning to think about making its way up again.

Jane took a deep breath and told herself not to be stupid. All she had to do was look through the photographs, speak up if she recognised the driver of the Bentley, or say at the end that she was terribly sorry if she didn't.

That was the theory, anyway. In practice it was harder. Every time she turned a page she had a sudden lurch of conviction that this, *this* was the page. And that man there, the one with the walking-stick, he, *he* was the –

But no, no, of course he wasn't.

Eventually, when she was two thirds of the way through the book, Jane saw the man immediately, and there was no doubt whatever in her mind. She saw his face in the photograph, one of a group of four talking to the King, and she remembered that she had seen him in Pont Street that afternoon, and that she had seen him in other places, at other times.

'Sir?' she said.

The King came to her side.

'This is the man.'

The King sighed. 'Oh,' he said. 'Westrow.'

'Oh yes,' said Jane. 'The Earl of Westrow. I knew I had seen him before. I just couldn't remember who he was.'

'Stay here, Jane,' said the King, and he went back into his study.

The King was gone for some time, and Jane had another attack of doubt. What was *happening* in there? Was the King telling them that she had made a fool of herself, that she had identified someone who was known to be in Australia, or who was *dead*? Oh God, she wished she had kept her mouth shut. And as for that bloody Seymour – who had only even *seen* the Princess once, and had fancied her something rotten because she was very beautiful, even if she was only fourteen – well, Jane thought, she was going to tell that bloody Seymour what she thought of him and his short-sighted identifications of royalty the next time she saw him.

The King returned.

'I've got them working on it,' he said. 'The Commander's gone back to the Yard. He's going to set about finding Westrow. And your father's organising everybody here. Those that can be trusted to keep their mouths shut and do a good job, that is – and there aren't very many of them.'

'Oh,' said Jane, in a rather small voice. 'Well I do hope I'm right, otherwise it will all be most embarrassing.'

'Oh I'm sure you're right,' said the King. 'I ought to have guessed really, but one doesn't like to think ill of one's fellow men. Especially when he's a peer of the realm.'

The King lit yet another cigarette and fell silent while he inhaled heavily.

'I see,' said Jane quietly. She stood up. 'Well, if you'll excuse me, Sir, I think I'd better get out of the way.'

'Oh no!' said the King hastily. 'No – please don't go, Jane.... If you leave, I shall have to go and face the Queen.' He pulled a rueful face. 'And I'm afraid I'm not quite ready for that. Not yet. Dreadful coward, you see!'

He sat down at the table, and motioned for Jane to do the same.

'What do you know about Westrow, Jane?'

'Um.... Not very much, really. Except that he's a Fascist, isn't he? One of those who admire Hitler and Mussolini for making the trains run on time.'

'Yes, he is. It's hard to know how black a villain he is, really. But I'm afraid I've misjudged him, very badly. You see, twenty, twenty-five years ago, this nation was fighting another war. And in the nineteen-thirties, when the international scene started to turn nasty, a lot of men were prepared to do almost anything to avoid a repeat of that war. Mr Chamberlain, Mr Kennedy, and so on. Even now that the second world war has begun, there are still people who will do almost anything to stop it. Mr Kennedy, for example, has been having talks with Goering in Vichy France.'

The King must have noticed that Jane's eyes opened wide in response to this piece of news about the American Ambassador to England, because he added: 'Oh yes, it's true. MI5 have been keeping a very close eye on Mr K., I can assure you.'

Jane couldn't help asking: 'What on earth were Mr Kennedy and Goering talking about?'

'Oh, their own self-interest, of course,' said the King. 'Dressed up in some hypocritical mishmash about peace in our time. Goering wants to take over from Hitler, I imagine, and Kennedy wants the war to end so that he can get back to making money on the New York stock exchange – though he manages to do pretty well here. He sells British firms short whenever it looks as if we're going to get beaten. Which is most of the time at present.'

'Oh dear,' said Jane, which sounded a bit feeble even to her own ears.

'Oh dear indeed. But my own brother is not much better behaved, I'm afraid. The Duke of Windsor and that wife of his sent their maid back to their house in enemy-occupied Paris – with the knowledge and approval of the Germans, if you please – just to collect some bloody crockery! I mean, one can hardly believe it. It's a breach of the Trading with the Enemy Act, for a start. That normally results in imprisonment without trial. But the Duke and Duchess seem to regard the war as a tiresome inconvenience, which ought to affect only the little people. They're just damned lucky that Mr Churchill is an old friend of the Duke's.'

'Well,' said Jane, 'if the Earl of Westrow is one of those people who would like the war to end, perhaps his heart is in the right place. And if he is the one who's kidnapped Princess Elizabeth, perhaps he doesn't really intend to do her any harm.'

The King sighed. 'Well that would be a very nice thought, Jane. But I'm afraid it's absolute nonsense. Let us not deceive ourselves. Westrow has already shot dead a police Sergeant – shot him in the back of the head, which is a coward's way – and I'm afraid he has no scruples whatever. He fooled me, you see. In the summer, when we arrested Mosley and all those other Fascist sympathisers, MI5 had Westrow on the list. But he came to see me, and argued precisely the kind of case you've just put. Said he was a loyal British citizen, prepared to do his bit, but he just had a genuine difference of view about the best form of government to make the people prosperous. So I – bloody fool that I am – crossed him off the list. I thought he was just a harmless crank. And then ten days ago he came to see me again – wanted me to make peace with Germany, peace at any price. And now look what he's done – kidnapped the Princess. And he'll want me to do something spectacular before he gives her back, you can bet on that. Though God knows what it will be.' The King looked crestfallen. 'The Queen is going to give me hell when she finds out.'

The King reached for his packet of cigarettes, found that it was empty, and immediately located another one on the mantelpiece. 'You see, the thing about you, Jane,' he said thoughtfully, as he lit perhaps his forty-first smoke of the day, 'is that you're twenty. You're at... Oxford, isn't it?'

'Yes, Sir.'

'And you've had a bit of a life. You've mixed with people. Done the simple, everyday things, like going shopping, going to the cinema, and dances. But Lillibet, you see, she's only fourteen. So she's still a child. Looks older, of course. But she's been nowhere, met hardly anyone outside the Palace. Poor girl will be scared stiff.'

'Don't worry, Sir,' said Jane. 'From what I've seen of the Princess, she's a very calm and sensible girl. I'm sure she'll keep her head.'

'Well, I hope so,' said the King glumly.

The door opened, and Alastair Padget announced that a few bags of mail had arrived. The promised letter, which would presumably set out what the kidnapper wanted in return for the release of Princess Elizabeth, might be among the pile which was now in the middle of the floor in the King's study.

Alastair and Jane got down on their knees and began slicing open the royal mail. So too did His Majesty King George VI, ruler of the United Kingdom of Great Britain and Northern Ireland, Defender of the Faith, and Emperor of India.

A quick glance was enough to determine whether each letter was the vital expected one, or just a piece of ordinary correspondence. All three of them wielded their letter-openers in silence.

They worked for some time, until Jane's knees began to ache.

Then, she unfolded one letter to find that the printed heading made it plain that it came from the office of the Earl of Westrow. She could scarcely believe that the man would be so bare-faced about what he had done. Talk about burning your boats!

She sat there, quite stunned, quickly scanning through the contents of the letter. When she was sure she said, 'Oh! I think this is it!' And she started to read it again.

After a moment her father coughed. 'Er, Jane,' he said. 'I rather think the King would like to read it for himself.'

Jane blushed furiously. 'Oh! Yes, yes,' she said. 'I'm so sorry, Sir.' And she handed the letter over.

The King pushed himself to his feet and walked over to his desk, where the reading-lamp provided a better light. He read the letter carefully, more than once.

Then he laid it down.

'Well,' he said. 'It is not good news.'

Part Two

October 1927 – June 1935

Chapter 4

It is a curious but little-known fact that, on the afternoon of Wednesday 12 June 1935, all those who were later to be involved – directly or indirectly – in the kidnapping of Princess Elizabeth were gathered together at an English garden party. Of course they didn't all know each other at the time; and, perhaps mercifully, they did not know that some five years later they would be forced by circumstances to take the action they did. Nevertheless, there they all were.

The host of the garden party was the Prince of Wales, and the place was Fort Belvedere, his eighteenth-century country house near Sunningdale. 'The Fort', as it was called, was ideally situated, being some six miles from Windsor and twenty-five miles from London. The Prince had been given the house by his father, King George V, and he had worked hard in the gardens and woodlands. He had made himself something of an authority on horticulture, especially on the growing of roses. As a result, the grounds provided a splendid setting for a social gathering on a warm June afternoon.

In 1935 the then Prince of Wales was undoubtedly the most famous and admired bachelor in the world. Slim, short, golden-haired and blue-eyed, he was, quite literally, the pin-up of many a young woman.

This bachelor Prince was just turned forty, and of course it was high time he was married. Every mother of an even halfway eligible daughter would tell you so without hesitation. And so would those who were worried about the royal succession, for the Prince would be King soon: George V was ailing.

The Prince was handsome, gay (in the old sense), debonair, charming, amusing, and likeable. He was a polished host, and every one of his guests felt welcome. Some of the women were hoping to catch his eye, but the Prince was, of course, spoken for.

Over the previous twenty years the Prince had enjoyed many close friendships with beautiful women – all of them married.

And now he had another mistress, and this time she was an American: Mrs Wallis Simpson.

For months the American and European newspapers had been full of gossip about Mrs Simpson, but the British press had tactfully avoided all mention of her. There was a long tradition in England that the press did not reveal what royalty were really up to. And besides, Mrs Simpson was so obviously unsuitable as a potential Queen that there wasn't the slightest chance – was there? – that the Prince would marry her. For one thing she had been divorced once already, and to be free to marry anyone else she would have to divorce again. Well, that ruled her out completely. And besides, she was an American, and therefore unsuitable by definition. But those who saw them together, on that June afternoon in 1935, were by no means so sure that the Prince would not, this time, commit himself permanently. And oh what problems would then ensue.

Wallis Simpson was therefore the Prince's consort for the afternoon. Wallis herself was no longer young: she was forty, but claimed to be thirty-nine, and was slim, dark, and vivacious. She had built her reputation by making herself attractive to rich and powerful men, and by now she had got it all down to a precise art.

Wallis was of course immaculately dressed in highly fashionable clothes (and the Prince himself was no slouch in these matters), but she was by no means flashy: she was discreet, elegant, and impressive. When she spoke, which she was not slow to do, she said what she thought, whether about world affairs or a lady's hat; but she said it sensibly, calmly, and without causing offence. She knew how to put people at ease. Those who had come to the garden party hoping to meet a vulgar, brash woman who would quickly cut her own throat were sadly disappointed.

There was another American there too: Joseph P. Kennedy. Joe was a hardened, ruthless Wall-Street financier, that is to say a crook. He had made his first big killing on the stock market in 1923, and another one a year later. On each occasion, Joe and a few insiders won; the suckers lost. Joe was smart enough to avoid the financial crash of 1929, and he had long since set up million-dollar trust funds for each of his nine children. (It was one thing to take money off suckers, but quite another to disobey his church's teaching on contraception.) Once he had made money, Joe had begun to buy political influence within the Democratic party. And now he was touring Europe, informally on behalf of President Roosevelt, trying to find out what the hell was going on, and whether there really would have to be another war.

Joe's long-suffering wife Rose was there with him. Rose was another fashion-plate, looking pretty good despite having given birth to nine children in seventeen years. Where sexual matters were concerned, her husband was what might be called a high-energy guy. Rose was well aware of this, and whenever Joe got himself a new girlfriend, or spent a night with a whore, Rose went out and bought some new dresses or a fur coat. This meant that she had for years been one of the world's great shoppers. She needed a lot of wardrobe space.

Germany's growing power in Europe was represented at the garden party by Hitler's principal adviser on foreign affairs, Joachim von Ribbentrop. The 'von' part of his name meant that he was an aristocrat. True, he had had to persuade a distant relative to adopt him, at the age of twenty-eight, in order to acquire this desirable prefix, but there it was, the visible and permanent proof of his true worth. Or so he thought. In fact, of course, he was just a jumped-up little wine salesman who had risen to power by supporting Hitler. Ribbentrop was enjoying the garden party no end. He spoke fluent English himself, and all the very best people were there. And there were no Jews.

Outside the inner circle of the rich, famous and powerful, there were perhaps a hundred lesser guests: Dutch diplomats, Russian exiles, Scout leaders, struggling musicians. These people had been invited not because they were friends of the Prince of Wales and Wallis Simpson, but because courtesy required that they be offered the chance to attend, as a reward for services, or as an encouragement to greater and more loyal service in the future. One of these lesser players in the social game was the Earl of Westrow.

Westrow was a dedicated admirer of the Prince of Wales: that is to say he admired the Prince's political views, and had a deep reverence for his royal status. He saw the Prince as a man who, when he became King, would be a true leader. If the Prince had clicked his fingers and said 'Westrow, lick my boots', Westrow would have said 'Yes sir yes sir', and got right down and done it, with a heart filled with joy. But he was not a man who pushed himself forward. He was aged thirty-four, but he looked ten years older. He loved food and drink, smoked heavily, and hated exercise. His lightweight suit was from Savile Row, and his valet had done his best to send him out decent; but by the time he had walked to his car Westrow had contrived to look scruffy again.

Westrow stood well back under the trees, a glass of wine in his hand, watching the others. He didn't approach strangers, and they, after a glance, didn't approach him. But he didn't mind. He was used to it. He had been alone ever since childhood – alone and not much liked. While most men are given a nickname or two at school, this man had never had one: he had always been Westrow to everyone. Westrow watched. And waited. And perhaps the most serious mistake that could have been made on that carefree June afternoon was to assume that he was as ineffectual and harmless as he looked.

There was one man at the party who was there, reluctantly, because he wanted to meet and get to know those people who, he suspected, would have to be dealt with sooner or later. This was Alastair Padget, Legal Secretary to the King. Alastair was plain Mr Padget, because he had turned down a knighthood, but if his wife had been alive he would certainly have accepted it, for she would have enjoyed the cachet of being a Lady. Instead of a wife, Alastair had brought his only child, a daughter.

Jane Padget was fifteen years old that summer, and she was as beautiful as an English girl can be at that age. Well turned out too – the French Ambassador's wife had helped her to choose a dress which was right for the occasion but not too expensive. 'Darling,' said Wallis as Jane was greeted on her arrival, 'you look absolutely fabulous. you really do. So keep well away from me, sweetheart – I'm the star of the show!' And she laughed. But she meant it.

Jane smiled politely and moved through the crowd. And the

odd thing was, the crowd parted to admire her on her progress. Nearly all the men who were present spent quite a lot of time thinking about what lay under Jane's dress, Joe in particular; Rose had to speak to him quite sharply.

A week later, on 19 June 1935, the Prince of Wales made a speech to veterans of the 1914-18 war, in the Queen's Hall. He spoke of his desire to have the conflicts of the great war forgotten; he spoke of stretching out the hand of friendship to Europe. He received a standing ovation.

The King was furious, as were many politicians, for the Prince's speech broke the convention that members of the royal family do not make public statements on political matters.

In Germany, however, the speech was welcomed. One week later, the Reichsmarschall des Grossdeutschen Reiches, Hermann Goering, addressed a huge crowd of 200,000 at Nuremberg. After savagely denouncing the Jews, he referred to the Prince's views. He declared that the Prince of Wales could be sure that the German people would 'grasp most eagerly the hand that was offered them.'

No doubt. Just as they grabbed everything else, whether it was offered or not.

Chapter 5

We have seen how all those who were involved in the kidnapping of Princess Elizabeth in 1940 were gathered together for an innocent garden party as early as June 1935. But to understand how the major participants in this affair came to be so assembled, we need to go further back in time still – to October 1927.

The individuals concerned found themselves, as the Chinese curse has it, living in interesting times.

Extract from FBI report to President Franklin Delano Roosevelt, ref. 35/2/198:

> Further to your request for information on Mrs Wallis Simpson, a U.S. citizen who is currently attracting some attention as the mistress of the Prince of Wales:
>
> Mrs Simpson has been of interest to British intelligence since at least 1923, when she appeared in Hong Kong. A summary of the information supplied by MI6 in London is attached.
>
> It is noteworthy in this context that our own records show that in October 1927, shortly after her first marriage ended, she had a brief liaison with Mr Joseph P. Kennedy in Los Angeles.

Wallis opened her handbag, glanced at the contents, and sighed. 'Gonna have to get out and hustle, honey,' she told her companion, an unemployed actress called Gloria. 'I'm down to my last few bucks.'

Gloria motioned with her head towards the other side of the restaurant. 'Maybe you ought to pay some attention to that red-headed guy over there. He keeps looking your way. Couldn't take his eyes off you when you went to the john. He ain't too handsome but he's loaded.'

Wallis slyly examined the guy in question, not directly but by looking at his reflection in a mirror. What she saw was a slim, upright man of about forty, with a freckled face, horn-rimmed spectacles, and a lot of teeth. He seemed to have a permanent grin on his face. 'Yeah,' she said. 'I've noticed him. You know who he is?'

'Joe Kennedy. Banker, money man. Comes from Boston. Has a big thing with my namesake, Gloria Swanson. Or so they say.'

'Hmm.' Wallis now turned and looked at Mr Kennedy directly. He caught her eye, grinned broadly, and waved. Wallis smiled back, and lifted her glass in acknowledgement.

Joe sent over a bottle of champagne.

Joe woke up at six the next morning to find Wallis sitting up in bed beside him, phone in hand, ordering breakfast from room service. He was impressed.

'Hell,' he said, 'I thought I was an early riser but you beat me to it. Most of you broads sleep till about ten.'

'Not so much of the broad,' said Wallis. 'You're talking to a lady.'

Later, when they were dressed and ready to leave, Joe reached into his pocket and drew out his wallet.

'No, no, no,' said Wallis. 'That is not how gentlemen behave. There's a little jewellery shop down in the lobby. Let's go there instead.'

They spent some time in the lobby, Joe restlessly looking at his watch, but not – definitely not – making a move to leave.

'Jesus fucking Christ,' he said, after Wallis had made her choice from the entire stock of the shop. 'You sure got expensive taste.'

Wallis gave him a big sloppy kiss on the cheek and hugged his arm. 'Oh yes I know,' she said. 'But I'm worth it.'

Joe didn't disagree, but he paid with a sigh. 'Gotta go,' he said. 'Got a meeting.'

Over dinner that evening they met again, and Joe gave Wallis his standard spiel about how well connected he was in the movie business, and how, if she played her cards right, he could make her a star. He didn't actually say 'Stick with me, kid,' but he came close. He was astonished when Wallis laughed in his face.

'But I don't want to be a movie star, Joe.'

Joe could hardly believe it. He had always found that line

remarkably effective in the past. 'You don't?'

'No.'

'What the fuck are you doing in Los Angeles then?'

'Looking for a man like you, Joe. But preferably one who's single.'

Joe had no answer for that.

Seven days later Joe returned to Boston, and Wallis went out to dinner with Gloria again. Wallis paid.

'Well,' said Gloria. 'You seem to have made out OK with Uncle Joe. You gonna see him again?'

'I doubt it,' said Wallis. 'A man with seven kids and another one on the way? No, I don't think so. I don't see him as any sort of a permanent answer to my problems. Still, I shall keep my eye on him. You never know when a man like that might come in useful.'

Joe Kennedy travelled back to Boston with a business associate who was also a Los Angeles resident. Working alongside Joe, this man had seen quite a lot of Wallis during the past week, and he thought it was worthwhile making a few enquiries in case she was still around when he got back. He asked Joe for an honest assessment of her moral character.

'Well, she's a very interesting broad,' said Joe. 'Been around a bit. Travelled in the Far East. Learnt a few fancy tricks out there too, I can tell you. Did things to me that I ain't never had done before.'

'Oh,' said the man, intrigued. 'A pretty good fuck then?'

'Oh yeah, terrific. Smart too. Wouldn't surprise me,' said Joe, 'if she went places.'

Chapter 6

Der Führer wanted to see him. Immediately! Instantly!! NOW!!!

Joachim von Ribbentrop fought hard to control the panic which rose within him when his personal assistant passed on this information. His head swam, his breathing became difficult, and the room seemed to darken around him. Ribbentrop forced himself to remain at his desk for a few moments. He took several deep breaths and tried to persuade himself that this call to see Adolf Hitler was good news.

You are, he reminded himself, the driving force behind the foreign policy of the entire German state. You have your own Bureau – the *Ribbentrop* Bureau – which works independently of the Foreign Office, and indeed is more influential than the Foreign Office. You are respected, admired, courted, because you have access to the Führer. People look up to you, *fear* you even, because of your position, your power. Furthermore, you were awarded the Iron Cross, First Class, in the war. There is no need for alarm, just because the Führer has asked you to speak to him. Of course not!

But there was, of course, very good reason to be alarmed when Hitler sent for you without warning. Only two months earlier (on 30 June 1934) Hitler had ordered the summary execution of Kurt von Schleicher, Ernst Roehm, and other Nazi party leaders, for participation in an alleged plot against him. Whether there had been such a plot was irrelevant. The fact was, the men were dead. Hitler was now the undisputed dictator of Germany. And no one, absolutely no one, could feel totally and utterly safe.

Now Ribbentrop was called. And the call must be obeyed. He rose to his feet and began the walk down the long, high, echoing corridors of the Chancellery.

At first sight, the signs were not good. Ribbentrop could see at once that Hitler had open on his desk the dark-red personal file which he maintained on all his closest associates. Dark red. The colour of blood. So Hitler would be reminded once again of Ribbentrop's background. Of his curious education, in schools in Germany, Switzerland, France, England. Of his sojourn in Canada. Of his modest first job, selling *Sekt*, a sparkling wine. Of his marrying the boss's daughter, struggling upwards, ever upwards.

The signs were not good, and Ribbentrop had already half-consigned himself to the grave.

But what was this? Hitler was effusive, chatty, cheerful. How was Frau von Ribbentrop? In excellent health, thank you. And yourself, Ribbentrop? Never better. And the Führer, how was he? He was well, full of energy, full of plans. Come. Look. See.

Hitler led his associate across the floor of the huge office to the west wall, which was filled by a massive map of Europe. It was massive, Ribbentrop reflected, probably because the Führer was somewhat short-sighted, and he never, ever, wore glasses. But no sooner had this disrespectful thought entered Ribbentrop's head than he immediately banished it to the back of his mind, wishing that he had never even noticed the Führer's little problem.

'Europe,' said the Führer, quite unnecessarily. 'See where we are, Joachim. See how we fit in.'

Joachim. So he was not to be executed today. Well, probably not.

Ribbentrop tried to concentrate. But what a fine figure of a man was the Führer. His military uniform was immaculate as usual. His presence was magnetic, the eyes piercing, the gaze hypnotic. His voice, above all, was what fascinated and held the attention. The Führer always spoke with great confidence, the confidence born of knowledge, experience, wisdom. This was a man who had seen much, understood it all, learnt everything that was important. And now he was setting out his plans, his vision, to his principal adviser on foreign affairs. Ribbentrop felt truly privileged to be in the presence of such a giant among men.

'See where we are, Joachim,' Hitler repeated. 'We have but a small space for such a large population. A growing population. We must find *Lebensraum*, Joachim. We must carve out an empire for ourselves, an empire which will provide sufficient vassals to service the German people. To give our people what they deserve, the wealth, the food, the space.'

Hitler picked up a long stick and began to point at the map. 'Before long, Joachim, we will expand to the east, and the west. We will regain our lost colonies in Africa. We will become strong. We will unite Europe, and we will defeat Communism. We will eliminate the inferior races – the Jews, the Gypsies, the scum. And then, in due course – strictly between you and me – we will conquer America, China, the world. But that will take a little time, of course.'

This was a joke, an excellent one, and Ribbentrop laughed uncontrollably. With relief as much as anything.

'But how are we going to achieve this, Joachim? You and I know that in the past, we have fought the British. We both served, with honour and distinction, in the great war.'

Ribbentrop nodded soberly. Fortunately, his service as a hussar on the eastern front was a mark in his favour. Hitler, who had risen all the way to the rank of corporal, admired those who had seen war at first hand.

'What a mistake that was, to have fallen into conflict with the British. What a pity it would be if they were to misunderstand, disagree with, and attempt to forestall our very reasonable drive for *Lebensraum*. Fortunately, in the Prince of Wales, we have a man who also saw the terrible waste which war between our countries represents. And the Prince is heir to the throne.'

Hitler moved away from the map towards a table, where he had spread out a genealogical chart.

'Have you any idea, Joachim, of just how close our two peoples are? The British and the German, I mean. Look here, at the kings of England for example. The royal family of England is a German family in origin. Their proper name is Saxe-Coburg-Gotha – they changed it to Windsor during the war, to avoid embarrassment. Queen Victoria married a German, Prince Albert. The present Queen is a German, Princess Mary of Teck. Our last Kaiser, Wilhelm II, still living in Holland, he is a cousin of King George. The Prince of Wales's favourite cousin is Charles, Duke of Saxe-Coburg-Gotha – a faithful member of the SS, incidentally. And do you know what, Joachim? I heard only recently that when the Prince of Wales speaks to his mother, they *speak in German!* Can you believe that! They *speak in German!*'

My word this was funny. The Führer and his friend laughed themselves silly over it. Roared till they had to wipe the tears from their cheeks. Then they sat down and drank coffee, after which the Führer got to the point. He didn't have time to waste.

'Your burden, Joachim, as my principal adviser on international relations, is a heavy one.'

Ribbentrop nodded. This certainly was true.

'I would not lightly add to your burdens. But you must understand one central, vital part of our strategy. We must avoid at all costs conflict with the British. We must bring them on to our side, and keep them there. This will not be impossible by any means. As I have indicated to you, from the top down there are many links between our countries. Many men of goodwill in England will go far to avoid another armed conflict, and that fact can be manipulated in our favour. There are also many high-ranking businessmen and men of property in England who see the growth of organised labour as a very powerful threat to their interests. They too can be made to work for us.'

The Führer looked thoughtfully out of the window.

'Before long, King George will die, and the Prince of Wales will be crowned. The Prince himself knows all the facts I have mentioned. His godfather, Tsar Nicholas II of Russia, was murdered by the Bolsheviks at Ekaterinburg, so the Prince is no friend of Communism. He is one of us. He thinks as we think. And your task, Joachim, is to keep it so.'

Ribbentrop took out a pen and began to scribble notes.

'You must master every detail of the situation in London,' Hitler continued. 'You speak good English. You have English friends and contacts. Use them. Read the papers. Cultivate our friends over there. Flatter them. Offer them, discreetly and in great secrecy, office in the greater German state, once we have absorbed them into our empire. Explain how they will then have the power to put things right. To get rid of those who have thwarted them, ignored them, persecuted them. Mainly the Jews of course, but others as well.... Work on their ambitions, their desires, their longings.'

Hitler turned to look directly at Ribbentrop, and his eyes seemed black and hard.

'Do you follow my thinking, Joachim?'

Ribbentrop leapt to his feet. During the past few minutes, as he had gradually realised that he was to be entrusted with yet further tasks, rather than be cast out into the pit, the blood had begun to zing in his veins. His pulse pounded in his ears, adrenalin pumped into his heart. He felt euphoric, inspired, rejuvenated.

'I do, mein Führer!' he cried. 'I do understand, and I will do everything that you command. I will do it to the greater glory of the German people.' He clicked his heels and raised his right hand high. 'Heil Hitler! Heil Hitler! Heil Hitler!'

Chapter 7

'The President will see you now, Mr Kennedy.'

Joe rose to his feet.

So, the President wanted something. Well, that was standard practice. Joe had written in, saying that he wanted to resign as Chairman of the Securities and Exchange Commission, and instead of writing back and saying OK, the President had sent for him. Which meant that he wanted something in return. Well, fine. Joe was used to doing deals.

The Secretary showed Joe into the Oval Office and the President greeted him effusively. Joe never knew whether to shake hands with the son of a bitch. It was awkward shaking hands with someone who couldn't get up out of a wheelchair, so he made do with giving the President a cheerful wave and a big grin. Usual stuff.

They chatted, fenced around for a while. How's Rose, how many kids ya got now, ho ho ho, that sort of thing. Joe made himself comfortable and waited. One minute thirty seconds of that, and then the President got down to business. Joe could have won money by taking in a stop watch.

The President picked up Joe's letter. 'So, you want to resign.'

'Yeah, had enough of that.'

The President didn't seem worried. 'Well, you've done a good job, Joe. And even though you've only served for one year, I'm not going to stand in your way.' He tossed Joe's letter of resignation aside.

And what's the catch? wondered Joe.

'As a matter of fact,' the President continued. 'There's something else I'd like you to do. Won't take long. How much do you know about Europe?'

'Not much,' said Joe. 'Been to England a couple a times. Tried to buy a film company there once. Rose goes to Europe all the time. Seventeen trips in the last four years.'

The President laughed. 'You keep count do you, Joe?'

'I should do. I pay the goddamn bills.... Whaddya want me to do in Europe?'

The President moved his position in the wheelchair, wincing as he did so. He wasn't getting any younger, Joe noticed. What was he now, fifty-four? Might get re-elected in thirty-six. After that it would be time for a younger, fitter guy. Someone with the energy to get things done. Not thinking of anyone in particular of course.

'I want you to go round and visit all the major players,' said the President. 'London, Berlin, Rome, Paris. See the political leaders, both those in power and those in opposition. And speak to the ordinary people too, I want to know what they're thinking. Take Rose, she's good at that.'

'Yeah, Rose'll go in all the dress shops and tell you what length of skirt to wear,' said Joe. But he didn't argue. He would quite like to know what the hell was going on in Europe himself. Information was money, that was one thing he had learnt a long time ago.

'You've got the connections,' the President continued. 'I'm sure you can get in to see these people, quite informally of course.'

'Of course.'

'If you have any trouble, get the embassies to help you. I'll give you a letter.' The President sighed and moved his position again, as if he were in pain. 'There's going to be trouble in Europe, Joe. I can feel it in my bones.'

'You're right,' said Joe. 'Unless we keep 'em in line, there's gonna be another goddamn war. And that's the last thing we want.'

'Don't worry, Joe,' said the President. 'You'll be too old to serve this time.'

Joe felt his cheeks redden, and he too stirred in his chair. In World War I, Joe had pulled every available string to avoid having to serve in the armed forces. He had eventually worked as an assistant manager at the Fore River shipyard in Quincy, Massachusetts. Now, in response to Roosevelt's sly reference to this, he felt like getting up and punching the son of a bitch,

President or no President.

The President laughed, not in the least rattled. 'Steady, Joe, steady. I don't want a war any more than you do. That's why I'm sending you to find out what the hell's going on. I want a report, detailed, confidential stuff. I read the papers, and I get all this junk from the diplomats. But I want the real stuff, and I know you can get it, Joe.'

The President swung round and picked up a file from his huge desk. 'By the way,' he said, waving the file. 'You'll be going to England, of course, and you're bound to run into the famous Mrs Simpson. The Prince of Wales's lady.' The President opened the file and looked up at Joe. 'You ever come across her before?'

Well, Joe had not got where he was today by telling dumb lies. Especially when the President of the United States had an FBI file in front of him. 'Yeah, I think I remember her. Bumped into her in Los Angeles some years ago.'

'I thought you might have.' The President leafed through the folder. 'This is some woman, Joe.' There was frank admiration in his voice. 'Born in Baltimore, of course. Good family, though her parents seem to have forgotten to get married until after she was born. First guy she married was a Navy man. Flew planes for us.'

'Yeah,' said Joe. 'I recall that.'

'But did you know that she was one of the Navy wives who worked for Naval Intelligence?'

Joe didn't know and he kept quiet.

The President consulted the file. 'She was in Washington in nineteen twenty-two – this was while she was married to the first guy, mind you – and had an affair with Prince Gelasio Caetani, the Italian Ambassador. Also had an affair with an Argentinian diplomat. Caused quite a fuss. Got her name known around the town.'

'Before my time,' said Joe.

'In nineteen twenty-three the Chief of Naval Intelligence picked her out for use as a courier. Sent her to Paris, London, Rome. Later she went to join her husband, who was flying planes for us in China. There was a civil war in China at that time – lots of shooting. Like all our people, she was constantly in danger, so she's a gutsy gal. She was in Hong Kong, Shanghai, Peking. In Peking she had an affair with Alberto de Zara, then a naval attaché at the Italian Embassy, now a leading Fascist. Later, back in Shanghai, she met another Italian Fascist, just a kid of twenty-one – Count Galeazzo Ciano. Got pregnant by him, had an abortion, spent time in the hospital in Shanghai. And apparently she was already a gun for hire.'

'What, selling sex?'

'Well, yes, but selling other things too. We have a report here from British Intelligence saying that she was suspected of spying for the Russians, who were our opponents in China. She approached British Naval officers, tapping them for information. The British also think she was involved in drug peddling. And she got rich men to back her for high stakes at the gambling tables. She was, it says here, notoriously a kept woman....'

The President leaned back and continued reading. 'Eventually she divorced her first husband and married this English guy, Ernest Simpson. Moved to London. Simpson's in shipping, travels a lot. Now Mrs Simpson mixes with, quote, a wealthy set which sees Fascism as Europe's only hope against Communism, unquote. And the funny thing is, Joe, while the American press is printing pages and pages about her, hardly a word has appeared in British newspapers.'

'Oh – why so?'

'Respect for the monarchy, I guess. And the Church and the politicians hate her guts of course. The German press hasn't mentioned her either – Dr Goebbels has forbidden it – which is interesting. Anyway, Joe, this Wallis is quite an operator.'

Joe scratched his balding forehead and tried to remember Wallis as he had known her – what, six or seven years earlier? As he recalled she had kept him company for a week in Los Angeles. A memorable week, certainly, and he remembered her OK, but there had been a lot of other weeks in between. Still, judging by the papers, she had that Prince of Wales by the balls OK. You had to be impressed by an American broad who could beat off all the Brits like that. Wouldn't make a gal too popular, stealing their number-one prize right under their noses. It would take some sort of an operator to do that.

'Yeah, well,' said Joe. 'I guess I'd better look her up, discreetly, and find out what she thinks about things. Woman like that is gonna have information. And opinions.'

'Damn right,' said the President, his nose still in the file. 'There's a lot more stuff in here too, some of it hard to believe. Makes you wonder what these guys have got filed away on you and me, eh Joe?'

Joe didn't answer. As far as he was concerned, there were too many goddamn snoopy people poking their noses into things that didn't concern them.

The President ordered a car to take Joe back to his office.

It was cherry-blossom time in Washington, and the trees were all beautiful, but Joe didn't notice. He was still thinking about Wallis Simpson. Gee, he thought, way things are going, pretty soon I'm gonna be able to say I fucked the Queen of England.

Only trouble was, about four hundred other guys would be able to say the same thing.

Chapter 8

In London, during their summer visit in 1935, Mr and Mrs Kennedy stayed at Claridge's. This was a five-star hotel well placed for Bond Street, Mayfair, and all the better class of shops. Rose chose it. Joe didn't give a fuck where he stayed so long as it was comfortable, and Claridge's was. And he was amused to find that at night, highly respectable though the district was, many of the streets were still lined with expensive-looking whores touting for business.

Joe spent two days meeting a succession of British politicians, both those in office and members of the opposition, plus a few businessmen. Most of them, he decided, were complete assholes. He was beginning to understand why the Irish had been treated like shit for all these years. These fucking Brits were just so goddamn arrogant, they thought the whole fucking world had to jump when they clicked their fingers.

Another thing. He had trouble with the plummy English accent. He could only understand about one word in three, and when he did understand them it seemed to him that the politicians talked mostly crap. The businessmen were a bit smarter. Only one good thing about any of them, they nearly all definitely did not want to fight another war. At least they had the good sense to agree with him that war fucked up business in the worst possible way. Except for the arms guys of course, and Joe assumed that everyone he talked to had had the sense to buy lots of armament-company shares years ago.

On the morning of the third day of Joe's stay in London, the phone rang at eight o'clock in the morning. Joe answered it, which was just as well.

'Good morning, Joe. This is Wallis. How are you?'

Well, there ain't too many women in the world called Wallis, so Joe knew who he was talking to. And he was pleased to hear from her.

'Hi Wallis,' he said. Rose moved in the bed and frowned.

After some preliminaries, Wallis invited him to lunch later that same day. 'There's someone I want you to meet,' she said. 'I can't say too much over the phone. But bring Rose. And tell her to dress smart.'

'Does she ever do anything else?' said Joe. He rang off and explained to Rose what was happening.

Rose was not pleased. She already had a lunch appointment with a Lady Somebody, who was apparently *the* hostess of the season, and the person everybody had to know.

'Cancel it,' said Joe. 'We've been invited to lunch with the most famous woman in the world. Nobody back home has ever heard of Lady Whatsit, but you'll be able to dine out on this one for years.'

'Dine out on the story of meeting the world's most famous adulterer?' said Rose bitterly. 'I couldn't get the words past my lips. And besides, who is it she wants us to meet?'

'She didn't say.'

'Probably her boring little husband. He can't be much of a man, to put up with the way she treats him. And how come you know Mrs Simpson anyway? You never mentioned her before.'

'Rose, there are twenny-eight thousand four hundred and fifteen people that I know that you don't know.'

'Where'd you meet her anyway?'

'Los Angeles, a few years ago. When I was in the movie business.'

Rose had never yet accused him to his face of going with other women, and he wouldn't have given a fuck if she did, but he could see that she was pretty damn close to it now.

'And what was this woman' – the words were hissed out – 'doing in Los Angeles? Up to no good, that's for sure. From what I hear, the less said about her past the better.'

'Rose,' said Joe. 'We're gonna go have lunch at her place. So just get used to the idea.'

Joe went out for a couple of meetings and then took Rose in a taxi to number 5 Bryanston Court, in George Street, where Mr and Mrs Simpson had a flat. He noticed that, although Rose made out she didn't give much of a damn for Wallis Simpson, she had had her hair done, and she was dressed in yet another new fucking dress.

When the taxi drew up at their destination, Rose claimed to be unimpressed by the neighbourhood, though in fact it was a good address. 'This doesn't look like much of a place,' she sniffed.

'It's discreet, is why,' said Joe. 'That's the way they do things in England. They don't flash their money around.'

But as they stood waiting for someone to open the door of the flat, Joe had to admit that Rose was right. Things didn't look too impressive. Everyone *said* that Mrs Simpson was the Prince of Wales's mistress. If so, he didn't seem to be spending much money on her apartment.

The door opened, and Wallis greeted them herself. She beamed, kissed Joe, kissed Rose, said how delighted she was to meet her, took her coat, hung it up, and was generally a gracious hostess. But Rose was still very stiff and formal, and Joe was beginning to wonder if this was all a waste of time.

But then he noticed that Rose had gone white. She clutched his arm, and he could feel her trembling. He was about to ask what was the matter when he realised that she was staring through the half-open door which led into the drawing-room of the flat. And when he followed her gaze, Joe saw why Rose was twitching. Standing there ready to greet them was a small, fair-haired man with a shy grin on his face.

Even Joe knew that this was the Prince of Wales.

Afterwards, Joe had to admit that he'd been a bit shaken up himself. He'd thought he was pretty used to meeting high-up guys, and he wasn't usually too taken by most of 'em, but even Joe found that he didn't remember too much about the first few minutes of that occasion.

Wallis introduced everybody, and she was entirely relaxed, even amused by the whole goddamn business. And the Prince, he couldn't have been nicer, more welcoming.

Rose dropped a curtsy – where had she learnt to do *that*? – and Joe found himself wondering what to call the guy. Eventually he settled on Sir, which seemed to go down OK. But as for Rose,

Christ he had never seen her so flustered, despite the curtsy.

One thing did stick in his memory. He had never seen anything like it, never in his whole goddamn life. The first course at lunch was a salad, and when the Prince of Wales picked up a piece of lettuce with his fingers, Wallis slapped his wrist. Jesus H. Christ! Slapped his wrist! And the guy was practically a king for Christ's sake! Well, if anyone wanted any proof that she had him right there in her hand, that was it. Joe was sold.

By the time they'd got through the hors-d'oeuvre, things had settled down a bit. Joe found that he was able to think straight.

For once in his life he heard Rose talking about something other than her nine children – at least she had the sense to keep off *that* subject – and the Prince kept her going with some chit-chat about clothes and where she and Joe had been and where they were going next.

Wallis, meanwhile, was sounding out Joe.

Joe told her why they were in Europe, who had sent them, and what he was trying to find out. He saw no reason to do otherwise. But the funny thing was, he had the feeling all the time that she and the Prince already knew damn well what he was up to. But then, of course, he remembered. This was a woman who had been dealing in sensitive, secret information for over a decade. And her boyfriend was *royalty* for Christ's sake. They probably read the intelligence reports in bed together. They probably read the Prime Minister's mail before he did.

Wallis was interested to hear of Joe's mission. She asked who he'd seen and what they'd said, and she gave Joe her own thumbnail impressions of people which filled in the background nicely. Then, when the talk got round to Joe's forthcoming trip to Berlin, the Prince took an interest.

'The man to see in Berlin,' he said, 'is von Ribbentrop. He acts as Hitler's principal adviser on foreign affairs. He speaks excellent English, so you won't have any trouble. You'll find him interested, helpful, and forthcoming.'

Wallis nodded. 'He's very well informed about the situation in Europe generally,' she said. 'You can't do better.'

Joe could hardly believe his ears. Wallis Simpson was giving him her personal opinion of a top official in a country like Germany! And telling him that the guy was pretty well informed! And yet he found himself prepared to accept it. In view of what he'd seen so far, he was quite prepared to believe that Wallis was in a position to pass judgement on this Ribbentrop guy.

At the end of the meal, over coffee, the Prince took control of the proceedings, and Rose had enough sense to stop chattering. It was obvious to Joe that this was the point of the whole goddamn meeting, the reason why the whole thing had been set up. He listened carefully. This was the message which the Prince wanted him to carry away.

'Those of us who served in the first world war, Mr Kennedy, will never forget the tragic loss of life which that war caused. We are determined that never again will that be allowed to happen. That's one factor in the situation. Another factor is that the German nation and the British people have very close links in history, not least through the royal family.'

Joe noticed that the Prince didn't talk like most Brits. He had a mid-Atlantic sort of a voice, with a half-American twang to it. Of course he had visited America, and no doubt he'd spent a lot of time with Wallis. Maybe she'd been giving him lessons in talking. As well.

The Prince moved the saucer of his coffee cup and looked down at it, gathering his thoughts.

'The post-war period has brought enormous problems in both countries. The loss of confidence in the German currency, massive unemployment, the great slump in trade. Solving those problems seems to many of us to require a new form of government. Democracy is all very well in its way, but can it cope with modern conditions? Some of us think not, and the German people evidently think not. That is why they have given extensive powers to Adolf Hitler, so that he can lead them out of their difficulties. That seems to me to be a sensible and appropriate development, given the troublesome times we live in.'

The Prince now looked up and gazed at Joe with his extraordinary blue eyes.

'And then, of course, we must never forget that facing us all is the threat of the Communist empire. Too many people in England seem to admire Russia, for reasons which are wholly lost on me. I have the fear that, within my lifetime, we shall have to defend ourselves against Communist aggression. Mr Kennedy, I say to you frankly that I hope to see much greater co-operation between Germany and Great Britain than has been possible so far. It seems to me that the two nations have much in common, and everything to gain by closer liaison, ideally through a formal alliance. I hope you will bear all that in mind as you continue with your talks.'

In the taxi back to the hotel Rose was ecstatic. 'Oh what a handsome, delightful man! Such charm. Such wonderful manners. And do you know, Wallis told me that the plates we were eating off came from the *Palace*. Can you believe that?'

'Very easily.'

'She showed me round while you were talking to the Prince. It's a beautiful place.'

Uh-huh, thought Joe. You weren't too fucking impressed when you arrived.

'The entrance hall is small, of course, but there's a nice large drawing-room, and the dining-room can seat fourteen. There are three bedrooms, two bathrooms and a good large kitchen. The servants' quarters are downstairs. It's all been decorated by Wallis you know. Such good taste. That Chinese vase came from Peking. And that cabinet with the Chinese ornaments is Chippendale. And the Queen Anne chair you were sitting in? With the striped seat? That came from the Prince's own house! Fort Belvedere. He gave it to her himself.'

That ain't the only thing he's giving her, thought Joe, but he didn't want to upset Rose by being vulgar.

'And the jewels he's bought for her! Did you see what she was wearing? Absolutely *dripping* with emeralds.'

'Yeah,' said Joe, 'I noticed. And yesterday I was told how much all those sparkly things cost him. Two hundred thousand.'

'Dollars?'

'Pounds! That's getting close to a million in real money.'

When they arrived back at Claridge's Joe went for a leak. As he came out of the bathroom Rose was on the telephone, trying to contact her friends in Boston. A woman who had been sneered at as an Irish mick by the old money in Boston and New York was not about to lose an opportunity of telling everyone how the Prince of Wales had kissed her goodbye.

'Gotta go,' said Joe. 'Got a meeting.'

Rose waved him away. But just as he went out of the door Joe couldn't resist putting his head back into the room.

'Hey Rose!' he crowed. 'Betcha glad I knew Wallis now, huh?'

Chapter 9

What did the Germans want? That was the question.

Joe thought he was beginning to figure it out. After just one day in Berlin he reckoned he knew what they wanted.

Everything. That was the answer.

Joe knew a few Germans back home of course. On the upper east side in New York there were whole streets of them. And there what they seemed to want was oompah music and food. Lots of it.

Pretty much the same here too. He had never seen so many goddamn greedy people in his life. Christ it made you feel ill just to sit in the same goddamn restaurant.

Today for example he had had lunch with a German businessman. A big wheel in the German equivalent of Wall Street. Fine. He gave the guy a rundown on the financial situation in New York, guy gave him some tips on the exchange rate and hot shares in Berlin. Joe made a couple of calls, figured he would come out covering the cost of the trip to Europe. OK so far.

But Jesus, just sitting opposite the guy was enough to make you a monk. The German ate about fourteen courses, drank about six steins of that foaming beer which Joe didn't care for – looked too much like piss for his taste – and stuffed himself stupid until his face turned purple and the veins stood out on his forehead. Wouldn't a surprised Joe if the guy dropped down dead on his way back to the office. Joe himself had stomach problems – he had had ulcers as early as 1917, and periodically they would play him up. And sitting opposite a guy like Fritz didn't help.

Anyway, that was over, thank God, and now Joe was on his way to do two things. One, get himself laid, and two, see Ribbentrop.

The German businessman had been most understanding when Joe had explained that it had been some time since he got his ashes hauled. Told him no sweat, knew just the right girl, spoke English and everything. Fritz the businessman had made the call, even told the taxi driver the address, and slapped Joe on the back, saying something crude in German. Like, shove it up for me, or something of that sort. Guy was so fat he could probably only screw by proxy.

Whatever, swell, Joe was on his way there. Thing was though, he only had to look out the window to see that his first impressions about what the Krauts wanted were right. Not only did they want all the food in the whole fucking world, wanted it right now, on a plate and warm, but Joe was also looking at a whole bunch of soldiers marching past. Goddamn taxi was having to wait while they all marched by. And what this proved was that the Germans not only wanted food, they wanted every other damn thing too.

Shiny boots, smart uniforms, straight lines, serious-looking guns. Joe had to admit the soldiers were impressive. He had never yearned for a uniform himself though. Uniforms were OK, did you no harm at all with the broads, but the snag was, every so often you had to go out and get your goddamn head shot off. So that was for suckers. Joe's view was, money beat a uniform any day of the week. It was a lot safer and just as effective.

Meanwhile there were flags going by. Swastikas everywhere. Perhaps it was some sort of national day or something. Or perhaps they did this every goddam day, just for fun. Either way Joe had it figured. These people weren't going to sit still and let themselves get shafted. Hell no. These people were going to go out and *take* it – take whatever they wanted. Take every fucking thing if the rest of Europe let them.

Joe sighed. FDR wasn't gonna like this.

Joe rang the doorbell. Nice-looking apartment block.

Door was opened by a big blonde. A *really* big blonde. Big tits, big ass, big everything. Well, nothing wrong with that a course. Joe went in.

She gave him a drink. It was true what Fritz the businessman had said: she spoke good English. 'You like to fuck or suck?' she asked.

'Well, to tell you the truth,' said Joe, 'I ain't got a lot of time. Got a meeting.'

Maisie or Freda or whatever the hell her name was, nodded. She quite understood. She led him into the bedroom.

It was a big bedroom, discreetly lit, lots of mirrors. Also whips, furs, black leather, all that stuff. Joe had never been into any of that and he wasn't about to start now. But Maisie understood. She was easy. Stepped out of her clothes, shook her tits at him a couple of times, reached for his fly, and boom.

Yeah, not bad.

Joe had to admit, if all German broads were like that maybe there was something to be said for them. He hadn't had a bang like that since – well, not since Wallis, come to think of it. Who was quite different – hardly any tits at all – but a sensational fuck, no doubt about it.

Joe had been thinking about Wallis. Thinking about her a lot since that lunch in London. And he remembered her now. Remembered her in bed in Los Angeles. Remembered how she had this trick of reaching down and doing something to you, right between your balls and your ass. And just when you thought you were going to come, somehow you didn't and you went right on fucking, and then a bit later just when you were about to shoot again, she did it another time. And again. And again. And again. A guy could get kind of used to that. If he had the time to spare, and didn't have to go to a meeting. And Princes could lie there fucking all day long if they felt like it. No wonder that goddamn Prince of Wales couldn't keep his hands off her, because the word on the street was, he used to come too quick. Too quick for himself and certainly too damn quick for his women. That was what they all said. Thelma, Lady Furness, for instance, having been dumped for Wallis, was inclined to complain about the size of the guy's dick and premature ejaculation and generally shoot her mouth off. So no wonder Wallis was indispensable.

The parade finished and Joe began to concentrate on the matter in hand. Namely Ribbentrop. The big wheel in German foreign affairs.

The interview with Ribbentrop was useful up to a point, but obviously a guy that senior wasn't going to give too much away.

What are the major issues facing your country, what do you hope for from us, how can I help you with your business connections. Those were the sort of questions posed and answered on either side.

Joe found Ribbentrop a bit too smooth for his taste, but there you were, what did you expect. Guy had to be pretty smooth to get where he was with this goofball Hitler running the goddamn place.

And then, at the end of their discussion, Ribbentrop asked Joe whether there was anything else he would like to mention.

'Well yes,' said Joe. 'As a matter of fact there is.... Ireland.'

'Ireland?' said Ribbentrop. His tone suggested that he had just about heard of the place.

'Yes,' said Joe. He got to his feet and crossed to the map of Europe which occupied most of one wall in Ribbentrop's office. Ribbentrop followed him.

'This place,' said Joe, pointing to it.

'Oh yes,' said Ribbentrop, as if he had only just noticed that there was an island to the left of England.

'Ya only got to look at it,' said Joe, 'to see that it oughta be one nation. Right?'

'Indeed,' said the German expert on foreign affairs. 'It has natural boundaries. Unlike Poland, for example.'

'Right. One country, with natural boundaries. But it ain't.'

'No?'

'No. All kinds a history there. I don't understand half of it myself, tell you the truth. But just take my word for it, it ain't one country and it oughta be. The fucking Brits control the north bit.'

'Brits?'

'Yeah, Brits. English. Englanders, ja?'

'Oh. Ja. Yes.'

'Now, see, all my folks came from Ireland, about three generations back. My wife's too. And there are lots of Irish in Boston. Thousands of 'em. Very influential politically. Ya wanna make progress in Boston, ya gotta deal with us. And what we want, see, is Ireland given back to the Irish.'

'Ireland given back to the Irish....' Ribbentrop absorbed the idea.

'Yeah, that's the thing. Now, what you should do, Mr von Ribbentrop, if I may give you a piece of advice, is file that bit of information away, see. Because it could be important. I mean, should you ever need my co-operation in the future. Most of the time I'm a businessman, as you know. But in international affairs, that's my ambition. A united Ireland. Or should you ever need any help from Dublin, then that could be a thing to remember. You follow?'

Ribbentrop followed all right. He might be ignorant but he sure as hell wasn't stupid.

'So,' he said. 'That is your ambition, Mr Kennedy. To see your homeland united, ja?'

'Ja,' said Joe. 'Ja with capital fucking letters.'

'Well,' said Ribbentrop, with a mock-serious face, 'I'm afraid I am not going to tell you what our ambitions are!' And he stepped back a pace and roared with laughter.

Joe joined in, slapped the guy on the back, made out that this was one hell of a joke. But inwardly he remembered the soldiers. And he remembered the businessman at lunch, stuffing his gut till he damn near choked.

No, he thought, don't tell me your ambitions, you goddamn son of a bitch. I know too fucking well what your ambitions are.

Joe laughed good-naturedly all the way out to the car that awaited him, and then, once he was out of sight of the Chancellery building, he stopped laughing.

Ho fucking ho, he thought.

Chapter 10

Such then was the background to the garden party at the Prince of Wales's country house, Fort Belvedere, on 12 June 1935.

Joachim von Ribbentrop knew most of this background, and it informed his thinking as he prowled around the party. He talked to some of the guests occasionally, of course, but for the most part he was just thinking.

And what was he thinking about? Why, he was wondering where he would live, after England became a province in the great German Empire. As it surely would before long.

Ribbentrop saw himself as the Governor, or the Viceroy – the natural ruler of this province, whatever he was actually called. It would be a role entirely fitting for the man who had overseen the transfer of the country, and all its many possessions, into German hands. To live in Buckingham Palace would be, perhaps, just a little ostentatious. But then who would live there? Perhaps it would have to become government offices. Or perhaps the Governor's *London* residence. But the Governor of the province would, of course, require a country house. And where better than Fort Belvedere?

Ribbentrop caught the eye of his host, the Prince of Wales, twenty yards away; the Prince was surrounded by pretty, chattering women. Ribbentrop raised a glass of wine to the Prince and smiled. It was, of course, a German wine: Deidesheimer Kabinett. None of that decadent French stuff here today, he was pleased to note. Yes, the Prince of Wales, soon to be King. What would the Third Reich do with him?

Well, of course, if the Prince's own vision was realised, he would become King of the United Kingdom of Germany and Great Britain. A mere figurehead, naturally. The Prince/King *imagined* that he would be able to take an active part in government – he and Queen Wallis saw themselves as people of wisdom and vision, after all, and that delusion must be fostered for some time. But once the political union had been effected, then, inevitably, they would be required to do as they were told. If they objected – well, the Führer had a favourite saying: Take a man to see one of his friends being hanged with piano wire on the end of a meat-hook, and it works wonders on his willingness to co-operate. Yes indeed.

Ribbentrop continued his silent wanderings around the lively party. He passed Wallis, and was favoured with a knowing smile. Yes, Wallis. He must do some more work on her. She was, when all was said and done, a woman, and moreover a woman who looked to him as if she might welcome a change from the interminable attentions of the Prince. Her relationship with the Prince was *work*, no doubt about it, and a woman of flesh and blood occasionally needed play. Ribbentrop would find it a pleasure to oblige her. Besides, Wallis was the conduit to the Prince's private and secret state information, the flow of which would be greatly improved when he became King. And Wallis spoke quite passable German, which she was anxious, she said, to improve. Perhaps he should offer her lessons.

Mr Kennedy's voice caught Ribbentrop's ear. It was a loud, brash, vulgar voice, and what a curious man he was. Not many men, Ribbentrop reflected, would have called in to see a whore in the half-hour before meeting a senior government official in a country they were visiting on behalf of their President. But Joe Kennedy had done so, without the blink of an eye. The woman had been interviewed afterwards, of course, and it seemed he had no perversions. Just straight up and down, in and out, and not very long about it either. Strange. And yet in the United States he was clearly a force to be reckoned with. Ambitious for political office himself, possibly even a presidential candidate, and certainly expecting his sons to enter politics. Extremely rich, with powerful connections within the Democratic Party. And, it was said, within organised crime. A wheeler-dealer, a deliverer of votes, a fixer, a funder, a friend, of sorts, of the President. Yes, Mr Kennedy would need to be cultivated.

And then, under the trees, there was that solitary fellow the Earl of Westrow. Another very rich man, pouring money into all the Fascist organisations he could find – and there were now quite a number in London. Ribbentrop had been told that he really ought to get to know Westrow, but he couldn't be bothered to do so; the man looked like such a fool.

In the next group, talking in much more sober, English tones, was Mr Alastair Padget. The power behind the throne, some said. Certainly a man capable of giving good advice to the King. And no particular friend of Germany, everyone was clear about that. Well, drink your wine, Mr Padget. Before long it will be the brick wall, the last request, and the firing squad for you.

As for your daughter – well, she's a pretty, fair-haired little thing. Bright, too, and alarmingly well informed about what was happening to the Jews. Ribbentrop had talked to her once, and had quickly terminated the conversation when she began to ask far too many searching questions about the fate of named individuals, and the location and purpose of certain not very well-known camps. A bit much from someone aged fifteen. Yes, she too was an obvious candidate for elimination, but it might be fun to keep her alive for a while. To have one's way with her – especially if she objected and had to be coerced – yes, that would be highly entertaining. A prim, pert little English girl, so contemptuous of everything foreign. Well, she would learn, learn like all her compatriots, what a mistake it was to underestimate the power of the German military machine.

Ribbentrop came to a halt on a slight mound, under the trees, where he could survey the whole scene.

It was, in many ways, a delightful vista. So many talented and experienced people. Well groomed, good-natured, friendly. Most of them English, and most of them doomed. Nearly all would stubbornly defend what they held, and what they valued so highly, and would therefore have to go.

Ribbentrop raised his glass to them. Enjoy your day in the sun, he thought. It will not last long.

Part Three

July 1935 – January 1936

Chapter 11

Alastair Padget was worried. He was never comfortable when he was asked to go and see his former boss, the Head of MI5: it usually meant trouble. And what, Alastair wondered, would the old boy want this time? The secretary who rang had given him no clue, but Alastair would have taken a bet that it concerned the Prince of Wales, his succession to the throne, and the problem of Mrs Simpson.

Following the call from MI5, Alastair left Buckingham Palace early that hot July afternoon. He told his own staff that he was going to see his tailor. Then he took a taxi to his club and went out through the kitchens at the back. He walked through an alley, across the next street, and up the steps of the anonymous office building which housed the nation's anti-espionage headquarters. It was all a bit cloak and dagger perhaps, and Alastair was never quite sure whether it was necessary; but he had been advised years ago to make sure that he wasn't observed when going into the MI5 building, and he had always stuck to that rule.

The head of MI5 at that time was Major-General Sir Vernon Kell. His military career had been ended by ill-health years earlier, and he had settled for a desk job. Kell was now in his sixties, suffering from asthma and constant back pain. Not surprisingly perhaps, he appeared grey-faced and weary, but he greeted Alastair warmly, genuinely pleased to see a trusted colleague. There were so many people these days whose loyalties were dubious at best.

Kell was never a man to waste much time on preliminaries, and as he poured Alastair a cup of lemon tea – brought in thirty seconds after Alastair's arrival – he asked about the health of the King, George V.

Alastair paused. 'Well,' he said, 'the silver jubilee celebrations have given the old man a brief burst of energy. But I'm afraid he's tiring again.'

George V had succeeded to the throne in 1910, and in May

1935 there had been a public celebration to mark the first twenty-five years of his reign. This had allowed the public to demonstrate their admiration and affection for their monarch.

'Don't forget he's seventy years old now,' Alastair added.

Kell sighed. 'Yes, we're none of us getting any younger. But the painful truth is, he won't live much longer, and we're going to have a great deal of trouble with his successor.' Kell glanced across the desk at Alastair. 'Do you think the new King will keep you on?'

'He might.'

'He'll be a fool of he doesn't. But then he is a fool. That's the whole point.'

Kell picked up a blue-covered file from his desk, and Alastair could tell from the way he handled it that at the end of the meeting it would be passed to him.

Alastair had to make a conscious effort not to sigh. Whatever the file contained, it would not be good news. In the past, such files had dealt with drug taking, unwanted pregnancies, theft, adultery, gambling debts – all of them within the royal household and all of them requiring time and hard work to deal with. With luck this new file would contain something that could be contained, resolved, and smothered. But that didn't seem to be the way of the world. Every year it seemed to be harder to keep things out of the newspapers, harder to persuade people not to sue or prosecute. Alastair rubbed his forehead wearily and tried to concentrate on what Kell was telling him.

'Well, Alastair, you know the international situation. The Germans are beginning to get restless. Again. Some of us thought we had settled all that in nineteen-eighteen, but apparently not. You were involved yourself, of course.'

'I was,' said Alastair. 'All four years. And my left arm still aches when the wind is in the west.'

'Ah yes. Still, you survived, which is more than most did. And here we are, looking straight into the mouth of more of the same. It's not a pretty prospect. The Saar has now been restored to Germany, and that, believe me, marks the beginning of their expansion. They have also repudiated the disarmament clauses in the Versailles treaty. There are those amongst us – and their voices are loud in the land – who say that what Germany wants is not unreasonable. Those who say that they were harshly treated in nineteen-eighteen, and that if we give them back a bit of what was taken away, all will be well. Complete nonsense of course. But most of that sort of talk comes from men who remember the tragedy of the great war with horror, and will do almost anything to prevent it happening again.'

Alastair nodded. He knew such men himself.

'And the awkward fact is,' Kell continued, 'the new King will want to be involved in all this. He's not like his father – not careful, punctilious about political niceties. He will not seek the best advice, ponder it, and digest it. He will just plunge ahead, following his own judgement. Interfering, influencing, participating. He's a loose cannon, Alastair. A dangerous man.'

'Yes,' said Alastair, 'I'm afraid you're right.' So the file was something to do with the Prince of Wales.

'Stability, Alastair. That's my concern. We can't hope to stop change, though God knows I'd like to, because most of it seems to be for the worse. But the old world ended in nineteen-fourteen, and since then it's been helter-skelter, scramble and scuffle, just trying to keep our heads above water or whatever metaphor you care to choose. There've been many mornings when I've woken up thinking, well, this is it, we can't hope to avoid disaster this time. But somehow we do. And so my ambition is to achieve stability – by which I mean we must try to avoid revolution, civil war, international war. Just to try to stop things going completely to pot. You follow me?'

'I do,' said Alastair. 'I share your views entirely.'

'And then,' said Kell, 'as if the political situation wasn't enough to deal with, we have to face the fact that the Prince of Wales is not yet married. Does not yet have an heir. Much less a spare. What we have is a bachelor playboy Prince, poncing around all over the place, a man who has made more cuckolds than any other fourteen fellows put together. A man old enough to know far better, but who shows no sign whatever of doing anything sensible about continuing the line of succession.'

So, it's the Wallis situation, thought Alastair. But what in the world am I supposed to do about that? Tell him to give her up? Fat chance.

'The newspapers tell us that the Prince of Wales is the most eligible bachelor in the world. But the foreign newspapers tell us that he is certain to marry Mrs Simpson. The British newspapers haven't yet printed a word about her – thank God.'

Kell opened the file, peering awkwardly at it through the bottom part of his bi-focal glasses. 'I've been concerned about Mrs Simpson for some time. It's not the fact that she is divorced, and American, and still married to this Simpson chap. Frankly I don't give damn about all that. But she's a woman with political views of her own, you know.'

'Yes,' said Alastair. 'I've heard some of them.'

'She fans the Prince's pro-German thinking,' said Kell, leafing through the papers. 'Believed to have worked for US intelligence in the past, and possibly other nations' intelligence services as well. Friend of Ribbentrop, you know. Met him?'

'Once or twice.'

'She corresponds with him. Well, she'll correspond with any handsome, rich, powerful man – that's her stock in trade. We open the letters of course.'

Kell evidently decided that he had had enough. He tossed the file across the desk towards Alastair, as if he were absolutely disgusted by the whole business.

'I asked our friends in Six to do some research on Mrs Simpson. There it is. Among themselves they've called it the Hong Kong file. I'm afraid you're going to have to show it to the King.'

'Thank you, Sir Vernon,' said Alastair drily. 'You're most kind.'

Chapter 12

The silence was disturbing.

Alastair had given the Hong Kong file to King George V a week ago. The old man must definitely have read it by now, and consequently he knew a great deal more about Wallis Simpson than he had done earlier. But he was saying nothing. Neither did his expression give anything away. He just continued as usual, pottering about, dealing with his mail, laying the odd foundation stone, shaking the hands of distinguished visitors.

Alastair was becoming anxious. What had the King done with the file? Alastair just hoped that the old man had it under lock and key. The contents of the file were truly appalling, and the thought of it lying around, possibly to be read by a footman or a chambermaid, was not a happy one. He decided that he would give the King another twenty-four hours. If nothing had been said by then, he would raise the matter himself.

No sooner had he made this decision than a familiar head was poked round his office door.

'Are you free for a moment?'

'Of course, Sir.'

The King came in. He was carrying the file. He sat down with a bump, and smiled. 'Old bones,' he said. The King had been seriously ill as long ago as 1928, and had not been in good health since.

Slowly, the King placed the blue-covered file on Alastair's desk.

'Read this, have you?' he asked.

'Oh yes.'

Long silence. The King was not made uncomfortable by long silences, though others, who endured them, certainly were. Alastair was used to the old man's ways and said nothing.

Eventually: 'Thing is, is it true? Could be, you see, that it's all invented. To discredit the poor woman.'

'I know,' said Alastair. 'That's possible. But personally I don't think so. There's too much detail.'

'And these interviews, with these... madams, I suppose you'd call 'em. Women who run the singsong houses – brothels in Hong Kong. Believe what they say, do you?'

'Yes.'

The King stirred in his chair. 'Used to hear about 'em in the navy, you know. Famous they were, even then.... It says here that Mrs Simpson was taught "perverse practices, i.e. the art of Fang Chung." Know anything about that do you, Alastair?'

'I can't say that I've had personal experience, no, Sir. But I gather that the art of Fang Chung involves massage with hot oil. It relaxes the body and heightens sexual pleasure.'

The King grunted. 'All sounds a bit foreign to me. Anyway, that's the least of it I suppose. These reports of her being involved in drug peddling, and selling information from one country to another, those are far more serious matters, wouldn't you say so?'

'I would.'

Another long silence.

Then: 'I suppose I've led a very sheltered life, you know. Being King. But I'm not a complete idiot. Learnt something about human nature, human weakness. For example....' The King paused. Then he looked up. 'When I was young, thing was, a chap caught buggering somebody was expected to shoot himself. Only decent thing to do. Now... place is thick with 'em.'

Alastair smiled.

'They tell me half the bloody actors are queer. Can't go to the theatre without shaking hands with 'em. Make sure I have a bloody good wash afterwards, I can tell you.'

Alastair chuckled.

'Mind you,' the King continued, 'I've had trouble in me own family, so I know that not everyone keeps their noses clean.'

Alastair said nothing. But he knew that the King was probably thinking of another of his sons, the Duke of Kent, who had had a little difficulty with cocaine.

The King pushed his chair back a bit and gazed thoughtfully out of the window.

'The real problem, Alastair,' he said, 'is not this woman – Mrs

Simpson. It's me son. And what he'll do when he's King. The British empire is huge, as you well know. Huge! One third of the world's population look up to me as their leader – King, Emperor or whatever. Hard to believe sometimes. And the main thing we have to do is to hold all that lot together. Stop 'em squabbling. Encourage the blighters to trade with each other. You agree?'

'I do.'

'And the King's role in that is not political – it's ceremonial. I'm a figurehead, you see. I stand for something. Though God knows what – I sometimes wonder meself. But I don't have to make decisions. Not day to day. I may have to take advice, and ask someone to form a government. Nineteen twenty-three was difficult, and so was thirty-one. But I took advice, then asked someone to do the job. After that, he got on with being Prime Minister. That's the thing about the monarch, you see. I'm not allowed to interfere in policy. That's not what Kings are for.'

The King paused again, looking down at the desk, gathering his thoughts.

'Now, the problem with the Prince of Wales is, he'd rather be Prime Minister than King. He wants to decide things, make political decisions, and he doesn't like ceremony at all. Can't stand it. But that's what being King is, mostly. Making speeches, shaking hands. Meeting little councillors and mayors and eating lunch with people. Bores you to death, but that's the job. And he hates it.'

Another long silence.

Then: 'What are we going to do about this file?'

'I will keep it,' said Alastair.

'Who's seen it here – you and me?'

'That's all.'

The King sighed. 'That's plenty. I won't show it to the Queen. Not yet. And what are we going to do about it?'

Damned if I know, thought Alastair. But he had to say something.

'As far as the security risk is concerned, MI5 are monitoring the situation, and they'll keep us informed. As far as the marital situation is concerned – well, at the moment, Sir, we are much too dependent on rumour and gossip. I will try to find out, directly, what the Prince's intentions are with respect to Mrs Simpson. And then we will speak again.'

The King seemed relieved that a suggestion had been made. 'Good idea,' he said. 'I can't do anything with the fellow myself. I've had him in, talked to him. Might as well talk to the wall.... What will you do, have him to dinner?'

'Something like that.'

'I hear young Jane acts as your hostess these days.'

'Yes,' said Alastair with a smile. 'She's old enough now – fifteen – and she enjoys social life. She's very capable.'

The King sighed. 'Must be nice to have a capable daughter. I wish I had capable sons....'

Alastair did not move, sensing that the King had more to say – when he was good and ready. Another long silence ensued.

'People tell me I did it all wrong, you know. Brought me sons up wrong. Perhaps they're right. But my father was frightened of his mother – Queen Victoria, that is – and I was frightened of my father. And I made damn sure my sons were frightened of me.... Thought that was the right thing to do, you see. But people tell me I was wrong.'

'I'm sure you did what you thought was best, Sir.'

'I did.'

Wearily the King rose to his feet, leaving the Hong Kong file on the desk. He moved slowly towards the office door, Alastair going with him to see him out.

At the door, the King paused. 'Mark my words, Alastair. When I am gone, the boy will ruin himself within a year. And I'm not talking about women. I'm talking about politics.'

Chapter 13

A dinner party for six, in Eaton Square on a warm evening in late July, could be a most delightful occasion. If all went well. But Alastair was just a *little* bit anxious. He had great confidence in Jane. She had acted as his hostess on quite a number of previous occasions, but this was more high-powered than any other party he had given. True, the cooking was being done by a professional – well, two professionals, actually – so all Jane had to do was chat to her guests. But tonight that task involved keeping up a sensible conversation with, on her right, the Prince of Wales, and, on her left, the man who was effectively the Foreign Minister of Germany. A formidable task for a fifteen-year-old girl.

However, by the time the meal had progressed to the dessert stage, Alastair had overcome his concern. Jane was coping perfectly. She had very sensibly confined herself to one small sherry before the meal, and had left her claret (a rather good Lafite '28) untouched. She was doing splendidly, and Alastair was proud of her. The only difficulty now was that whenever he glanced down to the other end of his dining-table he saw a disturbingly beautiful image. How like her mother Jane looked in the soft light generated by the candles. The fair hair and the blue eyes made Alastair remember, with a physical twist of pain in his heart, how much he missed his wife.

Alastair dragged his attention back to the guests nearest himself. On his right, Mrs Wallis Simpson. On his left, Frau Annelies von Ribbentrop.

The Prince of Wales was being charming to Annelies, and indeed he would have spoken to her in her native tongue all through the meal if Wallis hadn't told him off. But Frau von Ribbentrop didn't seem to mind what language she was addressed in: she was clearly entranced by the company of the world-famous man on her left. And every so often, of course, because he was possessed of perfect manners, the Prince would see to it that Jane was fully involved in the conversation.

On their side of the table, Joachim von Ribbentrop and Wallis Simpson for the most part took care of each other: they seemed entirely happy with their own conversation, much of it political, leaving Alastair to keep an eye on the wine and to fill in any brief silences.

Alastair took a moment to absorb his impressions of the relationship between the Prince and Mrs Simpson. There was, first of all, the question of her physical attraction.

Wallis had long since adopted a classical hairstyle which complemented to the best possible effect the shape of her forehead and her eyes. She was not exactly beautiful, but she was certainly stunning. Perhaps at least as important as her appearance was the fact that she was a brilliant conversationalist. She was renowned for her skill in bringing up just the right subject with anyone who met her, making them feel at ease and convincing them that what they had to say was of great interest.

It was said, on good authority, that Wallis had first attracted the Prince's attention when they were both guests at a weekend house party in Melton Mowbray. Wallis had been there with her husband, of course, the unremarkable but well-connected Mr Simpson. On being introduced to this American lady, the Prince had remarked upon the fact that the house they were staying in, like most English houses at that time, lacked central heating. He had asked Wallis whether, as someone used to her creature comforts, she missed it.

Instead of making some anodyne, simpering reply, Mrs Simpson had remarked sharply that every Englishman she met asked her that question, and she was greatly disappointed that the Prince of Wales couldn't be more original. All around the rooms mouths had fallen open in dismay at this outright rudeness; women went pale and men's hands started to tremble. But the Prince of Wales simply laughed. He was intrigued; and from then on Mrs Simpson had had his undivided attention.

Another story going the rounds – a very recent one – was that during the previous winter, while staying with Lord Somebody or other (the names varied), Wallis and the Prince had come in from a walk across some rather muddy fields. When they entered the house, Wallis was reported to have flicked her fingers at her companion and said, 'Here. Take off my dirty little shoes.' And the Prince had gone down on his knees to do so.

Alastair had heard this latter story from at least half a dozen different sources. Some of the people who told it were appalled (mostly the men), and some were highly amused (the women). Alastair had the distinct impression that all over London giggling women were saying to their husbands, 'George – take off my dirty little shoes!' And their husbands were turning exceedingly grumpy and telling their wives exactly what they could do with their shoes, dirty or not.

But the question now exercising Alastair's mind, and the principal reason for holding the dinner party, was this: Was Mrs Simpson just the latest in the Prince's long line of casual affairs – or did he intend to marry her?

Well, nothing had been said this evening, or on any other occasion to Alastair's knowledge, which would give a definitive answer to that question. It was all a matter of guesswork. But anyone who had known the Prince for years, as Alastair had, could see that in the past eighteen months or so there had been a distinct change in him. Whereas he had once been tense and irascible, now he was normally relaxed and confident. The increase in confidence was what struck one. Some people – the naïve and the prudish – had put this down to increasing age and maturity. But Alastair himself had no doubt that it was due to the fact that, at long last, the Prince had found a woman who could satisfy him sexually.

What the Prince and Wallis got up to in bed was anybody's guess. And lots of people *were* guessing, some of them out loud, even in mixed company. Some said that she had taught him 'Chinese tricks', whatever that meant. (And the Hong Kong file now gave some hints.) Others said that she whipped him. One or two said that they played disgusting games together, in which Wallis was the nursemaid and her lover was the baby. Others, no doubt remembering the latest story, muttered darkly and said that it was all to do with *shoes*. Few people seemed to think that the relationship between the Prince of Wales and Mrs Simpson involved straightforward sexual intercourse in the missionary position; the Prince had had plenty of that in the past, and both he and his partners had found it unsatisfactory and frustrating. There were quite a few married ladies, now feeling rather neglected, who would tell you about their experience if you asked. The Prince was often referred to as 'the little man' because of his stature; but his discarded lovers were inclined to use the phrase with cruel emphasis.

Whatever was going on between the Prince and Mrs Simpson, Alastair concluded, it was not just another affair. Only two days earlier Alastair had been told about a private visit to France. The Prince and his lover had stayed at the Hotel Miramar in Cannes. At one o'clock in the morning, the Prince had summoned the hotel manager, and had instructed him to contact the manager of the local branch of Cartier. The Prince and Mrs Simpson had then descended on the shop – it was two-thirty a.m. – and had selected an emerald and diamond charm for Wallis's bracelet. Plus a large number of other items which the Prince had doled out to his beloved over the next few weeks. Now it was said that the Prince had commissioned a couturier called Mainbocher, in Paris, to design a whole new wardrobe for her: it was to be severe, classical, timeless, the very opposite of the flamboyant creations currently favoured by most society ladies, and it was to be known as the Wallis look.

No, no, this was not a passing fancy. Alastair had the sinking feeling that this woman's grip on the heir to the throne was very tight indeed. And she was not going to let go. That was why, of course, Wallis was not disturbed by the Prince putting his head so close to that of Frau Annelies von Ribbentrop, and flirting with her outrageously. Wallis had seen it all before, and had beaten off better women than this. And Jane of course was too young to be a threat.

Jane herself was hoping for a breather. She was pretty sure that outwardly she appeared calm, but under the table her legs were twisted together in tension. She unwrapped them and instructed herself to relax.

When she was sure that everyone had finished their dessert she gathered together the dishes and excused herself to go and fetch the coffee.

Wallis offered to help, and followed her into the kitchen.

'Well, darling,' said Wallis. 'I do congratulate you on a splendid little party.'

Jane smiled politely and thanked her.

'I suppose you don't have servants living in?'

'No. Daddy and I normally cook for ourselves, and he eats at the Palace, or at his club when I'm away at school. But when we have a dinner party we employ a caterer. They go home after they've served dessert, and I see to the rest.'

'Very sensible.'

Wallis dipped her finger in the cream jug and then licked it, putting the whole finger into her mouth and then pulling it out slowly, erotically. Jane raised an eyebrow but said nothing.

'So you go to boarding school.'

'Yes.'

'Tell me, is it true that at English boarding schools the girls are punished by being caned on the bare bottom?'

Jane busied herself with the coffee percolator. 'Er, no,' she said. 'No, I don't think I've ever heard of that happening.'

'Oh, what a shame. I would so love to see it done. Do let me know if you hear of anywhere that does it.'

'No doubt some schools would be pleased to have such a distinguished visitor,' said Jane, rather sharply. 'Perhaps it might be possible to organise a display just for you. I'll speak to my headmistress. But don't expect me to be the victim.'

Wallis laughed. 'You're very bold,' she said. 'Very forward and outspoken. I like that.'

She then opened a wall cupboard and peered nosily in, inspecting the contents.

'You've got everything more or less right this evening,' she said thoughtfully. 'And you've done very well, Jane, considering you haven't got a mother to help you. But perhaps I might give you one or two tips?'

'Of course,' said Jane, gritting her teeth. A hostess, she told herself, must be tolerant of her guests' idiosyncrasies.

'First, the candles. Those Georgian silver candlesticks are lovely, but the guests can't see each other through the flame. The candles should be taller so that they're out of the line of sight.'

Then Wallis put her hand on Jane's shoulder and turned her round so that they were facing each other. She touched one of Jane's earrings.

'Next, jewellery,' she said. 'Very important at any time. And these are lovely ear-rings, a lovely necklace. Your late mother's?'

'Yes.'

'Very nice. But wrong for the evening, I'm afraid. Gold is for daytime. A woman should always wear platinum in the evening.'

'Oh?' said Jane, who was getting a bit fed up with being told what she'd done wrong. 'I haven't heard that before. Is that standard practice in America?'

'No,' said Wallis. 'It's standard practice for me. And soon, sophisticated women everywhere will be taking their lead from me.'

Jane concentrated hard on the coffee arrangements. She just hoped that her face didn't betray any emotion. Such as amusement and shock at the woman's sheer effrontery.

Wallis leaned back against the kitchen wall. 'What do you think of Joachim?' she asked. 'A lot of women find him very attractive. Handsome, isn't he?'

'Presentable, certainly.'

'Would you like to go to bed with him?'

Jane looked Wallis straight in the eye. She was damned if she was going to be shocked or intimidated by this vulgar bitch. 'I understood he was married,' she said calmly.

Wallis was undismayed. 'Oh yes, he is, but he and his dowdy little hausfrau have an arrangement. He makes love to whoever he wants to, and she stays at home and does the cooking.... The Germans are very disciplined you know. They make love by numbers, according to ze rule book. They take orders too. You tell them to wait, and they wait. That means they can go on a very long time. Which makes a change from some people, I can tell you. And nowadays they all say Heil Hitler after they've finished.'

Jane laughed. She preferred Wallis when she was being frivolous.

'I rather fancy Ribbentrop myself,' Wallis continued, 'but of course I'm committed elsewhere.'

Then, suddenly, while Jane had both hands full of crockery, Wallis leaned forward and put her left hand on Jane's right breast. She squeezed, assessing its size.

'Hmm,' she said. 'Real, not padded. And quite generously sized. How old are you?'

'Fifteen,' said Jane fiercely. Old enough, she thought, to kick you on the shins if you do that again.

'A nice little bosom,' said Wallis. 'Before long you will be fucked rigid by all the most handsome men in London, I'm sure.'

'Yes, well,' said Jane, 'we mature rather early in England. It's the sun.'

Wallis stared at her pensively. 'It's very fortunate that you don't know how to satisfy the Prince, Jane. Otherwise you would be very dangerous indeed.'

Fortunately the coffee was nearly ready, so Jane wouldn't have to wait long to get back into the dining-room.

'And in addition to a trim figure, you have a sharp little tongue. Several times you have been quite curt with me, and I can see you would have liked to say more. I like that. I like a spirited girl. But you must be careful. At the right time and in the right place a snappy reply can be very useful. But you must not let it get the better of you. Men don't usually like a woman who answers back. You're supposed to say yes sir, no sir, how would you like me, on my back or on my front?'

'Well,' said Jane, 'you would know.' Then she picked up the coffee tray and went back into the dining-room.

Afterwards, when the guests had gone and she and her father had finished clearing away, Jane was suddenly overwhelmed with exhaustion. She wanted to do nothing more than to flop straight into bed, but her father wouldn't have it. He sat her down and poured her a glass of port.

He seated himself opposite her. 'Now,' he said. 'I want you to give me your impressions of what went on this evening. I want them while they're fresh in your mind. And in particular,' he added, 'I want to know what Wallis said to you in the kitchen.'

'I don't think you want to hear all of it,' said Jane.

'Oh yes I do,' said Alastair. 'I want to hear everything. Every word.'

Chapter 14

This man is extremely wealthy, it said on the piece of paper. *He is firmly committed to our cause and should be used.*

Ribbentrop sighed. Yes, well, that's all very well, he thought. But how am I to use him? That's the question, and you haven't told me the answer. Underlings, he groaned with a sigh. You couldn't depend on anyone these days.

Ribbentrop opened the badly printed magazine which accompanied the file on the Earl of Westrow. There were now quite a number of Fascist organisations in England. They were aided and abetted by the German Nazi Party, which had its own office in London. Chief among the Fascist groups were the Link, headed by Sir Barry Domvile, who had formerly been in charge of naval intelligence; the British Union of Fascists, led by Sir Oswald Mosley; and the Nordic League, run by Archibald Maule Ramsay, a Scottish MP. All these bodies produced their own literature, and this particular magazine was a typical example of its kind: that is to say it was semi-literate, hysterical in tone, passionately complimentary about Hitler and Mussolini, hopelessly simplistic about foreign affairs, and generally an insult to the intelligence. The whole document offended Ribbentrop's sense of aesthetics. Nevertheless, he reminded himself, these people were the best friends that he and his master had in England. And the briefing paper prepared by the German Embassy underling was right: Westrow and all those like him should be used.

Ribbentrop turned the pages of the magazine until he found the article which was written, allegedly, by the Earl of Westrow. Ribbentrop had found that in reality most of these journals were written by one or two hard-working fellows who knew how to string a few words together. Then various names were attached to the articles, with the owners' permission of course, to make the whole thing look a bit more respectable.

The article by the Earl of Westrow was concerned with the

influence of the Jews in banking. It even quoted from the Protocols of Zion. That old chestnut. It was the usual rabid stuff. Ribbentrop read three paragraphs and then tossed it aside. No, there was nothing for it. He would have to see the man and come to some sort of conclusion.

He buzzed the intercom. 'Please ask the Earl to come in.'

Ribbentrop rose to receive his guest, adjusting his face into a welcoming smile as he did so.

He had chosen to meet Westrow in a tall, imposing room on the cool side of the German Embassy in London. It was a room heavily decorated with swastika flags, and a huge portrait of the Führer hung over the mantelpiece. It was the kind of room where English noblemen with right-wing leanings would expect to be received.

The Earl was admitted, introductions were made, and the two men were left alone.

The Earl was invited to say what he felt about the current political situation in England.

The man gabbled, Ribbentrop soon decided. He didn't so much talk as gabble. He went very red in the face, and got very excited, and he spoke so fast that Ribbentrop could hardly follow him. True, the man had begun to speak in slow, halting German, but his German was so execrable that Ribbentrop had quickly asked him to use his native tongue. Now the man was practically frothing at the mouth: little drops of spittle could be seen emerging as the tirade continued. Ribbentrop found himself wondering how long it had been since the man had had sex. Something was clearly troubling him – all this tension and fury must be motivated by something. Ribbentrop did not subscribe to the view that a good woman could rectify most emotional problems, but he really wondered whether this man had got past the stage of solitary masturbation.

Most of what the Earl of Westrow said was excessively effusive. It was along the lines of how deeply honoured he was to be received by such a close adviser of the Führer, a man whom he so deeply admired, et cetera et cetera. Then he got on to talking about the wickedness of organised labour. Why, there had even been attempts to persuade the men who worked on his farms to join a union, could you believe that? World Communism was on the march, it was vital for England and Germany to unite against this menace, yawn yawn.

Eventually Ribbentrop interrupted the flow. 'Now my friend,' he said kindly. 'The purpose of this visit is to find out how I may be of assistance to you. As you know, I have spent quite a lot of time in England recently, dealing with the Anglo-German naval agreement. So I have come to meet quite a lot of people who think as you do. Yesterday evening, for example, I had dinner with the Prince of Wales and his friend, Mrs Simpson.'

As Ribbentrop had expected, Westrow reacted as if he had been poked with something sharp. He sat up straight with a gasp, and his eyes lit up with a loyal glow.

'Yes,' Ribbentrop continued, having made his point. 'The Prince shares many of your views, as you know. And, although it gives me no pleasure to say so, he will be King quite soon.'

'Yes, yes,' said Westrow. His voice was hoarse with emotion. 'He will. Which is precisely what this country needs, a man like the Prince as its King. Think how successful the Führer has been in your own country in overcoming unemployment, for example. If we have any sense we will see to it that the King is given sweeping powers to put things right.'

Ah yes, thought Ribbentrop. What a happy turn of phrase that is. Sweeping Powers To Put Things Right. It could cover so many things: such as hanging people from meat-hooks.

'There are too many little men in politics,' Westrow continued. 'And not enough men of vision. But when the Prince is King, he will sweep away all those boring little nobodies and give power back to those who understand these things.'

Ribbentrop decided that Westrow himself could certainly not be included among 'those who understand these things'. It was amazing that so many English people knew almost nothing about their own political system. Westrow, Ribbentrop decided, clearly had a high opinion of himself which was not shared by objective observers. However, that in itself could be useful, because being sneered at generated bitterness and anger, both of them emotions which could be put to use by the Third Reich.

Yes, Ribbentrop concluded, the Embassy underling was absolutely right. This was a very rich man who was also an almost embarrassingly passionate believer in the Fascist cause, and he must indeed be used. It had been an error not to take him on board before, but since the man was so obviously a buffoon it was a forgivable oversight.

Ribbentrop leaned forward. He was, he said, about to convey to his visitor something highly confidential. Something which should not, under any circumstances, be made known generally. Could he trust the Earl of Westrow to be discreet?

He could. He certainly could.

Satisfied, Ribbentrop passed on his little titbit of information, and Westrow's mouth duly dropped open with amazement. Ribbentrop again requested confidentiality, and was again assured of it. He continued:

'It seems to me, my Lord,' he said smoothly, 'that you and I ought to have further discussions. We in Berlin are always delighted to find far-sighted men who share our view of the world. Indeed the Führer himself takes a personal interest in the political situation here in England. Perhaps, my Lord, perhaps I might be able to persuade you to come to Berlin? There I would be able to introduce you to people who can develop some of your ideas still further.'

The Earl of Westrow was quite pathetically grateful. His eyes shone with emotion, and his face suffused with blood at the sheer pleasure of having someone recognise his true worth. He had found, at last, a famous and powerful man who was willing to confide in him. What is more, this man was inviting him – inviting the ignored, despised, and sniggered-at Earl of Westrow – inviting him to go to Berlin, no less. As a guest of the German government. To discuss How To Put Things Right.

Westrow rose unsteadily to his feet. His new-found pride had evidently made him quite dizzy. 'Heil Hitler!' he cried, his right arm shooting towards the ceiling.

Ribbentrop was taken quite by surprise. 'Er – Heil Hitler,' he replied. But rather quietly and thoughtfully.

Chapter 15

Ribbentrop was quite clear about one thing. Not many men could say that they had ever exercised any control over Wallis Simpson.

Not her first husband, the drunken airman. Not any of her rich sugar daddies. God no – she had controlled them. And certainly not Ernest Simpson, her pathetic second husband, he with the Jewish blood in him which he was oh so careful never to mention. And definitely not the Prince of Wales! That much was quite certain, whatever the world might think.

But the Führer had urged him, Joachim von Ribbentrop, to achieve this apparently impossible task.

'The lovely Wallis is the key to the Prince of Wales,' the Führer had declared. Well, you didn't have to be psychic to know that. 'Control her, Joachim, and you control him. Become her master. Bend her to your will. And in so doing, you will ensure, through her influence on him, that England is delivered into our hands.'

Ribbentrop took the view that this was not a bad theory, as theories went. The problem lay in putting it into practice, since it had been repeatedly demonstrated over the years that Wallis did pretty much whatever she wanted.

However, he, Joachim von Ribbentrop, was not just any man. He was, after all, a German nobleman; he was effectively the Foreign Minister of the great German State, and a close associate of the Führer. And, by God, he was coming closer to controlling Wallis Simpson on this warm afternoon in London than most men. He wasn't going to be in charge of her for very long, perhaps. But for a few minutes the lady was entirely at his disposal.

Ribbentrop looked down at the naked, sweating woman who lay beneath him. She was quite an ordinary woman really, when you looked at her from this angle. Her eyes were closed, her famous hairstyle was all untidy, and her greedy mouth was open and wet with passion. He had the distinct impression that for Wallis Simpson it had been a long, long time between fucks. And now he was controlling her with his cock. Pushing it in and out. Slowly. Hard. Making her moan.

Ribbentrop held himself up on his elbows and watched Wallis's face. In. Out. Slow. Hard. He heard her gasp, felt her legs wrap around him. She squeezed him. Cried out. Shuddered. Relaxed.

Yes, he decided, it had been a long, long time. Then, when he was quite sure that she had had enough – for the time being at any rate – he brought the proceedings to a close for himself. Almost clinically. He had been holding himself back for so long that his cock seemed to have gone numb. He didn't enjoy it much. But finish he did. Then he eased himself off her and lay on his back.

The afternoon sun slanted in through the windows of the Bryanston Court flat.

Lunch had been served and digested. The servants had been dismissed. The Prince of Wales was safely peering down a coal mine somewhere. And Wallis Simpson and Joachim von Ribbentrop had got down to some serious sexual intercourse. Which was now finished. For the moment.

'You should cultivate him, you know,' said Ribbentrop after a while.

'Who?'

'Westrow.'

'Oh, him.'

'Yes.'

'A boring little nobleman.'

'Wallis,' said Ribbentrop firmly, 'noblemen are never boring.'

Wallis snorted with disbelief.

But Ribbentrop had worked hard for his own title, by God, and he wasn't going to have the aristocracy disparaged. Wallis didn't have a title at all. Not yet.

'Westrow is an absolute believer in the greater German empire,' Ribbentrop continued. 'I explained to him, swearing him to secrecy of course, that in my opinion the Führer would not be opposed to the future King of England being King of Germany too, while the Führer did all the practical work of running the whole of Europe. Westrow almost had an orgasm, right there on the spot.'

'Lucky him,' said Wallis. 'I wish it was that easy for me.' Then she sat up on one elbow and became more thoughtful. She was beginning to think about business again. 'What does he do for a sex life, this Westrow?'

'What does any Englishman do? It's a mystery.'

'Christ you can say that again.' Wallis spoke with some feeling. 'He's not married then?'

'No.'

Wallis was thoughtful. 'You think we can use him?'

'We certainly ought to. He is rich, passionate about the cause, and stupid.'

'Has all the right qualities then.'

'All.'

Wallis's brain began to get into gear. 'I think we should find him a woman,' she said. 'Someone who understands his needs. A nice big German girl perhaps. Joe told me he had a nice big German girl in Berlin. He was most impressed.'

'Joe Kennedy?'

'Yes.'

Ribbentrop thought back over his own meeting with the US President's informal ambassador at large. 'What do you make of him?'

'Oh, Joe's OK. You've just got to remember that he's only interested in two things. Business, and fucking.'

'What sort of business?'

'Any sort, so long as it makes money. Movies, property, the stock market, he's not too fussy. In the old days he wasn't even worried about it being legal, but I think he's cleaned his act up recently.'

Wallis sat upright and poured herself a glass of lemonade from the jug at the bedside.

She continued: 'Joe appears to be interested in politics, but really that's only because politics means power. And power means money. And money means sex. He's not too fussy about sex either. Joe will fuck anything wearing a skirt, including

Scotsmen and Greek soldiers.'

Ribbentrop laughed. 'I bow to your greater knowledge.'

'Yeah,' said Wallis. 'You better believe it.' She turned and looked down at Ribbentrop as he lay relaxed beside her. 'And speaking of fucking, have you got your breath back yet, you handsome German storm-trooper you?'

Ribbentrop laughed again. 'Yes, I think I might be tempted. Especially if you do some of your famous Chinese tricks for me.'

'Honey,' said Wallis. 'You ain't felt nothing yet.'

Extract from MI5 daily report to Sir Vernon Kell, 30 October 1935:

```
Mrs Simpson
-----------

Hitler's foreign affairs adviser, von Ribben-
trop, has arranged for 17 red roses to be sent
to Mrs Simpson, every morning, until further
notice. The flowers are often accompanied by
notes of open admiration.

Our banking contact reports that Mrs Simpson now
receives a substantial payment on the first of
each month from a numbered account at the
Reichsbank. It is believed that this is a re-
tainer to ensure that Mrs Simpson continues to
influence the Prince of Wales along lines ap-
proved by the German government.

The liaison between Mrs Simpson and Ribbentrop
will remain under surveillance.
```

Chapter 16

In 1931, King George V had made a live radio broadcast on Christmas Day. The speech had been relayed to every country in the British Empire: that is to say, it had been heard all over the world, by millions upon millions of people.

The Christmas Day broadcast became a tradition, and although the King was in poor health, he made his fifth and last such broadcast on Christmas Day 1935. It was a brief talk, lasting about ten minutes, and the BBC had set up a microphone in the King's study.

'We wish you all, my dear friends, a happy Christmas,' said the old King. 'It is this personal link between me and my people which I value more than I can say.... I feel this link now as I speak to you.'

After Christmas the King remained at Sandringham. January proved to be a bitterly cold month, and he became ill with bronchitis; his condition was not helped by his habit of smoking heavily.

On 16 January 1936, the Queen sent a hand-written note to the Prince of Wales, who was at Fort Belvedere with Wallis. It read: 'I think you ought to know that Papa is not very well.' Both the Prince and Wallis knew what this meant.

The Queen made appropriate arrangements. She was determined that Wallis should not have any of the royal jewellery. She therefore ensured that the King's will did not leave any of it to the Prince of Wales. Instead it was divided between the Princess Royal and the Duchesses of York, Gloucester, and Kent.

On the evening of 19 January, the King drifted into a coma. It was realised that, if he lived past midnight, the announcement of his death could not be included in the next morning's edition of *The Times*. In view of the old man's suffering, and in view of the passing time, Lord Dawson decided to inject three-quarters of a grain of morphine and one grain of cocaine into the jugular vein. It was obvious what effect this would have, and the nurse in attendance refused to do it. Lord Dawson did it himself, and within fifteen minutes the King had died; the time was 11.55 p.m.

On 22 January 1936, the accession of the new King, who was to be known as Edward VIII, was formally proclaimed in London. At 10 a.m. the balcony at St. James's Palace was draped in crimson cloth. The officers of arms, the heralds and pursuivants, appeared on the balcony in their scarlet and gold tabards. Trumpeters played a fanfare. A cannon boomed out repeatedly, firing one round for every year of the late King's reign; and Sir Gerald Wollaston, Garter Principal King of Arms, read out the proclamation that a new King now occupied the throne.

Edward VIII broke all tradition. He attended his own ceremony of accession, watching from a tall window in York House. And he brought Wallis Simpson with him.

As if to prove that everything was now to change, Edward VIII had already given a symbolic order. Nearly forty years earlier, his grandfather had decided that the minute hands of all clocks at Sandringham were to be kept permanently moved forward: he wanted to make sure that his guests got up in good time to go shooting. George V had never revoked this order, but now it *was* revoked. Clocks at Sandringham were henceforth to show the correct time, and no nonsense.

Most people in authority knew what this symbolic gesture meant, and most of them were depressed by it. The new King obviously intended to have everything done in his own way.

Part Four

March – December, 1936

Chapter 17

> 'When Edward VIII first ascended the throne he was the most widely known and the most universally popular personality in the world.'
>
> Lord Simon

By the spring of 1936 Hitler was beginning to flex his muscles. He had already broken the Locarno Pact of 1925 by introducing conscription. He had increased the size of his army from 100,000 men to 550,000, and had embarked on a massive programme of rearmament. Now he began to think about seizing new territory.

Looking at the map, Hitler saw that, if he was to be free to attack in any direction, he needed to cross the Rhine and occupy the demilitarised area which was known as the Rhineland; it lay between the western edge of Germany and the small countries of Holland, Belgium and Luxembourg. If German troops held that strategic position, they would then be perfectly positioned to launch attacks on nations further to the west, and they could also prevent the western powers from making good any agreement to assist an attacked nation on the eastern side of Germany.

On 7 March 1936, in contravention of the Versailles Treaty, Hitler ordered his troops into the Rhineland.

Hitler's intentions were obvious to all informed observers. The German army itself believed that the move was so transparent, so dangerous, and so patently illegal, that nations such as Great Britain and France would inevitably respond with armed force. The German generals were agreed that, if such a response came, they would depose Hitler.

But the politicians of Europe belonged to a generation which had seen war at first hand, not so very long ago, and they were sick of it. Only a few far-sighted men urged that military action should be taken. Winston Churchill, for example, writing in the *Daily Telegraph*, made it clear that this was a turning-point in history. 'Surely it is worth a supreme effort,' he said, 'to stop calamity upon the threshold. Stop it! Stop it now!! Now is the appointed time.' But the politicians of Europe made no move to eject Hitler from the land he had occupied; and the German generals allowed him to remain in power.

It was not long before this situation created trouble between the former Prince of Wales, now King Edward VIII, and the British Government.

When Alastair Padget received another summons to go and see the head of MI5, he groaned. What did Sir Vernon Kell want this time?

Kell did not take long to get to the point. 'I thought you ought to know,' he said, 'what our inexperienced new monarch has been up to....'

Alastair waited, already feeling depressed.

'On the seventh of March, Hitler invaded the Rhineland,' said Kell. 'We didn't like it, of course, and we began to negotiate. The Prime Minister spent a lot of time with von Hoesch, the German Ambassador. He thinks the man is a dreadful old queen, and so do I, but he *is* the Ambassador for Germany and so he's the one we have to deal with. Anyway, von Hoesch decides that the situation is very delicate, so what does he do? Well, naturally he trots round to see his old pal, who is now our King, and asks him to intervene. Our *King*, mark you. Did you know about this?'

Alastair sighed and shook his head.

'Not surprising,' said Kell. 'It was all done at night. Top secret, et cetera. Anyway, after hearing what von Hoesch has to say, the King then sends for the Prime Minister. *Sends* for him, for Christ's sake. Stupid little sod.'

Alastair now knew that Kell was deeply concerned, because the old man was deeply religious, normally respectful of the monarchy, and seldom swore.

'The Prime Minister was steaming mad about being summoned in this way, but out of an excessive sense of politeness he did agree to go round to see the King. There was then a fairly frank exchange of views,' said Kell, looking at Alastair over the top of his glasses, to make sure that his meaning was clear.

Alastair winced. He could imagine all too readily how imperious and foolish the new King might have been, and how plain-spoken the Prime Minister would have been in return.

'After the PM had gone back to his bed, the King – and I can still hardly believe this – the King telephoned von Hoesch at the Embassy. We recorded it, naturally, and I want you to hear what the nincompoop said.'

Kell pressed a button on his desk, and a technician came in to start up the playback equipment. The head of MI5 was well known to be wholly incapable of operating even a public telephone.

Alastair braced himself as the familiar voice of Edward VIII started to speak.

'Hello, is that Leo?' (Leo was the German Ambassador's first name.)

'Yes it is.'

'Do you know who is speaking?'

'Of course I do.'

'I sent for the Prime Minister and gave him a piece of my mind. I told the old so-and-so that I would abdicate if he made war. There was a frightful scene. But you needn't worry. There won't be a war. Have you got that? *There won't be a war.*'

Kell motioned for the recording machine to be turned off and the technician left the room.

The head of MI5 took off his glasses and rubbed his eyes wearily. 'Now,' he said, 'let us consider the implications of what we have just heard.... First, we have a new King who knows nothing about how our system of government works. Or, if he does, he chooses to ignore convention. He sees his role as one of direct intervention in the nation's affairs.' Kell again looked Alastair straight in the eye. 'Such a role, I can assure you, is unacceptable to the politicians of any party.'

'I'm sure you're right,' said Alastair, who was beginning to feel most uncomfortable. A lot of people were going to think that the King's Legal Secretary ought to have known about this nonsense, and should have put a stop to it at an early stage.

'Second,' Kell continued, 'I don't want to be too pompous

about it, but the King of England is now systematically committing treason. Every night, just like his father before him, he gets sent his red box, which contains all the most secret Cabinet papers. That's the way the system works – we keep the King informed of what his Government is doing. But now we have every reason to believe – *every* reason – that anything of the smallest value or interest to the Germans is being passed straight to their Embassy through this bloody Simpson woman.'

Kell paused and again rubbed his forehead. 'By God there are days when I look forward to retirement.... Anyway, as if that was not bad enough, we now have a situation whereby the King, having found out what the Government's intentions are, in the midst of a most difficult and vital round of negotiations, promptly gets on the telephone and tells the other side that they've got nothing to worry about! It beggars belief.'

Alastair remained silent. Kell was right. It was hard to believe that the King had acted as he did. Alastair had hoped that, once the former Prince of Wales took on the heavy responsibility which came with the Crown, he would calm down; become more mature; see things from a different perspective. But that was clearly not the case. Far from it. The new King's behaviour simply became more and more outrageous.

'Correct me if I'm wrong,' said Kell. 'And tell me if I'm taking this too seriously. But it is my considered view that the King of England is guilty of treason. And is it or is it not the case that the penalty for treason is still death?'

Alastair chose not to answer Kell directly. The old man was right, of course. Under the Act of 1351, treason was a capital offence. But Alastair knew that Kell was just giving vent to his feelings.

'What do you want me to do?' he asked.

Kell sighed heavily. 'Try to control him,' he said. 'You're his chief legal adviser. I know it's impossible, but you should clear your own conscience, and protect your own back, by telling him, once again, what the rules are. Put it in writing to him. And if he sacks you – well, so be it.'

Chapter 18

'I don't feel easy about asking you to do this, Jane,' said Alastair. 'But I suppose that if I have to justify it to myself, all I can say is that it's what our family does. It sounds rather pompous if I say that we serve the Crown, or serve the nation, but by and large it's true. The men in our family, and sometimes the women too, we have careers in the civil service, or in the armed forces. We don't by and large run businesses or work in the retail trade.'

Jane was beginning to get irritated. 'Daddy, you don't need to go on about it. Really. I understand. And believe me, lots of the girls I know would be only too delighted to have even seen Mrs Simpson on the other side of the street.' She went over to her clearly worried father and kissed him on the cheek. 'You don't have to worry, really you don't.'

The next day Wallis Simpson invited Jane to go shopping with her. Bearing in mind what her father had asked her to do, Jane cancelled her existing plans and went.

If Jane wondered why *she* had been asked, instead of someone more of Wallis's own age, she didn't have to wait long for an answer. As she and Wallis left the Bryanston Court flat, Wallis grumbled about the twitching curtains on the other side of the street.

'Look at them,' she said. 'Fascinated to see me, but too gutless to come out on to the pavement and stare. They just sit there all day, watching and waiting behind those dreadfully twee bits of lace.'

Wallis and Jane climbed into a taxi and headed for Harrods.

'I was spat at the other day,' said Wallis.

'No!'

'Oh yes. And I get called names. That's why I never go out alone. Not any longer. I'm supposed to wait until the King's detective is free to look after me, but I really can't live like that. And the hate mail I get – Jane, you wouldn't believe how disgusting some people can be.'

Jane was astonished. It was April 1936, and Mrs Simpson and the King had been lovers for years – probably three years at least. Even now, not a word about the relationship had appeared in the British press; but it was clear that the grapevine was working well, and not everyone was happy about what they heard. And perhaps some of Wallis's rich and influential friends were suddenly finding excuses not to go shopping with her. Why else would she choose as her companion a girl who was not quite sixteen?

Once their expedition got under way, Wallis cheered up. She and Jane tried on several dresses, some of them far more expensive than Jane could contemplate, and Wallis remarked again on what an attractive figure Jane had. But Jane was used to Wallis making personal remarks by now, so it didn't bother her.

By three o'clock Wallis was ready for tea, which she decided they would take at Claridge's.

'I want you to meet an old friend of mine,' she said. 'He's over here on some personal business, but if you're a betting girl you should put money on him being appointed as the US Ambassador before long.'

'Oh?' said Jane. 'What's his name?'

'Joe Kennedy.'

Joe gave Jane a big toothy grin.

He was an extraordinary man, she decided – quite unlike the Englishmen she was used to. He was aged about fifty, tall, balding, wore glasses, and seemed to have enormous numbers of teeth, which gleamed at you all the time because he seemed to be inordinately cheerful.

'Hi, Jane!' said Joe, pumping her hand up and down as they were introduced. 'Great to meet you.' He turned to Wallis. 'Can't stay long, honey. Got a meeting.'

'Yeah, yeah,' said Wallis. 'Siddown and drink your tea.'

Joe, it turned out, was on one of his business trips to Europe, this time without his wife. He talked a lot, addressing himself mainly to Jane, and Wallis listened, clearly amused by her little ploy of bringing her two friends together.

'You ought to come out to the States this summer,' said Joe. 'Come to my house on Cape Cod. You'd have a great time. Meet lots of young men. Hell, I got four sons myself, and two of 'em are your age. There'd be lots of sun, sea, dances, picnics. Whaddya say?'

'Thank you,' said Jane, 'that's very kind. But I do hope you're not labouring under any kind of delusion.'

'Er, delusion?' said Joe, as if he were unfamiliar with the term.

'Yes,' said Jane. 'Didn't Wallis tell you? I'm a lesbian.'

Wallis spluttered into her tea so much that a waiter had to pat her on the back.

The following week, Jane found herself in Wallis's flat. Wallis was getting ready to go and see a movie – *Anna Karenina*, starring Greta Garbo – and she apparently had no one to go with, so Jane had been recruited.

'How'd you get on with Joe?' Wallis called from the bedroom, where she was having trouble selecting an appropriate pair of earrings.

'Oh, fine,' said Jane.

'Where'd he take you?'

'Nowhere. We had dinner in his room.'

'Jesus, honey! You like to live dangerously!'

Wallis was intrigued enough by Jane's latest reply to come out of the bedroom and use the mirror in the drawing-room.

'What did he talk about? Or didn't he waste time talking?'

'Oh, we talked,' said Jane airily, as if she had had no problem with the man. Though in fact the memory of that evening still made her tremble a little. 'We talked about politics mostly. He wanted to know how young people of my age feel about war.'

She didn't add that Joe had also wanted to know every iota of gossip about Wallis. In particular, he had wanted cast-iron inside information on whether Wallis really was going to divorce the long-suffering Ernest Simpson, at last, and marry the King of England.

'Yeah, well, that's Joe for you,' said Wallis, who had now started on her lipstick. 'He likes to present himself as a man dedicated to world peace. All it is really, he's shit-scared that his precious sons will have to join the army, and that a war will knock the shine off his shares.'

'We also talked a lot about Ireland.'

'Oh yeah?' said Wallis. She sounded particularly uninterested. 'And at the end of the meal, did you fuck him?'

'Er, no,' said Jane. 'No, I told him it was the wrong time of the month, and anyway he had to go to a meeting.'

Wallis smiled. 'Poor Joe,' she said. 'He has a hell of a time getting laid in London. He could always use a professional of course, but he'd love to screw a duchess or two, and unfortunately they all think he's frightfully vulgar.'

Wallis came and sat down beside Jane. 'You could do a lot worse than play along with Joe,' she said confidentially. 'No offence, but you and your father are not exactly dripping with spare cash. Now with Joe, a good grope ought to be worth a piece of gold. He'd just love to cop a feel of a nice English rose like you. It would tickle him pink, as you say over here. And for a fuck, never settle for anything less than a diamond ring.' Wallis patted Jane's hand to emphasise the point. 'Come to think of it, you could do a lot worse than let Joe be the first one to screw you. Or pretend he's the first if he isn't. Joe would love that. A virgin fuck ought to be worth a whole handful of rings. And besides, you never know when a man like Joe is going to come in useful.'

The phone rang, bringing this homily to an end. Wallis went out into the hall and picked up the receiver.

'Oh, hello,' she said, when she discovered who was calling. And she pulled the door towards her so that Jane could not overhear the conversation.

However, Jane stood up, quietly crossed the room, and put herself close to the door, in a position where she *could* hear. Every word.

Afterwards they went to see the Greta Garbo movie. Wallis cried.

Another week passed, and Jane was alone in the Padgets' Eaton Square flat when her own phone rang. She answered it.

The caller was Wallis Simpson, and she at once began to shout and scream insults.

Jane was appalled. She was so taken aback that she held the phone away from her ear.

'You little cunt!' screamed Wallis. 'You filthy disgusting shit-eating whore! I'll cut your fucking throat! I'll have your face slashed! I'll have acid thrown in your eyes – you'll never see daylight again you cock-sucking little cretin!'

And more of the same.

After a few moments, when Jane had recovered her wits, she listened without replying at all. When the tirade was over she put the phone down.

Then she took the receiver off the hook for the rest of the day, so that it could not ring again.

She found that she was shaking from head to foot.

She went and made herself a cup of tea.

That evening, when Alastair arrived home, he saw at once that Jane was deeply distressed. When he asked her what was wrong she tried to speak and couldn't. She just burst into tears.

Alastair held her until the worst of the sobbing had subsided. Then he sat her down and got her to tell him all about it. The telling took a little while.

After Jane had finished, Alastair poured a glass of whisky for each of them, and then sat down again.

He sighed. 'Well, of course it's all my fault,' he said. 'I was probably asking too much of you. I tend to forget how young you are. However, having said that, I have a horrid feeling that your generation is going to have to grow up rather fast, so perhaps it's as well that you should get hardened to these things now. My generation had to go to war – yours may not have to, with a bit of luck, but you're certainly going to have to be quick on your feet to avoid it. So you might as well start young. Get in some practice.'

'The worst thing,' said Jane, wiping her eyes, 'was what she said about you. She said that she would see to it that you lost your job. You'd never work again, we'd be out on the streets begging, and all sorts of horrible things like that.'

'Yes, well,' said Alastair, 'I may very well lose my job. I'm not very popular with the King at the moment. But it's not because of anything you've done. And I shan't be short of alternative employment, believe me.'

'I'm sorry,' said Jane, the tears now falling again. 'I'm just not as tough as I thought I was.'

'Drink your whisky,' said Alastair. 'And then I'll tell you what this is all about.'

Alastair went into his study and returned shortly carrying two files, one blue and one green. He put them down on the coffee table in front of them.

'Short lecture,' he said. 'The King is unfortunately a fool. He has strong political views of his own, and he intends to interfere directly in the way the country is run. That alone would put him on a collision course with the Government. Side by side with that, he is carrying on this long-standing affair with a woman who has been divorced once and is still married to someone else. That woman is not just a pretty face. She too has political ideas and convictions. She too wants to get involved. And is involved, up to her neck. MI5 know pretty well what the two of them are up to, and they need to have them watched.'

Alastair paused. 'It's a very, very difficult situation, involving some very fine moral and legal judgements. Every citizen is of course allowed to have views about what should be done. But no citizen, not even the King, is allowed to betray his country's secrets. And when you and I report to MI5, as we have been doing – me directly, and you indirectly, through me – we are, in my opinion, doing our duty, as is only right and proper, because the King and his mistress are not doing *their* duty.... Let us give them the benefit of the doubt, and say that they are acting in what they believe to be the best interests of the nation. Even so, they're breaking the law.'

Alastair indicated the two files on the coffee table. 'Ever since the old King died, the new King has been getting his red box every day. You know what the red box is?'

'Yes, it's copies of Government papers isn't it?'

'Exactly. The King, whether it's Edward VIII or anyone else, sees what the Prime Minister sees. He knows all our secrets. But for the past few months, we have had reason to believe that any secrets of importance, and in particular any relating to our dealings with Germany, have been passed straight to the German Embassy.'

'The messenger being our friend Wallis,' suggested Jane.

'Precisely. File number one there, the green one, contains all the evidence which proves, beyond doubt, that Wallis Simpson – on the King's instructions mark you, not just on her own initiative – has been passing Cabinet papers, or the conclusions contained in them, direct to the Embassy. Last week, you overheard her on the phone, doing precisely that, and an account of what you heard is part of the evidence. But it's only a part. There's plenty more.'

'Oh,' said Jane quietly. 'So that's why Wallis screamed at me. She knows, or suspects now, that I overheard her, that I told you, and that you told somebody else – say MI5. And presumably the Government has now stopped showing the King any sensitive papers?'

'Indeed,' said Alastair. 'That's precisely what happened. The crunch point was not your report of the telephone call. That was only a small part of it. The crunch came when Sir Robert Vansittart was at a reception in the German Embassy, and one of the officials there quoted to him a so-called Foreign Office decision which had been made only the previous day.'

'So-called?' queried Jane.

'Yes. It was a plant. It wasn't a real decision at all. It was a made-up report which was included in the King's papers and nowhere else, and within twenty-four hours it was being quoted back at us by the Germans.' Alastair chuckled. 'There has been, to use a piece of English understatement, a bloody great row. From now on, the King will not be privy to top-secret information in his red box, and the Germans will have to find other means of informing themselves. And that is why Wallis screamed at you.

She would like to scream at the Prime Minister, but she doesn't dare.'

'I see,' said Jane. She looked down at her handkerchief, which was a damp, crumpled mess. 'And what do you think I should do now?'

'We'll wait a day or two,' said Alastair. 'We'll wait till your tears are dry, till you've met a few normal, sensible people and got your breath back. Then you will write a brief note to Wallis. We'll compose it together. You will say that you're sorry if you've offended her in any way, and you hope she's feeling better. These rages come and go. She'll speak to you again, don't worry.'

'I wouldn't care if she *never* spoke to me again,' said Jane with feeling.

'No, perhaps not,' said her father. 'But I care. We're not finished with this woman yet, not by a long chalk.... There's another file I want you to look at as well. I think it's time you knew exactly what sort of person you're dealing with.'

He reached forward and pulled the blue folder across the coffee table. 'Read this tonight and give it back to me in the morning.'

'What's this?' asked Jane.

'Oh,' said Alastair, 'the people who assembled it call it the Hong Kong File.'

Chapter 19

When under pressure, Wallis had never resorted to drink or drugs. She had seen too many people disintegrate to want to go down either of those routes. But sometimes she wished there was something available – some pill, or something you could take, to make you feel better. Because right now, Christ, she could use it.

Wallis had begun to realise, rather to her surprise, that Joe Kennedy was the nearest thing she had to a close friend – someone she could talk to, no holds barred. Someone who thought the way she did, looked after number one and fuck the rest of them. Someone with had come up the hard way and had no foolish illusions about the way the world worked. Trouble was, Joe was in the States mostly, and even now, when he was in Europe, the son of a bitch was in Paris.

She rang him at his Paris hotel. 'Joe, you coming back through London?'

'Tomorrow, if the goddam plane gets off the ground. Last one I went on was eight hours late.'

'Ring me, Joe. I need to talk to you.'

The next day, Joe arrived at Bryanston Court in the late morning. Wallis admitted him. She had made sure that she was on her own, with no servants to hear what was said.

She hung up Joe's hat and coat and sat him down.

'Joe,' she said. 'If you tell me you gotta go because you got a meeting, so held me God I'm never going to speak to you again.'

'Bad as that, huh?' said Joe.

'Bad as that.'

Wallis poured them coffee.

Perhaps it would help if I smoked, she thought. Perhaps that would relax me. But she hated smoking. She sat with her knees together, hands clasped, leaning forward, looking down.

'Joe,' she said slowly. 'I need advice.'

Joe sipped his coffee and listened. Which was not easy for

him. He was normally a talker.

Wallis didn't know where to begin. The hell with it, she thought. Tell him everything.

'Joe, the King has told me he wants to marry me.'

Mercifully, Joe didn't say anything. Which meant he understood that Wallis was suffering.

'So far, we've been lovers. I suppose that's the word. But now he has told me, definitely, that he wants to marry me. Now.... That means I've got to get divorced from Ernest.'

'Shouldn't be a problem, surely?' said Joe.

'Well, it's not as easy here as it is back home. Not by a long way. What happens here is, provided the husband will agree, the man goes to a hotel with a woman, who is well paid for her trouble. Private detective enters the room, sees the husband and woman in bed together. Then the wife sues for divorce, they all go to court, the detective testifies as to what he's seen, man admits adultery with woman, and the divorce is granted. Although it doesn't take effect immediately for some reason. You have to wait six months.'

'Oh. Ernest gonna give you any trouble?'

'No, Ernest will co-operate.'

'King gonna grease his wheels?'

'Yes.'

'How much?'

'A hundred thousand.'

'Dollars?'

'Pounds.'

Joe raised one eyebrow. 'Sounds more than reasonable.'

Wallis nodded. 'As you say, more than reasonable. So I can get divorced, and I'm then free to marry the King of England. In theory.'

'But?' said Joe.

'There are quite a few buts. To tell you the truth, Joe, nobody wants me except the King. His family hates me. His mother won't talk to me. His brothers' wives all hate my guts, particularly that bitch Elizabeth. And then there's the Church. The King is supposed to be head of the Church of England, though God knows why – something to do with Henry VIII, whoever he was. But that doesn't stop the Archbishops and whoever thinking they can tell him what to do. And apparently, marrying a divorced woman is one of the things the Church doesn't want him to do.'

'But he don't care, surely?'

'No, Joe, he doesn't.'

'Well then, no problem.'

'There is a problem, Joe, that's what I'm trying to tell you.'

Wallis twisted her hands together. It was as much as she could do to stop herself crying, and she was damned if she was going to do that. Joe would up and run if she did, and she needed his help.

She took a deep breath. 'The problem is, Joe, they're all going to gang up on me. The Church, the politicians, the royal family.'

'But you got the King on your side, honey. It's gonna be OK.'

'Is it?'

'Sure!'

Wallis desperately wanted to believe so. 'But what about the newspapers?'

'As I understand it, they ain't said nothing yet.'

'Of course not. Nothing has been said. Most of the people in England don't even know I exist. But how are they going to react when they do, Joe? That's what's worrying me.'

'Hell,' said Joe, 'they're gonna love you, honey. Why shouldn't they?'

'Well for a start, I'm not your average virgin girl. And I'm an American.'

Joe leaned forward. 'Honey, there's nothing wrong with that! Winston Churchill's mother was an American – nobody here thinks the worse of him. And Lady Rothschild's an American. She's doing OK.'

'So you think the British people might accept me?' Wallis could hardly get the words out – she felt short of breath. 'Tell me the truth now.'

Joe spread his arms out sideways in an expansive gesture. 'Honey, you know damn well that deep down I can't stand the fucking Brits. I'm an Irishman, or at least my granddaddy was, and no Irishman gives a shit about England. But as far as I can see, you got nothing to worry about. Nobody has come up to me and said the hell with Wallis Simpson. Far as I can see you're gonna be OK.'

Wallis sighed. She would dearly love to believe that Joe was right. But she had this dreadful nagging doubt. Somehow she could not convince herself that everything was going to turn out right.

Joe scratched his head. 'In any case,' he said, 'what's the worst that can happen? The worst is, the guy is told he can't marry you, because of some goddamn law or something. Is that gonna make any difference to the way he feels about you? He's treated you OK so far ain't he?'

Wallis had to agree that was true.

'OK, so let's say you can't be Queen of England. You're still gonna be the King's lady, like you are now. You're gonna get to go to all the dinners and dances and whatever, like you do now. Have a little faith in yourself, Wallis. You're a very attractive woman, and he's sold on you.'

'Yes,' said Wallis heavily. 'He is. But you see, Joe, if it turns out that the King can't marry me, he might decide to marry me anyway, and give up being King.'

She could see that Joe was having trouble with this concept.

'Can he do that? I mean, just stop being King if he wants to?'

'Certainly. It's called abdication. He's threatened to do it already, when he had a row with the Prime Minister about Germany.'

Joe waved his hand. 'Well, OK, let's suppose he abdi-whatsits. Then you just get to be the wife of a very rich man who's an ex-King. Could be a pretty good life, seems to me. You got anything better in line?'

'No.'

'Well then, quit worrying. And besides, I don't wanna be gloomy, but what the fuck can you do about it anyway? Ain't nothing you *can* do, seems to me. Things are gonna happen anyway, one way or the other. What I always say is, you do the best you can with a thing, and then, if that doesn't work, the hell with it. You're just gonna have to stop worrying, honey. Stick it out. Hold your head up high. Fuck 'em all, that's what I say.'

Wallis could see that Joe was getting restless. She sensed that she had exhausted this topic of conversation with him.

'Anything else I can do for you?' he asked.

'Yes,' said Wallis, 'there is.' Yet again, she felt that if she wasn't careful, she was going to burst into tears. 'You can take me to bed, just for old times' sake.'

For one dreadful moment she thought he was going to say no. But he only hesitated for a second and then Wallis relaxed. Her original conviction had been right: Joe wasn't going to pass up on her offer. Whatever happened to Wallis Simpson in the future, Joe was going to want to say that even when the King had proposed to her, he was still able to have her whenever he wanted. And you never knew when a man like Joe might come in useful.

They went into the bedroom.

'By the way,' said Joe. 'Seen any more of that Jane kid?'

Wallis almost exploded. 'Jesus *Christ*, Joe, you really know how to make a woman feel wanted!'

'Hey, I'm just asking is all. A little polite conversation while we get undressed.'

Wallis fairly snarled at him. 'Well, since you ask, yes I have seen some more of that Jane kid. I had a fucking great row with her, just last week, because she overheard me having a very private telephone conversation and went and told her daddy all about it. So I told the silly little shit what I thought of her.'

Joe roared with laughter. 'Hey, I wish I'd been there. She fight you back?'

'No, she didn't give me the satisfaction. She just wrote me a nice polite little English note afterwards, saying she was sorry if she'd upset me.'

Joe laughed so much he fell over his trousers as he pulled them off.

'I tell you what, Joe,' said Wallis. 'While we're doing it, you can think about fucking her, and I'll think about cutting her throat. That way we'll both have a really good time.'

Chapter 20

CUTIE SIMPSON CUTS OUT BLOODLESS BRITISH BLONDES IN ROYAL CHOICE

Daily News, New York

BALTIMORE BABE BAGS BIGGIE

Herald-Dispatch, Baltimore

KING'S PROPOSED MARRIAGE CREATES GRAVE CONSTITUTIONAL CRISIS

The Times, London

In March 1936, King Edward VIII began to plan Wallis Simpson's divorce so that he could make her his wife.

Legal advice was taken, and it was discovered that the London divorce-court calendar was so full that it might take a year to get a hearing; it was therefore decided to arrange for the case to be heard in Ipswich. Wallis took up 'residence' in Suffolk in order to enable matters to proceed.

The divorce hearing was held in October 1936, and it was a sickening, deceitful farce. Under English law, any collusion among the various parties would invalidate the proceedings and make divorce impossible. But of course there was collusion – there was a deliberate, calculated conspiracy.

In February 1936, Ernest Simpson had a meeting with the King at York House. The King declared that he intended to be crowned with Wallis at his side. (The Coronation was scheduled for 12 May 1937.) Edward swore to Ernest that he would be faithful to Wallis, and would look after her. Given these assurances, Ernest Simpson agreed to provide 'evidence' of his own adultery. He thus deprived the American press of the spectacle, which they had been gleefully anticipating, of the King of England being named by Ernest as a co-respondent.

After reaching this agreement, the King settled the sum of

£300,000 on Wallis. He also gave her a further £100,000 which she transferred to Ernest through a bank in Paris. (She used for this purpose a French lawyer called Armand Grégoire, a man who also represented Ribbentrop. Years later, after the war, Grégoire was convicted by the French authorities of being a Nazi collaborator and was sentenced to hard labour for life.) In addition, the King undertook to pay Ernest's legal expenses in connection with the divorce.

As a further sweetener, the King made it possible for Ernest Simpson to become a Freemason. Ernest had applied to join a socially prominent lodge, but had been turned down on the grounds that it was against masonic law to admit a cuckolded husband. The King now gave the lodge an assurance that his relationship with Wallis Simpson was platonic, and Ernest was finally admitted.

The divorce proceedings began on 27 October 1936. Giving evidence under oath, Mrs Simpson declared that her marriage had been happy until the autumn of 1934, when her *husband*, if you please, had begun to go away for weekends. (No mention of her own two-month holiday on the continent, in the summer of 1934, with the then Prince of Wales.) Wallis claimed to have found a love letter to her husband, from another woman, which had been put into the wrong envelope 'by accident'. She tearfully handed it to the Judge.

Later, two hotel waiters testified that they had served breakfast in bed to Ernest and a woman who was definitely not the poor neglected lady who was now seeking to be divorced from him.

The Judge was not impressed. He couldn't help noticing that the public gallery had been cleared. No one had been able to tell him who had ordered this, but his officials were quite *certain* that the public were not to be admitted. The press benches, on the other hand, were extremely crowded, and some of the journalists were obviously not English. Furthermore, the lady in the case was represented by a *very* distinguished barrister from London.

The Judge may or may not have heard the gossip about the King and Mrs Simpson, but he was certainly capable of smelling a rat, especially when it was crawling with maggots and located two feet under his nose.

'Well,' he said reluctantly, 'I suppose I must come to the conclusion that there has been adultery in this case.'

Dead right, your Honour, thought all the assembled news-hounds. *Got it in one.* It was just that the wrong party was putting his hand up and admitting it. If ever there was a case which exposed the nauseating hypocrisy of a divorce law which allowed rich liars to go their separate ways, while forcing poor and honest people to remain locked in a miserable marriage, this was it.

'Very well,' said the Judge wearily. 'Decree nisi.'

The standard practice at the time was that six months would have to elapse before the divorce became absolute.

The court hearing had been attended throughout by a large number of hard-drinking journalists who had written down every word of the evidence offered by Mrs Simpson. The American and continental papers printed it all (except in Germany, where Dr Goebbels kindly intervened). The British editors read their reporters' copy, sighed deeply, spiked it, and went out to get drunk.

Mrs Simpson's legal adviser had emphasised to her, over and over again, that her divorce might be invalidated if she was seen to have any contact, during the next six months, with the man who wished to become her third husband. She must maintain the appearance of being an aggrieved wife, and must not, under any circumstances, look like a woman who had made a deal.

Wallis ignored the advice. Such restrictions, she considered, were for *little* people. For *ordinary* people. They were not, in her view, binding upon the King of England. She got straight back into the large black Buick, which had been paid for by the King, and which was driven by the King's chauffeur, and had herself transported to Fort Belvedere. There she would spend the night with the man who was masterminding the operation.

At dinner that evening, the King presented Wallis with an engagement ring. It was not an unexpected gift, and Wallis had given instructions as to what she wanted. She had heard of a fabled Mogul emerald which had originally belonged to the ancient rulers of India. It was said to be one of the finest stones of its kind, and that was what she had ordered.

Wallis's wish was the King's command, and he had commissioned the great French jeweller Jacques Cartier to obtain the emerald for him. Cartier, after a lengthy search, had located the stone in Baghdad, where it had been bought from a syndicate at a substantial price.

Now Wallis wore it on her finger.

The divorce proceedings in Ipswich had made it clear to many highly placed persons in the Government, the Civil Service, and the Church, that what they had prayed would never come about was now about to happen.

For years they had hoped that the King would tire of Wallis. Or that he could be persuaded to marry some virgin Danish princess or somebody – perhaps a nice horsy girl from Scotland. Or perhaps he would die. Or Wallis would die. Or she might run off with a heavyweight boxer. Anything, please Lord, absolutely anything was preferable to the stupid bastard actually going ahead and marrying this ghastly, unspeakable, dreadful *cow*.

But no. No, the King had no sense. He remained just as infatuated as ever. And the Lord was not merciful. Nobody died. Worse, the virginal Danish princesses didn't have what it took to defeat the hard-nosed Baltimore babe. And so now there was going to be trouble.

The King telephoned his friend, the American newspaper proprietor William Randolph Hearst, and announced that he would marry Wallis Simpson on 8 June 1937. Hearst's *New York American* splashed the story all over its front page on the day Wallis was granted her preliminary decree.

Just to make the point *absolutely* clear to the royal family, the King had a meeting with two of his brothers, the Duke of Gloucester and the Duke of Kent. He told them too that he was going to marry Wallis.

'Um, er, well, er,' said Kent, who was better at stringing words together than his brother. 'Er, what will she call herself I wonder?'

'Why, what do you think?' replied the King. 'The Queen of England, of course. Yes, and Empress of India. The whole bag of tricks.'

'Ah,' said the brothers. 'Yes.... Well....' And they went away to think about it.

Meanwhile, the British press remained silent. Angry, bitter, and seething. But still, still, silent.

It was the Bishop of Bradford whodunit. He didn't mean to, of course. It was just that he was a divine innocent – an innocent divine. The Bishop's name, incidentally, was Blunt.

Bishop Blunt lived in the north of England, far from the gossip of London dinner tables. He had never heard of Mrs Simpson. He was, however, well aware that the King was to be formally enthroned at a Coronation ceremony to be held in May of the following year. And the Bishop was concerned to emphasise to his flock that the Coronation was not just a jolly event at which you waved flags and drank a lot of fizzy wine. Absolutely not. No. The Coronation was a *religious* ceremony, with profound Christian significance. And while he was sure – yes, quite confident – that the King himself was, at heart, a religious sort of chap, the Bishop did just wish – just occasionally, you understand, without in any way intending to be critical – he did just wish that occasionally the King would give more *evidence* of being interested in religion. Show a bit more willingness to go to church and so forth.

These remarks were made on Tuesday 1 December 1936, at the Bishop's diocesan conference.

Now, while the Bishop of Bradford might not have heard of Mrs Simpson, the editor of the *Yorkshire Post* certainly had. And so had the editor of the *Bradford Telegraph and Argus*. They, like every other editor in the land, had been regularly banging their heads against nearby brick walls in an agony of frustration at not being able to publish any details of what was undoubtedly the story of the decade. And they knew, as all good newspapermen did, that sooner or later a signal would come. It would not be a direct message – good heavens, my dear chap, this is England! No one would ring them up or write to them and say, 'OK, as from twelve tonight you can put that big picture of Edward snogging Wallis on the beach at Cannes all over your front page. Oh, and don't forget to get your airbrush chappie to cover up the erection.' No, no. Nothing like that would happen. It would all be *much* more subtle. What would happen was, somewhere, somehow, there would be a Sign Sent From Above. Somebody, somewhere, would have a word in the ear of someone in authority, and the chap in authority would purse his lips a bit and say, well, he thought perhaps a mention or two of Mrs Simpson would not now be wholly out of place. And that would be it. Open season on Wallis and Co.

So there they all were. The editors of the *Yorkshire Post*, the *Bradford Telegraph and Argus*, and many others. All waiting for The Sign From Above.

And now it had come. From the Bishop. Or so they thought.

If they had stopped to think, they might *just* have wondered whether it wasn't the tiniest bit unlikely that the Bishop of Bradford should have been deputed to do the job. But they didn't stop to think. They were men with deadlines to meet.

The *Yorkshire Post* published Bishop Blunt's speech in full, together with a leader which was, in itself, a model of restraint. The leading article did not even mention Mrs Simpson by name. But it did refer to rumours regarding the King which had been published in the more sensational American newspapers. And it did say that 'the King may not yet have perceived how complete in our day must be that self-dedication of which Dr Blunt spoke.' In other words, the editor of the *Yorkshire Post* was being bold enough to say to his sovereign: Forget about Wallis, sunshine, or forget about being King. It was a courageous step to take.

Meanwhile, the editor of the *Bradford Telegraph and Argus* circulated the text of the Bishop's speech to all the Fleet Street newspapers. And that was it. The whistle had gone.

Sad to relate, many historians have described the events which ensued by saying that 'all hell broke loose'. The use of this tired cliché is to be regretted, but the phrase does perhaps give some indication of the depth and extent of the furious public debate which followed.

Remember, please, that the vast majority of the British population had heard nothing of the King's intentions until they read their newspapers on 3 December 1936. Now, and for the next few days, they were to hear of, and discuss, little else.

Almost immediately, the public reaction became clear. It was one of profound disapproval.

The King rang the Prime Minister and asked him to stop *The Times* from publishing an attack on his beloved. The Prime Minister pointed out that the man who led the Government of the day, important fellow though he was, had no power to tell the editor of *The Times* what to do. However, the PM was a kindly old buffer, and such was the King's distress that he did indeed ring the editor. But only to say, 'You know, Geoffrey, the trouble is that the little man hasn't the faintest notion of the way this country is governed.'

No one in any position of authority got much sleep during the next week. But gradually, out of all the chaos, uproar, and snarling, there emerged a general view. A large majority of the British people did not want their King to marry Mrs Simpson. Furthermore, the consensus among the politicians was that if the King wished to marry Mrs Simpson he could not remain King. And although Wallis and the King were ever afterwards to believe that they were defeated by three wicked old men – the Prime Minister, the Archbishop of Canterbury, and the Editor of *The Times* – that was not true. The plain fact was, the British people simply could not stomach the idea of their King being married to a woman who had been divorced twice.

The knowledge that Wallis Simpson was an American and a commoner was not particularly crucial. It was the marital status which clinched matters. To have been divorced once might be thought a misfortune; to have been divorced twice looked like carelessness. And it simply would not do. It offended the non-conformist conscience of the nation; and, in many people's opinion, it offended the dignity of the Crown.

Wallis was not popular. Bricks were hurled through her

windows, and it was feared, by the more excitable, that vitriol might be thrown at her. It was therefore decided that for her own safety (and, belatedly, to protect the validity of her divorce) she should go abroad. She went to Cannes, travelling light: she only took one maid, sixteen trunks and thirty-six suitcases (as compared with her usual 150 pieces of luggage).

Once she arrived in Cannes, no less than four British newspapers reported that her solicitor had flown to join her, and that he was accompanied *by a well-known gynaecologist and an anaesthetist!*

Well, my dears – *what* a sensation. It wasn't true, of course. The doctor wasn't a gynaecologist, and the anaesthetist was just the solicitor's clerk, carrying a big Gladstone bag. Still, it was a jolly good story, and everyone enjoyed it no end.

It took the King a few days to get the message, but eventually he had no choice but to recognise the reality of the situation. And, once he realised where he stood, what he could do and what he couldn't do, he became a much happier man. Everyone remarked on it.

The lawyers and the politicians worked endless hours, and a scheme was bodged together. It later proved to be deeply flawed, but at the time it was acceptable to those involved. The King agreed to abdicate in favour of his younger brother, the Duke of York, who would become King George VI. The present King would cease to be Edward VIII and would assume the title of the Duke of Windsor.

On 10 December 1936, Edward VIII signed the Instrument of Abdication. That night, five hundred Fascists and Nazi supporters paraded outside Buckingham Palace, shouting 'We want Edward'. But there were too few of them, and the demonstration came too late.

Why was it that Edward VIII and Wallis Simpson lost the battle for power so quickly? There are several reasons.

First, neither one of them understood how the British political system actually worked. Wallis didn't understand because she was an American, and had made no effort. The King didn't understand because he was stupid, badly educated, and never read anything. At Oxford, where he was a poor student and didn't get a degree, he had had a tutor called Hansell (they were known as Hansell and Gretel). In later years, many a courtier had emerged from a discussion with the King, shaking his head and asking, 'What on earth did Hansell teach him?' The answer, apparently, was not much.

If Hansell had taught the King even schoolboy history, Edward would have known that the British people do not allow their kings to act as dictators. In 1215, King John had been forced to sign Magna Carta, which set out basic liberties for all his subjects. In 1649, Charles I, who had been getting much too big for his boots, had his head chopped off. Now, in 1936, Edward VIII was finding out that even he could not simply tell people what he was going to do and require them to accept it. Life was not that simple.

Another factor was that neither the King nor Wallace had any substantive support for their proposed marriage. The only politicians of note who were on the King's side were Sir Oswald Mosley and Sir Stafford Cripps. Mosley was a Fascist, and Cripps was a Socialist. They were unlikely bedfellows, and neither of them carried much of a punch.

Wallis too was without friends. Oh yes, she had a large circle of sycophants and hangers-on, but no one really *liked* her. Worse, she had made bitter enemies of every servant in every household that she had ever visited. Her endless demands, her ceaseless criticism, her snobbery, and her imperious manner had infuriated every butler and housemaid from Aberdeen to Plymouth. Many of these people had been eager to talk to the press. The more sophisticated of them had overheard conversations which, in their quaint, old-fashioned way, they regarded as treasonable; these people had made it their business to talk to somebody who knew somebody who worked in MI5. The telephonists at Buckingham Palace, for instance, had heard things said – quite accidentally, you understand, while checking the lines – which had upset them deeply. And these people needed little encouragement to move from accidentally overhearing things to co-operating in the recording of conversations verbatim. The result was that Wallis and Edward, while planning their next move, could not so much as cough without the Government and MI5 knowing exactly what they were up to.

Finally, of course, there was the attitude of the great British public. Ordinary people were well aware that they had been denied access to the facts for months, probably years, and they took a very dim view of that. They also did not think it appropriate that their King should set a poor example to his subjects.

And so the great lovers of our time lost their battle to remain as King and Queen, Emperor and Empress of India, the whole bag of tricks. But in a way they were fortunate. For if there had not been this hideous public row about the King marrying Wallis, there would assuredly, before long, have been a hideous public row about their attitude to Germany. That really would have been a constitutional crisis and might have spelt the end of the monarchy in Great Britain. And it would have been a far, far worse situation for the star-cross'd lovers. The end would have been the same – they would have been kicked out – but in the latter case their reputations would have been ruined for ever. As it was, they were able to sail off into a rosy sunset, holding hands, billing and cooing, with the softer-hearted members of the community waving them a fond farewell.

The departing King made a radio broadcast which was one of the great romantic performances of all time. He said that he had found it impossible to carry the heavy burden of responsibility and to discharge his duties as King 'without the help and support of the woman I love.' He added: 'I now quit altogether public affairs [which was a lie].... If at any time in the future I can be of service to His Majesty in a private station, I shall not fail [but he frequently did]. And now you all have a new King. I wish him, and you, his people, happiness and prosperity, with all my heart.'

Well, let us be generous, and assume that he meant it.

Part Five

February 1937 – 4 September 1939

Chapter 21

'Good luck, Daddy!' said Jane.

'Thanks,' said Alastair. 'I'm certainly going to need it.'

It was all going to be very difficult, that much was certain.

Strictly speaking, of course, the Duke of Windsor was not yet the Duke of Windsor: the title was not formally gazetted until May 1937. Nevertheless, 'the Duke' was what everyone was now calling the man who had once been King. And the Duke was going to be furious, Alastair had no doubt about that.

In late February 1937, Alastair Padget travelled to Schloss Enzesfeld, the castle near Vienna which was home to the Baron and Baroness Eugene Rothschild. It was here that the Duke of Windsor was now living. He was impatiently sitting out the months which had to pass until Wallis's divorce from Ernest Simpson became final. The lawyers had finally made the two love-birds understand that even a former King and his lady were not untouched by the laws of England, and that if they insisted on living together as man and wife before the beginning of May, then they would never be able to marry. So the Duke was in Austria and the Duchess-to-be was staying with another set of friends at the Villa Lou Viei in Cannes.

Alastair met the Duke late one afternoon. They were alone in a room set aside for the meeting.

Physically the Duke looked just as young and untroubled by events as he always had, but Alastair could see that he was tense and was concerned about what message Alastair might have brought from London.

Alastair said what he had come to say, and waited for a reaction.

Midway through Alastair's statement, the Duke had risen to his feet and gone over to the window. Now he returned to his seat, hitched up his trouser legs – a most uncharacteristic gesture – and looked Alastair straight in the eye.

‘So,’ he said, in a tight, slightly high-pitched voice. ‘Let me be clear that I understand what you have been sent to tell me.... First, when Wallis becomes my wife, she will not be recognised as a member of the royal family, and is not to be known as Her Royal Highness. Is that correct?’

‘It is.’ How fascinating, thought Alastair, that the Duke should wish to discuss that item first.

The Duke stared at the floor. He struggled visibly to contain his feelings and to find the words for what he wished to say. ‘I shall take legal advice about this,’ he managed to blurt out eventually. ‘I consider it wholly wrong. Completely outrageous. It goes contrary to everything I have ever heard, everything I have ever known about the right way to do things. I shall see what the lawyers have to say about it.’ He looked up at Alastair. ‘Do you follow me?’ The question was barked out.

‘I do.’

The Duke rose to his feet and went to the window again. The emotions surging through him were clearly far too powerful to allow him to remain stationary.

‘I know who is behind this,’ he said bitterly. ‘My brother would never have dreamed of this on his own. I know that. It’s his wife – that ice-cold bitch Elizabeth.’ He turned, seeking confirmation. ‘She’s the one, isn’t she?’

Alastair remained silent.

The Duke walked a pace or two nearer. ‘So. When Wallis and I are married, we shall have a situation whereby those who visit us will be obliged by etiquette to bow to me, and to address me as Your Royal Highness – but they will not be required to treat my wife in the same way. The ladies will not be expected to curtsy to her. Is that the strength of it?’

‘That is my understanding,’ said Alastair carefully.

The Duke snorted. ‘So, our friends and visitors will have to choose between disobeying their present King and insulting my wife and myself. We will see which they prefer.’

Alastair waited for a further reaction, as the Duke was evidently forming a statement in his mind.

‘You may tell your new sovereign,’ said the Duke when he was ready, 'that I shall not forget this. It is a deliberate, calculated insult, designed to hurt me, and hurt me it has. I shall not forget, and I shall not forgive.'

Alastair picked up his pen. 'I note what you say,' he said.

The Duke waited until Alastair had finished writing. Then he sighed. 'And now, I suppose, we must descend to the level of discussing the money.'

'Yes, Sir, I'm afraid we must.'

'Given what you have just told me, it is no surprise that my family intends to renege on the agreement which they signed. The property of the Crown is not in dispute. When I abdicated, all that property passed of course to the new King, and good luck to him. But I also, voluntarily, gave up my claim to the income from the Duchy of Cornwall, which is of the order of a hundred thousand a year. I did that to help my brother. And I did it on the understanding, embodied in a legal document which he and I both signed, that I would be paid a tax-free allowance of twenty-five thousand a year. And now you are telling me he doesn't intend to pay that money!'

Alastair paused. He knew that the new King, George VI, was on very weak ground here. 'Your brother's position, Sir, is that when he signed the agreement, he was assuming that the Government would agree to pay the sum in question from the Civil List.'

The Duke practically snarled. 'Was he indeed?'

'And now, I regret to say, it has become clear that the Government will not, under any circumstances, provide you with a Civil List pension.'

The Duke's pale-blue eyes narrowed in fury. In the past he had often been considered a soft man, a man little able to assert himself or to dominate a discussion. But this was a different man, one who was fighting for someone else's future in addition to his own.

'Well,' said the Duke, 'you can go back and tell my brother that if he chooses not to honour his own agreement, we will meet in court – the law courts I mean – and let a jury decide. If this is the age of democracy, let us do it that way. Tell him to think that over, and remember that this is another matter on which I shall take legal advice.'

Alastair nodded. 'But there is, perhaps, one way forward,' he put in.

'The Duke looked surprised. 'Oh?'

'Yes.... I understand, from an intermediary, that the King might find it possible to pay the allowance from his own resources, provided certain points were agreed.'

The Duke shook his head in amazement. 'Well,' he said, 'I always knew my brother was a bit dim, but I didn't realise that he would allow himself to be pushed around quite so soon. I suppose this intermediary wouldn't be called Elizabeth, would she?'

Alastair made no comment.

'Very well. Let me hear what the blackmailer wants.'

'It has been suggested that it might prove possible to pay the allowance if you were to sign an undertaking that you would never return to England except at the request of the King, who would only make such a request on the advice of his Ministers.'

The Duke gasped, rose to his feet again, and began yet another walk around the room. Alastair's last statement seemed to have knocked the stuffing out of him; the bravado had been only temporary.

'I can hardly believe all this,' he said. His voice was tearful. 'I can hardly believe it. Anyone would think they were dealing with a... with a tradesman – not with a former King, who is their own flesh and blood. I can hardly, truly, believe it.'

Alastair waited, and a long silence followed. Eventually the Duke turned towards Alastair again.

'You may take back the message that I do not agree to the proposed terms. And I will not agree to them at any time in the future. I shall keep the Fort open and ready, and my wife and I will reside there whenever we wish.'

'I'm afraid not, Sir,' said Alastair evenly. 'I'm afraid that will not be possible. Fort Belvedere will not be available to you in future.'

The Duke's mouth fell open. 'But it's *my* house! I own it! My father gave it to me. I've spent tens of thousands of my own money having it renovated. I worked in the garden with my bare hands!'

'All of that is recognised,' said Alastair as neutrally as possible. 'But the fact remains that the house is Crown property. And my instructions are to inform you that it will no longer be available to you.'

The Duke stared at him. 'Alastair, I have known you a long time, and I know that you are not a vindictive man. I know too that you are only the messenger in this matter.... So I will not insult you by asking your own views. But I do ask you to convey to those who have sent you that there is a limit to what I can tolerate. And apart from anything else, all this is going to make it very difficult for me to greet my family with any genuine pleasure when it comes to the wedding.'

Alastair now had to deliver his final piece of news. 'As to the wedding, Sir, I have been asked to make it clear that no member of the royal family will be attending.'

The Duke winced as if he had been slapped. 'None at all?' he asked.

'None, Sir.'

The Duke seemed on the point of tears, and he had visibly returned to the softer, more vulnerable persona which Alastair was so used to. *Abject*, his former lover Thelma Furness had called him. An abject little man, always blubbing over something.

The little man now waved a hand dejectedly. 'Well.... Well, so be it. God help those whose family turns against them. If I did not have Wallis to help me I would be lost. Utterly, utterly lost.'

On 4 May 1937, The Duke of Windsor and Wallis Simpson were reunited after several months apart. Edward 'Fruity' Metcalfe, a close friend of the Duke's who witnessed the occasion, described it as, 'Very touching. Very deep stuff.'

It was at this time also that the Duke announced to a journalist from the *Daily Herald* that he had plans to form a republic in England with himself as President and Wallis as first lady. Perhaps, the Duke wondered aloud, perhaps the Labour Party might be interested in this proposal? The editor of the *Daily*

Herald was too embarrassed to publish the story. The Duke also wrote a letter to Wallis in which he said 'WE will be back in our glory sooner than WE think.'

On 11 May 1937, the Duke formally announced his engagement to Wallis. He thoughtfully held the press conference on the very eve of his brother's Coronation in Westminster Abbey, thus stealing the headlines.

The Duke and Wallis were finally married on 3 June 1937, at the Chateau de Candé, France. (The chateau belonged to Charles Bedaux, a naturalised American. Bedaux was another friend of the Windsors who, after the war, was imprisoned on charges of trading with the enemy. He was faced with possible execution and he committed suicide in prison.)

The date chosen for the wedding was the birthday of the man who would have liked it least, the Duke of Windsor's father, George V. Although the Duke hoped, right to the very last minute, that his brother the Duke of Kent would be best man, he was disappointed. The entire royal family boycotted the event.

There was also a little problem about who should perform the ceremony. But eventually, a clergyman from Darlington defied his Bishop and travelled to France to do what was necessary for the former defender of his faith.

Shortly before her marriage, the bride legally resumed her maiden name of Wallis Warfield, by deed poll. In the application for a marriage licence she described herself as 'single'. But, despite her nominal return to virgin status, not even Wallis had the balls to wear a white wedding gown. Instead she chose a shade of blue. Mainbocher, who designed the dress, christened it 'Wallis blue'. It was said to be the same colour as her eyes. But those present, who knew about these things, couldn't help noticing that it was the same blue as the ribbon worn by the Noble Knights of the Garter.

The whole occasion, everyone agreed, was the wedding of the decade.

Chapter 22

Ribbentrop was invited to the wedding of the decade, of course. By this time (the summer of 1937) he had formally been appointed as German Ambassador to London. In that capacity, if for no other reason, his name was naturally high on the Windsors' guest list. But he couldn't go. Pressures of business, you understand. He sent the happy couple a handsome piece of German sculpture instead. It was one of those works of art which so impressed the Führer: an idealised bronze representation of the very best of German womanhood. A nude, of course. A perfect example of Aryan physiology – absolutely nothing Jewish about it at all.

So much for cementing relations with the once and future King of England. And – who could say? – perhaps the exiled Duke of Windsor would one day be King of Germany as well. Ribbentrop now turned his attention to another part of the plot.

Would she do? That was the question he pondered. Was this young woman exactly what he was looking for?

The woman concerned, Fräulein Helga Kronberg, sat opposite him, waiting patiently.

A week earlier, on one of his many visits to Berlin (for it wasn't wise to be away from the centre of power for too long), Ribbentrop had asked the people in his Bureau to find him a woman. And oh what fun that had caused. His secretary had blushed prettily and said Oh Sir! And his personal assistant had sniggered and said Did he prefer blondes? And the tittering had overflowed from the office all the way down the corridor. Good staff relations this was, and Ribbentrop was proud of himself. He liked to be loved by his people.

No no, he had insisted, after the fun was over. You misunderstand me! I require you to find a woman for a particular assignment. We need to find a nice German girl to assist the English aristocrat, Westrow. We will pretend she is Swiss, of course, so as not to alarm the English, but she will be German.

And she will be ours. And she will hold his hand, stand behind him, and push him forward, do whatever is necessary while he does important work for us.

So Ribbentrop's people had found their master a woman. And now she was sitting in front of him and he was reading her file. Ribbentrop hoped very much that she would be suitable because he was due back in London next week and there wouldn't be much time to find a replacement if there was any doubt.

Helga Kronberg.

Age twenty-seven.

Big, blonde, blue-eyed, creamy skinned. A bit beefy perhaps. But it was all muscle apparently, according to the file. An Aryan through and through. The Führer would be proud of her.

Helga came from a modest background in south Germany – good strong peasant stock probably – but she had eliminated the south German accent which might perhaps have hindered her career. She had begun to be noticed some years earlier as a leader in the Hitler Youth Movement – all that fresh air, drum banging and marching. Wonderful stuff. It did Ribbentrop's heart good just to think about it. He looked across his desk at Helga, pictured her wearing a pair of short shorts, and smiled. She smiled back. Wow.

Then she had joined the armed forces. Caught the eye of a Colonel, who marked her out for special duties. It said here. Ribbentrop suspected that special duties meant no more than being available to fuck the Colonel on two afternoons a week while his wife was out shopping, but never mind, it was a start. And we all have to start somewhere. The Colonel had passed her on to Intelligence. Probably after his wife found out.

Intelligence had trained Helga for sexual espionage. Well they weren't stupid, that lot. They could recognise a luscious fuck when they saw one. So for a while she'd been seducing visiting politicians, getting information, arranging incriminating photographs. Later they'd noticed another side to her, and had given her training in small-arms, judo, and assassination techniques. Then they sent her out to shoot a Jewish butcher and she came back in thirty minutes, job done, next one please.

Ribbentrop smiled at Helga again. Yes indeed, it would be a pity to send this young lady off to England *too* quickly. Perhaps a weekend in Berlin, with one or two personal briefings with the Ambassador to England, just to make sure that she knew what was required of her? Make sure she came up to scratch, hm?

Ribbentrop flicked through the rest of the file. Hobbies: popular music. It was dirty work, monitoring the filthy outpourings of the decadent American negro race, but someone had to do it, and Helga had bravely volunteered. She spent a lot of time listening to American records and trawling the radio stations on the short wave, and then she wrote reports about the appalling social attitudes which the music revealed. Fascinating stuff.

Favourite possessions. You could tell a lot about a person when you knew what their favourite possessions were. Helga's were handguns, knives, and whips. She was particularly keen on a South African sjambok, which was apparently a whip made out of rhinoceros hide. Could take the skin off your back in no time at all. She had asked to be sent to South Africa to see it in use in prisons for the coloured, but Intelligence had decided against it. Still, give the girl marks for initiative and keenness.

Sex life. Vigorous. Ribbentrop looked over his desk at big blonde Helga and thought about her being sexually vigorous. It made him feel a bit weak. A bit intimidated actually. Surely he wasn't getting as old as that? He was only forty-four. Must be the hot weather.

Languages. English passable. Intelligence had seen to that. Good, because that was an important factor. Ribbentrop addressed her in English and received a perfectly sensible reply, so he was reassured.

Yes, yes, the lovely Helga would do, he decided with relief. Provided, of course, that when she got to England she could remember that she was supposed to be a simple Swiss milkmaid called Schmidt, and not a hardened member of the great German military machine whose favourite spare-time occupation – after sex – was inciting gangs of young men to burn down Jewish-owned businesses.

'Well Helga my dear – you have talked to my subordinates and you have had this mission explained to you?'

'I have, Sir.'

'Essentially,' said Ribbentrop, 'your job is to act as our secret link with an Englishman who shares our vision of the future. Unlike most men, he is not motivated by greed or a desire for power, because he is rich already, and retiring in nature. In short, he is an idealist. What he wants is to do what is best for England, and best for the future of Europe. And in his eyes, that means co-operating with us. Are you confident that you can assist him in all that?'

'I am, Sir.'

'Good.'

Ribbentrop snapped the file shut and asked his secretary to send in the Earl of Westrow.

The interview with Westrow was difficult, because Westrow himself was such a diffident, awkward man. He wasn't exactly shy, though the presence of an alluring young woman like Helga definitely made him uneasy. No, it was somehow that he lacked confidence. Somewhere in his background, perhaps as a very young child, he had been cowed into submission. Probably whipped or otherwise abused by one of those dreadful nannies that the English inflicted on their children. Anyway, it was a bit difficult to carry him along with you, but between them Ribbentrop and Helga managed it.

Ribbentrop was pleased with Helga. She wasn't just a pair of tits – though they were quite remarkable tits, that much was obvious from the shape of her blouse, and he was looking forward to making a closer acquaintance with them. No, Helga was also adept at putting awkward, nervous men at their ease. Helping them to make up their mind to do those things which they knew they ought not to do, but which they very much wanted to do. And Helga had the knack. Ribbentrop could see that she would handle Westrow beautifully.

As a reward he took the pair of them along the corridor to meet the Führer. He didn't tell them where they were going in advance, because they would both have wet their knickers if he had, but they got the message as they walked along the corridor, and it amused Ribbentrop to see their faces change. Westrow went increasingly pale, and Helga's mouth popped open, until she became aware of what she was doing and closed it rapidly.

The Führer was taking a close personal interest in arrangements for the conquest of England (and all associated parts of the globe). Consequently he had set aside five minutes for the buttering up of this Westrow fellow who might one day prove to be useful, particularly if supported by a well-trained minion.

The Führer engaged the two visitors in conversation, overpowering them, as he overpowered everyone he met, with the force of his personality. Ribbentrop stood back and admired the master at work. This was truly a leader, a man with vision and the will to impose that vision.

The Führer emphasised the importance of the secret work which Westrow and Helga were to undertake. Helga, posing as a young Swiss woman seeking to improve her English, would be 'employed' by the Earl until the future status of England was clarified. No one could yet say in what way they would be asked to serve, or when. But they could depend upon it that their role was crucial. He, the Führer, would be watching their performance closely, and he had every confidence that they would not fail. He shook their hands earnestly and swept them out of the door.

Three minutes fifty seconds, Ribbentrop timed it, but there had been no sense of haste. It had been as if the Führer had all the time in the world, and his two guests were the most important members of his entire team. Brief though it was, it had been a meeting which neither Westrow nor Helga would ever forget.

In the course of time, after an extensive personal briefing by the Ambassador, Helga travelled to England. As far as the British authorities were concerned, she was a young Swiss woman called Helga Schmidt; she had all the papers to prove it. Once in England, she took up her position as 'personal assistant' to the Earl of Westrow, set up her secret radio-communications system in the loft of the Earl's country seat, and waited for instructions.

Westrow, meanwhile, made a speech in the House of Lords. It

was, both *The Times* and the *Manchester Guardian* agreed, quite the worst speech ever made in that House, in the sense that it rambled, was barely audible, and was full of *non sequiturs* and incorrect 'facts'. But at least its import was clear. The Earl had been to Germany. He had seen at first hand the wonders that were being performed there. He had stood in the crowd at Nuremberg. He had heard the drums, seen the flags, thrilled to the sound of ten thousand marching feet. It was all wonderful, wonderful, wonderful, and he couldn't wait for something similar to be introduced in England.

He was heard by a bare quorum of members. His audience included three bishops, two of whom went to sleep, four geriatric landowners, who ignored him, a handful of officials, and two journalists. No one took the slightest notice.

Chapter 23

Major-General Sir Vernon Kell stood at the window of his MI5 office, gazing down into the street below. Alastair could tell from his posture that the man was deeply dispirited.

'Thought we were rid of him,' said Kell in sepulchral tones. 'Some of us did, anyway. The stupid ones, like me. "I now quit for ever public life." Wasn't that what he said? Something like that. And what's the first thing he does after finishing his honeymoon? He gets himself invited to Germany! Bloody liar.'

Alastair said nothing, letting the old man vent his anger.

Kell turned away from the window. 'And who do you think's paying for this semi-state visit?'

'Well... The Duke, I imagine?'

Kell snorted. 'Him? He wouldn't pay his own bus fare if he could avoid it. Ran up huge phone bills at Schloss Enzesfeld, talking to his beloved, three and four times and day – and never offered a penny piece in return.... No, Hitler's the one who's paying, though no one's supposed to know. Top secret. The former King of England, official state visit to Germany – well, that's what it looks like to the public. Makes Mr Hitler look jolly respectable anyway – so Hitler's paying the bill. Unnamed account at the Reichsbank.'

Kell sat down at his desk. He was clearly disgusted and wearied by the news, now made public in that day's press, that the Duke and Duchess of Windsor were to visit Germany in October 1937. The official line was that the Duke wished to inspect some public-housing projects there, he being well known for his concern for the welfare of the working class.

'Anyway,' Kell continued, 'I'll try to waste as little of your time as possible. What I wanted to tell you is that there was a meeting to plan this visit to Germany. It happened a couple of weeks ago. Having completed their lengthy honeymoon, the Duke and his woman have taken up residence at the Hotel Meurice in Paris. And with the assistance of the French we've been able to put in microphones. The system doesn't work very well – we get a lot of plumbing noises – but it's quite useful.'

'Who attended this meeting?' asked Alastair.

'The Duke. Wallis. Ribbentrop. And Martin Bormann, who's Hitler's secretary. We've got a transcript of sorts.' Kell indicated a bundle of papers on his desk. 'You can take it away and read it. They all spoke in German of course, probably for Bormann's benefit, but we've had it translated. Bit difficult to tell what's happening in places, but the Duke can be heard telling his visitors that he's proud of his German blood, feels more German than British, is keenly interested in the development of the Third Reich, et cetera. Usual rubbish which we've all heard before. Bormann then asks him – *Bormann* please note, not Ribbentrop – whether he's willing in principle to return to the British throne, "should circumstances change." Nice little euphemism, that.'

'And I imagine the Duke said yes?'

'Oh yes, with alacrity. Emphasises that he's a man of peace of course. But he does remind his listeners that his family history is such that it would make perfect sense for him to assume the crown of both England and Germany, with Herr Hitler acting as political supremo of both countries.'

'Advised on the broader strategy by his king, no doubt.'

'No doubt.' Kell shook his head. 'This new super state would probably be called Gross-Deutschland – Great Germany. One doesn't know whether to laugh or cry.'

Kell paused, engrossed in his own thoughts, and this gave Alastair an opportunity to voice some of his own ideas. 'It seems to me,' he said, 'that the Germans have a clearly defined plan to expand the German state, both geographically and politically. An actual invasion of England would be difficult from a purely logistic point of view, so naturally they would like to arrange matters so that Edward gets back on the throne with their help. Some sort of internal upheaval. Perhaps a revolution of some sort. Then, if they can achieve that, Edward is hopelessly indebted to them. He's their man, and they control England and all our dominions and colonies, without going to the trouble of a military invasion.'

'That's about it,' said Kell. 'And the fact that Bormann attended the meeting means, to my mind, that this isn't just a fantasy dreamed up over dinner by Wallis and Ribbentrop. It means that Hitler is thinking along these lines too.'

Alastair paused. 'Do you think it could happen?' he asked. 'Are we really so politically unstable?'

Kell's eyes widened. 'Well, one likes to think not. Back in the old days, before nineteen-fourteen, it would have been inconceivable to think of any major political change. But then you have to look at what's happened in Russia, and Germany. And you see that dramatic changes in the way countries are governed *can* come about, with surprising speed. As for this country – well, in the early thirties there was deep social unrest. And at the moment we've got street fights between Communists and Fascists. If there is a war, and if we start to be on the losing side of it, then who can say what the outcome will be?'

Alastair smiled ruefully. 'Well, there's a happy thought,' he said.

Records recently released from the German state archives show that Ribbentrop and Bormann also arranged for the meeting at the Hotel Meurice to be recorded, probably by using a primitive machine contained in a briefcase. The two men no doubt hoped to inveigle the Duke of Windsor into making ill-considered statements which could, if necessary, be used to embarrass or blackmail him at a later date.

The German transcript shows that, at one point, Ribbentrop excused himself to go to the bathroom. Wallis followed him out of the room, leaving Bormann and the Duke of Windsor together. Later, as Ribbentrop and Bormann left the hotel, Ribbentrop thanked Bormann for 'covering for him'. He adds (translating literally from the German): 'She drank my lemonade very nicely.' This is believed to be a reference to fellatio.

'But,' says Bormann in astonishment, 'you were only gone three minutes!'

'Ah,' says Ribbentrop, 'but when a woman has a mouth like the Duchess, three minutes is all you need.'

Chapter 24

Joe Kennedy had for years had the ambition to be the American Ambassador in London. As the months of 1937 passed, Joe reminded President Roosevelt repeatedly of the services which he had provided and for which, as in the normal way of things, he expected to be rewarded. Surely, he said, over and over again, now was the time for him to go to London.

Eventually, after being endlessly pestered, Roosevelt grew tired of thinking up reasons why Joe's request should not be allowed. And there were, of course, certain advantages in sending Joe Kennedy abroad, the chief one being that it got the son of a bitch out of Washington. In early 1938, therefore, Roosevelt told Kennedy that he would give him six months in London, after which all the President's political debts to Kennedy would be regarded as paid. (In the end, Kennedy spent nearly three years as Ambassador.)

Putting a brave face on his action, the President tried to pretend that, in making this appointment, he was having a little fun. Kennedy was the first Irishman and the first Roman Catholic to act as Ambassador to London, and Roosevelt maintained that this was amusing. 'Isn't that just great?' he invited a dinner party to agree. 'Appointing an Irishman to the Court of St James's! That's just the greatest joke in the world!' There were polite smiles around the table, but no one else found it funny.

In the Ribbentrop archives in Berlin there is a report of a meeting held in the American Embassy on 21 November 1938. Joachim von Ribbentrop had recently completed his term of office as German Ambassador to London and had formally been appointed as Foreign Minister. Joseph P. Kennedy had just about found his feet as the US Ambassador to London. Ribbentrop initiated the meeting, and he wrote to Hitler about it afterwards.

Ribbentrop couldn't quite figure it out. Not at first. Couldn't see what the attraction was. But Joe soon explained.

‘Always wanted to come to London,’ Joe said. ‘And I was right. We’re having a great time. Everyone treats us real nice, you know? I’ve been made a member of the Athenaeum. And the Royal Thames Yacht Club.’

Ribbentrop smiled. He knew that Joe had been blackballed by every respectable American club, all the way from Boston to Miami, so naturally being admitted to the higher social circles in London would please him enormously. And Rose too.

‘Yeah,’ said Joe. ‘And the King and Queen have been real nice. They invited us to the Palace you know, for tea. And then a while later we spent a weekend at Windsor Castle with them. Gee, that was really something. We had a room in one of the towers, with a view of the park. And the servants all wore livery and wigs and everything. You know what I said to Rose? I said Rose, this is a helluva a long way from East Boston!’

Kennedy laughed uproariously, and Ribbentrop smiled. He was happy to let Joe meander on – it helped him to get the measure of the man.

‘And then we had the girls presented at Court you know. Kick, Rosemary, and Rose. Hell, they were really impressed I can tell you. They got all dressed up in tiaras and ball gowns and plumes in their hair and everything. Cost a goddamn fortune! Buckingham Palace was all lit up, with the Grenadier Guards and Beefeaters on the stairway. Boy, the girls won’t ever forget that, believe me. In fact all the kids are having a swell time.’

Ribbentrop now understood. Joe simply loved being His Excellency the US Ambassador to the Court of St James’s. It gave him status. Respectability. A title. Ribbentrop understood, at last, why Joe had come to London, and understood what he might therefore offer the man in any future deal. And there always would be deals. In politics there always were.

Ribbentrop put in a thought. ‘Yes,’ he said, ‘King George and Queen Elizabeth are most welcoming hosts, there is no doubt about it. But I have always thought it a pity that King Edward was obliged to abdicate.’

Joe’s face instantly became serious. ‘Oh, hell yes. Damn right. Yeah, that was a tragedy.’

'Do you keep in touch with the Windsors?'

'Oh, sure. Saw quite a lot of them this summer. We had a villa on the Riviera, and they were there having a yachting holiday. Had dinner with them several times.... The Dook and I think alike you know.'

'Yes?'

'Oh yes. Quite frankly, we think democracy is on its last feet. In the modern world you need a different sort of government. Something like yours in Germany, where a guy can get things done. Know what I mean?'

'Certainly. And I agree with you entirely. From that point of view, the Duke's tour of Germany last year was very useful. It enabled him to see at first hand what can be achieved if you have the necessary authority.'

Joe nodded gravely. 'Damn right. And let me say that I for one understand your problem with the Jews. See, I come from Boston, and quite a lot of the clubs there won't have Jewish members. So I understand, see. Where I think you go wrong is, you give it so much goddamn publicity. Know what I mean? Causes uproar back home. Gets Americans all worked up. Now if you did it nice and quiet, less of a problem.'

'I am sure the Führer will be interested to hear what you say. I will make a point of telling him.'

Joe nodded. 'Good. And when you do see him, tell him he can depend on me to do everything possible to avoid a war. If he wants any help in that regard, he's only gotta ask. Me, I'm a plain-speaking sorta guy and I say what I think. What I think is, Germany wants to dominate Europe, and that ain't no problem to me. Might do the place some good. Update the goddamn plumbing for one thing. All I hope is, you can do it without too much military action, because wars fuck up business something terrible. As for the Brits, well, they've been real nice to me and Rose, but if there is a war, they're gonna lose. That's my opinion, and I've told the President lotsa times, but he don't seem to take much notice. He thinks I'm biased see, because in the past the Brits ain't been too nice to my people.'

'You mean the Irish.'

'I sure do.'

Ribbentrop moved in quickly. 'Tell me Joe.... Suppose in the course of time, it was possible for Germany to assist in the unification of Ireland. If that happened, we would no doubt be looking around for someone to take charge. A man of experience and good judgement. Someone who thinks as we do, and who has an international reputation – a man of some standing. If ever that came about, and we were to approach you to be, let us say, the President of a new united Ireland – would you be interested in such a position?'

Joe gave a strange smile, for once keeping his lips together. 'Funny goddamn thing you know, but I was only thinking the same thing myself. Popped into my head while I was shaving, only the other day. Yeah, I'd be interested. Sure.'

Ribbentrop filed the information away. Something else that Joe wanted.

'Now, seems to me,' said Joe, 'what I heard, another thing you guys in Berlin want is some a your colonies back.'

'That's correct. Colonies that were taken from us at the end of the war.'

'I don't know a whole lot about that,' said Joe. 'Wanna give me a briefing?'

'Of course.'

Extract from Ribbentrop's report to Hitler:

> Mr Kennedy is our best ally in London and should be treated as such. He is sympathetic to the National Socialist style of government and hopes to see it introduced in all advanced countries including the USA. He understands about the Jewish problem. He hopes that it will not be necessary for us to initiate military action, but he will work with us to achieve our objectives in London, and elsewhere.
>
> As for Ireland, it is clearly a matter dear to his heart. He told me that he has close contacts with the IRA, 'through intermediaries' of course.

Before leaving London, Ribbentrop called at the town house of Lord Westrow.

It was an opulent place, as befitted a man who owned several acres of prime London property. The house was fairly discreet from the outside (in Brook Street) but it was dripping with wealth on the inside. Rather old-fashioned though. Ribbentrop had the impression that Westrow hadn't imposed his own personality on the place – perhaps it was left much as his parents had designed it.

Anyway, Ribbentrop hadn't come to admire the furniture. He wanted to see how Westrow and Helga were getting on.

Pretty well apparently. Westrow seemed unusually cheerful. And so he should be, given that he was allowed to fuck Helga whenever he felt like it, and by now she would presumably have got the hang of all his peculiar English perversions. Helga too seemed pleased to see Ribbentrop, and happy in her work.

Westrow, Ribbentrop, and Helga sat in the plush drawing-room at the back of the house, and drank tea while they talked. The tea came on a silver tray, borne by a wonderfully grizzled old butler.

'And how is the system of wireless communication working?' asked Ribbentrop, when the butler had retired.

Very well, it appeared.

'Good, good. We never know when it will be needed. But in the meantime, be prepared.'

Westrow and Helga solemnly agreed that preparedness was their watchword.

After tea, Ribbentrop suggested that it would be appropriate if he and Helga had a private meeting. Together. Alone.

Ah. Yes. It took a moment or two for Westrow's lethargic brain to work out what was required, but then he remembered that he had an appointment with his tailor. Wouldn't be back much before dinner as a matter of fact.

He left, and Ribbentrop had Helga strip off right there in the drawing-room. She marched around in her boots while he sang *Deutschland über alles* and toasted her bosoms with his teacup. They both had a lot of fun.

'The bosoms are holding up pretty well, Helga,' he told her. 'And your noble service to the state will not go unrewarded, I assure you. Is he very hard to please?'

Helga sighed. 'Don't ask,' she said. 'Once a fortnight, with luck.'

Ribbentrop sniggered. 'Oh dear oh dear,' he said. 'What a shame.'

'It's no so bad,' said Helga. 'There's a pub two or three streets away where you get a lot of soldiers in the evening, so I can always nip out when I get restless.'

Ribbentrop was decidedly restless. He was restless twice and then decided that he really must get back to work.

'Tell me,' said Helga, as he was about to leave. 'Everyone here thinks the Munich agreement has settled matters – that there will be peace in our time. But is there going to be a war against the English?'

'Oh yes,' said Ribbentrop. 'Yes, there will be a war. But it will be a short one. And we shall win.'

Chapter 25

As the year 1939 moved from spring into summer, Joe Kennedy found that the English became a little less friendly towards him. He was hurt and puzzled by this, but the reasons were not far to seek.

First, it became known in the higher levels of government and the civil service that the American President did not trust his Ambassador. Roosevelt had made an arrangement with the British whereby Joe's mail was read and his phone was tapped. Roosevelt felt obliged, not least by the value of the Irish vote, to let Joe remain in London. But by God the President was going to keep tabs on him.

The tabs proved interesting, and, to the British, disgusting. It wasn't just that Joe – the famous family man – kept a mistress (blonde, twenty-four, a model). The Brits could put up with that. No, it was the financial insider dealing which stuck in British throats: Joe was abusing his privileged position.

For example, in March 1939, Joe Kennedy, as American Ambassador, received advance information that Czechoslovakia was about to be occupied by the Germans. Well, hell, Joe wouldn't have been Joe if he had passed up an opportunity like that. Joe got on the phone and went short on Czech securities. Overnight he made a profit of some £20,000. The average British working man, in 1939, was being paid less than £4 for a 47-hour week. Thus in one afternoon, with one phone call, Joe made as much money as 100 British working men made in the whole of that year.

MI5 knew all about this instance of insider trading, and similar cases. So did the Cabinet. So did Roosevelt. The word got around, as the word often does, that Joe was acting improperly. The British had a very stuffy attitude towards that kind of behaviour, because for every big winner there are of course a large number of losers. Joe sometimes found, when he went into the Athenaeum, that one or two people got up and walked out.

If he had been asked to defend himself, which he wasn't, he would have said What the fuck? He had a wife and nine kids to feed (not to mention his mistress). And people might, just possibly, have given some weight to the argument. But they would still have maintained that, whatever else he might be, Joe Kennedy certainly wasn't a gentleman or a man of principle.

Europe, in 1939, scuffled and scrambled its way into chaos. Many British politicians were advocates of appeasement: that is say, they took the view that Germany should be given more or less anything in order to avoid a war. Joe Kennedy found his closest friends among this group. Some cynics might have said that what was to be given away wasn't his, or America's either, so it was easy for Joe to take the line he did. But a kinder soul would have said that Joe, and the rest of the appeasers, were doing their best to avoid another catastrophe like the Great War of 1914-18.

Whatever their motives, and whatever their tactics, the politicians of Europe failed to avoid another war.

On 23 August 1939, the British Prime Minister (Neville Chamberlain) warned Adolf Hitler that Britain would stand by Poland, which was then threatened with invasion by Germany. This warning was treated with contempt, and a week later German troops crossed the Polish border.

On Sunday 3 September 1939, Chamberlain made a radio broadcast. He explained that the British Government had presented a note in Berlin at 9.00 a.m. that day, giving Hitler until 11.00 a.m. to undertake to withdraw his troops from Poland. No such undertaking had been received, and consequently, said Chamberlain, 'this country is at war with Germany.'

This came as no great surprise to anyone, for the situation had been anticipated for months. France also declared war. America did not, and would not until December 1941.

Chamberlain's broadcast, announcing the beginning of the war, was heard by almost the entire nation.

In London, Alastair and Jane Padget listened to it in their flat in Eaton Square. Alastair tried not to look as horrified and distressed as he felt. He was appalled that, barely twenty years after the end of the last great conflict, which had wiped out a whole generation of able young men, Europe was about to repeat its mistakes.

Alastair thanked God that he didn't have a son. But he had a daughter of nineteen who was due to start a degree course at Oxford in a month's time. He just hoped and prayed that she could be persuaded to go on with her education, rather than join the armed forces. And he hoped and prayed that the war would be over before she finished her degree.

In France, the Duke and Duchess of Windsor were in the Chateau La Croë at Cap d'Antibes, a house which they had leased from Sir Pomeroy Burton. While they listened to Chamberlain, their late breakfast was served by servants wearing the red and gold livery of the British royal household.

The Windsors were well aware that the future was going to be difficult. Just to be on the safe side, they had bought some land in Hawaii.

They had mixed feelings about Chamberlain's announcement. The Duke said he feared that this would just open the door for Communism in Europe. The Duchess, silently, thought that the war would teach those fucking Brits a lesson, and serve them damn well right.

The Earl of Westrow and Helga Kronberg had gone to the Earl's country seat some days earlier, because they confidently expected that London would be bombed flat within a week or two. Helga was elated because at last she would have some real work to do. The Earl was subdued. The war was going to make a terrible mess of London, he was sure of that. He wondered if the Germans could possibly be persuaded to avoid bombing the property that he owned. Could Helga ask them perhaps?

In Berlin, Ribbentrop struggled to suppress his doubts. He couldn't help feeling just a little bit panicky. He knew it was wrong of him – it was treason really – but he did just wish that he felt a little more confident that Hitler knew what he was doing. Had Hitler *really* thought it through? Had he anticipated every reaction? Worked out all the logistics?

Ribbentrop turned around in his chair and stared at the picture of the beloved Führer on the wall behind him. He wondered if, even now, the Führer understood how much he owed to his Foreign Minister, Joachim *von* Ribbentrop. It was, after all, Ribbentrop who had negotiated the German-Soviet Nonaggression Pact of 23 August 1939, which had cleared the way for Hitler's attack on Poland. And did the Führer truly understand that? Did he *appreciate* it?

Eventually, as Ribbentrop gazed upon his leader's impressive features, his breathing began to lengthen and he felt secure again.

He began to hum to himself: *Deutschland, Deutschland, über alles....*

Joe Kennedy had been busy selling shares for the whole of the previous week. Shares in every goddamn British company that he could ever remember owning, and he had gone short on a lot more that he didn't own. Christ, what a godalmighty fuckup this was! Joe had never known anything like it. All the time and effort he had put into trying to avoid what had now happened! Joe had spent weeks, months, years even, talking to the goddamn Germans and the goddamn fucking Brits and now what had they done? Against his advice they had gone and started a fucking war, that's what. Rose and the kids were gonna have to be got back home, and then there were these fucking bombs that the Germans were gonna start dropping everywhere. And the fucking gas masks that you had to remember to carry with you! Because there was gonna be poison gas in the streets! The fucking Brits were gonna be beaten by Christmas, Joe was sure of it, so what the fuck did they wanna start a war for? For Poland? Who the fuck cared about a few fucking Polacks for Christ's sake? And so on.

Joe worked his Boston ass off that Sunday. Fixing this, arranging that, dealing with ten thousand and one things on behalf of the Embassy and his family. He worked long into the night of 3 September, and into the early hours of the following Monday morning. Then, at 4.45 a.m. London time, he phoned the President in Washington.

President Roosevelt could hardly believe his ears when he took the call. Joe was hysterical, rambling, incoherent, exhausted, and terrified, all at the same time.

'It's the end of the world!' wailed Joe to his President. 'It's the end of the whole fucking world!'

Part Six

October 1939 – early December 1940

Chapter 26

Frederick Jensen was not unused to meeting senior government officials and elected officers – ambassadors, senators, and the like – but this was the first time he had met the President, and he couldn't help feeling just a little bit nervous.

Fred sat in the White House corridor, waiting to be shown into the Oval Office, and tried to appear relaxed. But somehow he couldn't seem to concentrate on the print in the magazine in front of him.

It wasn't every day that the President asked to see you. 'The President would be glad if you would call at his office at ten a.m. tomorrow,' was the way it had been put by the secretary who rang. Well, gee, yes, sure. Tell the President that I think I can just about make it. And now here he was, Fred Jensen in person, without a clue as to why he was wanted.

Ten o'clock passed. And ten-fifteen. But at ten-twenty he was told that the President would see him now, and he was shown in.

'Hi, come in, welcome!' boomed Roosevelt.

'Er, thank you, Sir.'

The President waved his visitor to a chair, and Fred sat down. He crossed his legs, trying to seem at ease. Then he uncrossed them again immediately, because it seemed disrespectful to slouch. He sat up straight, which seemed too stiff. So he leaned back. Finally Fred decided to try to forget about his own appearance and concentrate on what was being said to him.

But the President wasn't saying anything yet. He was reading a file.

'You're a Harvard man,' said Roosevelt after a moment.

'Er, yes, Sir.'

'So am I.'

Actually Fred knew that already, but he didn't like to say so. And he was alarmed to discover that the President was reading his personnel file.

After a moment Roosevelt looked up again. 'How long have

you been in the State Department?'

'Just over twenty years, Sir.'

'Good.' Roosevelt tossed the file aside. 'The fact is, I have an assignment for you. Confidential. You could say top secret in fact. Calls for tact, diplomacy, a talent for picking up gossip without giving much away in return, and a strong concern for the welfare of the United States. Think you've got all that?'

'I... think so, Sir.'

'Well, your boss tells me so. He recommended you. You know England?'

'I've been a couple of times, Sir.'

'Good....'

'And I've just been giving a posting at the Embassy in London,' Fred continued. 'Defense Attaché. Starting next week.'

'Yeah. I know.'

Well he would, wouldn't he? The man has the file in front of him. Fred rebuked himself for stating the obvious.

Roosevelt turned and faced Fred head on. 'We have an Ambassador in London, Fred. Name of Kennedy. Heard of him?'

Fred grinned. 'Yes, Sir.'

'Yeah, most people have. Now the thing is, Fred, the United States has a foreign policy, and Joe Kennedy has a foreign policy, and the two don't always match up. Understand me?'

'Yes, Sir.' *Must stop saying Yes Sir.*

'Joe also has his own political agenda. His own ambitions. I think he'd quite like to be President himself, after I've had my turn.'

This was a joke, and Fred grinned again. Everyone in Washington knew that Joe Kennedy's appetite for power recognised no limits, and that he was manoeuvring for a shot at the presidency in due course.

'OK,' continued the President. 'Now what I want you to do is this. When you get to London I want you to prepare a confidential report for me, on a weekly basis. This is for my eyes only. When you leave this office you'll be given instructions on how to send it to me. And what I want to know is, I want to know all the things my Ambassador isn't telling me. I don't want you to do any spying, no breaking into offices or stealing papers. None of that. But I want you to keep your eyes and ears open. If Joe leaves London, I want to know where he's going, who he's meeting, and what they're talking about. If he makes a speech, I want to know what the ordinary Brit thinks of it – not what the newspapers say, because I can read that for myself. In other words, I want to know what the son of a bitch is up to, and what the London reaction is. I want the scuttlebutt, not the official whitewash. You follow?'

'Yes, Sir.'

'You think you can do that OK?'

'I'm sure I can, Sir.'

'Good.'

Roosevelt's body language indicated that this was the end of the meeting, and Fred stood up.

'Of course,' said the President thoughtfully, 'this is a hell of a time to send anyone to London. What with the war just started, and the bombing and everything. But there we are. Job's gotta be done. Is your wife staying here?'

'No, Sir. She says that if I'm going to be killed in the blitz she'd just as soon be there with me.'

The President seemed impressed. 'Good for her. And your boy...' He looked sideways at the file. 'Seymour....'

'He's going to stay here, Sir. With his grandmother.'

'Well, that seems sensible. You're going to send him to Harvard next fall, I see.'

Fred grinned, able to relax at last. 'Yes, Sir.'

The President smiled. 'Well, you and I are both Harvard men, Fred, and so I'd like to be able to say that he's bound to turn out just fine. That he'll get a good education, and become a man we can all be proud of. But since Joe Kennedy is a Harvard man too, I'm afraid we can't be absolutely sure of the outcome.'

Suddenly the President looked tired and worn.

'The magic doesn't always work, you see.'

Chapter 27

It was all very embarrassing, but the fact was, the Duke of Windsor wanted to do something useful. Now that Great Britain was at war with Germany, the Duke wished to be seen to be *doing the right thing*. He wanted to serve his country.

Everybody wished he wouldn't, and nobody knew what job to give him. Curses, curses, said all those who had anything at all to do with the matter. As if they didn't have enough to deal with already.

Eventually, after a good deal of head-scratching, it was agreed that the former King Edward VIII, now Duke of Windsor, would be sent to France, with the rank of Major-General. This had the advantage of getting him out of England, but of course the British army in France didn't have the faintest notion what to do with him when he arrived.

After further earnest discussion, an 'intelligence mission' was invented. It was decided that the Duke would survey the strengths and weaknesses of the French defence forces, including the Maginot line. In fact, this survey had already been carried out, but never mind, the Duke had to be occupied with something.

Consequently, for a few weeks in the autumn of 1939, the Duke of Windsor toured the three principal French army zones and inspected the regiments and the gun emplacements. He wrote reports about what he had seen. These were of no value to anyone, except of course to the Germans, who received copies through the Duchess.

The fact that this leakage of information was occurring soon became known in military circles. A French General, Alexandre Montagne, was sacked for revealing to the Duke secret information about how the enemy could break through the Maginot line. And the British Commander in Chief, Lord Gort, quickly realised that the Duke of Windsor was passing on to his wife a great deal of information which was subsequently making its way into

German hands.

By this time the Windsors were under constant surveillance by agents of the British Secret Intelligence Service (MI6), and they undoubtedly knew it. Nevertheless, the Windsors continued do what they felt they had to do.

And so matters stumbled on.

Early in 1940 the Duke was back in London, complaining about the futility of his military role. The role was indeed futile. That was the point.

While the Duke was in London, the royal family behaved as if he did not exist. He was invited nowhere.

The leakage of information continued. In February 1940, the German Minister to the Netherlands wrote to Berlin giving details of the British War Cabinet's discussion of what military tactics should be adopted by British forces if Germany invaded Belgium. The Minister openly stated that the information on the British intentions had been provided to him by the Duke of Windsor. Evidently some member of the War Cabinet had been foolish enough to trust his former King with details of military policy. And the former King didn't waste much time in passing on the information to the Germans.

In May 1940, the American journalist Clare Boothe Luce had dinner with Wallis, Duchess of Windsor. Mrs Luce commented on how sad it was that all those lovely English villages were now being bombed. 'Oh,' said Wallis, 'after what they did to me I can't say I feel sorry for them – a whole nation against a lone woman!'

Also in May 1940, Neville Chamberlain resigned as Prime Minister, and Winston Churchill took over that office to head a coalition government.

Churchill's policy was absolutely clear: it was to fight the Germans until they were defeated, and until they offered to surrender unconditionally. Churchill had no illusions whatever about the character and ambitions of Hitler and his cronies, and he was not interested in any form of negotiated peace. Consequently, he immediately took action to render powerless all those who favoured a *rapprochement* with Germany.

The Duke of Buccleuch was sacked from the royal household.

The Duke of Westminster was warned not to take part in any appeasement efforts. Sir Oswald Mosley and his wife were imprisoned. Major-General Fuller was warned to be inactive or face instant arrest. And Sir Samuel Hoare was sent abroad where, it was thought (mistakenly), he could do no harm; he was made Ambassador to neutral Spain.

On 28 May 1940, it was agreed at a meeting at 10 Downing Street, chaired by Winston Churchill, that both the Duke and Duchess of Windsor should be brought back to England immediately, to be questioned on their collaboration with the Nazis.

But the Windsors, meanwhile, were in the south of France. They were entertaining visitors at the Chateau La Croë: Maurice Chevalier came to lunch. No one actually took any action to bring them back to England, because everyone was far too busy fighting the Germans. Half the British destroyers had now been sunk, the U-boats were doing an excellent job at cutting off England's food supply, and Joe Kennedy was predicting that Hitler would be holding a victory parade through London by the end of the month.

The Duke of Windsor held military rank, and, in the eyes of most reasonable people, this meant that he had to obey orders. However, when he was informed by Lord Gort, the British Commander in Chief, that the task force to which he was attached was returning to London, the Duke said that he would not be going with them.

He went to Madrid instead.

Alastair Padget could see that King George VI was deeply depressed. And the King had good reason to be concerned.

At the end of May 1940, British troops suffered an almost catastrophic defeat at Dunkirk, on the French coast. By an extraordinary effort, and with a generous helping of luck, huge numbers of soldiers were evacuated safely back to England. They were carried in a vast armada of tiny boats, many of them pleasure cruisers and fishing vessels which were wholly unsuited to military use. But most of the British army's equipment had to be left behind. It was hard now to see how Churchill's aim of bringing the Germans to the point of unconditional surrender could ever be achieved.

On 10 June 1940, Italy joined Germany in declaring war on Britain and France. And, on 14 June, German troops marched into Paris, unopposed.

It would have been most surprising, in these circumstances, if the King had not been depressed.

Nevertheless, Alastair Padget knew that what was bothering George VI most was not the progress of the war, appalling and disturbing though that was. No. It was concern about the activities of his brother, the Duke of Windsor, which was occupying the King's mind more than anything. So Alastair was not in the least surprised when, on Tuesday 25 June, the King called him into his study.

Before speaking the King crossed to the fireplace, lit a cigarette and inhaled deeply.

'My brother,' he said eventually. 'And that wife of his....'

Alastair waited while the King gathered his thoughts. By common consent, George VI was not a man with a quick mind; in his naval college exams he had been placed 68th out of 68.

'Now, you see, my problem is that he is my brother. I grew up with him. Admired him enormously. And for many years I thought he could do no wrong. And as a matter of fact, that is still the natural bent of my thoughts. But – and it's a big but – I have to face up to reality.'

The King sat down and sighed heavily.

'Obviously, I would like to give the Duke every benefit of the doubt. And if I do that, then I have a picture of a man who wants to do his best for his country, which he loves. He hates war. He wants to bring about peace. Let us grant him all that. Nevertheless, even if we allow him all that, my brother has been, at best, very indiscreet. Very unwise. Very... careless. And he has allowed himself to be influenced by those who, I'm afraid, do not feel much affection for this country.'

Naming no names, of course, thought Alastair.

The King looked across at Alastair. 'You probably know more

about all this than I do, Alastair. I know you're kept informed by the powers that be, because they trust you. And rightly so. So forgive me if I state the obvious. The truth is, you see, I'm not a clever man. It's takes me a long time to understand things. But I do understand in the end.'

The King rose restlessly to his feet again and twiddled a globe until his hand fell on Europe.

'At the moment the Duke of Windsor is in Madrid. Now there's an awful lot going on in Madrid. Anybody can come and go, because it's a country which isn't involved in the war. And the question is, what is the Duke going to do? Where is he going to go?'

The King paused again, but Alastair said nothing. Alastair was now well used to George VI's moods and mannerisms. His sudden, violent rages over nothing at all. His usual cheerfulness. His habit of thinking aloud with agonising slowness, crawling step by step along a road which most people would have sprinted down. So Alastair waited.

'The fact is,' said the King, 'the Duke is in danger of being used by the Germans. Ribbentrop chiefly. They're in touch with him all the time. You do know that?'

Alastair nodded.

'Yes, well, as I say, you probably know more than I. God knows what they're planning between them. We can't find out much because that slippery bastard Hoare, who's the Ambassador in Madrid, he's closed down the Secret Intelligence Service – told them they can't operate in his bailiwick. Purely coincidental, of course, while the Duke is in Spain.' The King chuckled. 'Good name for him, isn't it? Hoare! Anyway, the Germans are sniffing round my brother, hoping to get him to do God knows what. Ribbentrop mostly, but Goering too is interested. They're offering to help him to come back as King if I stand down, and if he acts as the broker of a peace deal. That's about the gist of it. Christ only knows what they're up to.'

The King sighed heavily again, and paused for a very long time. He seemed on the point of tears.

'Of course,' he said eventually, 'we've heard endless proposals for peace. Every other person you meet seems to have a plan of some sort. Joe Kennedy and Neville Chamberlain came up with a so-called deal earlier in the year. And, to use an Americanism, it was crap. The trouble with all these peace packages is that they involve (a) giving the Germans a lot of stuff such as former colonies and money, which we don't want them to have and which they don't bloody well deserve, and (b) believing German promises. Well, not even I am dim enough to do that! Once upon a time I too wanted peace at almost any price, but not now. Anyone who believes what that man Hitler says deserves all the t... t... trouble they get.'

Another pause.

Then: 'This business with the Duke. The long and the short of it is, Alastair, we've got to put a stop to it. Now. If we don't there's going to be the most terrible disaster. There are people around who would like to see the Duke charged with treason you know. I've heard some very bitter comments, not least from my own wife. Well, I can't possibly have that. Not my own brother. Who was once my King. Think what a scandal that would be. It would go down in history.'

Alastair decided that the speculation had gone on long enough. 'What would you like me to do then, Sir?' he asked.

The King stubbed out the cigarette which he had furiously smoked to a dirty stub end in about four minutes, and lit another one.

'I've got another sh... sh... shitty little job for you, Alastair. One of the many that you've done for me, and I shan't forget you in my prayers. Fact is, we've got to get the Duke of Windsor out of Europe altogether. Send him somewhere where he can't be any trouble to anyone.'

'Australia?' suggested Alastair.

'That's about the right distance. But it's too prestigious. Important place, Australia. Sending us a lot of good troops. No, it's got to be somewhere unimportant, but a long way off. Somewhere which, to put it bluntly, is an absolutely insignificant little backwater. It hurts me to say this, but my bloody brother has got to understand that he's in trouble, and that, rather than put him up against a wall and shoot him, we're going to send him to guard some little brick out-house somewhere for the duration of this conflict. After that, we'll see.'

'Do you have somewhere specific in mind?'

'Well, Winston and I have been thinking about it. And we've decided that the Duke is to be offered the job of Governor and Commander in Chief of the Bahamas.... West Indies, you know.'

Actually Alastair did know where the Bahamas were, but he didn't say so.

'It's not as far as we would like,' continued the King. 'We would prefer Siberia. But unfortunately that is not a B... B... British possession. The Bahamas are also uncomfortably close to Miami, which might allow him to make mischief in America, but we shall have to put up with that.'

'I see,' said Alastair. 'And you want me to go and see the Duke and explain all this to him?'

The King smiled. 'I'm afraid I do.'

'And if he seeks to negotiate?'

'Oh, the Duke will want to negotiate. He will ask to be made Viceroy of India, or Governor-General of Canada.'

'But we say no.'

'We do more than say no, Alastair. You can tell him from me that if he refuses, the best we can offer him is a c... c... court-martial for failure to obey orders.'

Alastair Padget flew out of London on 3 July 1940. By then the Duke and Duchess of Windsor had moved on to Lisbon, where they stayed with Ricardo Espirito Santo e Silva, a man who had extensive Nazi connections despite his Jewish origins.

In Lisbon Alastair spent two days attempting to persuade the Duke of Windsor to see sense. He was not helped, of course, by the Germans.

Ribbentrop sent the Duke a message saying that the SD (German Secret Intelligence) had established that an official British order had been given that the Duke was to be killed as soon as he reached the Bahamas. In addition, Walter Schellenberg, head of the SD, was instructed to offer the Duke fifty million Swiss francs to co-operate with German plans. As Ribbentrop and Schellenberg spoke about these financial inducements, Hitler himself rang through on the phone. He told Schellenberg that the money could be increased, if necessary. And he also told Schellenberg: 'Bear in mind the importance of the Duchess's attitude. Try as hard as possible to get her support. She has great influence over the Duke.'

Alastair Padget never told anyone, not even his daughter Jane, precisely what went on during those two days in Lisbon. But he did once let slip a few hints to a member of MI5. Alastair said that he had warned the Duke that, unless he did as he was told, a court-martial would be the least of his problems. He assured the Duke that he, the Legal Secretary of both former and present Kings, would see to it that a charge of treason was brought. Alastair had taken with him to Lisbon details of all the extensive evidence which could be revealed if – God forbid – it was necessary to bring such charges against both the Duke of Windsor and his dearly beloved wife. The Duke promised to think things over.

As late as 20 July 1940, Herbert Claiborne Pell, the US Minister to Portugal, sent a telegram to the US Secretary of State. He had had dinner with the Windsors, and he described them as 'indiscreet and outspoken against the British Government.... They say that they intend to make propaganda for peace.'

On 26 July, Schellenberg arrived in Lisbon, his pockets full of nice clean German money. He offered a plan under which the Windsors would next travel to Germany, where they would be treated as honoured guests. A peace settlement would be negotiated, with the Duke playing the leading part, and he would then become King Edward VIII once again. Thus the Duke's native land offered him either a court-martial or a trial for treason; and the Germans offered him lots of money and his throne back.

In the end, not unnaturally, the Duke tried to have matters both ways. He told the Führer that he was in favour of the German strategy, but considered that it was 'inopportune at the present moment to manifest himself on the political scene.' His departure for the Bahamas need not, he explained, be seen as a rupture of negotiations with the Germans, since he could easily return to Europe in twenty-four hours via Florida. He offered to make himself available to Germany at once, when he received the appropriate code word.

The Duke kept the British waiting for a clarification of his intentions. But at the end of July 1940, the Duke and Duchess of Windsor finally had to make up their minds what to do. They had bookings as passengers on board a liner called *Excalibur*, which was due to leave Lisbon on 1 August 1940. It had been agreed with the owners of the ship that it would make a 350-mile diversion from its normal route in order to deliver the Windsors to their new home in the Bahamas. The cost of the diversion would be met by the British Government.

Typically, the Windsors played for more time, at other peoples' inconvenience. They asked if the sailing of the ship could be delayed for a week, but they were told that, sadly, this was not possible. No, not even for a former King of England. Sorry, but there were a few hundred other passengers who were anxious to leave the European war behind them as soon as possible.

When *Excalibur* sailed from Lisbon, on 1 August 1940, the Duke and Duchess of Windsor were reluctantly on board.

Chapter 28

'I wonder if the true story of Joe Kennedy will ever be known.'

Mrs Eleanor Roosevelt

Extract from a report to President Roosevelt by Frederick Jensen, Defense Attaché, US Embassy in London, 5 October 1940:

Mr Kennedy remains very defeatist in outlook. He is now predicting that the British will lose the war by Christmas. However, he was earlier predicting that Hitler would be having a victory march in London during August.

The truth is, life is very hard in England, but morale is surprisingly high. Were it not for the English Channel, this nation would certainly have been overrun by the Germans, as many European states have been. However, there are some twenty miles of sea, at the narrowest point, between England and mainland Europe, and that is a formidable defence barrier. For the moment England has a breathing space. The RAF was successful in defeating the Germans in the air (the so-called 'Battle of Britain' in August), and the British people are gathering themselves for further efforts, both to defend and to attack.

Despite Mr Kennedy's pessimism, my advice to you, Mr President, is that there is no likelihood of England being defeated in the immediate future. It is true that food is in short supply, as are clothes, petrol, and many other things which you and I take for granted. Everything of value is rationed. It is also true that German bombers cause havoc somewhere in London most nights. In the mornings people can see the smoking rubble as they go to work. Worse, they can see the dead bodies being brought out of the shattered houses. Nevertheless, there is a 'We can take it' attitude. People are not inclined to give in. The bombing seems to strengthen their determination.

You asked me to relay all the gossip, so here is a story which is going the rounds. A good deal of thought has been given to defending the nation, street by street, if the Germans launch an invasion. A popular idea is that if every citizen kills one German, the invasion will fail. The story is that Churchill went to see the King, and found him in the garden of Buckingham Palace, practising with a rifle. The King said that if the Germans came, he wanted to make sure that he could kill one before he himself was killed. Churchill said, 'Well, Sir, if that's your attitude, I'll get you a machine gun, and you can kill lots of Germans!'

Again, on the gossip front, it has not escaped notice that Mr Kennedy is terrified of the bombs. Well, the truth is, most people are. My wife and I certainly get very nervous when the air-raid siren goes. However, Embassy staff have to remain on duty at nights, and even when off-duty they have to remain in London. Mr Kennedy, however, has taken to leaving London at nights. He has found himself some accommodation about an hour's drive away, in a rural area not likely to be attacked.

This has caused a good deal of adverse comment among the staff. It has also become known in the community at large. I have twice been approached by people who said to me - telling a story which they had heard from a 'friend of a friend' - that the Prime Minister said 'I thought my daffodils were yellow until I met Joe Kennedy.' Sometimes the person making the comment is said to be the King. In any event, this is a widespread story, and Mr Kennedy's practice of leaving London each night is not admired. I would not be surprised if this gets into the newspapers before long.

Also, Mr Kennedy's view that peace must be brought about at almost any price has led people to think that he has no guts for a fight. People feel that his relentless campaign for a peace treaty is motivated by cowardice and self-interest as much as anything. War is bad for business, therefore he is against it.

More to the point, perhaps, I have heard, but have not been able to confirm, that Mr Kennedy went to France last week. The story is, he flew via Dublin. The story also is that he was on yet another 'peace mission', and that in France he had talks with Goering. This kind of information is very closely guarded, even within the Embassy, but I will try to find out more.

Jane Padget was a good horsewoman. She had a good seat, as her mentor in equestrian matters had frequently said, much to her annoyance. And this afternoon she was riding in Rotten Row in Hyde Park.

She was riding with a purpose.

Early in his days as US Ambassador, Joseph P. Kennedy had taken to riding in Rotten Row very early in the morning. But now that he had moved his sleeping quarters outside the city, his daily exercise had reportedly been shifted to the afternoon. And, yes, sure enough, there was the balding, bespectacled old goat right now. Dead on time.

Jane watched Joe as his horse gently walked through the golden autumn leaves. Even in wartime the Park was beautiful. It did the heart good.

Joe seemed preoccupied, totally wrapped up in his own thoughts. His head was down and he was hardly guiding the horse at all.

Jane trotted up behind him and greeted him. 'Mr Ambassador! Good afternoon to you!'

Joe looked up, recognised her, and grinned. He just *loved* that Mr Ambassador stuff. Jane had been told to lay it on thick.

'Oh hi, Jane!' said Joe. He perked up immediately. Wonderful what effect a pretty face will have on a man in his early fifties.

Jane and Joe exchanged idle chit-chat for a couple of hundred yards. Whereya bin, ain't seen ya for ages – that sort of thing. Oxford, eh? My boys go to Harvard. Not sure I believe in college for girls, but there ya go.

In due course Jane suggested that they dismount and sit down for a rest. Joe made no complaint about that. They sat on a bench, under the trees, admiring the sunlight as it streamed through the golds, reds, and browns.

'I'm glad I bumped into you, Mr Ambassador,' said Jane. 'I've been wondering how you saw things, now that we're at war. Of course in many ways the situation seems to be absolutely disastrous – but how does it look from your angle?'

Joe gave her an old-fashioned look, sideways, and she had the distinct impression that he knew perfectly well that this wasn't an accidental meeting, and that she had been asked to find out what he *really* thought – if she could.

'Well,' said Joe slowly, 'it ain't no secret that I didn't want this war to start. And now that it's started, I'm doing everything I can to get the damn thing stopped. In particular, I want it stopped before my own country gets dragged into it. So far we're not involved, and that's the way I want it to stay. Not that I get much thanks for any of this. Earlier this year Mr Chamberlain and I put together some proposals. Went to the King with it. Now you might think, in your innocence, that a guy putting a lot of effort into a deal like that would get some credit. But hell no. What happens? King gets on the phone to my President, asks him is this official US policy, and the next thing I know I'm getting my balls chewed off by FDR. You could be forgiven for thinking that the US President is just *dyin'* to get a lot of American boys killed. Course, being bawled out don't stop me at all. I do what I think is right, and the hell with 'em. But just goes to show that the world ain't the simple place you might hope.'

'I see,' said Jane. 'So you still think we ought to negotiate a peace treaty?'

'What the fuck else can you do?' said Joe. 'Excuse me using such strong language to an Oxford girl, but where the hell else ya gonna go? You can't beat the Germans, they're too damn strong for you. After Dunkirk you got no *matériel* any more. All left on the fucking beach. And the air force is only hanging on by the skin of its teeth. Can't say they're doing a very good job stopping the bombers, can we? How far'd ya have to go to find a bomb site? A hundred yards? Not more.'

Joe sighed. 'No, it just beats the hell out of me. Trouble is that guy Winston simply don't know when to quit. And the King's too fucking stupid to add two and two together.'

'But do you think Hitler is securely in power?' asked Jane. 'Isn't he a bit vulnerable? After all, you just mentioned Mr Chamberlain, and now he's gone. He's not Prime Minister any more. I'm sure that Reichsmarschall Goering would just love to take over from Chancellor Hitler.'

Joe gave her another old-fashioned look. 'Sweetheart, in

politics there *ain't* no security. Never. Gonna be an election for US President in three weeks' time. Is Roosevelt gonna win? And how long do you think Churchill's gonna last if the food runs out?'

Joe leaned forward. He was clearly getting restless and was preparing to move on.

'You know, kid,' he said, 'you're pretty good at pumping a guy – finding out what he thinks. I admire that. But if you really wanna know what a guy thinks, pillow talk is the thing. What ya have to do, see, is let a guy fuck you a few times. That gets him all loosened up, ya know. Indiscreet. Know what I mean? Now, for instance, if you and me was to go take a shower together after our ride, get between the sheets, and *then* have a little chat – who knows what might pop out?'

Jane gave him a thin smile and stood up. She realised that she had, as the Americans say, been rumbled, and she was annoyed with herself.

'Is it a deal?' said Joe. 'A quick fuck and I'll tell you what Goering's *really* gonna do.'

'Mr Ambassador,' said Jane. 'Go rub it up against a tree.'

Chapter 29

There was a small window in the box-room at the top of Blesserby Manor. Once, perhaps quite recently, the room had been home to some sad little serving-girl. She had no doubt slept here happily enough, after a long, hard day scrubbing floors and washing dirty pans. And in the morning, wakening refreshed – well, reasonably refreshed – she would have looked out on the Wiltshire countryside, as Helga Kronberg did now, and admired the beauty of the autumn leaves.

Yes, thought Helga. When the war is over, I will ask for this house as my reward. I shall enjoy that.

The box-room now had a pair of very powerful locks on the door, and a reinforced door too, come to that. Because that was where Helga kept her short-wave radio, the means whereby Berlin told her what she must do.

Having decoded the most recent message, Helga carefully locked the box-room door and went downstairs to find Westrow.

He was in the drawing-room, trying to do the *Daily Telegraph* crossword. The easy one.

'We're to go to Miami,' Helga told him abruptly.

'Miami?' Westrow seemed flustered. He did look ridiculous in his smoking-jacket. He was aiming for the Noel Coward look, but he came across as a fat and sweaty publican on his night off.

'Yes,' said Helga wearily. She would have bet money, had there been anyone to bet with, that Westrow did not know where Miami was. Geography was not his strong point. Neither was history. Or English, French, Latin, Greek, Maths, and Divinity. He had a whole set of school reports to prove it.

Westrow scratched his head. 'Miami. That's in America isn't it?'

'Yup,' said Helga. 'Don't think they've moved it. If they have they've kept quiet about it.'

'Ah. West coast?'

'East. Down south. It's hot.'

'Ah. Yes. Well....' A long pause. The Master was thinking. 'What are we supposed to do there?'

'We've been called to a meeting. Probably with Wallis and Joe.'

'Wallis and Joe?' queried Westrow. 'You mean the *Duchess* of Windsor, and *Mr* Kennedy, I take it?' Westrow preferred formality, although he and Helga had met the two parties concerned on several occasions and were on intimate terms with them.

'Yes,' said Helga sharply. 'That's right. I mean Wallis and Joe.'

Helga was not going to put up with any nonsense on this point. Helga knew all about Wallis, and Wallis knew all about Helga – what she was trained for and what she was good at. Ribbentrop had told each about the other. He had told Helga that Wallis was Germany's greatest secret weapon. So there were no illusions there. How much Joe Kennedy knew about who was working for whom, Helga wasn't certain. But if Joe was close to Wallis he was clearly in this business up to his neck. So, since they were all in it together, Helga had abandoned Anglo-German formality and had adopted American informality. It was Wallis. And Joe. If he wanted to argue about it, Westrow could shove it where it hurt.

But Westrow didn't want to argue. 'Hmm,' he said. 'So Mr Kennedy is going to be there, is he? In Miami?'

'He will be, shortly. He has a house in Palm Beach.'

'Ah. Yes. But how are *we* going to get there?'

Helga would also have bet money that Westrow had forgotten that America was not yet in the war. But she chose not to humiliate him. She didn't want to make an enemy unnecessarily. The man was needed by her country, and her job was to keep him sweet.

'Darling,' she said, 'we can fly. 'The Germans aren't shooting down American-owned airliners. Not yet.'

'Ah. Yes.' Westrow struggled with his thoughts for some time. Then: 'Why do you think they want to see us?'

'Well,' said Helga, 'it must be for something very important. They wouldn't drag us all the way over there for a face-to-face briefing if they wanted to talk about the weather.'

On 5 November 1940, President Roosevelt was re-elected with a huge majority of the votes.

Joe Kennedy had returned to the United States to assist the Democratic Party in the run-up to the election, and the following day he submitted his resignation as Ambassador to England. After nearly three years he had had enough. He agreed, however, that the resignation should not be made public until the new year.

On 8 November, Joe gave an interview to three well-known journalists. He made a number of statements which did not go down well with the American public.

'Democracy is finished in England,' said Joe. 'It may be here.' He predicted that National Socialism, as practised in Germany, would be introduced in England before long. There was, Joe maintained, a lot to be said for the National Socialist method of government. He said that he personally was against Fascism but in favour of National Socialism (whatever that meant). Above all, he sought to persuade the American public that the war in Europe was none of their business and they should stay out of it.

President Roosevelt, when he read the interview in the newspapers, told his cabinet that Joe Kennedy was convinced that Fascism would have to be introduced in the USA, so that the nation could survive in a world of concentrated and centralised power. If Joe had his way, said the President, America would be governed by a small committee of experienced men. Joe was not putting forward any specific names for the committee at this stage, but, if the call came, Joe would no doubt be willing to take his turn – purely in the public interest, of course.

When Joe felt the full force of the public reaction to his press interview, he tried to maintain that he had been misquoted. But he had spoken to three journalists, not just one, and they were all respected names. Joe was not believed. The result was that he had inadvertently killed off for ever any chance he might have had of running for high office himself. After that he had to concentrate on organising political careers for his sons.

It was at this time also that Joe had a major row with

President Roosevelt. The row may not have been wholly unconnected with a report which was passed to the President. Word had reached the FBI that Joe Kennedy and another Wall Street operator, Bernard E. Smith, had met Goering in Vichy France, and that after the meeting the two men had donated a considerable amount of money to the German cause. Both men were described in the report as anti-British and pro-German.

Joe's row with the President took place in a peaceful country setting. Joe had travelled by train from New York City to the President's house at Hyde Park, in New York State. He arrived at 10.00 a.m.

The two men began to talk, alone, in Roosevelt's small office at the front of the house. The President had had a lot of trouble with Joe during the election campaign. Joe had threatened to make anti-Roosevelt speeches and broadcasts unless he was given certain reassurances. This meeting was presumably to clear up the debris of all that.

After about ten minutes, the meeting came to an abrupt end, and the President sent for his wife. She had never seen him so angry. 'Get that son of a bitch out of here!' the President stormed. 'I never want to see him again as long as I live!'

Mrs Roosevelt was perturbed. She pointed out that Joe was invited for the weekend, that guests were due for lunch, and that there was no train back to New York until 2 p.m.

'I don't care what you do with him!' the President raged. 'Just keep him away from me!'

Mrs Roosevelt said later that the next four hours were the most dreadful four hours of her life. She took Mr Kennedy over to her cottage at Val-Kill, and entertained him to lunch on her own. Conversation was apparently a little difficult. Joe spoke mainly about the omnipotence of the German air force (a strange topic for a man who had lived in England during the Battle of Britain). Then, with a deep sigh of relief, Mrs Roosevelt put Joe on the train at Rhinecliff.

The President initiated a review of Joe's tax returns.

Wallis, Duchess of Windsor, had a toothache. That was the story, anyway. She would be travelling from Nassau, where her husband had recently been installed as Governor of the Bahamas, to Miami for treatment. But she would be incognito. This was not an official visit to the United States.

Mr Hoover (Head of the FBI) gave an instruction that every effort should be made to record the Duchess's conversations. These efforts were not always successful, but some transcripts were made available to the President.

Extract from a recording made in the Duchess's room at the Gloriana Hotel, Miami, 30 November 1940. FBI reference Sur/WW/40/192. Male speaker was believed to be Joseph P. Kennedy, US Ambassador to London, but was not positively identified by FBI agents on that date.

```
Man: Still wannabe Queen, Wallis?
Duchess: Sure. Why not? Teach those cocksuckers
a thing or two.
Man: Whaddya say if I became President of
Ireland?
Duchess: You? President of Ireland?
Man: Sure. Why not?
    Pause. Distortion on recording.
Duchess: Think you can swing it?
Man: Sure. Gotta deal. Deal is, I help get a
peace treaty - which I wanna do anyway - and
part of the package is, Ireland gets to be one
country. Then, naturally, they look around for
some guy they can trust who knows how things
work and is interested in doing the job for a
while.
    Pause. Sound of rustling (? Bed-sheets or
    clothes being removed?)
Duchess: Jesus, Joe. You pull that off, and your
sons and grandsons can be Senators in
Massachusetts for the next two hundred years.
Man: Yeah. I know.
    Shortly afterwards, bedsprings begin to
    squeak, indicating that sexual intercourse is
    taking place.
```

At the bottom of the transcript someone (possibly Mr Hoover) has scribbled in pencil 'How old are these people?'

And underneath that, in a different hand, someone else has

written: 'Old enough to know better.'

The Duchess of Windsor's dental treatment required a two-day stay in Miami. FBI records show that on the second day she had a meeting in her hotel room with three other people: a man now clearly identified as Mr Joseph P. Kennedy; an English nobleman called the Earl of Westrow; and a Swiss national, Miss Helga Schmidt. The 'Swiss national' was, of course, Helga Kronberg under her assumed name.

This second meeting was not recorded, even in part, because early that morning the Duchess had demanded to be moved to a different suite. The other one was, she said, too noisy. Helga Schmidt/Kronberg, however, wrote a very full account of the discussion in her diary. Well, she was a German, wasn't she? Thorough. Also, she didn't have much else to do.

Helga liked being treated as an equal by these people. And why not? She *was* their equal.

In fact, of course, she was far superior to Westrow, because she was a highly trained professional, and he was a rather bewildered and well-meaning amateur. But Wallis and Joe respected her professionalism. She could tell. They knew a pro when they met one. They were polite to Westrow, of course. But underneath she could see that they despised him as a simpleton.

As a matter of fact, she'd had a hard time getting him tuned up for this meeting. This was big-time stuff, and Westrow was smart enough to know it. And it scared him. It gave him the trembles, and he'd cut himself shaving. Several times. But Helga had helped him to finish it off. Dabbed his chin with a styptic pencil, given him one of those pills Dr Matthews swore by, and now he was ready. Here, paying attention, and looking reasonably alert.

Wallis made sure that everyone had a drink and then she sat down.

'OK,' said Joe, who was clearly going to chair the meeting. 'Let's get a move on.'

'Joe's got another meeting to go to,' said Wallis, and if Helga hadn't been so sure that no one with a title had any sense of humour she could have sworn that Wallis was sending the guy up. But the woman's face was straight enough.

Joe gave Wallis a quick glance and continued.

'Yeah, I do as a matter of fact.... Now, thing is this. We all know this goddamn war is disastrous. England has suffered a lot already. Germany has too for that matter. Bombs dropping everywhere, no one's safe, whole thing fucking A1 chaos, right from the beginning. And it ain't no secret that I wanna keep the US out of the war. But we got a President, now he's been re-elected, who given half a chance will take us into it. I wanna stop that. In fact, I wanna stop the whole war, period.'

Joe sighed. He seemed genuinely tired, Helga thought.

'I've tried lotsa times,' said Joe. 'Tried every goddamn thing I can think of. Come at it from every angle, and it still don't work. Tell you the truth, I'm beginning to run out of ideas. But it's worth one more shot, and that's why we're here today. The aim is, bring the war to an end, and get the Dook of Windsor back on the throne of England, which is where he belongs. And you know what I always say. I say, do the best you can with a thing, and if that don't work, then the hell with it. So that's what we're gonna do. Do our best.'

Joe looked round to make sure he had everyone's attention.

'Now, a few of us have put our heads together and we've come up with a proposal, which we think may do the trick. The way forward is this. We think King George VI oughta take the initiative. What he oughta do is this – use his Christmas Day radio broadcast to launch a peace proposal.'

Joe paused and looked across at Westrow. 'I've lived in England for a while, so I know that the King's Christmas Day broadcast is a pretty big deal, right?'

'Oh, certainly,' said Westrow hastily.

'It's heard all over the world,' said Wallis. 'Throughout the Empire. Millions upon millions sit by their firesides, soaking in the King's every word. It's the ideal opportunity.'

Helga couldn't quite figure out how King George VI was going to be persuaded to make a speech in favour of peace, given that he appeared to be totally in support of his Government's policy of pursuing the war to the point where one or other nation was utterly defeated. However, she thought, her doubts would presumably be dealt with shortly.

'OK,' said Joe. 'So what we do is, we persuade the King to use his Christmas Day broadcast to make this speech. The speech proposes – no, it actually *says* – that the Dook of Windsor will be in charge of negotiations with the German Government. It says that the British Government recognises that the war is futile, that it will destroy everything that Europe has rebuilt since the last war, and that it just opens the door to Communism. What is more, just to put the lid on it, the King will say that he, as head of the British armed forces, he is hereby instructing all the British soldiers – army, navy and air force – to lay down their arms and cease hostilities as of midnight that day.'

Joe paused and looked round the assembled faces.

'How's that for a Christmas present?' He grinned broadly. 'Not bad, eh?'

Wallis was strangely silent, looking down at her drink. Westrow, of course, was struck dumb. So Helga put in a few thoughts.

'You speak,' she said, 'as if this speech has already been drafted.'

'It has,' said Joe. He reached into his pocket. 'Got it right here.' He unfolded the papers. 'Quite a few of us have been working on this speech for some time. And I can tell you, Westrow' – Joe looked directly at the man – 'that the contents of this speech are wholly, one hundred per cent, totally acceptable to the German Government. They know what's in it, all the way up to the top. And I mean the top. And they're happy with it. If this speech is made, I can assure you that the proposals will be accepted. All fighting will stop, and peace negotiations will begin.'

Westrow made a croaking sound. Helga wasn't sure if he was actually trying to speak, or just clearing his throat. He was sweating and had gone unusually pale – insofar as a man with a blotchy red complexion can go pale.

Helga spoke for him. 'And what is our role in this? Westrow and me. What are we to do?'

Joe nodded. 'Good point. What we want the Earl of Westrow to do is go and see the King. You can do that, can't you?' he asked, looking at Westrow.

'Oh yes, yes. I can get in to see him,' Westrow managed.

'Good. Then what you do is, you go and see him, and you put this plan to him....' Joe leaned back, eyeing Westrow cautiously. Helga could see that Joe was trying to convince himself that the man chosen for this part of the job was capable of it.

'Don't worry about that,' said Helga quickly. 'The King will see the Earl, we can give you that assurance. And we will rehearse very carefully what is to be said to him.'

Joe was obviously pleased to hear that someone knew what they were doing. 'Good.'

'But I have to say,' continued Helga, 'that absolutely nothing I have heard so far convinces me that the King will agree to make this speech. The King is apparently a total supporter of Churchill, and is backing this new fight-them-on-the-beaches policy. How, precisely, is the Earl expected to persuade the King?'

Joe gave half a smile. A reluctant, sad smile. He glanced at Wallis. 'Well,' he said, 'that's where Wallis comes in. She knows the King so much better than I do.'

Wallis paused before speaking, and Helga had the impression that for Wallis too this meeting was something of a last-ditch manoeuvre.

'You are quite right,' said Wallis eventually. 'The King is not likely to want to make this speech. Not of his own free will. For one thing, it clearly implies that he and his wife will have to stand down. Go to Canada, or Australia perhaps. They will be given safe passage, of course, but in the new post-war world their services as King and Queen will no longer be required. His wife won't like that. They will be unhappy about the speech for that reason alone. And so...' Wallis sighed. 'They are going to have to be forced to do what they're told.'

'How?' snapped Helga. She was getting tired of all this pussy-footing around.

Wallis seemed reluctant to be specific. 'Well,' she said slowly, 'I have a number of things in my possession. Items which I have collected over the years. Put them aside for a rainy day, so to speak. They will be of value, and I will make them available to you.'

Helga felt as if she were about to go off bang. She had thought the English were mealy-mouthed, but this woman was an American for Christ's sake – why couldn't she say what she meant?

'What are these things? Photographs? Papers? Dead bodies?' It was like pulling teeth out of a rhinoceros.

'Letters mostly,' said Wallis. 'King George, like his father, has found it difficult to satisfy all his sexual requirements at home. After the second daughter was born, his wife seems to have closed the bedroom door. Not surprisingly, the King then went back to see one or two ladies who had been nice to him when he was a bachelor. I have a number of letters, and a few photographs, which make all this perfectly clear.'

'I see,' said Helga. They were getting somewhere at last. 'And these letters are sufficiently lurid, are they, to ensure that the King will co-operate? We can hardly threaten him with exposure in the popular press – the British newspapers wouldn't print a word of it. So all we can do is threaten to show them to his wife. Is that going to be enough?'

Wallis seemed to be reluctant to answer.

'Probably not,' put in Joe. 'But Wallis has got another suggestion. She'll tell you about it privately.'

Joe glance at his watch. 'Well guys, sorry but I gotta go.'

He stood up abruptly and left the room.

Helga gave Wallis and Westrow a very hard look. They were both silent and white-faced. At the beginning of the meeting Helga had assumed that there were three professionals present. Three people who could do whatever was necessary. Three who could point a gun, and if necessary, pull the trigger. Now she was beginning to wonder if there was, in fact, only one.

'I would be grateful, Your Royal Highness,' she said with undisguised venom, 'if you could explain to me, in words of one syllable, precisely how you expect me to persuade the King of England to make this fucking speech.'

Wallis sighed. 'Helga,' she said, 'it's very simple. You identify the person whom he loves more than anyone else in the world, and then you threaten – or rather, you *guarantee* – that if he does not co-operate that person will die.'

'Ah,' said Helga. 'At last. Now you are speaking a language I understand.'

When they returned to their own hotel, Helga and Westrow read through the speech which they had been given.

Westrow was now sweating profusely. 'He will never do it,' he moaned, almost sobbing with fear and despair. 'He will never, never do it. The King is *never* going to agree to say these things. I *know* him.'

'Not even with the letters?'

'No, not even with the letters. The letters will worry him, but he will tell me to fuck off. In precisely those words. He's a Navy man, he swears a lot.'

'Well then,' said Helga. 'We shall just have to do the other thing.'

'Oh God!' Westrow groaned and turned away.

Helga laughed. She felt quite relaxed. 'Don't be so pessimistic,' she said. 'Don't forget we're dealing with a man who never wanted to be King in the first place. He has a terrible stutter. Every public appearance is an ordeal for him. What he wants, more than anything, is to retire to a quiet family life in the country – the life he enjoyed before that selfish brother of his abdicated and forced him into the limelight. And you and I are going to give him the perfect excuse. We're going to let him look like a sincere, dedicated King who wants to do the best for his people. While all the time he's going to be doing exactly what he longs to do. It will work! Think positively. It will work like a charm. And it's going to be so, so easy, because the English are so, so stupid.'

Helga took off her blouse and unzipped her skirt. She was quite beginning to enjoy herself. She was really looking forward to their return to England. At last she had something important to do. Some real work.

Westrow watched her with some alarm as she shed her clothes. 'What are you going to do, Helga?'

'I'm going to go for a swim in this nice Miami sunshine. But first, my noble Earl, I am going to give you what the English call a bloody good seeing-to.'

Chapter 30

The early hours of Wednesday 11 December 1940 were a bad time for Eaton Square. Three houses were destroyed by German bombs. The bombs were probably intended to fall on more industrial areas, but either the navigator got lost, or the bomb-aimer panicked. Anyway, down came the bombs, the houses were almost flattened, seven people died, and others were injured.

Alastair Padget spent several hours helping to search through the rubble. He knew many of those who were resident in the houses, which were mostly divided into flats, and he was able to ensure that everyone was accounted for – either dead or alive. As a result he did not arrive in his office at Buckingham Palace until nearly noon.

'Watch out,' his secretary warned him as he came through the door. 'The language is a bit naval this morning.' This meant that the King was in a foul temper for one reason or another.

'Ah,' said Alastair. 'Thank you.'

What, he wondered, was the cause of the uproar this time? It was not unknown for the King to fly off the handle, and often the trigger of his rage proved to be something trivial. But the noise usually subsided quickly enough.

Shortly afterwards, the King came into Alastair's office and sat down. Having been warned that something was up, Alastair was not surprised by the visit.

A new cigarette was lit, as usual. The King could not survive for more than about three minutes without an intake of nicotine.

'Westrow,' said the King, after he had inhaled deeply and coughed. 'Miserable bloody man. Good mind to chase after him even now, and give him a bloody good boot up the arse.'

Alastair raised an eyebrow. 'What precisely is it that has annoyed you, Sir?'

'Oh, that bloody man Westrow,' muttered the King, too annoyed to be entirely coherent. 'Came to see me earlier today. Would have liked you to be there with me, but you were held up with your own problems. Anyway, Westrow asked to see me, to express his views about the war, as he put it, and I suppose I felt obliged to see the man. His aunt married my cousin years ago, so I suppose we're vaguely related....'

Another heavy cough.

'Trouble is, people seem to think I've got a magic wand, you know. They don't quite believe that I can cure the King's Evil any longer, but they seem to think I've got all sorts of influence that I don't really have at all.'

The King demolished a further half-inch of his rapidly diminishing cigarette.

'Anyway, there the man was, sitting opposite me, giving me the benefit of his views. People are weary of war – he says. Well, I think we knew that. No one has any appetite for continuing, he says. Food in short supply, everything rationed, U-boats cutting off our imports, position hopeless. Only way to avoid a catastrophic military defeat is to go for a negotiated peace treaty.'

The King waved at Alastair through a haze of blue smoke. 'That was the general drift of it. Heard it all before, Alastair. Many times. And if there is anything I am tired of, it's all this defeatist talk we hear so much of....'

Alastair waited while the King cleared his mind.

'Anyway, the man spoke quite well for a change. Normally I think of Westrow as a bit of a twit, but he'd clearly thought about what he'd come to say, and for what it's worth he seemed sincere. So I heard him out. I then pointed out that all these plans for 'an honourable peace' involve handing over the nation, lock stock and barrel, to Germany. Let's face it, we couldn't negotiate a peace treaty even if we wanted to. All we could do is surrender. We're not negotiating from strength – not at present. We would end up without any colonies or dominions, and without any independence as a nation. We'd be just a vassal state in the great German empire.'

'It goes a bit further than that,' said Alastair. He was pleased to hear what line the King had taken, and he wanted to reinforce it at once. 'Any peace treaty we might sign at this stage would lead to the Germans staging a victory march through London, just as they marched through Paris in June. It means occupation by German troops, and it means signing the death certificate of thousands of British citizens. You yourself, Sir, might well be allowed to retire to Canada or Australia. But let's not have any doubt about what Hitler would do with the Prime Minister, the Cabinet, and lesser lights like myself, right down to county councillors. We would all be shot, and our wives and daughters would end up in German brothels or concentration camps. So there can be no so-called peace treaty. It's fight or die time.'

'Exactly,' said the King. 'Told Westrow as much meself.'

'And what did he say to that?'

'Well, he brushed over the bit about the likelihood of people being shot. Said he was sure some assurances could be given. And the prospect of Hitler running Britain didn't seem to worry him at all. Quite welcomed it in fact. Said Hitler was a deeply misunderstood man, had dragged Germany up by its bootstraps, ought to be given a free hand to do the same thing with the rest of Europe, wipe out Communism, and so on and so forth.... And then – God, it makes me angry even now – then he said that of course he was sure I would be glad to lay down the burden of the Crown.'

The King stood up in his agitation, and began to pace about Alastair's office.

'Well, bloody hell, I nearly hit the man. I know I'm not the best equipped chap in the world, not for this job, but I like to think I'm m... m... making a stab at it. And now that the Palace has been bombed, just like everywhere else, I can look people in the eye and say that I know what it's like too. My wife and I share the c... c... common experience.'

The first cigarette was finished, and another one was lit.

'Anyway, Westrow saw he'd made a mistake there, so he backed off. Said what he really wanted to do was to ask me to intervene. Intervene personally, that is. Take the initiative. He wants me to set up a negotiating team to bring about the end of the war. What is more – and this is a bit of bloody cheek if you like – he said my Christmas Day sp... sp... speech would be a splendid opportunity to announce it. Well, by that time I'd had enough, so I told him to forget it. And at that point, it all began to get a bit messy. Wish you'd been there really.'

Alastair waited. What had the King done, he wondered? Punched Westrow on the nose?

The King took a deep breath. 'This next bit's confidential, Alastair. It's not to go any further, you understand. Agreed?'

'If you say so, Sir.'

'Very well. Westrow told me – and he was cool as a cucumber when he said it – that I had better agree to do what he suggested, or I would very much regret it. Oh, I said, and what did he mean by that? Well, he said, p... p... painful though it was, he felt it his duty to tell me that he had in his possession certain incriminating letters which, if I didn't co-operate, he would feel it his duty to show to my wife.'

'Well well!' said Alastair. 'Blackmail! First time we've had that.'

'Indeed.' The King looked uncomfortable and shifted his position.

'Did he say what these letters are?'

The King affected airiness, but Alastair could tell that he was very worried. 'Oh, billy-dooze, you know. Love letters. That sort of thing.' He smoked even more furiously.

'I see.'

'Said he would pass them to the Queen. Unless, of course, I undertook to initiate, on Christmas Day, the kind of thing he had in mind. He was sure I would agree, once I had thought it over. And when I did, he would come and see me again, and take the matter further forward. Said he had certain p... p... proposals to make, on the nature of the speech to be made. That sort of thing.'

'Hmm,' said Alastair thoughtfully. 'And what was your response?'

'Well, I'm afraid I rather lost my rag, I didn't quite hit him, but I very nearly did. I certainly told him a few home truths. I said he'd very nearly been imprisoned months ago, together with M... M... Mosley and Ramsay and all those other Fascist loonies. I told him he'd been on the list – which is true – and that the only reason we hadn't bothered with him was because everyone knew he was a bloody fool. And then I told him to fuck off back to Germany if he was so bloody keen on the place, and turfed him out.'

Alastair smiled. He rather wished he had been there to witness the exchange. But the matter was serious, there was no doubt about that.

'Did you get the feeling Westrow had been put up to all this?' he asked.

'Well, I don't think he could have dreamed it up all by himself, he's not clever enough. He's been mixing with that aristocratic Fascist bunch for years you know. Some of them are quite decent chaps really – just a bit off-beam. So I imagine some of them told him what to say.'

'But this threat of blackmail is all very unpleasant. Do you want me to get the police on to him?'

'Heavens n… n… no,' said the King at once. 'No no, that's the last thing I want. For one thing there's a war on, and the police have got far more important things to do. And for another, Westrow can't really do much damage. He didn't really say what he had by way of incriminating letters, but they can't be all *that* incriminating because I haven't written any.' The King paused and thought for a bit. 'Well, nothing *really* incriminating.'

'I imagine,' said Alastair carefully, 'that if these letters exist at all they take the form of brief notes which you wrote when you were single. They've probably been stolen, in some cases years ago, and passed through several hands. And if they were undated, as these things often are, they could be open to misinterpretation.'

The King's eyes lit up with relief. He had clearly not thought of this useful explanation. 'Ah, yes,' he said hastily. 'Yes, I expect you're right.' He puffed fiercely for a few moments. 'Still, I think it might be a good idea, Alastair, if you were to arrange for the Queen's mail to be checked for a while – just to make sure she isn't worried unnecessarily.'

'Leave it to me, Sir,' said Alastair. 'I can promise you that nothing will reach her which will cause her distress. And what about Westrow? Any further action on him?'

The King sighed. 'No, I don't think so. I got very batey with him, but I think he's a harmless fool really.'

'I agree,' said Alastair. 'So we'll leave him be.'

'Yes.'

Later, Alastair and the King would agree that this was the most serious mistake they ever made.

Helga was waiting at the wheel of the Rolls-Royce when Westrow emerged from the Buckingham Palace door.

She watched him as he walked across the yard towards her, and she tried to guess, from the way he looked and walked, how the interview with the King had gone. But she couldn't. Westrow was that much his own man.

Helga had to admit – and no one was more surprised than she was – that a change had come over the Earl of Westrow in the last few days. For years everyone had thought he was a complete buffoon – she had thought so herself. But since the visit to Miami he had suddenly acquired a new stature, both literal and metaphorical. He stood up straighter for a start. He was more articulate. And he acted with determination and purpose. He was able to make decisions, and even tell her what to do. It was all very unusual.

Helga had spent quite a lot of time trying to figure out what it was that had brought about this change. And she decided, eventually, that Westrow had been given his new sense of confidence because someone, at last, had entrusted him with something important.

After all, she thought, when we were in Berlin, the Führer himself told us that one day we would be needed. It was years before the time came, but now it has come. Berlin told us to go to Miami, and there we got our instructions. We were instructed by some very senior people – people who operate on the same level as the Führer himself. And the plan is a good one, undoubtedly. It is clear, simple, realistic, and achievable. And Westrow has been told that the Führer, Wallis and Joe, they all look to him to pull it off. To do what has to be done.

And it was that which had effected a change in the man.

Overnight, Westrow had pulled himself together. He had panicked a bit on the day they met Wallis and Joe. He had felt overwhelmed by the size and difficulty of the task. But the next day he was OK. He was in command of himself. He had thought it through, and he knew that he could do what he had been asked to do.

He stopped drinking. He stopped wolfing down huge meals. And he started to think. Started to ask questions. Started to work things out. He began to anticipate what the King might say. What shall I do if he says this? What's the best response if he argues this way?

Westrow had also begun to harden himself psychologically. He seemed to have come to terms with the fact that in war there had to be casualties. He was not what you might call a philosophical man, but two days earlier, while walking in a London Street, he and Helga had come across a team of men digging an elderly couple out of the basement of a bombed block of flats. As they stood there, Westrow had said aloud, but almost to himself, 'People do get killed in a war, you know. It's inevitable. And what is one death more or less, Helga – yours, mine, or someone else's – if at the end of it, the world is a better place?' He seemed to be preparing himself, both physically and mentally, for what he had to do.

Yes – Helga was reluctant to admit it – but Westrow was a different man. He was well on his way to becoming – well, he was *part* way to becoming – a true professional.

Westrow slid into the front passenger seat of the Rolls, and Helga eased the car into the Mall.

She waited.

Westrow looked out at the leafless trees, peering at them as if he had nothing on his mind but the inexorable progress of the seasons. His silence and his self-control were quite impressive. There was no immediate babbling out of what had happened between him and the King. He was taking his time.

Maybe, thought Helga as she drove carefully through some temporary traffic lights, maybe we have all misjudged this man. Seriously underestimated his will and his determination, now that he has been an entrusted with a major, major task.

Eventually, when the Rolls came to a halt outside Westrow's town house, he turned in his seat to look at Helga. He was wearing a wonderful camel-hair coat, a simply beautiful cloth. Helga decided that she would buy one for herself. Soon. When the war was over.

'He turned me down,' said Westrow.

'Refused to co-operate?'

'Yes.'

'And you mentioned the embarrassing letters?'

'Of course.'

'But they didn't worry him?'

'They worried him, but not enough. He became angry, but not foolishly angry. He told me that he would not co-operate, that I could do what I liked with the letters, but he would not change his mind. Publish and be damned, he said. I think that's a quotation from somewhere. I've heard it before.'

Helga leaned back in her seat. 'Well, that's a pity. Still, it's pretty much what you expected.'

'Yes.'

'What now?' asked Helga. And it was interesting, she thought as she said it, that she had moved instinctively from *telling* Westrow what to do to asking him. What now?

'Now,' said Westrow, 'we do what we always thought we would have to do, in the end. We find out how much the King cares about the welfare of his elder daughter – the delightful Princess Elizabeth.'

Part Seven

Late December, 1940

Chapter 31

Extract from the American Embassy staff newsletter, 10 December 1940:

> We offer a big welcome to 19-year-old Seymour Jensen, son of Defense Attaché Fred Jensen and his wife Katie. Seymour is in his freshman year at Harvard, and has hitched a military flight to London for the holiday. These days, most of the family traffic is definitely going the other way, so we offer warm congratulations to Seymour for braving the London blitz to spend Christmas with Mom and Pop.

Extract from Jane Padget's report to the King, 3 January 1941:

> I first met Mr Seymour Jensen three days after he arrived in England, that is to say on Thursday 12 December 1940. I already knew his parents, and indeed they had been to dinner with my father and myself more than once. Mr Seymour Jensen and I saw each other socially on several occasions prior to the events which are the subject of this report. I formed the view that he is a trustworthy and sensible young man who is very sympathetic to the British cause in the present war.

On the night of Monday 23 December 1940, Jane's mind was whirling when she returned to the flat in Eaton Square. Seymour had been right about seeing Princess Elizabeth in that car, dammit. That was the irksome thing – and unfortunately the blighter was entitled to know that he'd been right.

She rang him up.

'Seymour, are you in bed yet?'

'No.'

'Got anyone else with you?'

'No!' He sounded shocked.

'Think your Mom will let you out again?'

'My Mom's not here. She and Dad have had to go up to

Liverpool. They left me a note. A liner's been sunk off Ireland by the Germans, and quite a few American citizens are among those who've been rescued. So Dad's been sent up there to help sort things out. Mom's gone with him because there are women and kids among the passengers.'

'Gosh I'm sorry to hear that. Still, it means you're free.'

'Free?'

'Yes. Get your beautiful smooth adolescent little ass round here. I've got something to say to you.'

Seymour sounded astonished. 'What do you mean?'

'I mean, Seymour, you should come round and see me. It's only a ten-minute walk, and I'm sure even you can find your way in the dark. If you get lost, ask a policeman. I've got things to say to you. About what we saw this afternoon. And about what's been happening at the Palace. I don't want to say any more on the phone.'

'Oh.' Seymour sounded interested. 'Well, yes, I suppose I could come.'

'Yes, you might very well,' said Jane. 'And bring your toothbrush.'

'Princess Elizabeth's been kidnapped,' said Jane, as soon as Seymour had crossed the threshold and she had closed the front door.

'What?'

'Well don't sound so surprised. You're the one who swore blind you saw her struggling in the back seat of the car.'

'Yes, well, I know, but....'

'So you were right, Seymour. And I was wrong. I apologise.'

'Well, gee, hell....'

'Come inside,' said Jane. 'I'll make you a cup of tea. Before we do anything else.'

Seymour kept gaping like a fish. Jane really wished he wouldn't do that. Every time she told him something else, he nearly dropped his half-finished cup of tea, his mouth fell open and his eyes bulged. Anyone would think he was a simple country boy rather than a Harvard freshman.

'Hell,' he said. 'This is really amazing. So this guy – what's his name?'

'Westrow.'

'This guy Westrow has kidnapped Princess Elizabeth, and is threatening to kill her unless the King makes a speech promising to stop the war?'

'That's about the drift of it.'

'But she's the heir to the throne, isn't she? I mean, Princess Elizabeth is going to be Queen one day.'

'That's right. And she and the King have a very special relationship. Believe me – I've seen them together.'

'Jesus. I mean, excuse me, but it's not every day you hear something like that.'

'No,' said Jane. 'It isn't. Mercifully. But you mustn't tell anyone, Seymour.'

'Oh gee, no, of course not.'

'It's a state secret. We'd probably both be sent to the Tower if we breathed a word of it. But I thought you ought to know. Especially as you're going to help me.'

'Help you?'

'Yes.'

'To do what?'

'Well, we're all going to have to think about where she is. I mean, Commander Mantle and his men are going to be doing all they can, but there is a war on and there's a shortage of man-power. So you and I are going to do our bit. After we've had some sleep.'

'Sleep?'

Jane *did* wish that he would stop repeating what she said. 'Yes, Seymour,' she said firmly. 'You and I are going to make mad passionate love, and then we are going to sleep for a while, and then in the morning we're going to think about how we can assist in the search for Princess Elizabeth.' She made a move towards the bedroom, switching off the kitchen light.

'Oh, but er – ' stammered Seymour as he stumbled after her.

'Oh but er what, Seymour?'

'Well, I, er – '

'Did you bring your toothbrush?'

'No.'

'Why not?'

'Well, I didn't think you meant it. And your Dad....'

'My Dad's going to be staying at the Palace. He won't be sleeping much till this is over. And he certainly won't be coming back here tonight.'

'Ah.'

'And your Mummy and Daddy are elsewhere. So no one will know what a bold seducer you are, Seymour.'

'No, well, perhaps not.'

'Oh shut up, Seymour, and take your clothes off. We'll get undressed in the dark if you like. Saves electricity anyway.'

A few moments later she said, 'You see, what it is, Seymour, it's the war. It has brought about a total moral collapse, to the extent that otherwise highly virtuous people go about fucking more or less complete strangers whom they would never even have acknowledged with a nod of the head in the past. That's what war does, you see. It changes things. Before the war, there was never, in the entire history of England, a single recorded instance of premarital sexual intercourse. But don't worry. You'll soon get used to this new way of doing things.'

'I doubt it,' said Seymour, from somewhere in the gloom. 'And if we're going to – well, have sexual intercourse....'

'Fuck each other,' said Jane.

'Have sexual intercourse,' said Seymour heavily. 'What happens if you get pregnant?'

'Darling, I can't get pregnant three days after a period, and especially not if you're wearing a rubber johnny, which you will be.'

'Rubber johnny?'

Jane sighed. 'Never mind. Just lie back and think of Mrs Roosevelt.'

The next morning, just as it was getting light, Seymour whispered in Jane's ear: 'You know, Jane, I don't know whether I ought to tell you this – but I'd never actually done it before.'

'Really?' said Jane. 'Gosh, I would never have guessed. You were jolly good, Seymour. For a beginner.'

They ate breakfast: a boiled egg each, and toast. There was margarine, but no marmalade.

As they ate, Jane filled in some of the details which she had omitted the night before.

'The official story is that Princess Elizabeth has appendicitis. That will satisfy the staff in the Palace.'

'What about the newspapers?'

'They'll be told the same thing. But they won't publish anything until they've been told that the appendix has been dealt with, and she's returned home.'

'And you said, yesterday,' began Seymour haltingly, 'that you and I were going to help.'

'So we are. Either officially or unofficially. You wash up while I phone my Dad and find out what's happening.'

Chapter 32

Her Royal Highness the Princess Elizabeth Alexandra Mary, aged fourteen, awoke with a start.

It was now Tuesday the twenty-fourth of December. Christmas Eve. And it was just beginning to get light – or at least Elizabeth thought so. The only window in the room was covered with a crude sheet of plywood nailed to the outside frame. The plywood hadn't been very expertly cut, and light was beginning to creep in around the edges, but she couldn't see enough of the sky to judge whether it was properly daylight or just dawn. Anyway, the night was over. And the trouble was, what had happened to her hadn't all been a nasty dream after all.

Elizabeth now realised that her situation was real, and it wasn't very satisfactory. That bloody man Westrow really had locked her up in a small, cold bedroom, and she wasn't very pleased with him. And the door was firmly locked too – she knew because she had tried it, several times, turning the handle quietly and then pulling it hard. But it was no good. She was locked in.

That wasn't the only thing to complain about either. The bed was horrible and lumpy, the sheets were scratchy, and there was no carpet on the floor, just a small rug. Of course she was the Earl of Westrow's prisoner rather than his guest, Elizabeth understood that. But even so, there were limits to what one was prepared to put up with, and Elizabeth decided that she would give the bloody man a piece of her mind when she next saw him.

At least, she would *probably* give him a piece of her mind. The truth was, she wasn't in a very strong position for ticking people off. She could see that now.

Elizabeth sat up in bed and hugged her knees.

Well, at least she had slept. Sort of. Fitfully. Fitfully – she thought that was the appropriate word. She had decided that it was no good throwing oneself on the bed and weeping and calling for Mummy. That was going to get one nowhere at all. So she had told herself firmly that she must get some sleep so that she would not be exhausted, and then she would wake up the next morning with enough energy to do something. Do something about escaping, and getting back home again.

And now the next morning had come.

Home. Yes, she would like to go home.

A tear trickled down her cheek, and she brushed it away angrily.

But she wasn't at home. She was here, in this ghastly cold little bedroom. She had had a sleep, it was now morning, and what was she going to do about getting away?

The first thing to do, Elizabeth decided, was to get dressed. She slipped quietly out of the bed, abandoned the hideous flannelette night-gown which that Helga woman had given her, and put on her clothes again. They were the same clothes as yesterday of course, and therefore not ideal, but one had to make the best of one's circumstances.

When she was dressed, Elizabeth listened. She listened for sounds of movement elsewhere in the house. Listened for birds, traffic, farm animals, anything. But she couldn't hear a sound. So no clues there.

The fact was, Elizabeth didn't know where she was, except that she was upstairs in a sort of cottage somewhere, about two hours from London. Or at any rate they had driven for about two hours, and she didn't think that Westrow and his lady friend would have driven in circles. They had blindfolded her for the last part of the journey, even though it was dark, so she hadn't been able to see where they were going, but she rather thought they had gone west.

There was a little more light creeping through the window now, and Elizabeth's eyes were getting adjusted to it, so she went carefully all around the room. She identified the few pieces of furniture, the rug on the floor, and the single light hanging from the ceiling. It was minus a bulb, unfortunately. Big help. And in the room as a whole there was nothing she could use to help her escape. At least, nothing she could imagine how to use.

After Elizabeth had concluded that there was nothing within

the room which was of the slightest assistance to her, she suddenly found herself moaning aloud, with a fresh set of tears streaming down her cheeks. She was astonished at herself, and decided that this would not do at all. She was getting hysterical, and there was nothing worse than a hysterical woman. Papa had often said so.

'Stop it!' she said to herself. Her voice echoed in the featureless room. 'Stop it at once. It won't help at all.'

She instantly stopped the moaning, wiped her cheeks with the back of her hand, and tried to calm her breathing.

Well, that was very silly, she thought. Papa would be ashamed of me.

Elizabeth understood now the meaning of what her father had often said to her. That none of us ever knows the fate that awaits us. But we must deal with it as best we can, when the time comes.

And now she must deal with this.

Elizabeth sat down on the edge of the bed and began to think over what had happened. Yesterday, she had gone to dancing class as usual. The day had been perfectly ordinary up to that point. Coming out of the dancing class, she met Sergeant Wilson at the door, and they walked round to the back of the building where the car was parked. It was still daylight, although rather a dark day.

As she walked forward down the passageway between two buildings, with the Sergeant slightly behind her, there was a sudden bang. It made her jump, and it made her heart pump faster now, just to think of it.

She turned round, and saw Sergeant Wilson lying on the ground. And there was blood – yes, it must have been blood, though she hadn't realised it at the time – there was blood pouring out of his head.

Elizabeth thought he'd collapsed. She had thought so to this very moment. But of course that was silly. The truth was, poor Sergeant Wilson had been shot. She could understand that now.

Poor man. She hoped he would be all right.

But no. That was silly too. It was no good thinking like that. Sergeant Wilson was dead. Nobody could be shot in the back of the head, not like that, with the blood pouring out, and survive. He was dead. And Westrow had shot him.

At least it was *probably* Westrow. But now that she thought about it, Elizabeth decided that perhaps it wasn't him after all. Perhaps it was Helga.

Surely not? Surely a woman couldn't shoot a man?

Elizabeth tried to remember what had happened next. But it had all happened so quickly, that was the trouble.

There had been the bang. It made her jump. She turned round and... Yes, it was the woman. Helga. She was the one who was standing there, looking down at Sergeant Wilson, a gun in her hand. And it was Westrow who seized Elizabeth's her arm and spoke to her. And she listened to him because she knew him.

'Your Royal Highness, you know me don't you? Westrow.'

And, yes, she did know him.

'Sergeant Wilson has collapsed. You must come with me, in my car. At once.' And he bundled her into the back of his Bentley. With the woman following her in.

The door was slammed shut and they set off, driving at a great pace.

And at first she was totally bewildered. 'What happened to Sergeant Wilson?' she asked.

No answer.

She looked directly at the woman, the one she now knew was called Helga. 'What happened to Sergeant Wilson?' she asked again. 'Is he ill?'

'Don't ask questions,' snapped Helga.

Don't ask questions! What kind of a way was that to speak to anyone? Especially – well, if she did say so herself, and one didn't like to make too much of it – it was especially no way to speak to a Princess. It was disrespectful. That wasn't the way you were supposed to speak to people. At least Westrow had addressed her properly.

And now they were speeding through the streets of London, going far too fast. And she had been silent for a while, unable to catch her breath. She seemed to be breathing so much faster than usual, and when she wanted to speak she opened her mouth and tried but nothing came out. And she wanted to say *Stop! Let me out! I don't want to go with you! You're going the wrong way! I want to go home! I feel... I want...* And she couldn't speak. Couldn't breathe. Couldn't see. The streets swirled and swam before her eyes as they swept along, everything out of focus, blurred, meaningless, frightening. The car was going far too fast, Westrow blasting away on the horn, cutting corners, going through red lights, and she wanted to get out, be free, escape....

And she couldn't.

Elizabeth realised that she was panting and moaning again.

Stop it, she told herself. It won't do any good. We never know what fate awaits us, and we must deal with it calmly, and with dignity, as best we can.

Dignity. Yes, that was the word. Dignity. And calmness. We must remain calm. If I do that, whatever happens, Papa will be proud of me.

They were driving in the Bentley. Going much too fast. And then she realised that they were going entirely the wrong way, not towards the Palace at all, and she shouted and began to scream and struggle. Not very dignified or calm at all. Rather hysterical in fact. Sorry about that, Papa, but I will try to do better. It was the shock, you see. And then the Helga woman hit me! Yes, she actually did! She hit a Princess of the realm! Well, it just goes to show, as Crawfie often says, that you learn something new every day.

Elizabeth decided that she was going to have to watch out for this Helga woman. First, difficult though it was to believe, Helga had shot poor Sergeant Wilson. And then she had slapped the face of a Princess. Jolly hard too. It had hurt. So there was no knowing what she might do. And then when Elizabeth tried to open the door of the speeding car, and failed, because it was somehow locked and couldn't be opened from the inside, Helga smiled and said, 'I wouldn't try that if I were you, dearie. You wouldn't look so pretty if you fell out of a car going this speed, now would you?'

Elizabeth sighed. Perhaps she had been very foolish and naïve.

But on the other hand, what else could she have done? She had been told that, in emergencies, she should do exactly what Sergeant Wilson told her. But Sergeant Wilson had been shot. And no one had told her what to do when that happened.

When the penny dropped, and she realised that she was being – well, kidnapped was the only word for it – she struggled and kicked and screamed, and she had been bashed about the head for her trouble, until in the end she subsided into exhausted sobbing.

That Helga woman was very strong, and very ruthless. She didn't care how much she hurt you, she was just determined to stop you doing what you wanted to do. And she could do it. She could force you to be silent. And be still. Even when you wanted to scream and shout for help. Because somehow she cut off your breath and made it impossible for you to speak. You opened your mouth and tried to cry out, but nothing happened.

Be silent, Helga said. And be still. Or I will handcuff you and throw you on the floor like a dog.

That's what Helga said. And she clearly meant it. And could do it. And Westrow, looking over his shoulder, advised Elizabeth, very politely, to do as she was told, because it would make everything so much simpler. And it had. In a way. She just sat there in the back of the Bentley, crying silently, the tears growing cold on her cheeks, unable to speak, unable to gesture, too feeble even to signal for help from passers-by or other drivers. Because it was the shock, you see. She understood that now.

And soon it grew dark, and soon after that they blindfolded her as well, and told her to lie down on the back seat, which had smelt of leather and perhaps cigar smoke, and then they arrived at wherever it was, and they had given her some soup and locked her in the dark, cold room, which didn't let in much daylight even now.

Oh dear. Elizabeth felt that she hadn't distinguished herself yesterday. She ought to have struggled harder, and made it more difficult for those who were carrying her away. But somehow she hadn't had the strength. So today she must do better.

There was another oh dear too. She knew that if someone

didn't come soon she was going to have to use that dreadful pot thing under the bed, the one that Helga had pointed out to her with a disgusting snigger, and she was pretty sure that she would rather die than do that.

Elizabeth peered around the room, searching in the gloom for something.... What a pretty pass she had come to. She was searching for something to *hit* that dreadful Helga woman with. Something hard. And if anyone had said to her, even at two o'clock yesterday afternoon, that she would ever *dream* of hitting anybody with anything, she would have called them a liar and worse, and now here she was positively longing to find something big and heavy and hard which she could use to crack that ghastly Helga woman right over the head. And then – well then she was pretty sure that she could run faster than fat old Westrow.

Suddenly there was a rattle as the key was put in the door, and it was opened by Helga.

'Ah,' said Helga. 'You're dressed. Good. Come downstairs and have some breakfast.'

'Um,' said Elizabeth. 'Is the bathroom free?'

Breakfast consisted of cereal and toast, and Elizabeth ate rather a lot of it. For one thing she was very hungry, and for another she wanted to build her strength up. Because if she got even half an opportunity she was going to run away, as far and as fast as she possibly could.

Towards the end of her meal Elizabeth decided to try to find out a little bit more.

'Where is Westrow?' she said.

'Mind your own business.'

'Well, as a matter of fact, I think the whereabouts of the man who kidnapped me *is* my business.'

'Nonsense. Eat your breakfast and keep quiet.' And Helga smiled.

She enjoys this, thought Elizabeth. She enjoys bossing me about. It makes her feel important.

Elizabeth ate silently for a while, and poured herself another cup of tea. She was beginning to feel stronger already.

'And who are you?' she asked. 'I know who Westrow is, but who are you?'

'I am his secretary.'

Hmm. A likely story. Secretary? Nonsense. Mistress, more like. Elizabeth wasn't absolutely sure what a mistress was, but she knew it evidently wasn't very respectable, because of the way people spoke about these things. So Helga was almost certainly Westrow's mistress, because if ever Elizabeth had met anyone who wasn't respectable, it was Helga.

When she had finished her breakfast, Elizabeth said, 'I suppose you realise this is treason?'

Helga raised an eyebrow. 'Dear me,' she said. 'Now you've got me really worried.'

'Well I hope so,' said Elizabeth, 'because treason is a very serious crime. They tell me you can be hanged for it. And if kidnapping the King's daughter isn't treason, then I don't know what is.'

Helga began to gather together the dirty crockery, putting the plates and cups on to a metal tray. 'Well, *Princess,*' she said, 'treason or no treason, you can help me to wash up.'

When the tray was full Elizabeth said, 'You're not English, are you?'

Helga looked at her sharply.

'I know what you are,' Elizabeth continued. 'You're a German. I can tell from your accent. And your demeanour.'

Helga curled her lip. It was a sort of snarl rather than a smile. 'Demeanour!' she said. 'That's a long word for a girl your age. But then you are terribly posh, aren't you?'

She jerked the tray upwards off the table, as if she were lifting weights.

'And in any case,' she said, 'what if I am a German? It takes one to know one.'

Chapter 33

They were in the King's study at Buckingham Palace: the King, Alastair Padget, and Commander Mantle, who was the Scotland Yard officer responsible for the security of the royal family.

It was 8 a.m., Tuesday 24 December, a little over thirty hours before the King was due to make his Christmas Day broadcast.

Each man had had about three hours' sleep.

'The problem is,' said the King slowly, 'where is my daughter?'

Alastair waited patiently. He had found it best, over the years, not to hurry the King but to let him work his own way round a problem.

The King sighed. 'I saw the Queen just before I came in here. She is not a happy woman. She is never an early riser, but today she intends to stay in bed all day with a case of the vapours.'

The King glanced at his companions guardedly. 'The Queen has made it clear,' he added, 'that unless Princess Elizabeth is returned to her unharmed, she will never speak to me again.'

Privately, Alastair could think of far worse fates than that, but he kept his thoughts to himself. This was no time for levity.

'She thinks I have a magic wand, you see,' continued the King. 'In her heart she knows it's nonsense, of course, but the shock of recent events has had a bad effect on her. She chooses to pretend that I can give an order – a simple click of the fingers – and the impossible will be achieved.' The King sighed again. 'You and I know it is n... n... not so easy. But the purpose of our meeting this morning is to clarify exactly where we have got to, and where we go from here.'

The King reached into an inside pocket of his jacket and took out the letter from the Earl of Westrow which had been received the night before. He opened the envelope carefully, as if anxious not to damage the contents in any way.

Alastair noticed that, both last night and this morning, the King had been unwilling to let anyone else handle the letter and the proposed Christmas Day speech which it contained. The King had kept it very much in his own hands, and no one seemed inclined to ask him to hand it over. Alastair certainly wasn't about to.

'This letter,' the King began. 'I wondered, at first, why the Earl put his name on the thing, quite openly. It's treason, of course, intending harm to the Sovereign's heir, and he's condemned himself out of his own mouth, so to speak. But I realise now why he did it. He did it so that we will understand that this is not a letter from a crank or an amateur. It's from someone we know. Someone with a lot of money behind him, and close connections with the Germans. When you think about it, this is just the sort of thing he would do.'

The King looked up.

'We've all underestimated him,' he concluded. 'At least that's my opinion. But perhaps in the cold light of a new day you have a different view?' He glanced from Alastair to Mantle and back again. 'Westrow claims to have kidnapped my daughter, the Princess Elizabeth. Do we believe him?'

Mantle answered. 'The Police Sergeant who was guarding the Princess was shot dead. The Princess was seen being taken away in a car driven by the Earl. And we have his letter. So, yes, I think it would be quite wrong to believe anything else. Princess Elizabeth is held by the Earl.'

The King nodded. 'So, we assume that Westrow holds her. And the t... t... task thus becomes one of finding him, because she is presumably there too.'

'Correct,' said Mantle. He was about to say more, but the King continued, taking his own good time, and sorting out his thoughts as he went. Alastair glanced at Mantle and saw that he too was sensible enough to let the King take the lead in the conversation, even if the experience was frustratingly long-winded at times.

'So,' said the King slowly. His head was down, and he held Westrow's letter in front of him. 'We have let it be known in the Palace, to a select few, that the Princess has appendicitis. I told Miss Crawford myself. She of course will tell others, in strictest confidence, so word will gradually percolate downwards. If it leaks out to the newspapers, I'm sure we can depend on their discretion.'

'Agreed,' said Alastair. 'Any enquiries to verify the story are likely to come to me. I'll make sure that nothing appears in the press.'

The King, his head still down, nodded. 'Good. And we have made a p... p... policy decision, between the three of us, that we will not inform the Prime Minister or indeed anyone else. Now, let us think about what Westrow says.... He tells me, in his letter, that if I make a special speech on Christmas Day – a speech which he has thoughtfully written for me – he will return my daughter unharmed. Otherwise he w... he w... he will shoot her. And – '

The King paused for a moment to gain control of himself.

'And he is very specific about it. The threat is, he will shoot her in the b... b... back of the head. Just like Sergeant Wilson, you notice. Another reason, I think, for taking the man seriously.'

Alastair was becoming increasingly worried. At the moment the King was speaking sensibly enough, apart from the usual stutter. But if the Princess was not returned, how was this man going to make any sort of a speech tomorrow? The King's difficulties in public speaking were notorious, and Alastair could foresee him being rendered helpless by the emotion of the occasion. He made a mental note to work out a fallback arrangement. Perhaps the Duke of Gloucester might be able to step in?

'Now,' said the King, 'let us consider the p... p... proposed speech itself. The one Westrow has drafted. I have read it through several times. Very carefully. To see whether I could reasonably make this speech instead of the one which has been drafted here in the Palace.'

The King spread out the papers on the desk in front of him, flattening them slowly with the palm of his hand.

'After the usual opening courtesies, the speech refers to the general sense of weariness with the war. It speaks of the relative weakness of our position. The need to avoid senseless slaughter. It goes on to say that, to bring the whole horrible business to an end, I will dismiss Mr Churchill and his government. I will appoint a new Prime Minister with a brief to negotiate peace. I will put my brother, the Duke of Windsor, in command of the day-to-day negotiations with the Germans. I will order all my armed forces – army, navy, and air force – to cease all hostilities with effect from one minute to midnight tomorrow, Christmas D... D... Day. I will express the hope that, once the war has been ended in this way, the British and the German peoples will unite to make the world a stronger and better place.'

The King looked up, but only for the briefest of glances.

'The Earl doesn't exactly say so, but presumably he is thinking that we and the Germans will unite to overcome Communism and the threat of the little y... y... yellow men in the East.'

The King paused, and both Alastair and Mantle waited.

'I must say,' said the King at last, 'that perhaps the most worrying aspect of all this is the thought that there must be quite a number of people who think as Westrow does. Some of them, the extreme Fascists, are safely in prison, but some of them unfortunately aren't. And if I did make this speech, I have the uneasy feeling that we should not be short of volunteers to serve in the new cabinet. I guess that there are sympathisers in P... P... Parliament, the BBC, and so forth.'

The King shrugged and waved his hands wearily, as if matters were entirely beyond his control.

'Anyway, while I am not an expert on the law, the Earl of Westrow does seem to me to be a little bit naïve about constitutional niceties. Tell me, Alastair, what in your opinion would be the effect of this speech, were I to make it?'

Alastair spoke immediately. 'It would be catastrophic,' he said. 'The King's Christmas Day broadcast is an absolutely vital part of the war effort, particularly this year, when things have gone badly. It is listened to by virtually all your subjects, Sir, all over the world. The early parts of Westrow's speech, the bits about the people's weariness of war and the wish to avoid needless slaughter, those parts would strike chords in the hearts of many listeners. But as a constitutional monarch you can do none of the things that Westrow would have you do – dismissing the Prime Minister, telling the armed forces to stop fighting and so forth.

And if you were to try to act in that way it would bring about the most disastrous rupture between Crown and Government. Parliament simply would not stand for it. You would be overthrown in one way or another. And in the meantime there would be the most terrible confusion in the minds of those serving in the armed forces. At the very least, the Germans would be able to take advantage of that confusion.'

The King nodded sadly. 'Well, I imagine you will be relieved, Alastair, to know that I was thinking p... p... pretty much the same thing myself. I have no intention of making this speech. If my brother were still on the throne, I dare say he would take a very different view. He was all too ready to meddle in politics, and would probably have been delighted to run the armed forces as well. But that is not my style. No. I will not make this speech.'

The King seemed to Alastair to be trying to convince himself as much as anybody.

'I will not make this speech. Come what may. *Come what may....*'

Alastair thought it was time to try to defuse the emotion of the situation. 'As far as I am aware,' he said, 'Westrow has given us no means of communicating with him?'

The King shook his head, temporarily unable to speak.

'As I thought,' said Alastair. 'So we can't negotiate any sort of terms. But if the Earl does get in touch, of his own volition, I think we can agree that we will play along with him? Give him some hope that we are willing to do as he says?'

'Absolutely,' said Mantle. 'That's the line to take.'

Seeing that the King's head was still lowered, and that he was wrapped in his own thoughts, Alastair ploughed on. 'Perhaps,' he said, addressing Mantle, 'perhaps you could give us an account of where we are in terms of the police search for the Princess.'

'Certainly,' said Mantle, who had clearly been itching to do just that since he entered the room. 'We've raided Westrow's London house, with no result. No one there except a few servants. The same with Blesserby Manor, the Earl's country house in Wiltshire. From there, we've widened the search to include all property which the Earl is known to own. The trouble is, there's a great deal of it. He has houses in Scotland and Northern Ireland that we know about, and of course he is the ultimate owner of an enormous amount of leasehold property in Kensington and Chelsea, the so-called Westrow estate. We think he owns about fourteen streets and five squares in all. Quite a lot of that property is vacant. Either people are selling because of the war, or they've moved to the country till the bombing stops, or whatever. So the Earl could be lying low in any one of those houses, and it's going to take some considerable time to search all those premises. However, we're doing our best, and using every man we can get hold of. The searchers don't really know what they're looking for, except that we're trying to arrest the Earl under Defence Regulation 18B.'

Alastair nodded, well satisfied with what he had heard. 'Good. Well we're going to have to leave that part of things to you, Commander. I'm sure you understand the urgency. Meanwhile,' he continued, looking pointedly at the King, 'the office here will make arrangements for the King's Christmas Day broadcast to go ahead as planned. The BBC will be here later today to set up their equipment.'

Mantle glanced at his watch. 'We've still got a bit of time,' he said. 'About twenty-four hours, realistically.'

The King roused himself from whatever thoughts had been occupying him and looked up. 'Yes,' he said, addressing no one in particular. 'Twenty-four hours. And if we do not succeed within that time, let us not be in any doubt about the outcome. Westrow is determined enough to have killed a decent policeman. So I have no doubt that if we do not succeed, I will lose my daughter.'

The King gathered together the sheets of paper in front of him and put them back in his pocket.

Chapter 34

At ten o'clock that morning, Christmas Eve, Jane returned to Eaton Square from the Palace. Her father had rung up at about nine, asking for some clean clothes and shaving gear to be taken over there, and she had naturally obliged. Apart from anything else she wanted to sense the atmosphere of the place.

In the meantime, Seymour had quickly returned to his own home. He wanted to make sure that his parents' house was still intact after last night's bombing raid, and to check the mail, but now he too was back.

'Well,' said Jane as she took off her coat, 'everyone at the Palace is remarkably calm. But then I suppose they have to pretend to be, because it's all so deadly secret.'

She put the kettle on to make them a cup of tea.

'Daddy was too busy to say much, but I gather the King is determined not to give in to blackmail. At least he is at the moment.' She glanced at Seymour, who looked worried. 'As the deadline for his speech approaches, he'll probably begin to have doubts.'

Seymour was being given a refresher course in tea-making because Jane had found his earlier attempts quite useless. One cup he had served up had been brewed with water which was not boiling. 'Well,' Seymour had said defensively, 'it's quite hot enough to drink.' Honestly, Americans. So now he was being retrained. 'Warm the pot first, Seymour,' she told him.

Seymour carefully poured some hot water out of the kettle and swirled it round the teapot.

'Anyway, I asked Daddy if there was anything we could do, and he said not at the moment. They're not calling for volunteers at present. Though of course there *are* things we can do, and we shall start in a minute.'

Seymour looked alarmed, and seemed about to drop the teapot. Jane sighed. 'Do watch what you're doing, laddie.'

'*How* are we going to help?' asked Seymour.

'Oh, we shall think of something. Anyway, Scotland Yard have organised a huge search, as you might imagine. The trouble is, this Westrow fellow seems to own half of London, so there's a lot to do.... There, now we let it stand for about four minutes.'

As they drank their tea, Seymour repeated his question. How were he and Jane going to help? He seemed to be apprehensive about becoming involved in the search for Princess Elizabeth. He especially didn't think it was appropriate for an American citizen to start meddling in another country's affairs. His father had always taught him that diplomats, and their families, should remain neutral and objective, and not allow themselves to be drawn into the domestic politics of a foreign state.

Jane tried to reassure him. 'Look, Seymour, that's all very well in theory, and normally I would agree with you. But this is a quite exceptional state of affairs. For one thing the nation is at war, and for another it's not every day that someone grabs the King's daughter and whisks her away. And for better or for worse, you *are* involved. You're the one who actually saw the Princess in the back of the car. And because of that you're one of only about half a dozen people who actually know what's going on.'

Seymour was clearly unconvinced. A worried frown remained on his forehead. 'Well....' he said.

'And in any case, all we're going to do at first is think.'

'Think?'

'Think.'

'What are we going to think about?

Jane took out a pad of paper and a pen. 'Well, we're going to try to put ourselves in the position of the Earl of Westrow, and work out what his plan was.... Now, supposing you were the Earl, and you decided, misguided fool that you are, that you were going to kidnap Princess Elizabeth. You would need somewhere to take her, wouldn't you?'

'Ye-es.'

'OK. So where would that be?'

Seymour sighed. He had evidently concluded that there was to be no escape for him. 'Well, we kidnapped her in London, right?'

'Right.'

'And we saw them driving – where, west?'

'Mmm, roughly. But don't place too much reliance on that. We saw them in London, and the streets go every which way. They could have been going anywhere.'

'OK,' said Seymour slowly. 'So the thing is, were they going somewhere within London, or out into the country?'

'My guess is the country.'

'Why?'

'Just a hunch. I just have the feeling that Westrow is happier in the country than in the town. Look at his *Who's Who* entry. He's not a City man. No directorships. It just says that his interests are fishing and shooting. And how often does he attend the House of Lords? Hardly ever. No, I think he would take her somewhere out of town.'

'Does he have a country house?'

'Yes. Blesserby Manor, in Wiltshire.'

'Presumably the police have searched that.'

'Yes, first thing this morning.'

Jane stood up and began to pace about.

'What we have to remember,' she said, 'is that the brains behind this enterprise is not Westrow himself, but his so-called secretary, a woman called Helga Schmidt. Or she calls herself Schmidt. She was thought to be Swiss, but Scotland Yard now think she's actually German. She had radio equipment in Blesserby Manor, which makes it pretty clear. Of course she ought to have been caught in the general sweeping up of aliens at the start of the war, but she was missed. Probably Westrow used his influence to protect her. So now they think she's the one who's been doing the planning of all this.'

'How does it help us to know that?'

'Well, apparently – according to Daddy – apparently the view is that this woman is a trained spy. A professional. She will have arranged to set up a base somewhere. It would have to be within reasonable reach of London – they couldn't have driven all night. But it won't be anywhere obvious. In other words, it won't be in a house which can easily be identified.'

'So it won't be one of the many houses that Westrow owns then?'

'No.'

Seymour raised his eyebrows. 'Well, that widens the options considerably. They could be anywhere.'

'Yes, but think, Seymour, think. How long do you think they've had to plan all this? A week? A month?'

'I don't know. Perhaps they've been planning it for years.'

'No! Nonsense! Events are moving fast, Seymour. There's a war on. Countries have been invaded in ten days flat. No, my guess is they've had a week. At most. Now, if you had a week to set up a hideaway somewhere, what would you do?'

'Well.... Rent somewhere?'

'Yes. I think so. You'd rent somewhere. Not a house next door to where you're living. But not too far away either, because it's not as easy to move around the country as it used to be. For one thing you can't get the petrol.'

'I still don't see how that gets us anywhere.'

Jane snapped at him. 'Of course it does, Seymour! Don't be so feeble. It gives us a starting point. We assume that Westrow planned all this from his country house in Wiltshire. We assume that he would rent a place, not too far from his home, but in a remote spot. See? That's as good a line as any.'

'Well, supposing it is. What do we do about it?'

'What we do is ring up all the estate agents in the area round Blesserby Manor, and ask them whether they've rented a place in the last month to the Earl of Westrow.'

'Won't they tell us to get lost?'

'Probably. But we'll tell them a sob story. Say it's vital to contact the Earl, important business matter. Whatever. I'll pretend I'm my father's secretary, and you can pretend you're his personal assistant.'

'Me?' croaked Seymour. 'I'm not going to do any of this.'

'Seymour,' said Jane firmly. 'You will do as you're bloody well told.'

Unfortunately, Jane's attempt at locating the Princess through the application of logic proved to be very frustrating. A quick visit to the reference section of the nearest public library located a book which listed estate agents by geographical area. To Seymour's horror, Jane stole it and brought it home.

'Don't worry, Seymour, I'll take it back after Christmas.'

Then they began telephoning the likeliest firms in the book. This was a slow, painful business. In those days there was no long-distance dialling. All so-called 'trunk' calls had to go through the operator. And what with it being the day before Christmas, and some of the central London exchanges having been damaged by bombs, getting through to the firms concerned was difficult.

Even when she did get connected, Jane found that it was not easy to extract information. All she wanted to know was whether the estate agents had or had not had recent dealings with the Earl of Westrow.

Sometimes Jane pretended to be the Earl's mother, slightly dotty, and unable to remember where the dear boy had gone for Christmas. Sometimes she was Detective Sergeant Guinevere from Scotland Yard. And sometimes she was Miss Waggoner, from *The Times*, anxious to interview the Earl about bomb damage to his London home. Nothing made the slightest difference.

Seymour did marginally better, when he tried. The American accent proved to be an asset. It seemed to lead people to expect that he would naturally ask impertinent and unusual questions, and it seemed to imply, in some mysterious way, that he had a bucketful of money which he would immediately empty over the head of anyone who helped him. But, despite the higher degree of co-operation which Seymour elicited, some two and a half hours' work in the morning got them nowhere.

By one o'clock Jane had had more than enough. And besides, she was hungry. She took Seymour out to a nearby restaurant where, for a price, you could still get a hot lunch.

Chapter 35

How was she going to get away? Princess Elizabeth could think of nothing else. The question went round and round in her head, like a cracked gramophone record.

How am I going to get away?

Elizabeth had come to the conclusion that she would have to help herself because no one else was going to come to her rescue. At least, not quickly. Sergeant Wilson had been there to help, and the poor man had been shot. And now here she was in some sort of a cottage.

Elizabeth reviewed what she knew. She still wasn't sure where this cottage was located, but it was clearly in the country somewhere. There were no other buildings visible from the ground-floor windows, and no traffic noise could be heard, so it was evidently quite a long way from anywhere. It didn't seem likely that people would be walking past or coming to the door. There would be no one she could appeal to for help, and no one to assist her in getting away.

So, she was going to have to do it herself.

Much to her annoyance, she'd been put back in that nasty drab room again, the one where she'd spent the night. There was a little more daylight to see by now, but not much. She looked at her watch: nearly noon. She'd been in here several hours.

She'd already had a good look round, several times, and had discovered that there was nothing in the room that could be used as a weapon. So, the first thing she was going to have to do was to get downstairs. Somehow or other.

She decided to call out. Politely. 'Helga. Helga?'

No answer.

Elizabeth called a few more times, until it was obvious that she was going to be ignored.

So. Nothing for it but to be thoroughly rude and annoying.

If she dared.

The one object of furniture in the room, apart from the bed, was a pine chest of drawers. All the drawers were empty.

Elizabeth took one of the top drawers out, sucked in a deep breath to bolster her courage, and began to use the drawer to bang on the door.

Bang! Bang! Bang!

This was quite unlike anything she'd ever done before, and it was surprising really what a lot of fun it was!

Bang!

You swung the drawer round, gave the door a good old wallop, and... Bang!

It made a tremendous noise, echoing right through the house, she was sure. And she was positive that Helga wouldn't put up with that for very long.

Nor did she.

Bang! Bang! Bang!

Helga came pounding up the stairs – Elizabeth could hear her, because they were wooden stairs, with no carpet, and Helga was a biggish woman – and then Helga was standing outside the door, shouting at her.

'Stop that! Stop that at once! Do you hear me?'

Well, normally of course Elizabeth wouldn't even have started. Banging drawers against doors was distinctly anti-social, and in normal circumstances one would never have dreamed of doing such a thing. But there was no point in stopping now.

Bang! Bang! Bang!

Elizabeth gave the door three more resounding wallops, swinging the drawer round from right behind her. She was pleased to see that one of the panels in the door was beginning to crack. If she went on like this the door would eventually be demolished.

But she didn't have to go on like that.

There was a clink of keys and Helga threw open the door. She stood in the opening, eyes blazing, hands on hips. 'What *do* you think you are doing?'

'I'm attracting your attention. I want to come downstairs.'

Helga's eyes narrowed. 'If I had my way we'd have got rid of you yesterday evening. I said you were trouble right from the start.'

'I won't be trouble if I come downstairs,' said Elizabeth, trying to sound confident. 'It's cold up here. And it's dark, and it's boring. At least if I come downstairs I shall be in daylight.'

Helga turned away. 'Oh, very well,' she said, flouncing down the top three steps. 'Come downstairs if you must.'

Elizabeth smiled a little smile, making sure that Helga didn't see her.

Back in the kitchen Helga turned on an ancient radio which stood on a rickety table in front of one of the windows. The radio crackled fiercely as Helga turned the dial. Eventually she found a German station, though the reception was poor and the signal varied in volume.

Then Helga motioned to Elizabeth to sit down. 'You are right,' she said. 'It is boring. This is the most boring assignment I have ever had. And believe me, that is saying quite a lot.'

Elizabeth sat down at the table.

Helga went to her handbag and pulled out a pack of playing cards.

'Here,' she said. 'Do you play patience?'

'Yes.'

'Then play with these.'

Elizabeth took the cards gratefully and began to lay them out on the table. Helga lit a cigarette and inhaled.

After a moment Elizabeth said casually: 'Where has Westrow gone?'

'I told you before – mind your own business.'

Pause.

'Why are you holding me here? Am I being held for ransom?'

'Sort of.'

'But surely Westrow is a rich man? He doesn't need the money.'

'Oh God,' sighed Helga. 'Why must you ask these questions?'

'Well you can't expect me not to be interested. After all, I am being held prisoner....' Red nine on black ten. 'Am I a hostage then, if it's not for ransom?'

Helga inhaled hard. 'Yes, you are a sort of a hostage.'

'Oh. You want someone else released, do you? Are we to do a swap? I've read about that in books.'

No answer. Black six on red seven.

'I bet it's Mosley, isn't it? Papa and Mr Churchill had him put in prison.'

'No,' said Helga, in tones which sounded bone weary. 'No, it is not Sir Oswald Mosley.'

'Oh. Someone else then.'

'You are being held here,' said Helga eventually, 'so that your father will follow instructions. To keep you safe, he must take certain steps. So, naturally, he will take them.'

'Oh. I shan't be here long then?'

'God,' said Helga, 'I certainly hope not.'

'Later today do you think?' Two aces at once – gosh.

'Tomorrow!' shouted Helga. 'Tomorrow, Christmas Day, you stupid, inquisitive little nobody!'

If she had been able to, Elizabeth would have danced a short jig. She was so pleased to know that she was getting under Helga's skin.

Helga picked up the packet of cigarettes from the table and began to turn it round and round in an agitated manner. 'Tomorrow, if your father says what he is supposed to say during his Christmas Day broadcast, then we will let you free.'

'Oh, I *see*,' said Elizabeth, keeping her head well down, so that Helga should not see how dismayed she was. 'So that's it.'

Well, that really was it, there was no doubt about that.

Elizabeth began to feel short of breath again, just like she had in the car yesterday, because if there was one thing her Papa wouldn't be able to cope with, it was somebody telling him at the last minute that he had to say something special – something *different* – in his Christmas Day broadcast.

Obviously Helga didn't know, but Papa found that broadcast awfully difficult. It was a very hard thing to do, talking to all those millions of people over the wireless, and Papa had to practice every day for a long time, and the words had to be rearranged for him in a different order so that he didn't stutter and sound silly, and if anyone thought they could make him say something different at very short notice – well, it just wasn't possible, that was all. He needed help to get the job done at all, and it simply wasn't possible to change it at the last minute. And if you couldn't change it, and if Papa didn't say what Westrow and this woman wanted him to say....

Elizabeth saw again, in her mind's eye, the body of Sergeant Wilson. That was what happened to people who didn't do what Westrow and this woman wanted. They ended up dead. And if Papa didn't, or couldn't, do what they wanted, then that was the way she would end up too. Being a Princess didn't matter at all. She would have thought it did. Yesterday morning she would have been quite *sure* that it did. But now she could see that being a Princess made absolutely no difference whatever. She was going to end up dead.

Unless of course, she could get away.

She didn't even think about it. Didn't plan it, rehearse it in her mind, judge the distances, think through the possibilities, didn't do any of that.

She just sprang to her feet, picked up the light wooden chair she was sitting on, raised it up high, and smashed it down on Helga's head.

Or at least she tried to. Helga saw it coming, of course.

As Elizabeth jumped to her feet, Helga's eyes opened wider, wondering what her prisoner was up to. And then, as the chair went up in the air, Helga realised what was going to happen. She let go of the cigarettes and her lighter. And as the chair came down towards her head, Helga raised her arms to protect herself.

What happened after that, Elizabeth didn't wait to see. She ran to the back door, turned the handle, and pulled.

Of course, she didn't know whether the door would be locked or open. She hadn't paused to think about that, hadn't tried to find out before making a run for it. And if the back door had been locked, she would have ended up looking rather foolish.

But the door came open, and beautiful fresh cold air came flooding in, and Elizabeth sprinted over the doorstep, down the path, round the side of the house, on to the rutted drive which led towards a clump of trees at the junction of the drive and the road, and then when she reached the road she turned left – didn't pause to think which way was best, left or right, didn't know which way led to the nearest house, nearest village, nearest town, didn't bother to think – just turned left, and ran and ran and ran, down a long straight road.

She panted as she ran, drawing great mouthfuls of cold winter air into her lungs, ran as fast as her legs could carry her.

She had gone about two hundred yards perhaps when she began to pay some attention to the countryside around her.

It dawned on her that this was a long straight road.

And that on either side of the road there were broad flat fields.

And that nowhere, neither in front, nor to the left, nor to the right, could she see anything.

Not a tree.

Not a house.

Not a telegraph pole.

Nothing.

And then she heard the car.

By that time she had gone – what, perhaps half a mile? She didn't know. What she did know was that she was running out of puff. And that there was nowhere to go.

The car came up behind her.

Elizabeth ran until she was *really* out of puff.

She could have gone on, of course. She could have gone on until she was exhausted. But that would have been futile. Silly. It would have been... undignified.

So she stopped.

Back in the cottage, Helga examined her arm, where it had been struck by the chair.

'Well,' she said. 'You didn't quite break the bone, but you had a good try.'

Helga gazed at Elizabeth with a new expression. It wasn't menacing exactly, but it was cold, and hard.

‘If it was left to me,’ she said, ‘I would strip you naked and whip you unconscious. But that is not what I am instructed to do. I am instructed to keep you here, in good order, until tomorrow afternoon. And that is what I will do, because I am disciplined, you see. Trained. But then, after three o’clock tomorrow....’

Helga smiled, and suddenly it was a very menacing smile indeed.

‘Well, then we will see.’

Anyway, after she had been brought back to the cottage, quite exhausted and a bit muddy, Helga took her upstairs again, to that nasty, dark little room, and tied her to the bed.

‘There,’ said Helga smugly, as she finished the last knot. ‘You can stay there until you learn some manners. When you’re ready to apologise, you can come down. But until you apologise – and really mean it, you can stay there.’

‘But what if I want to use the bathroom?’

‘You can wet your knickers for all I care. But if you do apologise – if you convince me that you are really, really sorry for what you did – then I might think about letting you use the bathroom. And perhaps even come downstairs.’

Helga moved towards the door.

‘It’ll be rather dark in here, I’m afraid. But that’s what happens to girls who don’t mind their manners. They get punished.’

Then she went out but almost immediately came back in again.

‘Oh – I nearly forgot to tell you. I do hope you don’t mind spiders, because I saw quite a few of them in here the other day. In the dark they won’t be able to see you, and they’ll probably crawl all over you. What a pity your hands aren’t free to brush them off. And there are rats too. Quite big ones. I hope they won’t bite.’

And off she went.

Elizabeth lay in the darkness.

At first, of course, she cried.

Well, she was allowed to, she told herself. It wasn’t a crime to cry. Lots of people did it. Perfectly normal.

So she cried, being very careful not to make any noise about it. She wasn't going to give Helga the satisfaction of hearing her.

Time passed.

She began to think about spiders, and that made her laugh, strangely enough. What a fool that Helga was, to imagine that she would care about spiders! Lots of people *were* frightened of spiders, of course. But Elizabeth *certainly* wasn't bothered by them. She'd had a pet spider once, until Crawfie found it and screamed the place down. Which had proved very useful afterwards, because if ever she wanted to get rid of Crawfie all she had to do was mention that she had seen a particularly hairy spider just over there, and Crawfie would rush off somewhere else for the rest of the afternoon.

So spiders were not a problem.

Rats, on the other hand, she was not keen on.

Not that there *were* any rats, she was quite sure of that. Helga had just said that because she'd been hit over the head and wanted to get her own back.

No, there were no rats.

Elizabeth listened carefully, just to make sure. Was there any rustling to be heard? The scampering of tiny feet?

No, there were no rats.

Well, probably not.

Some time later, Elizabeth had an idea. She began to call out to Helga.

'Helga? Helga!'

Nothing happened, of course, not for ages. She didn't expect it to. So she made her calling sound a bit more urgent. As if she was really desperate.

'Helga! HELGAAAA!'

Eventually the door opened.

'Oh. Need to do a little wee-wee do we?'

'No, we don't as a matter of fact.'

'Oh? So why are you bawling? Ready to apologise?'

'No. I'm not.'

Helga seemed surprised. 'Oh. Well you can stay there then.'

'I don't think so.'

Helga turned towards the bed, bringing her head forward as if she needed to read Elizabeth's lips. 'I beg your pardon?'

'I said, I don't think so.'

'Oh, and why not, *Princess*?'

'Because,' said Elizabeth calmly, 'unless I keep quiet about what happened, you're the one who's going to be in trouble.'

Helga snorted. 'Oh, I am, am I?'

'Yes. You are. I don't think the Earl of Westrow would be very pleased to know that you very nearly let me escape. Would he? You're the one that's supposed to be guarding me. And if I tell him what a jolly rotten job you did of it, he's not going to be very pleased, is he?'

Silence. Helga was taken aback.

'So?' said Helga eventually.

'So, if you untie me, and let me go to the bathroom whenever I want. And if you let me play patience and sit downstairs with you, and listen to the radio and so on – then I promise not to tell him what happened.'

'Oh.' Helga sneered, as if she was not impressed. 'Quite the little negotiator, aren't we?' She sat down on the bed. 'Well my dear, I don't do deals with smart-arse little Princesses. But I am under instructions to keep you in good order. I told you that before, didn't I? Otherwise I would have whipped you. And I still might whip you, as a matter of fact, because a few stripes on your bum aren't going to bother anyone. But I've been thinking it over. And if I leave you here to lie in your own shit, no one's going to be very pleased with me. They want you in good order, you see. And good order is what they will get.'

Helga began to undo the ropes which held the Princess to the bed.

'You can come downstairs, with me.'

Westrow did not appear at the cottage at all on Christmas Eve. Where he was Helga would not say.

The time passed slowly, with much playing of tedious games of patience, and only the radio to occupy them. Most of the time, Elizabeth was kept firmly tied to a chair, tied by both feet and one hand, in a position where Helga could see her, even when she was cooking.

Elizabeth kept her ears pricked, but there was no sound of any human activity outside the house. Not a car or a tractor passed down the lane. It was a desolate spot, and the day was short: it was dark by five o'clock.

Elizabeth was now a *little* wiser as to her whereabouts, because a sign at the gate had said that the name of the building was Plain View Cottage. But just *where* she was – England, Scotland or Wales – she had no idea. She was beginning to wonder if they might have travelled further than she thought.

Even if she escaped from the cottage again, she was evidently miles from anywhere. Still, she was going to have to try. And it was going to be much harder now. The only thing she could think of was grabbing a knife, cutting the ropes which held her to the chair, and then *stabbing* Helga. All three actions were difficult even to imagine, especially the last.

First, she would have to grab a knife. That seemed impossible. Helga kept Elizabeth well clear of anything which might constitute a weapon.

Then, even if she got a knife, she would have to slice through some quite thick rope. That was not going to be easy.

And finally she would have to... Well, she would have to *stop* Helga chasing her. She had already tried to knock her out with a chair. And that hadn't worked. So next time she would have to...

Well, she would have to do something even more drastic. And Elizabeth didn't think she could.

She stopped thinking about it. About that last stage. There was no point in thinking about it unless she had the *chance* to escape. And she wouldn't get the chance unless she managed to get hold of a knife and cut herself free. And there was no likelihood of that. On the few occasions when Helga herself went to the bathroom, she tied *both* Elizabeth's hands to the chair. So it was hopeless.

Absolutely hopeless.

Chapter 36

'We're not going to do any more telephoning,' said Jane firmly, as she and Seymour tucked into their treacle pudding with custard. This particular dessert was a speciality of the restaurant they were eating in; the owner had stolen the recipe from the House of Lords, where their lordships were particularly fond of it on account of them having enjoyed it so much at school.

'Oh,' said Seymour, who had a remarkably healthy appetite despite being somewhat slim. 'What *are* we going to do then?'

'I think,' said Jane, 'we'll go out to Blesserby Manor and take a look around. We agreed that Westrow probably planned his dirty deed from there, and we're getting nowhere speaking to these stupid estate agents. Let's see what we can find on the site.'

Seymour was by now sufficiently well trained not to object to any of Jane's proposals, no matter how bizarre they seemed. But he did just raise an eyebrow. 'This place Blesserby,' he asked. 'Is it far?'

'Couple of hours' drive. Out in Wiltshire.'

'You say drive. You have a car?'

'My father's.'

'I thought petrol was rationed and impossible to get hold of.'

'It is. But what else is the American Embassy for, Seymour?'

Jane left a note for her father, though she expected to be back home before he saw it. Then she backed her father's blue Humber Super Snipe out of its mews garage, and drove it round to the American Embassy.

There Seymour used his father's name to fill the car with petrol, and he added a couple of cans in the boot as an afterthought.

'I thought you didn't believe in taking advantage of Embassy privileges for your own benefit,' Seymour teased her.

'I don't, but this is an emergency.'

Seymour smiled, and they set off down the A4.

It was getting dark as they turned into the long drive which led up to Blesserby Manor. However, there was enough light left to show that the house was modest by the standards of the great country houses. It was evidently an ancient dwelling which had been extended and modernised at around the turn of the century; though not, Jane decided, by Lutyens.

'Well, now we're here,' said Seymour. 'What are we going to do?'

'See if anyone's in first.'

There were no lights to be seen in the house, and Jane did not expect their ring to be answered. But after a minute or so, a light appeared in the hall and the front door was pulled open by a middle-aged, motherly-looking woman who was evidently the housekeeper.

Jane was ready. She had taken out of her handbag a security pass which she was supposed to show whenever she went into Buckingham Palace but never did because most of the doormen knew her.

'Miss Padget,' she said. 'MI5.'

She heard Seymour gulp beside her, but at least he had the sense to keep quiet.

'And this is Mr Jensen,' she added. 'From the American Embassy.'

The housekeeper seemed unsurprised and quite willing to co-operate. 'Oh,' she said. 'And I suppose you want to look around too?'

'That's right,' said Jane, picking up on this useful cue. 'Are the police still here?'

'No, Miss, they went at lunch-time. Said they'd finished.'

Jane decided to take advantage of the housekeeper's very natural assumption that she and Seymour were officialdom and therefore entitled to do whatever they wished.

'Yes, well, I'm afraid there are still one or two things we need to check. Sorry to trouble you.'

The housekeeper stepped aside. She smiled good-naturedly. The fact that the police were investigating her employer did not seem to trouble her in the slightest. 'Never you mind about that, dear,' she said. 'You come on in, Miss, out of the cold.'

Jane and Seymour entered the house.

In the hall was a suitcase, with a woman's coat and hat laid on top of it.

'Fact is,' said the housekeeper, 'I was just off to see my sister. Lives in Clapham, you see. A widow now she is, like me, so I thought I'd keep her company over Christmas. What with the bombing and everything she's having a hard time. So I was wondering, Miss, will you be long?'

'We might be,' said Jane, looking round. 'It depends. When are you leaving?'

'Half an hour, Miss. Bus passes the end of the drive, takes me right to the station. I would have gone earlier.' She motioned towards the interior of the house. 'But what with the police arriving at the crack of dawn and everything, it's put me all behind. Took a lot of stuff away they did, I'm surprised there's anything left for you to look at. And what the Earl will say when he comes back I really don't know. If he does come back,' she added darkly, peering into Jane's face. 'They do say as how he might be in trouble.'

'Oh, I couldn't comment about that,' said Jane.

'No, well,' said the housekeeper hastily. She clearly didn't want to be thought to have spoken out of turn. 'The house is closed up really. The Earl ran it all down when the war started. Stopped having guests and put most of the rooms under sheets. He and Miss Schmidt just lived in a few of the rooms. He got rid of all the servants too,' she added, addressing Seymour. 'All except me and two ladies from the village what comes in to clean. No butler any more. Them days is over, you see.'

'Yes,' said Seymour. 'I'm sure you're right.'

Jane was anxious to get on. Left to her own devices, the housekeeper looked as if she would stand here gossiping for some time.

'Well,' said Jane, 'I suggest you just carry on as planned, Mrs...?'

'Perkins.'

'Mrs Perkins. Mr Jensen and I will do what we have to do and then close the front door after us. When were you expecting the Earl to be back?'

'In the new year, Miss.'

'I see. And I don't suppose you know where he's gone?'

'No, Miss.' The housekeeper smiled. 'The police was very anxious to know that too. But I couldn't help them at all. And I don't think they knew where he was even after they'd looked through all his things. Very disappointed they was.'

'No doubt,' said Jane.

After further debate Mrs Perkins was persuaded to catch her train, leaving a key to the house in Jane's care. Jane undertook to see that the front door was locked when they left, and promised to push the key back through the letter-box.

When Mrs Perkins had gone, the old manor house fell strangely silent. It was cold too.

Jane and Seymour went into the kitchen, where an ancient stove was still giving off some heat as the ashes died down. Knowing how difficult it would be to find anywhere to eat in wartime Britain, Jane had brought a few provisions with her from the flat, so they were able to make themselves a modest meal of cheese on toast, with two apples to follow. The latter items were supplied by Mrs Perkins, who declared they 'wanted eating'.

Afterwards Seymour asked Jane where they were going to start their search and what they were looking for.

Jane sighed. 'Goodness knows. Now that we've got here, I don't honestly know what to do, Seymour. The police have evidently been here for hours. Mrs Perkins said there were scores of them, both uniformed and plain clothes, like us, as she put it. And they took away a whole van full of papers. So to tell the truth we're probably wasting our time.'

'Hey,' said Seymour. 'This isn't like you. Don't be so depressed! Let's go find the Earl's study. According to Agatha Christie, country policemen are not as smart as they might be – so who knows what we'll find?'

Jane tried to summon up the energy to be enthusiastic. 'Yes,' she said heavily. 'I suppose you're right. That's what we ought to do. But the truth is, Seymour, I think I'm out of my depth.'

Jane rubbed her eyes wearily. The plain fact was, she was having trouble staying awake after eating some food. She could really do with a nap. But she told herself she must concentrate.

'This business about Princess Elizabeth being kidnapped,' she said at last. It's a serious, deadly business, Seymour. Not a game. And in a way I've been treating it as a game. As a bit of a lark. But I realise now that it's not. And unless we find her, the poor girl is going to end up dead.'

Seymour came over to Jane and literally pulled her up off the wooden kitchen chair.

'Damn right,' he said. 'Everything you've said is true. All the more reason to get off our butts and go to work.'

Seymour led the way through the house, switching on lights as he went. Jane followed, not wanting him to see how close to tears she was.

She had thought that once she got on her feet she would get her breath back. But she hadn't. The long drive and the loss of nervous energy over the last twenty-four hours had left her very tired. She really wanted nothing more than to go to bed.

But Seymour was different. He had got his second wind from somewhere, and was poking his nose into everything. Having once been a most reluctant participant in this entire enterprise, he was now taking the initiative.

Before long they found what was clearly the Earl's study. It was a man's room. It smelt of cigar smoke.

Seymour went through the drawers of the desk, and then through the bank of filing cabinets. All the files had obviously been thinned out by the police. Sometimes whole drawers of the cabinets had been removed. Meanwhile Jane sat at the desk and read some of the material which he passed to her.

Before long Jane concluded that she was reading rubbish. Rubbish, that is, in the sense that the papers had no bearing on the whereabouts of the Earl and Princess Elizabeth. There was correspondence with banks, letters to the agents who looked after the Earl's extensive property interests, circulars sent out by Fascist groups, newsletters from the parish council. There were leaflets, pamphlets, booklets, the occasional vulgar magazine – all the debris of a man of property with right-wing political interests who seldom threw anything away. It was depressing to sit and contemplate it all, especially when you knew that the police had already undertaken the same search and had presumably carted away all the most promising material.

After a while Jane grew too depressed to go on reading. She asked Seymour to continue searching the study, and she herself went upstairs.

As the housekeeper had told her, most of the rooms were 'closed up'. That is to say, the doors were not locked, but the furniture was covered in dust-sheets. The light bulbs in those rooms were dim, the air seemed damp and cold, and the atmosphere added further to Jane's sense of depression. She could have done with a stiff whisky.

Speaking of which, she thought, there must be some hard liquor somewhere.

Eventually Jane found the main bedroom. The merest glance showed that this room was used by both the Earl and his 'secretary', Helga Schmidt. The wardrobes contained a selection of both male and female attire, and a fire was laid in the hearth.

As she stood there in the bedroom, contemplating the intimate details of two other people's lives, Jane suddenly realised that she felt more than tired: she felt completely exhausted. As a member of the Oxford University women's hockey team she had trained several times a week during the previous term, and she had thought she was pretty fit. But now, suddenly, all her strength had left her.

She took down a box of matches from the mantelpiece and lit the fire in the hearth. She had no intention of leaving Blesserby Manor tonight – she was far too tired – and a warm bedroom would be most welcome. The bed looked as if it had been made up with clean sheets, ready for the Earl's return, but she would have used it whatever its condition. It was as much as she could do not to flop down on it right now. But instead she went back downstairs.

Sure enough, the Earl's study had a drinks cabinet, and she poured large whiskies for herself and Seymour.

'Found anything?' she asked.

'Not much. Nothing useful anyway. What about you?'

'I've found somewhere comfortable for us to sleep. And a bedroom cupboard full of artificial penises, whips, and high-heeled boots.'

'You're kidding!'

'No,' said Jane wearily, 'I am not. But don't get any funny ideas, Seymour, because I'm far too tired.'

Seymour glanced at his watch. 'Ten o'clock.'

'Bedtime,' said Jane. 'Seymour....'

'Yes?'

Jane turned to face him. 'I'm sorry if I've treated you badly.'

Seymour looked at her in astonishment. 'I didn't think you had!'

'Yes I have. I've spoken to you as if you were an idiot, more than once. I've dragged you out here on a very foolish search for goodness knows what, and I've done things, like pretending to be an MI5 officer, which could get us both into a lot of trouble. And I just want to say I'm sorry.'

And then, to her acute embarrassment, tears began to flow down her cheeks and she let out an involuntary sob.

Seymour looked at her in amazement. Then he chuckled, as if reassured to discover that she was human after all. And finally he came over and gave her a hug.

'Hey,' he said as he put his arms around her. 'You really are pooped, aren't you? This isn't the old you, Jane. Not the real you at all....' He pulled back a moment and looked in her face. 'Hey, I tell you what,' he said. 'You finish your whisky, and then I'll carry you upstairs to bed. And in the morning, after you've had a good night's sleep, you'll be snarling at me just the same as usual. You see if you aren't.'

Chapter 37

Extract from Jane Padget's report to the King, dated 3 January 1941:

```
In the end, we found the papers about the
cottage quite by accident.
```

Jane slept as if she had been hit over the back of the head with something heavy. Better, in fact, because her sleep was dreamless, and the next morning she awoke without any trace of a headache.

Outside it was just beginning to get light. Beside her, Seymour slept peacefully, with the hint of an adenoidal snore now and then. Jane lay still for a few minutes, thinking over where they had got to in their search for the Princess, and what they might sensibly do next. Then she rolled over and gave Seymour a dig.

'Happy Christmas!' she said. 'It's Christmas Day, sleepy.'

Seymour awoke slowly. 'Huh?'

'I said, it's Christmas Day.'

'Huh? Oh, yeah. Happy Christmas.' And he yawned. 'Hey – you think I could call my Mom and Pop?'

Jane laughed. 'You can try. But don't bet on it. The English telephone system is primitive at the best of times. We don't believe in making communication too easy. It leads to over-familiarity.'

'Gee, I hope all those people off that liner that sank are OK. This is a hell of a Christmas for them.'

'Get dressed, Seymour. You can't do anything for anyone till you've had breakfast.'

Seymour and Jane washed and dressed quickly, because little was left of the fire which had warmed them last night, and outside there was a frost. Not a hard one, but enough to give the semblance of a white Christmas.

Seymour shaved with a gold safety razor which he found in the bathroom, and Jane advised him to keep it as a souvenir.

'All property of traitors belongs to the state anyway,' she told him.

Once downstairs, Jane cooked breakfast for them. Yesterday evening she had deliberately not used the four eggs and some bacon which she had brought with her from Eaton Square. That meant that they could now have these items fried, with toast. To drink there was the best part of a bottle of milk. Jane was delighted that she had not used up her supplies the night before: it was so much more valuable to start off the day with some protein in their stomachs.

While Jane was cooking Seymour tried to phone his parents. He knew the name of the hotel they were staying at in Liverpool, and he was able to get the number from directory enquiries. But that was as far as he got. The local telephone operator was polite, but not able to do much. 'There's been a lot of trouble with the lines,' she said. 'What with the air raids and everything. And it's Christmas Day, Sir. Only a skeleton staff.'

After a few minutes Seymour gave up. He figured his parents were probably on their way back to London anyway.

After Seymour's attempt to make contact with the outside world had failed, Jane tried to ring her father in London. But it was the same story. Only a few lines were open, the operator advised. There was a war on, and it was Christmas – as if anyone was likely to forget either of these circumstances. The current waiting time for a connection to London was said to be ninety minutes. Jane said she wouldn't bother to wait, thank you. But she would dearly have liked to know whether the police had made any progress in locating the Earl of Westrow and rescuing the Princess.

Jane sighed. 'We shall just have to assume,' she said, 'that nothing has happened, and carry on trying to do our bit.'

Somehow, the task of searching the Earl's house seemed easier in the bright frosty daylight; it also seemed much more likely to yield something useful. But after a couple of fruitless hours, Jane's initial optimism had vanished.

She took Seymour back into the Earl's spacious study. Then

she stood in the middle of the floor and surveyed the scene.

'You know,' she said, 'I'm certain that, if there is anything to be found, it's in here somewhere.'

'Assuming the police haven't taken it.'

'Yes, assuming that.'

Jane scratched her chin. 'Suppose you were the Earl, Seymour. And you had some incriminating, secret papers. And you knew that one day someone might come looking for them, and you wanted to keep them hidden. Where would you put them?'

Seymour sighed and peered around. 'Darned if I know. But the woman, Helga what's-her-name – she's supposed to be the professional. Where would she have hidden these things?'

Jane looked around also. 'Well, not in any of the obvious filing cabinets or cupboards, that's for sure.'

'Under the carpet?'

They looked, without success.

'On top of the bookshelves? On the very top, I mean, near the ceiling.'

With difficulty, Jane clambered on a chair placed on a table, and scanned the top of the high bookshelves which held the usual country-house selection of leather-bound volumes. She saw nothing except a great deal of dust, undisturbed for years.

They pottered and poked around, growing less and less sure that they were going to have any success.

Half an hour passed, and Jane grew restless.

'Perhaps there's a safe,' she said. 'Let's look behind the paintings.'

There were nine paintings in the room. They moved them all aside, or took them down, revealing... nothing.

'All right,' said Jane. 'If the safe isn't hidden by a painting, perhaps it's behind the books.'

But there were an awful lot of books in the Earl's study. It would take most of the day, and a great deal of physical effort, to move them all. So instead, Jane stood in the centre of the room, with Seymour beside her, and told him to look carefully.

'Look carefully for what?' asked Seymour.

'I don't know. Something different. Some dust marks. Or an

absence of dust marks. Something that shows the books have been moved recently. Or not moved. A row of fake books, hiding a pornographic picture – or whatever. I don't know.'

So it was untrue then. What Jane wrote in her report to the King. They did not find what they found entirely by accident. They found it after quite a lot of hard work, through the application of reason, and after a systematic search.

'What's that, over there?' said Seymour.

'Where?'

Seymour crossed the floor and went to a line of books four feet off the floor. He pointed, and lifted a book off the shelf. 'Oh, it's nothing. Just a book with a loose cover. From a distance it looked as if it might be a ribbon you could tug. Or a bookmark.'

A ribbon you could tug, thought Jane. *Or a bookmark.*

She looked around. No bell pulls. No curtain cords. No lights operated by ceiling switches. But there was...

There was a bookmark visible. In one of the lower shelves. In the large Oxford Dictionary.

Well, it wasn't actually a bookmark. It was a small gap between the pages, as if there were something tucked inside the book.

She went over, and drew the volume out.

After they had found the papers which led them, eventually, to the cottage where Princess Elizabeth was being held, Jane tried once more to phone the Palace. That was, after all, the correct thing to do. The obvious thing. The sensible thing.

What she wanted to do was to contact her father and tell him that the Earl of Westrow had, within the past ten days, rented a cottage on the edge of Salisbury Plain; that he had done it under a false name, paying cash for a month's rent; that he had concealed the correspondence in the large OED; and that this cottage would surely merit investigation by the proper authorities.

But there was no telephone access to London. The operator (a different one this time) said she was terribly sorry, she was having to disappoint a great many people, but the raid last night had damaged one of the most important exchanges, and there were *some* lines working, but the waiting time for a call to London was now estimated at two hours, and if Jane would care to be added to the list, she, the operator, would make sure that she was put through just as quickly as possible, but you see it was Christmas, and what with the raid, and people very naturally wanting to speak to their family on Christmas morning, and there only being a skeleton staff, because naturally anyone with a family wanted to be at home and not working – well, it was all very difficult, wasn't it? Jane thanked the operator for her kindness and hung up.

'It's no good,' she said. 'It's a complete waste of time. But this cottage is only about twenty miles away. Let's go there. It's probably all a false alarm, anyway. The Earl probably rented this cottage as somewhere to run to if the police got on to him in London. I don't suppose the Princess is being held there for a minute. But when we get there we can alert the local police and let them check it out. That's the best thing to do.'

Seymour agreed.

Chapter 38

Christmas Day brought a joyless dawn to Princess Elizabeth The day was cold, drab, and lonely.

Helga seemed just as depressed as Elizabeth was.

After breakfast Helga lit a fire in the living-room of the cottage. She and Elizabeth made that their base for today, rather than the kitchen. This alone made Elizabeth realise that something was going to happen soon. She wondered what it might be. Probably, she thought, Westrow would appear.

But there was still nothing to do but wait. And Helga made sure that her prisoner was always tied to a chair.

Elizabeth wished she was at home with her family. She thought about what they would be doing at this very moment – or rather, she started to think about it, but it made her want to cry so she stopped immediately.

Eventually, at about eleven o'clock on the morning of Christmas Day, Westrow did arrive. Elizabeth saw him through the living-room window. He came in a car – no longer the big black Bentley, but a smaller grey vehicle, less noticeable. He strode into the room, pulled off his overcoat, and greeted Elizabeth quite cheerfully.

'Good morning, Your Royal Highness.'

'Good morning,' said Elizabeth politely. The fact that this man was a traitor who would shortly be hanged was not, she decided, sufficient reason for abandoning her normal standards of decorum. But she saw no reason to wish him a happy Christmas.

Westrow rubbed his hands and handed his overcoat to Helga, just as if she was a servant. Which, of course, she was. Elizabeth could see that now. Helga just stood there, the coat over her arm.

Westrow seemed to ignore Helga and addressed Elizabeth. 'And how are you this morning, Ma'am?'

'I am well thank you.'

'Good. I hope Helga has been treating you well?'

Elizabeth glanced at Helga, whose face was a blank, without

expression. 'Helga has treated me as well as I would expect in the circumstances.'

'Good. Good.'

Westrow continued to rub his hands, as if he were slightly nervous. 'I think,' he said to Helga, 'that we might release the Princess from her bonds now that there are two of us here to watch her.'

Helga said nothing, but she bent to untie the ropes which held Elizabeth to her chair. Then Helga turned away, saying that she would go and make a cup of coffee.

Westrow sat down at a small card-table, opposite Elizabeth.

He paused for a moment, as if making up his mind what to say. When he did speak, he obviously felt that Elizabeth deserved some sort of explanation.

'Perhaps I ought to tell you,' he said, 'why we have brought you here.'

'That would be very much appreciated.'

Westrow smiled briefly. He seemed slightly embarrassed by Elizabeth's self-possession. Even a little intimidated. But then he was, Elizabeth reminded herself, addressing royalty. She tried to put on her best Queen Victoria expression.

Westrow tapped his fingers on the table in front of him. 'Yes, well.... The fact is, you see, it's all very difficult.' He paused, and then leaned forward. 'You're old enough now, Ma'am, to understand about the war. And many of us feel, you see, that it's a tragic waste. Waste of men's lives, waste of resources. So we want to stop it. Now, you might think that was easy enough. Just contact the other side, propose terms, talk about it a bit.... But the sad thing is, some people don't want to settle things round a table. Mr Churchill, for example. As far as he's concerned, it's all rather gung-ho. Men like him, they'd rather fight to the death. And they don't seem too fussy about whose death it is.'

Westrow looked at Elizabeth earnestly. She could see that he wanted some sign that he should continue.

'Yes, I understand that,' she said. 'And I would like the war to end too. So would Papa. But what does that have to do with me being here?'

'Ah, well, you see, I have tried to persuade His Majesty – and many others have tried to persuade the politicians – that the war should be brought to an end. But we haven't succeeded. So what we have decided, some of us, is to apply pressure. We want to concentrate people's minds. In particular, we need to gain the attention of your father, the King.'

'And was it really necessary to kidnap me?'

Westrow sighed. 'Yes, I'm afraid it was. I tried the polite way, and it didn't work. So what I have said to the King, now, is that if he wishes to have you returned to him, he must use his Christmas Day broadcast – ' Westrow glanced at his watch ' – in about four hours' time, to announce to the world that the British government will stop fighting and will start to negotiate a peace treaty.'

Elizabeth's eyebrows went up. 'So that's what Papa has to do, is it? He has to use his speech to say that we'll make peace with the Germans?'

'Yes!' Westrow appeared delighted that she had cottoned on so quickly. 'If the German and the British people combine, you see, instead of fighting each other, then we shall be in a position to deal with the *real* threats to our civilisation. Such as Communism. That's what Hitler understands, and what so few people in England *can* understand. The Führer sees the bigger picture.'

'I see. And if Papa makes that speech – the one you've told me about – I will be released?'

'Yes. So this afternoon the three of us will go into the kitchen and turn on the radio. And listen for ourselves. We will see whether he makes the speech which has been written for him by my associates. Or not.'

'Oh.'

Elizabeth tried to look cheerful, as if she was quite hopeful that what Westrow wanted to happen *would* happen. But she didn't feel at all cheerful. What Westrow had said was more or less what Helga had said the day before, though with a bit more explanation. And Westrow obviously didn't have a clue, any more than Helga did, about how much thought and planning went into the Christmas Day broadcast. If Westrow imagined for one moment that Papa could just change things to suit himself then he clearly wasn't very well informed. The Christmas Day speech was worked on for *weeks*. Mr Churchill himself wrote parts of it. And then Mr Padget put it into sentences that Papa could say.

But she tried hard not to convey any of that.

'Oh, good!' she said brightly. 'Well I'm sure Papa will want me back, so I'm sure he'll do what you say.'

Westrow smiled. 'Yes, I think so. With a bit of luck you'll be home soon.'

He paused.

'But, just in case things don't work out.... Just in case your Papa isn't allowed to say what we want him to say.... And we have to be prepared for that, you know, because life doesn't always go according to plan – perhaps I ought to tell you what will happen in that eventuality.'

Elizabeth shuddered. *If Papa wasn't allowed to do what Westrow asked....* But who would stop him? And then of course, she remembered once again how complicated everything was. She remembered how many people were involved in preparing that Christmas Day speech. How much Papa *hated* it, and because he hated it, how much she too loathed and feared it, now more than ever. And she remembered how hard she and every other member of the family had to work to *disguise* how they felt, to keep from showing to each other how very afraid they were that poor stuttering Papa would not be able to do it, and how humiliated poor Papa felt every time he *tried* to do it, because he knew he didn't do it very well. Everyone said that even professional broadcasters felt quite terrified when they sat there alone in the front of the microphone, so it wasn't surprising that Papa found it difficult. And now here was this ghastly disgusting fat stupid slobbering man Westrow making life even more intolerable for Papa and it *just wasn't fair.... It just wasn't fair*.

'Would you like me to do that?' repeated Westrow.

'Hmm? Like you to do what?'

'Explain to you, Ma'am – explain what will happen if, for whatever reason, His Majesty the King is unable to co-operate in our peace initiative.'

Elizabeth's head whirled, and she felt dizzy. There were noises in her head – a roaring sound – and Westrow's voice seemed distant and tinny.

She fought hard to concentrate.

'Yes,' she heard herself say. 'Yes, I would be grateful if you would do that.'

Westrow clearly sensed her unease, and it appeared to cause him pain. He would not have upset her for the world, his expression seemed to say. Not if he could have avoided it. He was so sorry.

'Well,' he said, 'we have had to make a plan. A contingency plan, it's called. And the plan is, if your Papa does not make the speech which I have left with him, we shall have to leave the country.'

'Leave the country?'

'Yes.'

'Who will leave?'

'The three of us. You, me, and Helga.'

'Where will we go?'

'To Germany, of course. It won't be for long, because the war cannot continue very long. And I'm afraid England will lose. And then all our people will lose everything. Far more than if we negotiated for peace now.'

'But how will we leave the country?'

'Oh, we will go in a plane. It's a private plane, with a neutral pilot. It's all arranged. That's where I was, yesterday and this morning. Making the final arrangements. There are a lot of people who think as we do. A lot of rich and influential people, all of them determined to bring the war to an end. And that's how the plane has been arranged. Through my friends. Those who want to end the war, as I do.'

'But why do I have to go with you?'

'Oh, so that the RAF will not shoot the plane down, you see. They won't. Not with you on board.'

Chapter 39

Christmas Day in Buckingham Palace was proving to be difficult.

The story that Princess Elizabeth had appendicitis had worked its way round the staff. Given that the Princess was ill, a certain amount of gloom and worry on the face of King George VI was only to be expected. And the staff could certainly see that he was gloomy and worried. Indeed the man had seldom looked so awful. His face was grey, heavily lined, and only occasionally visible through a blue haze of cigarette smoke. Alastair had the distinct impression that if the King could have smoked three cigarettes at once he would have done so.

Also there was the little question of the King's Christmas Day broadcast to be dealt with. Everyone knew what an ordeal His Majesty found that. And so, on every Christmas morning, the cheerfulness of the occasion would always be muted by the prospect of the King having to address a few hundred million people shortly after lunch. Not until that was over would the King, or any of his close family, really be able to relax.

Moreover, in addition to all these very sensible reasons for there being a sense of tension in the air, Alastair could readily detect a growing feeling on the part of many of the staff that something else was wrong. Something big was brewing.

For example, it was known that Mr Padget was sleeping in the Palace. Quite a lot of people knew that. Two nights he'd spent here now. And he hadn't got much sleep on either night. And Commander Mantle, that uniformed man from Scotland Yard, he was in and out all the time, face like a graveyard dog. What was bringing him here?

No doubt rumours were already circulating. Alastair just hoped that they weren't anywhere near the truth. Only a handful of people knew exactly what was going on, and that was too many. Life was quite complicated enough without having anyone else in on the act.

The King came into his study carrying a tray, and behind him were two footmen with more trays, each of them piled high with food.

'It's twelve o'clock,' said the King. And her M... M... Majesty the Queen has instructed us to take a light lunch. To keep our strength up, she says.' He put down the tray on his desk. 'Well, I suppose she's right.'

The Queen's idea of a light lunch for three would have fed a family of four for several days. Wartime restrictions seemed to have had little influence today. There were three kinds of sandwiches (egg, chicken, and spam), sausage rolls, two varieties of fruit cake (one of them iced), apples, lemonade, and coffee.

Alastair and the King had now been rejoined by Commander Mantle, who had spent the morning at the Yard, and for a few minutes they made a half-hearted attempt to eat. Though it turned out that none of them had much appetite.

'Well,' said Mantle, as he drained his coffee cup, 'I'm here until after the speech now. There's a lot of trouble with the phones all over London, but I've set up a special link with the Yard, so communication is good on that front.'

Alastair himself was already pretty well informed about what was happening in the search for Princess Elizabeth – he'd made sure that he was given regular briefings. But he thought it advisable to keep some kind of a conversation going because he didn't want the King to have time to get introspective. So he asked: 'What's the latest state of play on the search of Westrow's London property?'

Mantle wiped his mouth with a napkin. 'Well, we've leaned jolly hard on Westrow's agents in London. There's a firm which looks after all his property holdings for him, and we've got them to give us a complete list. So we're working our way through it. Every house should have been visited by the end of today, though it may run into tomorrow.'

'Tomorrow!' exclaimed the King. 'Tomorrow's no good! I've got to make this sp... sp... speech at three o'clock!'

Mantle said nothing. What could he say? Only that he could not achieve the impossible. He didn't have the manpower, and even if he'd had the manpower there was a time factor. In any case, neither Mantle nor Alastair believed, in their hearts, that Princess Elizabeth was being held in London property which was actually owned by the Earl of Westrow. His lordship was not over-intelligent, but he wasn't as dim as all that. No, the London search was just a formality.

The King was getting twitchy again. Alastair could see it at a glance.

'What's the time?' said the King, though he knew perfectly well because he was peering at his watch every three minutes. 'Twelve o'clock.... Hmm.'

Alastair decided to reinforce the points which he had been making to the King, directly and indirectly, all morning.

'While you were at the Yard,' he said to Mantle, 'the King and I were looking at the options. Thinking over what he might do. We've agreed that the King has three options. One is to make no speech at all. And that, we've agreed, is out of the question. The whole country, indeed the whole Empire, is expecting a broadcast to be made, and therefore it must be made. To do otherwise would cause undesirable speculation. To make no speech at all wouldn't even help in terms of securing the safe return of the Princess, because it would just antagonise Westrow.'

'Agreed,' said Mantle, who was taking his lead from Alastair.

'Second, the King could, in theory, make the speech which Westrow has drafted for him. That would, again in theory, secure the safe release of the Princess. But it would cause untold havoc in political and military circles. The King has agreed – indeed he agreed yesterday – that he will not make that speech come what may.'

Alastair looked directly at the King when he said this, but the King refused to meet his eyes. Alastair just wished that the King would hand over the text of the Westrow speech – or better still take it out of his pocket and tear it up. But no. The King clung to those few sheets of paper like a child hanging on to his teddy bear. So long as that speech remained in his pocket, the King was able to convince himself that his beloved daughter would be returned to him safe and sound. And for that reason alone it was probably best to allow him to hang on to it.

'The third option,' Alastair continued, 'and the one which we will put into effect, is that the King will make the speech which has been prepared here in the Palace. The one we have worked on for some weeks past, which has been approved by Mr Churchill, and which says all the right things. In particular, it tries to encourage the people to prepare themselves for a long war. A war which will be costly, but which is very much worth winning. That,' said Alastair, looking directly at the King again, 'that is the speech which the King will make.'

The King lit another cigarette.

A long silence followed, and Alastair began to sweat. He knew, though Mantle didn't, that this year the King's speech referred to Christmas Day as 'above all, Children's Day.' In view of the large number of children who had been evacuated from the cities, for their own safety, and were now living with strangers, the King was expected to say: 'I am sure that we shall all do our best to make the day a happy one for our children, wherever they may be.' Alastair had some difficulty in imagining that the King was going to cope with that particular sentence.

Eventually the King spoke. 'What is the police view,' he said slowly, 'as to what will happen to my d... d... daughter, if I make the proper speech? That is to say, if I ignore the speech Westrow has written for me. Do you think Westrow will carry out his threat to kill her?'

'No, Sir, I do not,' said Mantle.

You think he's bluffing?'

'Certainly. If you fail to do as he demands, Westrow has no motive to harm the Princess. What's the point? The opportunity will have passed. You won't be making another broadcast for twelve months.'

'No, thank God,' muttered the King. 'So that is your considered opinion, is it? As a professional? If I ignore Westrow, make the speech which Alastair wants me to make, the Princess will be safe?'

'That's correct,' said Mantle. 'That is my professional advice.'

Alastair was delighted. This was precisely what he wanted

Mantle to say.

'What is more,' Mantle continued, 'I am confident that we will find the Princess very soon. After all, we still have nearly three hours before your broadcast begins. And even if we don't find her by then, I think you'll find that pretty soon afterwards the Princess will be dropped off at a railway station somewhere and told to find her way home.'

The King smiled ruefully. 'Yes....' he said. 'That is what I would expect you to say. You put it very well. And as you say, there are still three hours to go before I have to make my speech. But you see, I find myself in a quandary. If I do what Westrow suggests, I deliver my country into the hands of the Fascists. If I don't do what he suggests, I lose my daughter.'

The King looked up and stared frankly at his two advisers.

'The plain fact is, I'm afraid I can't share your optimism, Mantle. I really can't. I fear very much that unless I do as Westrow asks, I am condemning my daughter to death.'

Chapter 40

In those days, traffic was not heavy in rural Wiltshire – and it was especially light on Christmas Day, in wartime. As a result Jane was able to travel fast as she drove from Blesserby to the village of Hattley, on the edge of Salisbury Plain.

Jane enjoyed driving the big Humber, and she hammered the car hard on the winding roads. As she drove, she went over in her mind the events of the past few days.

It was always possible, of course, that now, at this very moment, she and Seymour were wasting their time. Perhaps Princess Elizabeth had already been found and was safe back home at the Palace. If so, the King would be happy and confident. He would be feeling well able to handle his broadcast to the waiting millions at three o'clock. But Jane doubted it somehow. She didn't believe it in her bones, and she didn't envy her father the task of motivating the King to speak to the world when all the time the Princess was being held prisoner.

A rare signpost indicated that Hattley was one mile away. 'What's the time Seymour?' she asked, not wanting to look at her own watch. In places there was still frost at the edge of the road, and she was cutting the corners as close as possible.

'Twelve-thirty,' said Seymour.

'Twelve-thirty,' repeated Jane thoughtfully. 'Church just about finished, everyone at home thinking about the turkey. If they could find one, which of course this year they couldn't. So it'll be chicken if they're lucky – and a boiled egg if they're not.'

A minute later the Humber entered the small village of Hattley. Not more than a few dozen houses and a church. There was no one about. But there, on the far side of the village green, Jane suddenly spotted a sign which said 'Police House'. This, she guessed, indicated the home of the local bobby.

'Here we are, Seymour. Just what we need. Official assistance.'

Jane parked the car outside the small detached house, which looked as if had been built about ten years earlier, and walked up the short path. On the muddy front lawn was a child's football, and inside she could see a light. There was evidently someone at home.

Jane's ring on the doorbell was answered by the village policeman himself. He was on the short side for a police officer, and broad with it. He was wearing his uniform trousers but no jacket. His braces were bright red.

'Yes, Miss?' he said in a friendly enough tone. 'And what can I do for you?'

Jane took a deep breath. She had decided to tell as few lies as possible. She took out her Buckingham Palace pass again, and handed it over.

'My name is Jane Padget. My father is Sir Alastair Padget, Legal Secretary to the King.'

Now that wasn't *strictly* true. Alastair Padget wasn't a knight, but he had turned a knighthood down, and Jane felt that somehow or other she had to get this man's attention and co-operation. She thought a title might help.

The Constable took the proffered pass and began to examine it.

'And your name is?' asked Jane. She didn't want him spending too much time reading the small print.

The Constable glanced up. 'Brown, Miss.'

'Well, Constable Brown, this is Mr Jensen from the American Embassy in London. The fact is, we're out here on official business, and I need to get in touch with London as quickly as possible. May we use your phone please? I take it you've got one?'

'Yes,' said Constable Brown slowly. He continued to look at the Buckingham Palace pass. 'Yes, we've got a phone all right. They put it in last year. Wouldn't have bothered for me, I don't think, but my missus is the district nurse, you see. Sometimes needed in emergencies.'

Two small children, aged about six or seven, had appeared behind Constable Brown's legs, and they now peeped cheekily out, anxious to know what was going on. The smell of cooking also drifted out of the front door.

'Well perhaps,' said Jane, 'perhaps you would be kind enough to allow Mr Jensen to phone London? I'm afraid it's rather urgent.'

Constable Brown frowned. He clearly found all this rather irregular, and who could blame him? He was just looking forward to sitting down to a nice Christmas dinner with his family, and bang – Sod's Law strikes again. But he was quite familiar with that legal principle by now. He handed back the pass, evidently having concluded that Jane was indeed someone official. She was confident, articulate, well educated, personable, and connected to Buckingham Palace. It was highly unlikely that such a person would be chasing about in the middle of Christmas Day without a good reason. Failure to co-operate might prove fatal to his career.

Brown stood to one side. 'Yes, Miss,' he said cheerfully, 'you may certainly use my phone. Come you in.'

Jane put Seymour to work, trying to phone the Palace, while she asked to speak to Constable Brown in private. The two small children were shooed away into the kitchen, where their aproned mother was briefly visible. Brown took Jane into a tiny front room.

This was clearly the room reserved for special occasions, when visitors were present, and obviously no visitors were expected today because the fire laid in the grate was unlit.

'We've just driven over here from Blesserby,' said Jane. 'Were you aware that Blesserby Manor was searched by the police yesterday?'

'Yes, Miss, I was as a matter of fact. It's a good step away from here, and I didn't go myself, but a lot of the force from round here was called in special. They had a lot of men over there. Fair took the place apart, I understand.'

'Yes, that's correct. So you know that the police are very anxious to interview the Earl of Westrow.'

Brown's face gave nothing away, other than the fact that he was a man who spent much of his life outdoors: his complexion was ruddy and shiny. 'Yes, Miss, I knows that.'

'And you know that he has not been located yet?'

'I've been told to keep my eyes open, Miss. To tell you the

truth, I don't remember seeing the Earl in the flesh, but I've been issued with a photograph. I've been told to arrest him on sight. Apparently there's a woman with him too – name of Schmidt. Claims to be Swiss, but there's doubts about that. Rumour is she's a German spy. She's to be arrested too, if seen.'

Jane nodded. 'Good. Well now, Mr Jensen and I have discovered that the Earl has rented a cottage near here. He rented it under an assumed name, ten days ago, and we believe he may be hiding there.'

'With the woman?'

'Possibly. Mr Jensen and I want you to guide us to the cottage, and help us to check it out.'

Brown became thoughtful. 'Hmm. You mean search the place?'

'If necessary.'

'Hmm. I don't know as how I could permit that. Unless of course you've got a warrant?'

Jane didn't want to get into all that. If Brown started questioning her authority, wanting to know who she was and who gave her permission for this and who assented to that, they would be there all day.

'Look,' she said, 'no offence, Constable, but I'm not asking your permission or seeking your advice. I'm simply telling you that Mr Jensen and I are going to go to this cottage, and under the terms of section four, paragraph twelve of the Defence of the Realm Act we're going to go in and search it if necessary. All we want you to do is help us to find the place with the minimum of fuss.'

Jane was gambling that the Constable's familiarity with the various sub-sections of recent acts of Parliament was even vaguer than her own. And one look at his face told her that she was right.

It wasn't that Brown believed her exactly. In fact he probably didn't believe her – he looked downright sceptical. But he was prepared to assist her on the basis of his assessment of her character – not because he was convinced by her legal references.

'Fair enough, Miss,' he said.

At that point Seymour came back into the room. He shook his

head. 'Phones are hopeless,' he said. 'No chance of getting connected to London until – and I quote – towards the end of the afternoon.'

'Right,' said Jane. 'Constable, are you coming, or are you just going to give us directions?'

Constable Brown was not a man to be hurried. 'Now, now, Miss. I didn't say as how I wasn't coming. What did you say the name of this cottage is?'

'Plain View Cottage,' said Jane. 'Off the Devizes road, apparently.'

'Ah yes, I knows it. You've got a car, I see.'

'Of course.'

The Constable sighed. All thought of that nice hot Christmas dinner was fading rapidly into the distance. 'Well, if you'll just hold on a minute,' he said, 'I'll get my coat and hat.'

Chapter 41

Nothing in life is simple. Alastair had always known that, but today he was having it proved to him. The hard way.

Lunch was over. Very little had been eaten, because none of the three men had any appetite for it. The King had tried an egg sandwich and a glass of lemonade. Commander Mantle had demolished three sausage rolls and several cups of coffee – he was a big man, after all. And Alastair had done his patriotic best to consume some spam.

Now here they all were, sitting in the office which adjoined both the King's study on one side and Alastair's office on the other. All three men were concerned, consciously or unconsciously, with one simple issue: how to fill up the two hours and twenty minutes before the King was due to give his speech.

Conversation had dried up.

The King excused himself and left the room. Alastair hoped that his monarch would have the good sense to go outside and get some fresh air, but he didn't like to suggest it. Later, perhaps even during the broadcast, he might have to tell the King precisely what to do, and he wanted to interfere in the King's conduct as little as possible until then.

After the King had gone, Alastair turned to Mantle. 'Look,' he said, 'I've got a bit of a problem.'

Mantle smiled grimly. 'Only one?'

Alastair grinned back, though he didn't feel at all light-hearted. 'This BBC producer I told you about....'

'The one you knew at Cambridge?'

'Yes. I've been worried for some time about what we should do if the King suddenly takes it into his head to use Westrow's speech instead of the approved one. And, for that matter, what we should do if he starts to improvise some variant on it. So I had a word with the producer a bit earlier on. I didn't tell him anything specific – I certainly didn't mention the existence of an alternative script. But I did say that at some point, if the King appeared to be making a hopeless botch of the job, I might have to give the producer a signal. He would then have to pretend there was a technical hitch. What we would do, I said, was allow the King to go on speaking, but at a signal from me I would expect the technicians to cut off the broadcast.'

Mantle grunted sceptically. 'Huh! And what did your friend say to that?'

'Well, he seemed puzzled, and surprised, but at first it was, Of course, old boy, whatever you say. I'll take my lead from you. That sort of thing. As a matter of act, the BBC already has a drill worked out in case there's a real technical hitch. An announcer at Broadcasting House will come on and say how sorry the BBC is that contact with the Palace has been lost, and then suitable music will be played. But now, you won't be surprised to hear, my producer friend is having second thoughts.'

Mantle laughed out loud. 'No, I'm not in the least surprised! All of a sudden he's realised that a technical hitch in the middle of the most important broadcast of the year might do his career no good. Interview with the Director-General, up before the Board of Governors.'

'Precisely.'

'I know just how he feels!' said Mantle, as cheerfully as he could manage. 'That will be my fate too unless we find the Princess soon – career in ruins.'

This was undoubtedly true, but Alastair didn't want to make matters worse by agreeing. Instead he said: 'Well, right now the producer is wandering around puffing his pipe worse than the King, jangling the coins in his pocket and asking to speak to me urgently. I don't want to tell him even half the truth. What do you suggest I say?'

Mantle rose to his feet, and his enormous bulk seemed to fill a large part of the room. 'What you will tell him, Alastair – not now, but five minutes before we start – is that you and I are not pissing about. You will tell him that the King is under enormous pressure to make a speech which differs from that approved by the government. A speech which will lead to the surrender of this country to the Germans. You will tell your friend that you and I have no intention of allowing that to happen.'

Mantle began to pace about, hands behind his back, his huge feet thumping down on the carpet.

'I've had a very close look at the King's study, where this broadcast is going to be made. When the broadcast starts, there'll be four people in there. The King, the producer, and two technicians.'

Mantle bent down and seized his large leather briefcase. He opened it and held it out for Alastair's inspection.

'You see that?'

'Um, yes,' said Alastair, his eyes widening.

'I drew that out of the armoury this morning,' Mantle continued. 'My main job is to find Princess Elizabeth, not to control what happens in relation to the King's speech. That's your area. But I am not prepared to put up with any nonsense from anyone, and that includes the King. The King is a human being, and he has his limits, like you and me. If he cracks under the pressure, and tries to use the Westrow speech, then I personally am going to go in there and impose my will on the proceedings.'

'Well, for what it's worth, I'll back you,' said Alastair.

'I hope it will amount to no more than ripping the wires out by hand,' said Mantle. 'But if necessary I will heave the King out of his seat and dump him outside his office. The office has a good strong lock on both doors, and I've got the keys. If necessary I will lock the King out, and you and me in. And then you will make the King's speech for him.'

'Me?' gulped Alastair.

'Yes, you! You can read, can't you? And it will come as no great shock to anyone if we announce that unfortunately his Majesty the King is not able to speak in person, and that his speech will be read for him. They will just think he's been overcome by nerves. Everybody knows it's a struggle for him.'

'I see,' said Alastair. 'And what about the revolver?'

'That's a last resort,' said Mantle. 'But if I have to persuade the BBC men to co-operate by pointing a gun at their heads, then that's what I'll do.'

Alastair closed his eyes. He tried to remind himself that, at this very moment, members of the armed services were risking their lives, all over Europe. The problems he had to deal with were minor compared with theirs.

'Very well,' he said. 'You and I must keep a clear head. But we will do whatever is necessary. We will see that the prepared speech is made, whatever happens and whoever makes it.'

Mantle sat down again.

'By the way,' said Alastair. 'Do you really believe what you said about Princess Elizabeth?'

'What did I say?'

'That Westrow will release the Princess unharmed, even if the King refuses to make the speech that Westrow wants.'

Mantle grunted again. 'Huh! No, I don't really believe that. If the speech isn't made, then we're in serious trouble. I'm having the ports watched, of course, but it's my belief they could be gone already.'

'Gone?' echoed Alastair. 'Gone where?'

Mantle looked at him in astonishment. 'Why, to Germany, of course. Where else?'

Alastair suddenly felt sick. 'Oh,' he said faintly. 'I'm afraid I hadn't thought of that.'

Further speculation was cut short by the return of the King.

Wherever the King had been, it didn't seem to have done him much good. His face was anguished, and he sat down heavily.

'Alastair,' he said. 'I've b... b... been thinking. Is there any way we might c... c... compromise? Go some way towards satisfying the Earl. I mean, we m... m... might sort of rewrite the official speech so that it goes some *way* towards what this man Westrow wants. Do you think that's possible?'

'No, Sir,' said Alastair firmly. 'No, it is quite impossible. Allow me to enumerate the reasons.'

Chapter 42

Extract from Jane Padget's report to the King, dated 3 January 1941:

```
Afterwards, of course, it was easy to see how we
might have done things better.
```

'What's the time now?'

'Quarter to one,' said Seymour from the back seat.

'Oh hell.' Time was running out.

'There's a deadline, is there, Miss?' asked Constable Brown.

'Yes, there is.' Jane pushed her father's blue Humber a little faster round the bends.

'By the way, Constable,' she said. 'I told you that we want to search this house.'

'Plain View Cottage.'

'That's the one.'

'It's about another two miles,' said Brown. 'Two minutes, speed you're going. Assuming we meet nothing coming the other way.'

'Yes, right. Well,' said Jane, 'I don't think I told you why we need to search it.'

'Looking for the Earl, aren't we? Him and his lady friend.'

'Yes, we are. But we're also looking for someone else. A girl, aged fourteen.'

'Ah.'

'She's believed to have been kidnapped.'

'Ah, I see.'

'Your superiors didn't tell you about that?'

'No, Miss. Just said to arrest and hold the Earl, if we sees him.'

Jane changed down into third and accelerated hard; the note of engine rose alarmingly.

'What we'll do, Constable, is this. When we get to this house, you and I will go to the door. If the Earl appears, we'll arrest him. And likewise the woman.'

Constable Brown thought about it.

'I see. And are they likely to come quietly, Miss? I mean, if kidnapping's involved....'

Jane didn't answer.

'Slow down,' said Brown. 'Two turns of the road ahead.... Now, pull in here.'

Jane did as she was told, parking in a small bay at the side of the road. A tall hedge was to their left.

'The cottage is over there,' said Brown, pointing. 'You can see the chimney from here. Smoking too, so someone's living there.'

Jane rubbed her eyes. 'Yes, you're quite right, Constable. I should have thought of that. The truth is, these people are probably armed and dangerous.'

Constable Brown blinked. 'Don't get many firearms round here, Miss. Only shotguns.'

'Yes, well, I'm just saying,' said Jane, 'that we need to be careful. In an ideal world, we would surround this cottage with twenty men and tell anyone in there to come out with their hands up. We can't do that, I'm afraid. We haven't time. But, for what it's worth, I've got a gun.'

She reached into her handbag and produced a small pistol. 'It's only a two-two, I'm afraid. It's not a man-stopper.'

There was a shocked silence from both the men.

Then Seymour said: 'You didn't tell me about that!'

'Shut up, Seymour.' In the mirror, Jane could see that his face was quite pale.

'Well,' said Constable Brown, speaking even more slowly than usual. 'You looks as if you knows how to use that, Miss. Which is more than I do. So you'd better hold on to it. Let's you and me go and see if anyone's in there first. Then we'll see where we go from there.'

He began to get out of the car, and Jane swung the driver's door open.

'What do you want me to do?' asked Seymour.

'Stay here,' said Jane. 'Mind the car. Keep hold of the keys.'

Chapter 43

Princess Elizabeth was sitting in the living-room of Plain View Cottage, reading one of the magazines which the Earl had thoughtfully brought with him. He had evidently seized a pile on his way out of wherever he had been to before coming here. By a happy chance, many of these magazines were of the entirely unsuitable variety which the fearsome Crawfie never allowed her charges to read. So Elizabeth was sitting there glued to the page. There were, it seemed, certain advantages to being kidnapped after all.

However, Elizabeth was not so engrossed in her reading that she failed to notice movement out of the corner of her eye. She looked up and saw – yes, she really *did* see them, it wasn't her imagination – she saw a policeman and someone beside him walking up the path to the front door. She couldn't quite see who the other person was, because the window was covered with lace curtain, and the angle of view was wrong.

Elizabeth instantly pretended not to have noticed anything. Fortunately the Earl of Westrow, who was reading *Country Life*, had his back to the window. But it was a *policeman*!

Elizabeth could hear that roaring noise in her ears again.

There was a loud rat-a-tat on the door-knocker.

Westrow leapt up as if someone had stuck a pin in him. 'What's that?' He almost ran out into the hall, where he met Helga coming from the kitchen. 'Who is it?' he hissed.

Neither Westrow nor Helga could see who had knocked because the door was solid, with no glass in it.

Elizabeth stood behind the Earl. Her hands had started to shake.

'You go into the kitchen,' said Helga fiercely. She was very much in command. 'And take the girl with you.'

Westrow turned, put his arm round Elizabeth, and ushered her into the kitchen. When she got there, Elizabeth put herself in a position where she could just see what was happening in the hall.

Helga's large leather handbag was hanging on a peg near the door. She reached into it, pulled out a pistol, did something to it which made a sharp click, and held it behind her back in her right hand.

Then she moved to open the front door with her left hand.

At the last moment, Westrow realised that Elizabeth was looking down the hall, and that she would be visible from the front door when it opened. He pulled her roughly to one side.

Westrow himself watched what was happening by holding the kitchen door open an inch.

The English, of course, do not shoot first and ask questions afterwards. That is not their way. But Helga Schmidt/Kronberg was not English. She was not even Swiss. She was German, and she had been trained by the SS.

All of this Jane realised only when it was far too late. And she blamed herself bitterly for her hopeless, foolish naïvety.

The door was pulled open and Constable Brown said politely, 'Good afternoon, Miss. Are you Helga Schmidt?'

And he had no sooner said these words than Helga brought her right hand out from behind her back and fired once, shooting him in the chest.

Brown was knocked backwards about five feet and fell sprawled on the ground.

Jane, driven by pure reflex, hurled herself sideways, away from the door, seeking shelter under the window.

The front door slammed shut.

Loud shouting could be heard from inside the cottage.

Elizabeth heard the shot, and she knew what it was. She was used to the sound of guns – shotguns, mostly. She had used one herself. And besides, she had seen Helga take the pistol out of her bag, so it was perfectly obvious what had happened.

And Elizabeth did not hang about. In the first few seconds after being pulled back into the kitchen, she had made up her mind what to do, and now she did it.

She kicked Westrow hard on the shins and broke free of his grip. She pulled open the kitchen door before Helga had even slammed the front door, and raced up the stairs.

That nasty cold dark little room in which she had been locked for so many hours had one feature which was both a drawback and an advantage: it had a key. And Elizabeth knew where the key was: it was hanging on a peg, outside the door.

Elizabeth tore up the bare wooden staircase, leaving the shouting and the uproar behind her. She grabbed the key, went into the room, banged the door shut, and locked it. On the inside.

There was noise and shouting below. Westrow apparently tried to chase after her. She heard him clumping up the stairs with his big flat feet. Then he seemed to change his mind and go back down.

Helga was screaming at him: 'Get out the back, get out the back!'

And he was bawling: 'But what about the Princess? She's gone upstairs!'

'Fuck the Princess, get to the car!'

Dear me, thought Elizabeth fleetingly. What language! Nearly as bad as Papa when he lost his temper.

Jane lay sprawled on her side, under the window of the cottage. She swore in the most violent, obscene language she had ever used in her life as she struggled to get the small pistol out of her handbag. Then, when at last it was ready for use, she held it in both hands.

Constable Brown groaned and made an effort to raise himself. He couldn't.

Jane looked around her. No sign of movement anywhere.

Inside the cottage, shouting from both Westrow and Helga. All Jane could make out was 'car' and 'Princess'.

Jane crouched down low. She moved sideways, away from the window, and stood up, her back to the wall of the cottage.

There was a bang, which made her jump. But it wasn't a gunshot. It was – what? The back door slamming?

Then there was the sound of car doors closing – two slams –

and a car engine started up at the rear of the cottage. They would be coming round to the front and going down the drive! Jane held herself ready, pistol in both hands.

Next, with a speed and a roar which took her entirely by surprise, a small grey car shot past her, skidded on the gravel drive, straightened, and was powered recklessly towards the road. Two people in the front, Man and woman. Westrow and Helga.

Jane braced herself and fired two quick shots into the back of the disappearing car.

A pistol was brandished from the front passenger-side window, and a shot was fired back. But it was wild. A gesture rather than an aimed shot.

Then the car was gone. It turned left at the end of the drive, and was driven away fast, hidden by the high hedge.

Jane stamped her foot. *Goddamn bloody fucking SHIT!*

And then she began to have the most awful, terrible doubts. Why in God's name had she shot at the back of the *car*? The Princess might have been in there! Tied up in the boot perhaps, or lying flat on the back seat! Supposing she'd shot *her*?

'Oh God,' Jane groaned aloud. Everything that possibly could have gone wrong had gone wrong. She felt sick.

Constable Brown waved an arm, which had the merciful effect of taking Jane's mind off her own problems. She went over to his side and knelt down.

Brown's eyes were closed, and the front of his uniform was already dark with blood. But he was breathing.

'Can you hear me?' Jane asked.

Brown nodded, with difficulty, and winced at the pain.

Seymour came running up. 'What on earth's happened?' he gasped.

'I'm afraid poor Constable Brown has been shot,' said Jane. 'It's all my fault. And Westrow and Helga have got away.'

She stood up.

'Look after him for a minute. I have to go inside the house.'

Seymour bent down to attend to the Constable and Jane tried to open the front door. It wouldn't move.

Leaving Seymour to do the best he could, Jane ran round the side of the house, seeking another way in. At the rear she came to the back door, and this one did open when she turned the handle.

Jane went into the kitchen.

Kettle still sitting on the cooker, gas turned on under it. Jane turned it off.

No one in the kitchen.

Holding the pistol ahead of her, finger on the trigger, Jane went out into the hall. Empty.

Living-room, dining-room, empty. Cupboard under the stairs. Nothing.

Upstairs still to search.

Jane went up, slowly, half expecting to get her head blown off by a shotgun. But all was silent. Still.

Bathroom. Cold. Deserted.

Bedroom one – not only empty but unfurnished.

Bedroom two – unmade bed. No one under it.

Bedroom three.

Bedroom three? Door locked.

Jane stood well to one side. If there was anyone in there she didn't want to get shot through the door. She tried the handle again. It wouldn't open. It was definitely locked.

Hmm.

Why would Westrow and Helga have left this room locked? Seemed odd. But just to be on the safe side, she called out: 'This is the police! If there's anyone in there, come out now, with your hands above your head!'

Silence for a moment, and Jane was about to go in search of a key, when she heard a rattle. The door was being unlocked.

The door opened, and Jane pressed herself back against the wall of the landing, pistol in hand, ready....

Princess Elizabeth Alexandra Mary put her head out and looked around.

'Oh, hello, Jane!' she said brightly. 'I didn't expect to see you here.'

Chapter 44

One o'clock at the Palace.

The King's mental agony was palpable. His eyes were half-shut, his forehead deeply lined, his expression grim.

A few minutes earlier he had gone into his study and emerged with a photograph of Princess Elizabeth. Now he held it in front of him and stared at it.

'You know,' said the King thoughtfully, 'Westrow is a fool. He doesn't really know me at all. If he did, he would know that I would be much more likely to co-operate if he sent me some sort of evidence that Elizabeth is still alive. A n... n... note in her handwriting, for example.'

Alastair had had enough. This mawkishness would get them nowhere. 'That's very true, Sir,' he said briskly. 'But, in the circumstances, unhelpful.' He stood up. 'You and I, Sir, are going for a walk.'

The King looked up in astonishment. 'We are?'

'Yes. We are. Get your coat.'

Such was the King's state of mind that he obeyed without question.

Alastair took the King out into the Buckingham Palace garden. Such sunshine as there had been had now disappeared. The sky was a dreary grey, the air cold and biting. But it proved to be just what was needed.

Both men walked quickly to get warm. To Alastair's relief, the King made no attempt to smoke.

They walked in a large circle, roughly following the perimeter wall. And for the most part they walked in silence.

Eventually the King said: 'Did I ever tell you the story about the tommy-gun?'

'No Sir.' Not quite true, because the tommy-gun story had been told and retold, but Alastair was not going to interfere with the King's train of thought at this stage.

'I was up at Sandringham one day, in the early summer, and Winston came to see me. It was soon after he became PM. I've got a small rifle range up there you know – in the woods. Anyway, there I was, popping away with a handgun. And Winston heaves up and says, I didn't know you were interested in pistol shooting? I'm not, I said. But if the Germans invade, the idea is that every able-bodied Englishman should kill one of them, and I'm getting ready to do my bit. Oh, says Winston. I'm very pleased to hear what you say. And if that's your attitude, I'll send you a tommy-gun – then you can kill lots of Germans!'

The King chuckled and Alastair laughed with him, out of relief as much as anything.

'And did he send you a tommy-gun?'

'Oh yes. And I use it too. Bit of a handful, mind. And very inaccurate. You press the trigger and fifty bullets go all over the bloody place. Shot three keepers and a fox the other day.'

Alastair could not have been more pleased. The King seemed to be in complete control of himself again. And the stutter had disappeared entirely – for the moment.

'Anyway,' continued the King. He came to a halt and looked about him, as if assessing the size of his kingdom. 'Point is this. If that bloody man Westrow harms my daughter, by God I will kill him myself.'

Chapter 45

Jane took Princess Elizabeth downstairs. Once there, Jane opened the front door of Plain View Cottage and looked out.

Seymour had heaved Constable Brown into a sitting position, so that his back was against the wall of the house. He had opened the policeman's tunic, which helped the man to breathe more easily but also demonstrated that Brown was bleeding copiously from his chest wound.

'Oh dear,' said Jane faintly. 'Oh dear, the poor man.'

The Constable opened one eye. 'Sorry, Miss,' he said. 'It all happened so quick.'

'Not your fault,' sighed Jane.

Well, this would not do. It was no good standing around apologising for past mistakes. Jane took a deep breath.

'I'll go and get the car,' she said. 'We'll take you to hospital.'

The nearest hospital, it emerged, was ten miles away. Constable Brown said that if it was all the same to Jane he would sooner be taken home to his missus, she being a district nurse; and, he added, there was a doctor in the village who was likely to be available. So they made the policeman as comfortable as possible in the rear seat of the Humber and headed back towards Hattley.

Five minutes later Jane brought the car to a halt outside the police house. Not surprisingly, Mrs Brown was hovering at the window, wondering where on earth her husband was when he should have been enjoying his Christmas dinner, and she immediately came bustling out.

For a moment, inevitably, she was horrified by what she saw. Both hands went to her face, and when she took them away her normally rosy cheeks had gone chalk white. But her professionalism soon took over. Wiping her eyes with the backs of her hands, she didn't waste any time by asking what had happened. She just said: 'Right, let's have him out of there and into the house.'

The fact that a wide-eyed Princess Elizabeth was sitting in the front seat of the Humber escaped Mrs Brown's notice – even when Elizabeth leapt out and did her best to help move the Constable into his home.

They sat the wounded man in an easy chair. His two children hovered nearby, their eyes round and their mouths open but silent.

Mrs Brown made sure that her husband was comfortable and then straightened up. 'Now then, you two,' she said, addressing the children. 'Sarah, you get the kettle on. Wilfred, you run down to Dr Mackenzie's and tell him your Dad's been shot in the chest and would he kindly come if he can.' Then she began to unbutton her husband's shirt.

Jane watched for a moment and then looked at the old-fashioned clock on the mantelpiece: it showed one o'clock.

'Look,' she said. 'I'm really sorry, Mrs Brown, but I've got a young lady with me, and I've got to get her back to London. It's an emergency. The fact is, you see, she was kidnapped, and her parents are really worried about her. Are you going to be all right if I leave now?'

Mrs Brown didn't even look up. 'We'll be well enough,' she said. Her daughter had returned from the kitchen, and stood waiting. 'Sarah, go next door and ask Mrs Watson if she could come and give me a hand, would you?'

Jane took this as a dismissal, which was welcome, but.... 'I'm afraid there is one other thing,' she said.

Mrs Brown brushed her hair out of her eyes. She was frowning, and looked as if she would be glad to see the back of Jane. 'Well?'

Jane groped in her handbag, found a pencil and a scrap of paper, and scribbled her father's telephone number on it. 'As soon as you can, please get someone to ring this number. Ask for Mr Padget, and if he's not available leave a message. Tell them, Jane Padget says Elizabeth is safe.'

Mrs Brown took the piece of paper. 'Jane Padget says, Elizabeth is safe.'

'Yes, that's right.'

'Well I'll do my best, Miss.'

'Thanks.' Jane turned to go.

'Oh, and Miss....'

'Yes?'

'I'm sorry if I sound a bit short. It's just the shock, that's all.'

Jane went out to the car. Elizabeth was now in the back seat, looking anxiously towards the house. Seymour stood pale-faced, waiting by the front passenger door. He had the road-map in his hand.

Coming along the road were young Wilfred and a middle-aged gentleman carrying a Gladstone bag.

Jane hoped that they had done everything they could. But in any case, they had to go.

Jane began to drive fast again. She put her foot down flat whenever possible and generally treated the dignified Humber with a marked lack of respect. The engine whined abjectly at this unaccustomed abuse.

After about five minutes of being rocked from side to side as they hurtled round tight country bends, Seymour lodged an objection. 'Look,' he shouted above the noise of the engine, 'it's not just you and me in the car now, you know. We've got Princess Elizabeth in the back seat. And her life is surely worth preserving, even if ours aren't.'

Jane bawled back at him. 'There won't be any traffic coming the other way, you stupid ignorant colonial! No one's got any petrol, and anyway it's Christmas Day. They're all either eating or sleeping it off!'

Elizabeth leaned forward and tapped Seymour on the shoulder. 'Jane's quite right, Mr Jensen. And at least you've got me away from that horrible cottage. Do try to look on the bright side.'

Seymour groaned. He took a final glance at the speedometer, noted that it was reading seventy on a high-hedged, narrow, winding lane, and decided to concentrate on the map instead.

Jane told Seymour to guide them towards the main London

road, the A4. After about ten minutes they found it, though more by luck, she felt, than good navigation.

Once on the main road, Jane began to push the Humber towards its top speed along the wide, empty highway.

Miles and miles went by. They were still a long, long way from London, but fortunately the road was almost clear.

Jane overtook a solitary lorry. 'Time?' she enquired.

'Quarter to two.'

Pause while Jane did a mental calculation. Then: 'We might just about make it.' She addressed Princess Elizabeth over her shoulder, without taking her eyes off the road. She raised her voice to overcome the noise of the engine. 'I want to get you back to the Palace before your father has to make his speech, at three o'clock.'

'I know,' said Elizabeth. 'Westrow explained it all to me. But Papa won't do it, you know. He won't make the speech that Westrow wanted.'

'I'm sure he won't,' said Jane. Though privately she was sure of no such thing. 'And I asked the policeman's wife to phone and tell the Palace that you're safe. But she may find it hard to get through – and I want to get you back there anyway, to put His Majesty in the right frame of mind.'

Elizabeth looked at her own watch. 'Do you think we'll be in time?'

'We'll try.'

Back at the police house, Constable Brown was only semi-conscious and Dr Mackenzie was watching his breathing carefully. Mrs Brown was on the phone, wanting to know where that ambulance was.

'Must make that phone call,' the Constable murmured. 'Tell them Elizabeth is safe.'

'Don't you worry about phone calls, old son,' said the Doctor. 'Plenty of time for that.'

When the ambulance did arrive, and Constable Brown was loaded into it, Mrs Brown went with him.

Halfway to the hospital, Mrs Brown noticed that her husband wanted to say something. She bent closer to hear. 'Yes, dear?'

'Don't forget to phone.'

'Oh – no, dear. Don't you worry. I've got that piece of paper. Somewhere.'

Only when her husband had been wheeled into the operating theatre did Mrs Brown even think about using the telephone, and then because she wanted to ring home and tell her children that Daddy was being well looked after. That done, she searched for the scrap of paper that Jane had given her, eventually found it, and tried conscientiously to get the trunk-call operator to connect her.

'I'm sorry, madam. There's still a one-hour delay on calls to London.'

'Oh,' said Mrs Brown. 'Oh well, thank you. I'll try again later.'

The BBC producer was puffing smoke at an even faster rate than the King, though in the producer's case the smoke came from a pipe.

'How is His Majesty?' the producer asked Alastair.

'Much better for a spot of fresh air,' said Alastair, thinking that the producer himself could do with a large whisky to calm him down. 'How about your side? Any technical problems?'

'No, no, all ready to go.' The producer jangled the loose change in his trouser pocket. 'Amazing thing, really.' Puff, puff. 'The King speaks here in the Palace, and is heard all over the world. Australia, Canada, West Indies, South Africa. Impossible fifty years ago.'

'Yes indeed.'

The producer glanced at his watch. 'Um, still an hour to go, but do you think the King would be willing to do a few tests? We want to get his voice level right.'

'Fair enough,' said Alastair.

Tactfully, they asked the King if he would mind taking his seat in front of the microphone. They suggested that he might read aloud from a newspaper or a magazine, just to test the equipment.

The King took his time finding something suitable to read, while everyone waited.

'When you're ready, Sir.'

The King was not ready. He shuffled his papers. Cleared his throat. Had a drink of water. Then he picked up the preferred text – a passage from *Country Life* – and opened his mouth.

Nothing came out.

Not a sound. Not even a croak.

The blood left the BBC producer's face like water draining out of a hand-basin. A basin with a large plug-hole.

Alastair went to the King's side. 'I think I've got a few throat pastilles in my room,' he said. 'I find them quite useful when I do any public speaking myself. If you'd like to come through, Sir, I'll find them.'

The A4 was being dug up. Not at that very moment, of course. But it was in the process of being dug up, both before and after Christmas. Today, it being Christmas Day, there were no workmen present. But there were temporary traffic lights. And the traffic lights were red.

Jane fumed. If she could have seen the other end of the road-works, and if there were no other vehicles visible, she would have blasted on through, regardless of the red light. But there was only room for one lane of traffic, and if there was even one car coming the other way and they met it head on there would be even further delay. So she was obliged to wait. And fume.

She looked at her watch. Two-thirty.

At last the light changed to green.

And as it did so, a solitary figure pushing a bicycle stepped into her path. Judging by his dog-collar, it was the local Vicar, on his way to minister to some lonely parishioner.

Jane blasted on the horn to get him out of her way.

The only effect this had was to cause the Vicar to come to a standstill. He frowned at Jane through his horn-rimmed spectacles. Even without any great skill in lip-reading it was clear that he was urging patience upon the driver.

Jane wound the window down and put her head out. 'Get out

of the fucking way, you stupid bloody moron!' And she gave him another blast on the horn.

Well, whether it was the language, or the sudden realisation on the Vicar's part that both he and his precious bicycle were about to be severely mangled, no one will ever know. But whatever the case, the Vicar showed a remarkable nimbleness in a middle-aged man and shifted himself smartly to one side.

Jane drove on.

Seymour was appalled, and he could not resist a swift glance backwards to see what effect this incident had had on the heir to the throne. He found that the Princess was grinning broadly.

In response to Seymour's enquiring glance, Elizabeth leaned forward and tapped him on the shoulder. 'Jane swears just like my Papa!' she said. And giggled.

Fortunately the Vicar proved to be the last of their major obstacles, and they made good time on the rest of their journey, even in central London. The combination of Christmas and wartime conditions ensured that traffic was light, and Jane ignored all speed limits.

By the time they reached Hyde Park Corner, Jane thought they were home safe with time to spare. But no – bomb damage had closed a road, and they were forced into a mile-long detour along Piccadilly and down the Haymarket. This made the air blue once more. But finally they reached the east end of the Mall – that long, wide road which runs from Admiralty Arch to Buckingham Palace itself.

'Time?' shouted Jane.

'Five to three,' her passengers chorused.

'I think we might just make it.'

Headlights full on, horn blaring at the least sign of trouble, Jane powered the Humber down the final half-mile of its journey. She touched ninety on the last hundred yards.

She slammed on the brakes, rounded the Queen Victoria Memorial with tyres screaming, flashed past two guardsmen on duty at the open main gate, made a wide turn in the forecourt of the Palace, and came to a violent halt outside the south entrance.

The two guardsmen came racing after these unauthorised entrants, swinging their rifles down from their shoulders as they did so.

Jane, the Princess, and Seymour all leapt out of the car.

'Halt!' bawled one of the guardsmen. 'Stay where you are!'

'I think, Sir,' said Alastair patiently, 'you should now take your seat at the microphone.'

The King looked like a man about to be executed. All that was missing was the Chaplain to give comfort, and over the last half-hour Alastair had done his best in that regard. Now, for better or for worse, the matter was in the King's hands alone.

'Oh,' said the King. V... v... very well.' He shuffled towards his position. So poor was his morale that even his gait was affected.

The King sat down at his desk. He did not look at the microphone, which was a large, box-like object on a formidable stand.

The speech which he was due to make – the *official* speech – was laid out ready for him. The other speech – the one which had been sent to the King by the Earl of Westrow, together with certain demands and threats – that speech was still in his pocket. And to Alastair's dismay, the King now took out that speech also, and laid it down beside the other one.

Three minutes to go.

Alastair sighed. He went and sat himself down in the room outside the King's study. He positioned his chair so that he could clearly see the King, though not the rest of the room.

Commander Mantle drew up a second chair and sat beside Alastair. He had with him his briefcase, which he now opened. Inside it, Alastair could see a gleam on the barrel of the revolver which Mantle had shown him earlier.

'I suppose there's no word of the Princess?' asked Alastair quietly.

'None,' whispered Mantle. 'And how did the voice tests go?'

'Badly.'

'Well, suck a throat pastille, laddie.'

Dear old Mr Redpath was the security man on duty at the south door. He was a widower, lived alone, and would much rather be at the Palace than at home, which was why he'd happily agreed to work on Christmas Day.

Three figures ran past Redpath at a bewildering speed. The poor old boy hardly had time to look up from the letter he was writing to his sister in Newcastle. *Dear Sis, Sorry to be late with your Xmas card....*

'Sorry, Redpath, no time to explain.'

That was Miss Padget, wasn't it? Tearing past at a great rate of knots. And Princess Elizabeth – always running she was, till Crawfie made her stop. And who was that other fellow? Looked a bit familiar, perhaps he was in a couple of days ago, but you couldn't have people running into the Palace just any old how. 'Oy! Have you got a pass?'

Too late. All three were gone.

Their departure was followed almost instantly by the arrival of two guardsmen, puffing and panting and worried sick about what the Sergeant would say when he found out they'd let a car get by without so much as a 'Who goes there?'

They wanted to go chasing after the three intruders, naturally, but Redpath put his foot down.

'Oh no you don't, lads,' he said firmly. 'King's about to make his speech. Not having any uproar while that's on.'

Jane and the Princess, who knew where they were going, belted up the stairs of the south wing, and headed, still running, down the long corridor which led to the King's office. It was a *very* long corridor. People had been known to say that you needed a bicycle to live and work in the Palace.

Seymour, convinced that he would be stopped and thrown out at any moment, panted along self-consciously in the wake of Jane and the Princess. He was certain, just as he had been two days earlier, that he had no right to be here at all.

The corridor was empty and all three of them ran *headlong* towards the far end.

Then a woman in a green cardigan emerged from a stairway

on the left, and stepped back with a squawk just in time to avoid being trampled.

'Oh! Lillibet!' cried the cardigan.

'Later, Crawfie!' called the Princess over her shoulder.

'Much, much later,' she added, *sotto voce.*

They ran.

On the left an office door was open and a radio was switched on. The volume was turned up high. Big Ben, the great bell after which the clock in the Houses of Parliament is named, was beginning to sound the hour.

They reached the outer office which led to the King's study. The door was closed.

The Princess stopped running.

Jane came to a halt.

Seymour stood well back.

Elizabeth turned the handle of the door and went into the room.

Inside the room, Alastair Padget and Commander Mantle turned to see who was entering. When they recognised who it was, they rose to their feet.

A loudspeaker was relaying the BBC broadcast into the room. Big Ben had completed the preliminary sequences of booming notes which denote the end of another hour, and there was a hesitation before the huge bell began to ring out three times to denote that the King's speech was due to begin.

Princess Elizabeth Alexandra Mary walked through the outer office, knocked on the open door of her father's study, and went in.

She had just run flat out for over a hundred yards, including a flight of stairs, but you would never have known. She was not out of breath. And Princesses, of course, do not sweat. Neither do they perspire. They simply glow. Elizabeth glowed.

Big Ben struck once.

The King, bent over the desk in his misery, looked up. His face changed and he became a different man.

Elizabeth went to his side and he took her hand.

‘Hello, Papa.’

‘Hello, my darling.’

Big Ben struck a second time.

‘Are you ready for your speech?’

‘I am now, yes.’

Big Ben struck for the third time.

‘I will talk to you afterwards,’ said the Princess.

‘Yes. I shall like that.’

The BBC announcer spoke. ‘This is London calling the world. His Majesty the King....’

The King picked up the speech which had been sent to him by the Earl of Westrow, tore it in half, and dropped it into the waste-paper basket beside his desk.

It was estimated that the King’s speech was heard that year by over a hundred million people, but of course no one could be sure of the total. It was heard in all the obvious parts of his Empire: in Great Britain, Canada, India, Australia, South Africa, and New Zealand. But it was also heard by British subjects in more obscure places: Bechuanaland, the British Virgin Islands, Sierra Leone, Papua New Guinea, Tonga, Cyprus, Mauritius, and the New Hebrides.

Most listeners remarked on the fact that the King sounded so much more relaxed than usual: he hardly stuttered at all. He urged his people to prepare themselves for difficult times ahead. But he gave great hope that, in due course, the war against Germany would be won.

Given the dark circumstances of the war, most listeners thought that the King sounded remarkably cheerful.

Joachim von Ribbentrop heard the speech in Berlin. Afterwards he told his secretary to cancel the appointment with the Führer which had been scheduled for the following day.

The Duke and Duchess of Windsor heard the speech at Government House in Nassau, in the Bahamas. After it was over, the Duchess went down into the local high street (accompanied by one police officer) and bought a picture-postcard. She addressed it to Mr Joseph P. Kennedy at his residence in Palm Beach, Florida, and this is what she wrote:

> Dear Joe,
> The hell with it.
> Love, Wally

Chapter 46

There was, of course, a great deal to be said afterwards, and Jane said it all, several times, formally and informally, to the King, the Queen, Princess Elizabeth, Commander Mantle, her father, and others.

Seymour also had a lot of explaining to do, not least to his parents, who had now returned from their mission to Liverpool. Alastair took Seymour to one side, told him about the Official Secrets Act (which did not apply to Seymour, since he was an American citizen) and asked him to be suitably discreet. Seymour gladly agreed. He would have agreed to more or less anything by that time. Then Alastair spoke to Mr and Mrs Jensen, whom he knew well, and told them enough to stop them worrying about where Seymour had been and what he had done, but not enough to give them any real information. Then Seymour went home.

By seven o'clock that evening Jane was exhausted to the point where she thought she was going to fall over. She begged to be allowed to go home too. Whatever else needed to be done and said could be done and said tomorrow. Alastair, who knew that his daughter did not often plead fatigue, arranged for a car to take her to their flat. He himself still had work to do.

When Jane went down to the south entrance of the Palace to be driven to Eaton Square, she found Commander Mantle just coming back from another visit to Scotland Yard.

'Good news!' he said. 'The Wiltshire police have just caught Westrow!'

Jane was astonished. 'But the Princess said he was supposed to be catching a plane. What happened to it?'

'Well, I rather think the noble Earl's rich and powerful associates suddenly got cold feet. It's one thing to help an old friend, but quite another to run the risk of being hanged for treason. Anyway, for some reason the plane didn't appear at the appointed time and place, and the Yard got an anonymous tip-off as to where they might find him.'

Jane slid into the back seat of her waiting car – a royal Rolls, no less.

'Well,' she said, 'that is good news. And you've caught Helga too?'

'No. She's disappeared into the woodwork. Too canny, that one. I expect she'll go north. Liverpool or Manchester. That's what I would do in her position. She'll be able to make a living up there, working the streets.'

Mantle closed the car door and then leaned forward. Jane wound the window down to hear what he had to say.

'You've done a marvellous job, Jane,' he told her. 'I personally am very grateful to you.' He stood back and saluted. 'Take care,' he said.

The car took Jane to Eaton Square.

She half-hoped that the neighbours would be watching as she arrived in a royal Rolls, but of course there were no streetlights, and all her neighbours had far better things to do than peek out at the darkness on a cold Christmas Day evening.

Jane let herself in at the front door of the flat and switched on the light in the hall.

The place felt empty and unlived-in. The air was chilly. She went into the living-room and lit the gas fire. It would soon warm up.

She moved on into the kitchen and put the kettle on. She had had a few sandwiches at the Palace, but she was dying for a cup of tea. What she also needed, she decided, was a good hot bath.

What with it being wartime you could never tell whether there was going to be any hot water. The supply came from some mysterious boiler deep in the basement, servicing all the flats in the house. However, when Jane ran the tap to test its temperature she soon found that the water was as hot as she'd ever known it. Obviously someone had made a special effort for Christmas, so she decided to take advantage of the situation at once.

She went into her bedroom to get undressed, pushing open the door and reaching for the light switch.

But before she touched the switch she saw a sudden gleam of light – a moving, swinging, split-second gleam of light, reflected in the full-length mirror on the far side of the room. It was an upward movement in a room where there should be no movement.

Jane was tired, but she was still wound up tight inside. She was so tense she would have jumped three feet in the air at the sound of a doorbell. All day she had been living on the very edge of her nerves. She had been driving at excessive speeds for hours. She had been shot at and had shot back. She had chased, hunted, despaired, found, rejoiced, worried, explained, cried, and laughed.

And now, when she saw a sudden, unexpected, swinging gleam of light, she reacted instantaneously, by instinct. At the subliminal sight of something steely moving through the air towards her, she dropped to her knees. A hand, moving violently downwards, brushed against her back.

Jane rolled sideways on the floor, aware now that someone else was in the room. She threw herself hard against the knees of the person standing just inside the door, beside the bed, knocking that person backwards on to the bed.

It was Helga.

Jane could smell her. She had smelt that perfume in the hall of Plain View Cottage, and now the scent was here, here in her *bedroom* in the flat in Eaton Square.

Jane reached up and grabbed the hand holding the knife, the hand which had swung down seeking to stab her, the hand which held the knife which had gleamed faintly in the reflected light from the hall as it curved down towards her, the hand which had brushed against her back as the stabbing motion missed its aim.

Jane gave a great snarl of rage. Adrenalin gushed into her veins as she realised who was here in the room with her and what Helga was trying to do. The filthy, disgusting *effrontery* of the woman! The sheer bloody *cheek* of it! Here, in my bedroom! Trying to kill me!

Jane seized Helga's wrist and gripped it tight.

But Helga was powerful, fit, trained, and ready. She brought her right knee up and kicked Jane off the bed, sending her sprawling on to the floor.

Helga came forward again, the knife slashing down.

Jane twisted away and the knife clunked heavily into a chest drawers. It went into the wood so hard that it stuck, causing Helga to use both hands to pull it free.

As Helga tugged, Jane picked up a vase and smashed it over Helga's head with all her might.

The vase shattered into a hundred china pieces.

Helga pulled the knife free, swung it round in a slashing arc. Jane leaned back, felt the air move as the blade went by, felt it nick her somewhere under the chin.

Helga grunted, swore, turned around, lunged, and missed as Jane side-stepped.

Jane punched Helga on the side of the face as the momentum of her lunge carried her past, the blow landing by chance rather than by good timing. Helga stumbled.

Jane shoved her in the middle of the back, sending her forward into the door.

And the door was a solid, old door. It was not a modern softwood item. It was made of oak and it hurt. The collision dazed and confused Helga.

Jane reached back, trying to find in the half-light from the hall the heavy walking-stick which stood beside her bed, the one her father had put there years ago saying you never knew when it might come in useful.

But it didn't come in useful today, because Jane never reached it. Helga turned round, still dazed, and kicked her in the ribs.

Jane gasped loudly and buckled over, winded. She collapsed across the bed.

Helga stabbed at her again.

It was a huge, vicious, bitterly angry swing, a swing that came from right up high. How *dare* you, it said, how dare you fight back! This will teach you not to fight against me, Miss Padget!

The swing started so high and came down in such a long arc that the knife, had it connected, would have passed clean through Jane's chest and into the mattress below.

But the long swing took time to complete, and once started on its way its direction could not easily be changed.

Jane rolled sideways to her left and struck backwards with the point of her elbow, hearing something – a cheek-bone? – something actually crack.

Helga cried out in pain, let go of the knife, and clutched her face.

Jane grabbed her by the neck with both hands and hurled her on to the floor.

Helga bounced once, banging her head against the wall.

Jane threw herself on top of the woman, seized her by the throat, and banged her head backwards against the wall a second time.

Helga's knees came up and she tried to shove Jane off.

Jane held on to the throat and banged the head against the wall again. Hard.

Helga twisted and tore at Jane's hands. Choking noises came from Helga's throat – a hoarse, frothy, spluttering sound.

Jane bashed the head hard against the wall. Plaster came off. She could see it cracking in the light from the hall.

Helga kicked and twisted again.

Jane bashed and bashed again, tightening her hands on the throat.

She bashed and bashed and bashed.

Until, in the end, she was exhausted, panting, unable to move.

And Helga lay silent and still beneath her.

Chapter 47

Two days later, on 27 December 1940, Hitler sent the *Luftwaffe* to attack London. A hundred bombers came over. They dropped 111 tons of high explosive, and 11,000 incendiaries. As a result, 1,500 fires were started. The flames were visible from a distance of 60 miles. There were 600 civilian casualties.

On 29 December there was a further raid, concentrated on the old City of London. This time 120 tons of high explosive were dropped, together with 22,000 incendiaries. Over 500 people were injured, and 160 killed. Much of ancient City was destroyed.

On the afternoon of 30 December, Alastair was called in to see the King.

'Ah, Alastair. Come in. Please sit down.'

The King continued reading for a moment. Then he said: 'Good work, this, you know. Mantle's given me a copy of the police report about the capture of the Earl of Westrow. And I understand that the Constable who was shot is beginning to recover. Brown I think his name is?'

'Yes, Sir. We're told he's doing well. The bullet seems to have glanced off his ribs and made him bleed a lot, but did no serious damage.'

'Good. I'm very pleased to hear it. I hope you'll see that he gets some sort of award for bravery.'

'It's being considered, Sir.'

'Ah,' said the King. And paused. 'That means you don't think he *should* get an award.'

'The least said about this whole business the better, Sir, in many ways. We don't want any word of this incident to leak out.'

'No. Quite. I see. Well, the police will have to decide what to do about their own man. Whether to recognise his bravery formally, or not. But then there's young Jane, of course. I'd like to give her something. I was thinking of the George Medal.'

'Oh no, Sir.'

'No?'

'No, Sir,' Alastair repeated. 'Definitely not. Quite inappropriate. For one thing it would attract public attention – people would want to know why she'd got it – and that's the last thing we want. And for another, Jane was simply serving the Crown. And that's what my family does, by and large. Some families farm, some go into the Church. My family serves the Crown, often pretty directly.'

'Ah. Yes. I see. Well, what about young Jensen? Think we might stretch to a medal for him?'

'No, certainly not. For much the same reasons, only more so. I have already sworn him to secrecy, and he has promised never to reveal to anyone what happened during those two or three days. Not even to his family.'

'His parents were a bit concerned about him, I gather.'

'Yes. They tried to get in touch with him on both Christmas Eve and Christmas Day, and couldn't, so naturally they were worried about him. But I've spoken to them at length, and explained that, although I can't tell them precisely where he was or what he was doing, the Palace is very pleased with him.'

'Yes. I see. But no medal?'

'No medal. You thanked both those young people personally, and very warmly, after your speech on Christmas Day. That is sufficient. You should leave it at that.'

'Well, I certainly won't leave it at that,' said the King boldly. 'Not as far as Jane is concerned. Every time I see her I shall give her a big kiss. P... p... provided the Queen isn't watching of course. And when Jane gets married I shall have to stop. But until then it will be the Order of the Big Kiss. Every time.'

Alastair smiled. 'That, I think, would be permissible.'

'Good. And, er, one other thing....'

'Yes, Sir?'

'I know you want to bury all this,' said the King. 'Pretend it never happened and so forth – but I would like Jane to write a full account of the story, from her point of view. Just so's I have it in my own files. Will you allow that?'

Alastair paused. Then: 'Yes, I think that would be harmless

enough.'

'Good. Perhaps you'd ask her to do that then?'

'I will.'

'Thank you. And as for young Jensen, I think I'll ask him to tea. Americans like that sort of thing.'

'Yes indeed, Sir. But no medal.'

'Oh no no, certainly not. No, we've established that. Quite inappropriate.'

The King shuffled the papers on his desk.

'Now then, Alastair, this document you want me to sign.'

'Yes, Sir?'

'I see, from what we have here, that the Earl of Westrow and Miss Kronberg have been tried in camera for their various crimes, one of which was the murder of Sergeant Wilson.'

'Yes, Sir.'

'The authorities didn't waste much time, did they?'

No, Sir. Action this day is, I believe, Mr Churchill's motto.'

'Yes, quite. Anyway, they've been tried, it appears, and found guilty.'

'Yes, Sir. Guilty under the Treachery Act, which was passed earlier this year. Both of them made statements admitting that they were present when Sergeant Wilson was shot, but each said the other did it. They also gave us a very full account of the plot to kidnap Princess Elizabeth and the thinking behind it.'

'Yes, I see.' The King looked somewhat embarrassed.

Alastair continued. 'These documents will, of course, be kept secret more or less for ever.'

'Yes. I suppose I agree.' The King now looked very much embarrassed. 'I don't think I want to know the details about who dreamed it all up.'

'No, Sir. You don't. But Miss Kronberg clearly felt that by confessing everything she would save herself from the death penalty, and the Earl seemed positively eager to tell us that Mr Hitler is a close personal friend of his.'

'Cheeky blighter.'

'Quite, Sir.'

'Anyway, I see that, to complete the formalities, I am asked to sign this... this... d... d... death warrant, I suppose you'd call it.'

'Yes, Sir.'

The King fiddled with the piece of paper, screwing up his eyes to read it.

'Tell me, Alastair,' he asked eventually. 'If I sign this, will history see me as vindictive?'

'No, Sir. The Earl of Westrow and Miss Kronberg are guilty of treason, after all. Miss Kronberg is a self-confessed German spy, and Westrow has freely admitted his crimes.'

The King sighed. 'Yes, I suppose so. And this Kronberg woman did her best to kill Jane, of course.'

'Yes, Sir.'

'How did she knew where to find her?'

'Well, Westrow knows Jane, of course. He recognised her at the cottage. And as he and the Kronberg woman drove away, he told her who Jane was and where she lived. Kronberg swore that she would kill Jane, for ruining their plans, and then she was going to disappear into the underworld.'

'Yes, I see.' The King stared out of the window. 'I don't know why I'm hesitating really. This morning I went out to see the damage from last night's raid. Mile after mile of London is still burning. You can't breathe anywhere for smoke and fumes. Hundreds of people have been killed, most of them burnt to death. And all of that has been done by the people that Westrow and Kronberg worked for.'

The King picked up his pen and signed his name at the foot of the execution warrant. He had a slow, laboured hand, and his signature was almost childish in form. Then he handed the document to Alastair.

'Thank you, Sir.'

The King put the top back on his fountain-pen. 'They tell me,' he said, 'that when a peer of the realm is hanged, they use a silk rope.'

'Yes, Sir.'

'I think, on this occasion, we might extend the same privilege to the lady. Don't you agree?'

'I'll see that it's done, Sir,' said Alastair.

EPILOGUE

by

George Digby

The novel written by my friend Anthony Dorner ends on the previous page. But you will recall that I promised my friend, as he neared the end of his life, that I would write both an introduction *and* an epilogue to his book. It seemed to me that readers would want to know a certain amount about the fate of the principal characters. In particular, they would wish to know what happened to Seymour Jensen and Jane Padget.

This epilogue makes good my promise. But I will begin by relating what happened to the other characters in this story – the shits, as Anthony so bluntly called them.

As indicated in the previous chapter, the Earl of Westrow and his accomplice, Miss Helga Kronberg, were tried and sentenced to death with almost indecent haste. However, we must remember that it was wartime, and there was no doubt about their guilt.

A few months later, it was discreetly made known to the public at large that the Earl of Westrow had been 'killed by enemy action'. Which was true, in a sense. The fact is, he was executed in Pentonville Prison at dawn on 31 December 1940.

Miss Kronberg followed him to the gallows a few minutes later. It was, of course, highly unusual (perhaps unique) for a woman prisoner to be held and executed in Pentonville, but, as I say, the circumstances were exceptional. A whole wing was apparently cleared to house the two of them in complete isolation.

No word of the execution appeared in the newspapers at the time, or for that matter afterwards. If it had been known that Westrow had been convicted of treason people would have had to know what form the treason took, and that would never have done. So silence was the order of the day.

The authorities tried to pretend that the two executions had never taken place. For example, the public hangman of that time, Mr Albert Pierrepoint, makes no mention of the Earl and Miss Kronberg in his published memoirs. However, in the course of my own researches into this matter (and I like to think that, as a professional librarian, I am rather good at following up references), I was able to obtain access to Mr Pierrepoint's original journal on which he based his book.

In his journal, Mr Pierrepoint's entry for 31 December 1940 reads as follows:

> I was called upon to execute two people in Pentonville Prison. One was a peer of the realm, no less, and the other a German lady who had been spying on us for some years. The whole operation was surrounded by great secrecy, and for once not even the other prisoners knew exactly what was happening. The peer made a short speech. He denied that he was a traitor, and said that he had done the best he could for his country. He was in full command of himself, and went to his death with dignity. The lady, unfortunately, was not a lady. She cursed me in excellent English, and as I put the hood over her head, she turned and spat in my eye.

Consistent to the last, then.

Joachim von Ribbentrop survived rather longer.

To my mind, Anthony Dorner did not get Ribbentrop quite right. In the novel he comes across as a cultured, rather a charming sort of chap – a man who was an English gentleman at heart, perhaps a bit out of place in Berlin. The truth is rather different.

Ribbentrop was, of course, one of Hitler's leading henchmen. He gloried in the cesspool that was Nazi Germany, and he occupied a very high position in the hierarchy from 1933 until the very end.

When the war ended he panicked and ran, like most of his kind, but he was captured by Allied troops in Hamburg on 14 June 1945.

The British government favoured summary execution for

captured Nazi leaders – put 'em up against a wall and shoot 'em. However, the view of other, more 'civilised' Allies was that legal methods should prevail; consequently the top men were tried for war crimes by the International Military Tribunal at Nuremberg.

During his trial Ribbentrop claimed (of course) that he had never had the remotest idea what happened to the Jews after they were deported. Then he contradicted himself and said that he had had 'terrible arguments' with Hitler over the fate of the Jews. No one believed a word he said, and on 1 October 1946 he was sentenced to death by hanging.

On the night of 15 October 1946, Goering committed suicide in his cell, and so, in the early hours of 16 October, Ribbentrop was the first of ten men to go to the scaffold. Mr Pierrepoint again officiated.

After all ten were dead, their bodies were taken to Dachau concentration camp. There the gas ovens were lit for one last time, and the bodies of these worthless scum were transformed into smoke and ashes. Later, the ashes were scattered, in secret, into a river.

Next we come to Mr Joseph P. Kennedy.

Joe never did become President of a united Ireland, which was a pity really. The Irish government at that time was composed mainly of men who were hard-nosed, Brit-hating, hypocritical-Catholic, confused-thinking, self-serving mediocrities, and Joe would have felt entirely at home in their company.

As we have seen, Joe's technique was to live a life totally dedicated to self-interest while presenting himself as an altruist, public servant, and statesman. This technique was widely adopted by his children.

Unfortunately for Joe, but fortunately for the rest of us, his foolish press interview about the death of democracy destroyed his personal chances of any political advancement in the United States. From 1941 on he was therefore obliged to concentrate on trying to obtain office for his children. In this he succeeded, largely because he employed the same ruthless tactics in politics as he had in business: that is to say, he lied, bribed, and cheated his way towards the desired objectives.

Joe had a stroke in 1961, and took no further part in business or politics. He died in 1969 at the age of 81.

The Duke and Duchess of Windsor deserve no more respect than Joe Kennedy. They were shits too.

The Duke remained at his post as Governor of the Bahamas for the duration of the war. Occasionally he angled for something better. He told the American press that he would accept the post of Ambassador in Washington if it was offered. But – surprise, surprise – it wasn't.

In 1944, Berlin radio helpfully announced that the Duke would be appointed as Viceroy of the United States when that country was conquered by the Germans and the Japanese. But that didn't happen either, so the Duke was disappointed once more.

After the war the Windsors devoted themselves to the social whirl. They became full-time professional members of café society. They entertained lavishly at their home in Paris, and they travelled widely, moving restlessly from capital to capital. They were frequently photographed in glittering night-clubs, surrounded by glamorous but morally dubious companions.

In short, they lived lives of extraordinary emptiness. They were admired by those who knew nothing of their sordid and treacherous past.

It was made abundantly clear to the Windsors that they were not welcome in England, and so, thank God, they never came here – except for the occasional funeral, and then the visit was brief and low-key.

The British royal family used to be adept at protecting its public reputation. After the war, a man called Anthony Blunt (who was considered *terribly* discreet) was sent to Germany to destroy all traces of the Duke's collaboration with the Hitler and his merry men. The mission was largely successful.

Unfortunately Blunt later turned out to have good reason for being discreet: he had spent several decades spying for the Russians. And despite Blunt's best efforts, the truth eventually emerged. Well, hard luck; it was a good try.

The Duke of Windsor died in Paris, in 1972. He was buried at Frogmore, within the grounds of Windsor Castle.

Wallis, the Duchess, lived on. And on, and on, and on. In her later years she was 'cared for' by her French lawyer, Maitre Suzanne Blum, who was nearly as ruthless and single-minded as the Duchess herself. No visitors were allowed to see the ailing Wallis, but it appears that she gradually fell into a state of senility.

She eventually died in 1986, aged ninety. The funeral service took place in St. George's Chapel, Windsor, at which occasion her name was never once mentioned. She was buried beside the Duke at Frogmore.

After the death of the Duchess of Windsor – she who was never Her Royal Highness – her collection of jewellery was sold by Sotheby Parke-Bernet. It was an occasion that Wallis would have revelled in. *All* the best people were there, and they positively *fought* to buy her possessions.

The Mogul emerald engagement ring which the Duke (then King) had given to Wallis on the evening of her decree nisi at Ipswich went for $2.1m. Princess Diana was reported to have set her heart on two rather gorgeous panther ear clips, but Elizabeth Taylor outbid the Prince of Wales for them. Hard luck again!

At the end of two days, the total realised by the sale of Wallis's jewellery was just over $50m. How proud she would have been.

Having dealt with all the disgusting people, let me now turn to those who deserve our admiration.

I suppose, for the benefit of younger readers, I ought to say that, on the death of her father in 1952, Princess Elizabeth became Queen Elizabeth II, and began her long and successful reign.

And what of Jane Padget and Seymour Jensen? My friend Anthony Dorner must have known what happened to Jane – the title of his book alone reveals that – but for some reason he chose not to complete the story. I will now remedy his deficiency.

In the summer of 1941, after she had come of age, Jane decided that two years at Oxford was quite sufficient when there was a war on. To her father's dismay, she left the University and volunteered for service in the Women's Auxiliary Air Force.

Very soon, her exceptional intellectual abilities were recognised, as were her physical toughness and courage. After six months her commanding officer therefore asked her if she was interested in serving in the Special Operations Executive (SOE). She gladly volunteered.

The SOE was an independent British secret service which had the task of conducting subversive warfare in every German-occupied country in Europe. Having spent most of her schoolgirl summers in France, Jane was a fluent French speaker. She was therefore trained to be parachuted into that country, where her brief was to assist the resistance.

Jane successfully landed in France on 19 October 1942. For some months she carried out her clandestine mission, helping the Maquis to sabotage German military bases.

On 10 April 1943, Jane was captured by German troops. She was handed over to the Gestapo. Following their normal practice, the Gestapo tortured her for two days, trying to extract what information they could. But Jane did not betray her friends.

In the early hours of 13 April 1943, Jane Padget died from the wounds inflicted upon her. Just before dawn, a German lorry drove into the marketplace of a village near Besançon, and there her blood-stained, naked body was dumped on to the cobblestones. At first light, the women of the village took her indoors. Later that day they buried her in the nearby churchyard.

When I became aware of these facts, I made it my business to visit the village in question, last summer. When I arrived there, I asked for directions to the churchyard, and as I walked up the main street I wondered if it would be difficult to locate Jane's grave. But not at all. It lies under a splendid, sheltering tree, which seems to give comfort with the shade of its widespread arms. The grave is well tended, and, on the day I was there, fresh flowers had been placed upon it. Jane Padget is not forgotten.

The spot is marked by a simple upright stone, and the stone is engraved with just four words. On one line is her name: Jane Padget. And beneath that, in English: Beautiful Lady.

Tracing Mr Jensen was a harder task. During the course of my researches, I came across an unsupported rumour that, despite Alastair Padget's best efforts, King George VI had nevertheless awarded young Seymour the George Medal.

I tried to obtain either a confirmation or a denial of this rumour, but I quickly discovered that there is still strong resistance on the part of the authorities to admitting that anything untoward happened to Princess Elizabeth in December 1940.

In the end, I traced Seymour Jensen by accident. I happened to be glancing at a copy of *Time* magazine, in my University Library, when I noticed a reference to a certain *Senator* Jensen, who was reportedly a long-serving member of the Senate of the United States. Further enquiries revealed that this man's first name was Seymour, and that he was apparently the right age.

I undertook further research. It appeared that, when America entered the war, Mr Jensen left Harvard and joined the US Navy. He served with some distinction.

After the war, he completed his studies at Harvard and began a business career in the Midwest. Later, he entered politics, and in 1968 he was eventually elected as a US Senator, an office which he still holds.

Senator Jensen seems to have had a relatively uneventful life while representing his state in Washington; he is not a high-profile national figure, at least as far as we in England are concerned. However, I was amused by one incident which came to light. Mr Jensen had never married, and on one occasion, when he was standing for re-election, he was accused of being a 'closet gay'. In fact, an attempt was made to 'out' him.

This was quite obviously a dirty trick on the part of one of his opponents, and it backfired badly. Within a few days, a group of ladies had announced themselves as 'The Friends of Senator Jensen.'

There were 14 of these ladies to begin with (more joined later). They all signed affidavits in which they testified that, to their certain knowledge, Senator Jensen was not a homosexual. It was well known to his friends, they said, that in his youth he had hoped to marry one particular person. That had not proved possible, and from then on he had led a bachelor life.

However, they continued, a bachelor life did not mean a celibate life. Senator Jensen, the ladies affirmed, was a gentleman, and would never approach a married lady. But any attractive woman who was single, separated, divorced, or widowed could depend upon it that Senator Jensen would treat her with charm, courtesy, and generosity.

At the election, a month later, the Senator was victorious with an enhanced majority.

After discovering these facts, I was by now fairly sure that I had the right man. I therefore wrote to him, and rather than embark on long and involved explanations I simply asked him whether he could confirm that he was the same Seymour Jensen to whom the King of England had reportedly given the George Medal in January 1941. There was, of course, no mention of it in any of his campaign material.

After a few weeks I had given up hope of a reply. But just before this book went to press, I received a letter from the Senator. I think it is worth reprinting in full.

Dear Mr Digby,

Thank you for your recent letter about the events of late 1940. I delayed replying because, quite frankly, it is distressing for me to think about those times.

I am now 79 years old, and I think it will do no harm to any party, at this stage, if I say that I was indeed the recipient of a medal from King George VI in early January 1941.

I am quite certain that I did not deserve it. I doubt whether the King had the legal authority to give it to me. However, when you are 19 years old, an American citizen, and the King of England wants to give you something, it is hard to say no.

I was asked to keep the matter secret at the time, and I have done so until now. I took the medal home to the United States with me, but I seldom looked at it because of the memories which it brought back.

Then, various circumstances brought me to the realisation that I would not live for ever, and

I was troubled by my continued possession of the medal. And so, in the summer of 1995, fifty years after the end of the war, I travelled to a small village in the east of France. There, with the aid of the village priest, I left the medal in the care of that lady to whom, in my mind, it had always truly belonged. She was very beautiful, and I loved her very much.

Yours sincerely,
Seymour Jensen

That was all the letter said. But then, I suppose, when you think about it, there is nothing further to say.

Except perhaps this. It is sometimes argued that, whether good or bad, handsome or ugly, rich or poor, the dead are all equal now. But that is not true. For the dead are not equal in our memory. Some are despised. Some are forgotten. And some are remembered with affection and respect.

Author's Note

The novel which you have just (I hope) finished reading is a work of fiction set within a factual framework. December 1940 was indeed a time of crisis for the British people, and there certainly were those who argued that the government of the day should seek a peace treaty with Germany, rather than fight on towards what seemed like certain defeat; but there was not, so far as I know, a plot to kidnap Princess Elizabeth and so bring pressure to bear on the King. The events described in this novel should therefore be regarded as having taken place in a parallel universe, where history does not assume quite the same shape as in our own.

As indicated within the text, some of the characters who feature in this book were historical personages, as George Digby chose to call them; and there may be some readers who consider, in common with George, that I have been unfair to individuals who are now dead. In response to such criticism, I would say that, as a rule of thumb, I have taken care not to paint historical figures as being any blacker than they actually were. The likes of Ribbentrop, the Duchess of Windsor, and Joe Kennedy may not actually have plotted to kidnap Princess Elizabeth, but, by my reading of history, they were certainly capable of it, and far worse. Those who doubt this conclusion are invited to research the period for themselves.

There may also be some British readers who think it vaguely improper to feature our present Queen in a book such as this. The point is arguable, but since I portray the then Princess Elizabeth as a rather charming teenager (which I think she was), with a particularly strong sense of love for and loyalty to her father (which I think she had), I cannot see that any great harm is done. In any case, Her Majesty quite often appears in fiction; in one instance – not one of my own books – she features as a detective who investigates a murder in Buckingham Palace.

Listed below are some of the books which I found particularly useful when researching the period covered by this novel. Some of the specific incidents which I relate are recorded in these books, and, where the authors have given what appear to be authoritative accounts of what was actually said at the time, I have used their dialogue. For example, the telephone conversation between the then King Edward VIII and the German Ambassador (page 115) is attested to by both Sencourt and Higham. The two authors give slightly different versions of the exact words spoken, but the import of the conversation is the same in both cases.

I am happy to acknowledge my considerable debt to the authors of the following books:

Ralph F. De Bedts: *Ambassador Joseph Kennedy, 1938-40*. New York: Peter Lang, 1985.

Michael R. Beschloss: *Kennedy and Roosevelt*. New York: Norton, 1980

Caroline Blackwood: *The last of the Duchess*. London: Macmillan, 1995.

Michael Bloch: *The secret file of the Duke of Windsor*. London: Bantam Press, 1988.

Lady Colin Campbell: *The royal marriages*. London: Smith Gryphon, 1994.

Nigel Hamilton: *JFK – reckless youth*. London: Century, 1992.

Charles Higham: *Wallis – secret lives of the Duchess of Windsor*. London: Sidgwick and Jackson, 1988.

Rose Fitzgerald Kennedy: *Times to remember – an autobiography*. London: Collins, 1974.

Robert Sencourt: *The reign of Edward VIII*. London: Anthony Gibbs & Phillips, 1962.

Gwynne Thomas: *King pawn or black knight?* Edinburgh: Mainstream, 1995.